"She's over h

Case tugged on the b[...]
stepped out of the car. "She?"

"Driver's licence says her name is Kelly. Heather Kelly. She also has a card to the Antler Club in her wallet."

Case followed his deputy over to an old VW that sat in a corner of the lot. He let out a low, sympathetic whistle as he crouched to look in. "Awfully young," he said to himself. "Who reported this?"

"A jogger. About an hour ago. The man saw her in here and thought she was passed out. Then he went to the nearest phone."

"You have his name?"

"Yep. Got a full statement from him, too. Not much help."

"Okay," Case said, still crouching, looking at the body. Indeed, Heather Kelly could have been passed out. Her blonde head lay tilted to the right and back, against the headrest, and her eyes were closed. Except for her ashen pallor she sure could have been asleep.

But she wasn't. Heather Kelly would never wake again.

As college students, Carla Peltonen and Molly Swanton spent several years travelling the world. As bestselling authors, they have drawn on those experiences more than 30 times, and their pen-name—Lynn Erickson—has come to mean glamour, excitement, intrigue and passion to their millions of fans the world over. Based in Colorado, this dynamic writing team turned closer to home for the inspiration of *Aspen*. They believe "everything is possible in Aspen—there's a kind of freedom and exhilaration in the blue sky and the towering mountains." Read as Lynn Erickson delves behind the glittering façade of Aspen to expose a world of ruthless ambition and murderous desires.

LYNN ERICKSON

ASPEN

MIRA BOOKS

All the characters in this book have no existence outside the imagination
of the author, and have no relation whatsoever to anyone bearing the
same name or names. They are not even distantly inspired by any
individual known or unknown to the author, and all the incidents are pure
invention.

First published in Great Britain 1995
by Mira Books

© Carla Peltonen and Molly Swanton 1995

ISBN 1 55166 054 7

58-9512

Printed in Great Britain by
BPC Paperbacks Ltd

ASPEN

ONE

The day it all began it was threatening to snow. A man and a woman were skiing down Ruthie's Run on Aspen Mountain. It was a gray day, the clouds rolling in ominously across the white peaks. She was slight and graceful: he was a strong skier with perfect technique. They stopped, and the woman laughed at something he said while he leaned close, his white teeth showing in a smile. He put a gloved hand on her arm in a familiar manner.

They continued skiing down, down the white slopes toward Aspen, curving through the moguls, down Spring Pitch and Straw Pile and Magnifico, down to the bottom of the mountain, where they clicked out of their bindings, hoisted their skis to their shoulders and walked toward Billy Jorgenson's condominium.

His place was messy, but Beth Connelly didn't look closely. She pulled off her hat and gloves and goggles and shook out her dark hair. Billy unzipped his distinctive red ski instructor's parka and dropped it on the floor, took off his heavy boots and removed his ski pants. Soon Beth's shiny green suit, turtleneck and sweater also littered the floor. She looked at the heap of skiwear and laughed, then went to Billy. His body was bronzed and lean and muscular; he took good care of himself.

She wound her arms around his neck and pressed against him, and he kissed her deeply.

"Can you stay the night?" Billy ran a hand along her hip.

"No. Duty calls, I'm afraid," she said reluctantly. "I have to meet the clan at the Antler Club in an hour or so. A command performance. That's the place where the rich and notorious gather, after all."

She kissed him again, enjoying his expertise, but all too soon it was time to dress and prepare for the inevitable.

The threat of snow became a reality that night of December twenty-eighth, fat, spiraling flakes that rushed to earth, and every powder hound turned up his face to catch tiny, melting bits on his tongue and grinned, thinking, tomorrow. Tomorrow they'd be in the lift line early, before the Silver Queen gondola even started, stamping in the cold air, impatient, jostling for position, joking with friends. It would be the Face of the mountain first, no, the Back of Bell. Hell, no, the Dumps. Searching for that elusive dream of perfect powder. But now it was dark, nearly midnight. Aspen lay like a brilliant jewel nestled in white velvet and black satin, the bulk of Aspen Mountain rising over her like a petrified wave, her downtown lights glittering. Above the town, on the slopes of Red Mountain, huge stone-and-glass and redwood homes were lit up for the season—the two weeks of the year they were used. And down the long Roaring Fork River Valley, away from town, the lights thinned, becoming farther and farther apart, to where horses and cattle stood patiently in dark fields, backs to the storm.

And it kept snowing.

Locals, people who lived in Aspen year-round, were home in bed or, if they had night shifts, were pouring drinks behind bars, driving taxis, waiting on tables or answering hotel switchboards. The tourists were out on the town, crowding the door at Mezzaluna to see George Hamilton or Kurt Russell; sitting at tables inside the fogged-up plate-glass windows of the Ute City Banque, having a nightcap at the Red Onion or the Golden Horn; dancing to a rock band at Club Soda or merely strolling the snow-covered malls, window-shopping, staring at Rolex watches, cashmere sweaters, Bogner ski suits, fine paintings, snakeskin cowboy boots, butter-soft leather jackets, six-hundred-dollar powder skis.

A man and a woman in their thirties, swathed in identical full-length dark mink coats, strolled by as a waiter in black pants and parka hastily thrown over his white shirt walked swiftly on his way home. A couple of local high school boys in torn jeans stood near the mall, smoking, jeering at rich tourists. The snow fell on them all, wetting faded denim jackets, sitting lightly on fur, glistening on hair and eyelashes.

In the heart of downtown Aspen, on the corner of Mill and Hopkins, was the stately old Victorian building that had for most of its existence housed a hardware store; now it was refurbished into boutiques and, downstairs, the Antler Club. Dark green walls, dim lights, old English decor and chandeliers of elk antlers made the club elegant, restful and private. People of Aspen, of course, knew that anyone could belong; it only took money.

They walked by the old building and shrugged, wishing they could still buy faucet washers there.

Downstairs, inside the secure womb of absolute comfort, a fire crackled in the stone hearth. The bar was full, the Great Room dotted with groups of people drinking and talking. In one corner a loud gathering of people partied on, not entirely oblivious to the surreptitious stares directed their way.

Beth Connelly joined their party, hurrying in late. She smiled, said hello to everyone, gave her mother a quick kiss and sat down at the table. She was deceptively innocent looking, with white skin, huge dark eyes and silky straight dark hair that swung with every movement. As Matt Connelly's stepdaughter, she was a fully vested member of this clan, for better or for worse.

"Look, it's what's-his-name, that senator," a man sitting nearby said to his wife.

"Connelly, Matt Connelly," she said. "God, he looks so short."

"Doesn't he though?" The man finished his drink and waved at the waiter for another. "That must be his wife, what's her name? Soused."

"I heard she's got a problem."

"Well, she sure as hell does tonight," he replied.

Matt saw the man's glance, saw the sneer as he looked at his wife, Lee. He was amused and flattered and resentful, a mixture of emotions he always felt as a figure under constant public scrutiny. He was the senior senator from New York, chairman of a select senate committee and head of the large, unruly Connelly clan, and he was never sure which position gave him the most grief.

Matt Connelly was sixty years old, a fireplug of a man, built like a bulldog with only a little flab around his middle. His face was square and strong with thick brows over fine dark eyes and a wide, sensual mouth. He was almost completely bald, yet he still had the aura of a young man, a vital, sexy man, charismatic and in control. Women were drawn to him—and he to them.

He raised his snifter of brandy to his family, gathered around the low cocktail table. "Come on, time to toast good old Aspen," he said in his most avuncular voice, his New York accent unabashedly evident.

"Every year," his son, Terence, said, raising his glass.

They all held up their glasses and drank. The Connellys were great imbibers, handling large amounts of alcohol with ease. Except for Matt's wife, Lee, but then, she wasn't a real Connelly. She was, in fact, his second wife; his first had died years ago, a tragedy that had earned him voter support for his first senatorial bid.

At the moment Lee Connelly was sitting on a velvet settee, a drink in her hand, her eyes staring unfocused into the dimness of the room. She was a small, beautiful woman, blond and impeccably turned out.

"So, you just got back from where this time?" Terence asked his stepsister. "I can't keep track."

"Africa," Beth replied, punching him lightly on the arm.

"Sure, I knew that."

Terence was a true Connelly, not too tall but handsome as any movie star, black Irish, heavy across the shoulders like his father. A real charmer, a lady's man with no intention of settling down even though he was thirty-one, he habitually hid the slight tension between Beth and him with light banter, teasing, superficialities. Still, they saw nothing of each other except at family functions.

"Why did Ellen have to go home so early?" Beth asked no one in particular.

"Oh, you know her, always the healthy life," Matt answered. "Unlike the rest of us."

"Too bad, I wanted to see her," Beth said.

An older couple who had an air of prosperity and self-satisfaction made their way through the crowd toward the Connelly table, the man rough-featured, running to fat like the ex-football player he was, the woman heavyset and handsome.

"Hey, hey, hey," Matt said, "look who finally made it."

The man was Buzz Crenshaw; his wife, Cynthia, was Matt's older sister.

"We had to drop off the kids," Cynthia said, peeling off her fox coat without her husband's help. "The kids" were their son, Edward, and his wife.

"Where'd you eat?" Matt asked.

"The Golden Horn."

"Um. Good?"

"Marvelous," Cynthia gushed.

"Too damn nouvelle for me," Buzz growled.

They sat down and ordered drinks. The conversation picked up. Buzz, always good for a new dirty joke, was in top form. He and Matt were great pals, cronies. They made money together, too.

"Didja hear the one about the nun with big tits?" Buzz was asking.

"Buzz, for God's sake," Cynthia said.

"No, listen. See, she's got this problem...."

Cynthia rolled her eyes, and Beth looked down to hide the inadvertent twist of her mouth. The Connellys were at it again. Beth would give them one thing, though. They sure had fun. Put the entire clan in a room together, and there wasn't a family in America that could get as much mileage out of a good party.

"So, Beth, where were you?" Cynthia asked. "I thought you had planned on going out to dinner with us."

"Oh, you know me, I got tied up. You didn't wait, I hope?"

"Not long," Cynthia said dryly. "The kids wanted to get home early. You know how Edward is."

Oh yes, Beth knew how Edward was. Cynthia's pride and joy, her son the congressman, was spoken of inside the Beltway of Washington as a possible presidential candidate. Edward was uptight and repressed and a pain in the neck, but he was a damn effective politician.

More people entered the affluent sanctuary of the Antler Club, snow melting on their expensively clad shoulders. Many of them knew one another. They waved across the room to friends, stopped at tables and leaned over to chat, smelling of expensive brandy or wine, perfume, after-shave and the fresh, cold scent of the outdoors. More than a few stopped to speak to Matt. He was well-known in Aspen because he'd been coming here for years. He was one of them.

"Mom, you feeling okay?" Beth Connelly asked.

Lee's mouth formed the semblance of a smile. "Sure, honey, I'm fine." She took a gulp of her drink then subsided into paralysis again.

"Dad, I think . . ." Beth began, but Matt was off on a story, one of his Washington insider stories, his voice louder than it needed to be, so that everyone nearby heard him whether they wanted to or not.

"So there he was, this poor slob from some dinky town upstate. He's telling me his town doesn't want to be cleaned up by the EPA. They'd rather live with the pollution. They're used to it, see, and they don't want to move. Well, what could I say? I tried to explain.... Picture this—there I am with this guy, this farmer in overalls, and I'm trying to tell him there's no way to stop the EPA once it gets rolling, and he says, 'But, Senator, it's our taxes that pay the EPA, so how can they do something we don't want?'"

"Christ," Buzz Crenshaw said.

"Yeah, so what can I do?"

"Dad, I think..." Beth tried again.

"What is it, hon?" he asked.

She gestured toward Lee.

"Ah, she's fine. Yeah, sure, we'll go soon. It's early. Relax, kiddo." He leaned forward. "Lee, Lee, baby, you okay?"

The beautiful blue eyes came into focus, the perfect mouth curved. "I'm fine, fine."

"See?" Matt said.

Beth shrugged. She'd long ago learned that Matt heeded nobody's needs but his own. Terence was cut from the same cloth. But Matt had a fire, a love of life, a largeness of spirit that made people forgive him; in Terence that fire was banked, the love turned inward, the expansiveness diminished to empty gestures. Terence was intelligent, a perpetual student, but not shrewd like his father, and he had not a whit of the driving ambition that marked Matt or his cousin Edward Crenshaw.

Beth took another drink of her rum and Coke. She felt the coldness hit her stomach with a stab of pain and winced. Coke was supposed to be good for a queasy stomach, wasn't it? Damn dysentery. She'd gotten it in Africa. It was better now, but it still flared up from time to time. And she hated taking the pills. They had codeine in them, to slow up her digestive tract. Well, they did that, but they slowed her up, too. God, she'd slept for three days when she'd gotten back this time. Wrung out. Sick. Embarrassed over her inability to stick it out.

Beth looked around. She recognized a billionaire from California, an aging movie star with a young ski instructor, a visiting royal couple, so very anonymous except for the gaggle of Secret Service men at the next table, and a CEO of a huge communications conglomerate whose sleek Learjet had landed just before the Connelly plane had touched down at the small Pitkin County Airport.

She was bored. Matt was telling another Washington story, about a lobbyist who'd offered him his pick of young girls if he'd support the latest bill proposed by his association.

"So I went to the guy's place and, by God, there were six, yeah, six, unbelievable broads. So I said to him, 'Mister, Mister,' I said, 'I go with one of these young girls and I won't live long enough to pass your bill!' Then I left, walked right out. Jesus, you shoulda seen his face."

"Matthew," his sister, Cynthia, admonished.

"You coulda called me," Buzz said, his voice booming.

"Oh, those men," Cynthia said, turning to Beth. "How are you feeling, by the way? You were sick, your mother was telling me."

"Oh, I'm coming along," Beth replied.

"Now, which country were you in this time?"

"I was in Kenya, in the refugee camps," Beth replied.

"Awful. How can you stand to do it?"

"Well, I try to concentrate on the good I can do. But sometimes it's hard," Beth said, and a scene she could not avoid flashed through her mind: a child crying weakly, crying endlessly, with flies on its face. And dust. Dust everywhere. She could smell it and taste it and feel it grit in her teeth. She took another drink.

"Lee should put a stop to your gallivanting around like that," Cynthia said in her decisive way. "It's dangerous."

Beth laughed lightly. "She's tried, believe me."

"When are you going to settle down, Beth?"

"Probably never, Aunt Cynthia. There's too much to do."

Their conversation ended abruptly. Matt was on a roll, regaling them with yet another story: "He's got this thing about guns, see, loves 'em. Likes to wave them around, target shoot, blast trees on his farm. And there he is, the hypocrite, in his three-piece suit in front of the Senate, going on and on about gun control. Did I tell you about the time he nicked his driver with his Uzi? Well, I'll tell you, he paid the poor bastard off bigtime...."

"Dad, we've all heard that one," Terence was saying.

Beth felt another pang in her belly and tried to ignore it. She glanced at her mother. There was a peculiar blank sheen in Lee's lovely blue eyes. God, what a family!

"Ellen was looking well," Cynthia was saying.

Ellen Connelly, Beth's stepsister, was Matt's oldest child; she lived in Aspen year-round and owned an art gallery. She'd stopped by the house earlier that evening with her newest lover in tow, and left shortly afterward. Ellen had a problem with family get-togethers.

"She does look great," Beth said. "I saw her yesterday when I got in. I went to the gallery."

"She seems happy with her ... uh ... new friend."

"Yes, she says he's very talented. A genius."

"He's a bit..um...flamboyant, isn't he?" Cynthia ventured.

Beth laughed. "Yes, he sure is." A tall, elegant man with a long black ponytail, pencil-thin mustache, soulful black eyes and a silver-studded, quasi-gaucho get-up, Manuel Ortega had cut quite a figure. He looked like Zorro. Good for Ellen, Beth thought. She was the only one of the younger generation of Connellys who'd gotten out, escaped. She had her own business, which she loved, and a life, a real life, here in Aspen.

And now she had Manuel, whom she'd discovered. His sketches and paintings sold for five figures—soon to be six, according to Ellen. He was the new Southwestern rage, his wildly colored impressionistic stuff fresh and vigorous, but with the simplicity of Spanish-Indian tradition. So what if he was prone to an occasional artistic tantrum? The public reveled in his antics.

Ellen was crazy about Manuel, anyone could see that; it was a real change for the rigidly controlled, ambitious woman to reveal her feelings so openly. Beth liked Ellen better than any of the other Connellys and had since her older stepsister had taken her under her wing when Beth had been swept into this overwhelming new family with Lee's remarriage. But that had been fifteen years ago....

Matt and Buzz were laughing about something. Cynthia was even smiling, and Lee lurched a little to one side, then straightened abruptly, spilling a few drops of her drink.

Suddenly Beth wondered what she was doing in this place with these people. She drained her drink and rose. "Excuse me, I've got to go to the john," she said.

The light in the ladies' room was flattering, thank God. Beth searched her purse for her pills, unscrewed the top of the little plastic container and spilled one out into her hand. She swallowed it, then bent over the marble sink to splash water on her face. Patting her skin dry with a paper towel, she stared at herself in the mirror. White, she was so white, despite the months she'd spent in the African sun.

She could see the circles under her eyes despite the subtle lighting. She suddenly felt old, ancient. What was she doing here? She should be in Somalia or Bangladesh or Laos. Somewhere she was needed, somewhere worthwhile. Yet when she was in those hot foreign places with the disease and the heat and the filth, she always wondered the same thing. She didn't seem to belong anywhere.

She grinned, a mocking twist of her mouth, shook her head, her hair swaying like a dark silk veil, and took a last look at herself in the mirror. The hell with it.

Beth straightened as the door opened, and a woman came in with a rush of strong perfume. She was wearing black tights and high-heeled ankle boots and a black-and-silver tunic. Her face, partially obscured by long dark hair, was vaguely familiar. Beth smiled.

"Excuse me," the woman said.

"Just leaving." Beth stuck her pill container back into her purse and pushed the door open. A scene popped into her mind—a movie, a murder mystery, sure, that woman . . . what was her name . . . had been the killer. Well, she sure looked younger on the big screen.

The bar was just to her left, crowded with people, ringing with riffs of laughter, loud voices. Inviting. Beth squeezed between a couple of men and caught the bartender's eye. "A soda and lime, please," she said.

She saw Terence then, at the other end of the mahogany bar, leaning negligently, his hands clasped around a glass, his white smile turned on full. The other bartender was talking to him, a female bartender with curly blond hair.

Leave it to Terry, Beth thought.

Her drink came. "Put it on the Connelly tab, please," she said.

"You're one of those Connellys," a voice said in her ear.

She turned, hating it, but she was always polite. Not a Connelly trait, but Lee's influence. Her mother might be a drunk, but she was a blue-blooded Philadelphia drunk, an uptight WASP with impeccable manners. "Yes, I am," Beth said, not bothering to explain about being adopted. It never did any good.

He was middle-aged and good-looking, with a close-cropped dark beard. His hair was long and his shirt was made of expensive gray silk. "Consider yourself forgiven," he said, laughing at both of them, at the pretension.

She warmed to him, lifted her glass. "To Aspen," she said.

"To Aspen."

"Is it still snowing out?" Beth asked.

"It was a half hour ago when I got here," he told her. "I'm Dennis, by the way."

"Beth," she said.

Terence was coming toward her, making his way through the throng. Smiling, handsome. Slick.

"Hi, Sis," he said deliberately. He never called her "Sis," for God's sake.

"This is your brother?" Dennis asked politely.

"Terence Connelly," he said, holding out his hand in that politician's gesture he'd learned from Matt.

"Are you in politics, too?" Dennis asked Terence.

"Uh, not really. I'm getting my doctorate right now in foreign affairs at Georgetown," Terence replied. He made it sound commendable, when indeed he'd been a student for thirteen years, starting over, failing courses, never finishing his thesis.

"I'd love to talk, but someone's waiting for me at the Ute City Banque," Dennis said to Beth regretfully.

"Too bad you can't stay," Beth said with elaborate insincerity.

"Yeah, too bad. Look, here's my card," he said, taking one from his pocket. "Call me. You ski?"

"Sure."

"We'll get together. Nice meeting you, Terence." He smiled, pressed Beth's hand and made his way through the crowd.

Beth glanced at the card. Dennis Metzler, Beverly Hills, California. Casually she dropped it on the bar where it soaked up spilled Scotch.

"Too bad," Terence said. "He seemed nice."

"And married," Beth said dryly. She turned to the bar and swallowed her drink. Terence sidled up next to her. The cute blond bartender appeared as if by magic.

"Need another?" she asked, smiling, a dimple in her cheek, her hair gleaming golden in the dim light, a mass of riotous curls. The requisite white bartender's shirt pulled tight across her breasts, and her cheeks were pink.

"No thanks, sweetheart, I'm fine for now," Terence said. "Beth?"

"Later. I'm going to rejoin the folks."

"By the way, this is Heather. She lives here," Terence was saying.

"Hi, Heather," Beth said politely. Another of Terry's conquests, she thought.

"Oh, hi, nice to meet you." Heather's hands fluttered; she was shy. Ah, yes, Terence would like that.

Terence leaned across the bar and said in a breathy voice, "You have the most gorgeous hair, you know that?"

Beth looked away. It was like watching a lion close in on its kill—in the natural order of things but distasteful to witness.

Heather said something in a low voice, giggled a little, then she was called away by a waitress.

"God, she's cute," Terence said.

"Be nice," Beth said.

"Nice." He grinned wolfishly.

Beth left him at the bar and sat down at the table with the family. Matt's face was red, his voice louder. Buzz had a shine to his eyes and they didn't quite focus. "God, it's getting late," Matt said suddenly. "We have to ski tomorrow, right? It's a date?"

"Ski? Sure," Buzz said enthusiastically, although everyone knew his skiing consisted of a run from the Sundeck bar to Bonnie's bar, a long rest, then up the lift to the Sundeck bar again.

Everyone rummaged around for coats or purses. Buzz creaked upright, thick-necked, grizzled, battered, a lopsided grin on his face. Lee stood, sat down abruptly, then stood again, swaying a little. Out of habit Matt took a firm grip on her arm.

"Who's driving?" Cynthia asked.

Matt slapped his coat pocket. "I've got the keys, Cyn."

"You've had too much to drink," she said.

"Listen, Cyn, I've driven in Washington traffic drunker than a skunk. No problem. My car, I drive."

"Oh, for God's sake," Cynthia retorted. "Act your age, Matthew!"

"Not on your life," he said flatly.

Terence came over to the table. "Going, huh? Listen, I'll be along soon. Heather, the bartender, well, she's off in a few minutes. She's going to change and drive me home. Okay? See you there?"

Matt waved a dismissive hand at his son. "You kids."

Terence's mouth stretched into a feral smile. His blue eyes gleamed, his well-shaped head and heavy shoulders were as sleek as an animal's. He moved with a renewed litheness. "Well, catch you later."

The clan moved through the crowd, Buzz stumbling once, Lee listing but holding on to Matt's arm, Cynthia stalking, frowning, meeting every glance with the hard Connelly stare. A procession, Beth thought, a royal procession.

They piled into the big Range Rover, squeezing together. It was still snowing, and the car's headlights made twin tunnels in the black night, catching the tumbling crystals, momentarily freezing them in their descent. Matt drove well, steering past the shops and bars and restaurants, along the streets where revelers still walked, arm in arm, an army of people searching for excitement and glamour, for a touch of that star quality that was Aspen.

Matt turned east, out of town, along the highway that quickly became dark. The road was snow-packed, piles on either side, the oncoming traffic sparse at this time of night. It was only a mile or so past town to the Preserve, that elite subdivision along the Roaring Fork River where large houses were built on larger lots. Privacy, scenery, views, security.

The Connelly house had been built only five years before. Previously the clan had used condominiums in town, but that had become cumbersome. This house, Matt's pride and joy, was a gigantic place, with soaring ceilings, wooden beams, stone and glass. Downstairs was a rabbit warren of bedrooms and baths. A family bastion.

Buzz had dozed off in the back seat and had to be awakened as they drove up to the house. The cavernous garage echoed with their voices as the door slid down behind the car automatically, cutting off the Christmas-card scene outside. Into the house, through the huge mudroom with skis lined up on wall racks and pairs of boots neatly set side by side with built-in boot dryers inserted in each pair, past the vast, dark kitchen with its polished granite counters and built-in appliances, into the living room with its snow-shrouded view of the dark slumbering mountains and bright gaiety of downtown Aspen.

"Lights!" Matt said, flipping on the recessed lighting.

"Cameras, action!" Buzz cried.

"Nightcap anyone?" Matt asked.

Lee went off to bed, saying, "I'm fine, dear, just fine." The rest started in on a bottle of ancient brandy that had been a present to Matt from the Kuwaiti ambassador, a Muslim teetotaler.

Beth was feeling a heavy dullness—those damn pills. A brandy now? Bad idea. She declined the drink and ignored Matt's teasing.

Edward Crenshaw, Buzz and Cynthia's son, joined them in his bathrobe, and they sat around and gabbed and sniped, all the familiar old stuff. Buzz leaned back and swallowed a mouthful of sweet, burning brandy. "Shit, that's good," he said with satisfaction.

Beth yawned and watched the family with her usual detachment. Movers and shakers, smart, worldly people. Drinkers, carousers, the men sexually irresponsible with a penchant for tabloid headlines, which somehow the voting public kept forgiving . . . and forgiving. Close, tight, with ferocious family loyalty, they bickered constantly and hurt those closest to them with amazing regularity.

And yet Matt and his nephew, Edward, served their country with insight and liberal-minded social consciousness. Sure, there were back-room maneuvering, trade-offs, marginally unethical bits and pieces that politicians were prone to, but that was hardly exclusive to the Connellys.

There was a sound at the front door then—Terence. Beth rose to open it, and he burst in, laughing, his arm around the pretty blond Heather, who was hanging back, blushing, embarrassed.

"Hi, everyone!" he called out, stamping snow off his boots. "This is Heather Kelly."

"Hi," she said shyly.

"Come on in, get a load off," Matt said cordially.

The family members were drifting off now, yawning, upending their glasses for the last few drops of brandy. "Nice to meet you, Heather. Take it easy, kids. Still snowing, huh?" And they straggled, red-eyed and mellow, down the broad staircase to their rooms.

Beth left when Matt did. She could barely navigate the stairs, dulled by codeine. Matt joshed her about being a cheap drunk, not knowing about the pills. He was proud of the younger Connellys' notorious ability to hold their liquor.

"Must be the altitude," Beth said, an old joke. Aspen was at eight thousand feet, the thin air notorious for bad hangovers.

"Yeah, sure, hon. Sleep tight," Matt replied.

In the living room Terence poured a snifter of brandy for Heather. "Try this," he said.

Terence watched her with a predatory intensity. He sat close to her on the leather sectional and ran his hand through the glorious tangle of her hair. Leaning close, he whispered, "God, I've wanted to do that all evening."

He could feel her shiver a little, and her skin seemed to glow, to heat up. What a tender morsel this one was.

He stood, pulling her to her feet. "Come on, I want you to see the Jacuzzi. Maybe we can relax in it."

She looked down. "I don't have a suit."

"So?" He pulled her hand. "Come on."

She went with him, of course, down the stairs, along the dark hallway, his finger to his lips as they passed closed doors. He stopped at his and opened it. "Come in for a sec, I'll get towels," he said, and she did.

He closed the thick oak door behind her with a satisfying snick.

"This is nice," Heather said, looking around.

He actually found a couple of towels and thought about leading her out to the Jacuzzi—to see her nude, all slippery and gleaming.... But he couldn't resist her right there in front of him, now, with the door shut.

He approached her with care, took her in his arms, murmuring. She melted against him, all soft flesh and youth. "You're beautiful," he said, nuzzling her white neck.

"Oh, Terence."

"Terry," he whispered, "all my friends call me Terry."

He ran his hands down her back, cupped her buttocks, moved across to his bed so that her legs were against it. A gentle push, and she lay on it, with him beside her. She stiffened a little and said, against his lips, "I thought we were going to the Jacuzzi."

"We are, we are."

He kissed her again and ran his hands over her hips, her breasts. She withdrew a little; he could feel it.

"Terry," she said, "please, I don't want—" But he silenced her with his mouth. God, she was soft and warm. He reached for the zipper of her jeans and began to tug gently. She put her hands on his chest then and looked him in the eye. "No," she said, and put her hand over his.

"Oh, come on, a little fun, that's all. Heather, be nice," he wheedled.

"I think I'd better go now," she said, sitting up.

"Not yet, please," he said in his best little-boy voice. "Terry..."

Blood beat in his temples, in his groin. He ached deep inside. They always said no and meant yes, always. And he always had them in the end because they really wanted to be mastered, taken. "Heather, honey, you're so beautiful. Don't go."

He pushed her back down and rolled over on her, covering her face with kisses. She shoved at him, and a tiny flare of anger ignited in his gut. Stubborn female. "Stop," she breathed, scared now, rolling her head away, but he put a hand in that tangle of golden hair and pinned her down, pulled her sweater up, her zipper down, yanked at her bra and freed her white, round breasts. He moaned, beside himself.

She bit his hand and cried out. He yelped and put a hand on her throat to stop her. He was hard as iron, powerful, his muscles infused with blood.

She got free, pulled her knees up, panting, slapping at him, thrashing. She started to really yell—he could see her mouth open, her muscles tense. He grabbed her, locking her neck in the crook of his elbow, put his other hand on her mouth and squeezed, shutting off her cry. Finally she stopped fighting him and lay there quiescent.

Power surged through him. He ripped at her clothes, at his own. She lay there so quiet he knew she wanted it. They always did. He kept a hand on her neck so she wouldn't cry out, and he entered her, pounding at her soft body with his strength. He orgasmed so quickly it almost surprised him, and he lay there panting for a minute, drained.

She said nothing, never even moved. Terence raised himself on his elbows and warily loosened his hold on her neck.

"That was good," he crooned.

Something was wrong, though. The girl lay there too silently. He looked closely at her, leaning over. "Heather," he whispered, and a tiny curl of fear moved inside him. He shook her gently, then harder. Damn female, playacting like this. "Heather!" he said sharply, slapping her. Nothing.

My God, the stupid girl was... It hit him like a sledgehammer, took his breath away. He scrambled backward off the bed, zipping his pants savagely. Panic welled, ugly fear, stark and inescapable. Dead, she was dead!

Terence stood there and stared down at her. Conflicting thoughts raced crazily in his head, ricocheting off the inside of his skull. He hadn't meant to, he hadn't! It was an accident!

Oh, damn it! Why? What was the matter with her? He hadn't really done anything, nothing really. If she hadn't fought . . .

Call an ambulance! No, the police. Oh Jesus, no, they'd arrest him, blame him. Murder! No, an accident!

A calmness came over Terence then. The story formed itself in his mind as he stood there, and his awful trembling stopped. Sure, everyone had seen him with the girl, but she'd left, yes, she'd gone home. He knew nothing more, she'd gone, left him because . . . because she was a cokehead and he didn't do drugs. Sure, she'd gotten mad at him and left.

Her car! Her battered old VW! Outside—in front of the house!

He threw his jacket on, straightened Heather's clothes, carefully zipping, hooking, smoothing. Found her purse and coat and the car keys in the pocket. He had a brainstorm then and quickly rushed into his bathroom, fumbling for a pill bottle that contained cocaine. Good thinking, he told himself; this would help corroborate his story. He went back to her lifeless body and smeared some of the white powder beneath her nose, just a little, though, don't overdo it.

Yet he was thinking frantically: What in hell good was the coke on her nose going to do when there was none in her bloodstream! Stupid! But it was too late to worry about that now, too damn late. . . .

He straightened, took a calming breath. He could pull this off. Gloves, he thought abruptly. He was going to drive her car. Yes. Gloves. He put on his driving gloves and hoisted her up over a shoulder. Heavy.

Thank God everyone was asleep. Quietly, quietly. No one even knew she'd been in his room. No proof. He'd stayed upstairs with her. He walked swiftly along the carpeted hall, her hair hanging down, tickling his chin, that beautiful hair. Almost to the stairs. Quick now.

A door opened so suddenly his heart almost burst. Beth stuck her head out into the hall, all tousled and heavy-eyed. She saw him and said, "Terence," and then her eyes widened and she froze as white and still as marble.

"She passed out," he said with a quick smile. "I'm taking her home."

"Oh...I...uh-huh...just thought I heard something," Beth said, backing into her room. "Uh, good night."

"Yeah, sweet dreams," he whispered, sweating now, and he continued on, up the stairs, cursing Beth because now he'd have to say that sure, Heather had come to his room. Okay, he thought, he'd tell everyone she'd started that business about taking coke in his room and he'd told her she'd better go....

No. Beth had seen him carrying her. Damn it!

Beth, he thought, fumbling with the front door lock, he'd have to somehow handle her, maybe say Heather had been walking out—okay. Beth had seen it all wrong. Beth was so damn fanciful. And everyone knew she was secretly taking those stomach pills and drinking on top of them.

Yeah, Beth could be handled.

He closed the door quietly behind him, Heather's deadweight in his strong arms, and went out into the night, the snow still falling, smoothing all the rough edges, obliterating everything.

TWO

Case McCandless was a quiet man. As sheriff of Pitkin County, which included the town of Aspen, his wait-and-see attitude fit the bill just fine.

He was a man of simple tastes and simple needs, rock-solid in his embrace of the old-time virtues of family and security and honor and a fulfilling job. He had most of what he wanted, and his job was perfect for him; he possessed the touch, the perfect mixture of ethics and laissez-faire needed by a small-town sheriff. It was as if he knew automatically what to do in awkward situations, how to handle people in trouble.

Oh, there was crime in the county, although not the big-city kind. Despite the most elaborate and costly security systems installed in the multimillion dollar homes, there were still robberies, ski and bicycle thefts, shoplifting. Occasionally a car with the keys left in it would turn up a few blocks away, stolen and then abandoned. Men got drunk and struck their wives or lady friends, and due to an inordinate number of liquor licenses per capita, there were late-night bar brawls that could spill out into the picture-perfect malls. Traffic accidents were numerous, especially in the winter, but you hardly needed an academy-trained cop to take down names and help exchange insurance company information.

Of course, every seven or eight years or so someone was murdered, and in Aspen, a well-known name was invariably involved.

It was odd, Sheriff McCandless was to think later, but he'd been contemplating just that fact, wondering if there was going to be some sticky incident this holiday season with all the celebrities in town, when the call came in over the patrol car's radio early that morning.

"Pipe down," he said to his two kids in the back seat of the county's Jeep Cherokee. He picked up the mike. "I'm not telling you again, Nate."

"Case, you there? Over."

"Yeah, I'm on my way to drop the kids at the ranch. What's up?"

"We have a report of a dead body in the parking lot of the Aspen Health Club. Over," Beverly, the dispatcher, said.

The radio reception was breaking up as Case drove the narrow Maroon Creek Valley. "Say again. Over."

"A dead body, Case, parking lot at the Aspen Health Club."

"Hell," he muttered. He pressed the button on the mike. "Send Loren. Over."

"He's there. Wants you ASAP. Over."

"I copy that. I'll drop the kids off and be on my way. Twenty minutes. Over and out."

Seven-year-old Nate and five-year-old Amanda were still going at it in the back seat. "Nate . . ." Case said, his voice calm but authoritative despite his preoccupation with this new problem—obviously something his capable deputy Loren didn't want to handle without his boss's presence. "Now look," he said to his children as he drove the icy road, "your grandma is real busy, and I want you monkeys to behave today."

"Grandma's always busy," Amanda said, and she pushed at Nate.

The McCandless guest ranch lay a mile ahead now, nine miles from Aspen up the narrow, twisting valley that was bracketed by precipitous pine-covered mountains. At the top end of the valley sat the Maroon Bells, reportedly the most photographed peaks in North America, three massive pyramids of striated rock that rose more than fourteen thousand feet into the thin atmosphere and claimed the life of at least one rock climber a year.

"Can we go snowmobiling today, Dad?" Nate asked, leaning forward. "Uncle Nick said—"

"Your Uncle Nick's busy. Don't bug him today."

It had been hard on Case for the past three years, being a single parent. At thirty-five he was feeling the pressure of balancing a career and raising his children properly. Of course, over the Christmas holiday when school was out, his mom, Dottie, was a lifesaver—and so were his bachelor brothers—but they couldn't do it all.

Dottie met them at the door. As always at seven-thirty in the morning, she was cooking breakfast for the guests, gingham apron tied around her ample hips, her gray pageboy held back with two big, brown bobby pins.

"Hi, babies." She beamed and gave both of her grandchildren huge hugs as her son shot her a quick smile, then headed out to his car and straight back along the same route he'd just taken. He crossed Aspen without using his flashing lights. If there was a body up at the Aspen Health Club on the far side of town it was no use rushing through the heavy Christmas traffic and causing an accident, not for the dead person's sake, anyway.

He saw Loren's white Cherokee, just like his own, immediately upon pulling into the parking lot of the plush health club, and behind it the yellow bands of the police barrier to keep the public from the crime site.

Loren strode up to his car. "She's over here," he said, blinking in the snow that was still drifting down.

Case tugged on the brim of his Stetson as he stepped down out of the car. "She?"

"Driver's license in her purse says her name is Kelly. Heather Kelly. The picture matches. She also has a card to the Antler Club in her wallet."

"Um," Case said, thinking about that as he followed his deputy over to an old VW that sat in a corner of the lot. The car was covered with snow, Case noted, but he could see that not too long ago someone—Heather?—had cleared the windshield.

He opened the door, aware of a couple of cars pulling into the lot. Shortly it would be full, but in nonchalant Aspen, people were trained not to stare.

He let out a low, sympathetic whistle as he crouched to look in. "Awfully young," he said to himself. Then, "Who reported this?"

"A jogger. About an hour ago. The man saw her in here and thought she was passed out."

"I take it he looked at her?"

Loren nodded. "That's what he said. And then he went to the nearest phone, which was in the club."

"You have his name?"

"Yep. Got a full statement from him, too. Not much help."

"Okay," Case said, still crouching, looking at the body. Indeed, Heather Kelly could have been passed out. Her blond head lay tilted to the right and back, against the headrest, and her eyes were closed. Except for her ashen pallor she sure could have been asleep.

But she wasn't.

Case straightened and put his hands on his jean-clad hips. "You call the coroner in Glenwood Springs yet?"

"No. I thought you'd want to see her first."

"Okay, go ahead and contact Aspen Valley Hospital, get an ambulance, and tell them not to hurry. No point in speeding through town. Get them to contact the coroner in Glenwood. I want an autopsy."

Loren raised a brow.

"See those marks on her neck?" Case said. "I'm no expert, but something doesn't look quite right."

Loren frowned and headed off to his vehicle. Case leaned down again and eventually squatted on his haunches next to the driver's side, studying the girl's face. Snow collected on his hat and shoulders, settling gently. His breath came out in white plumes, slow and easy. He felt a little sick, not that he'd ever let on to anyone. Still, he stared at her, seeing those marks on her neck more clearly with each passing second. And could that be a white, powdery substance around her nostrils?

After a time he stood up again and carefully closed the door. Lester Wiggins, the coroner, would tell them about the powder.

It was then that Case studied the surroundings. He couldn't help wondering when Heather had pulled her car into this lot, and why. Of course there remained the big question: how had she died?

He walked around the area, his cowboy boots half-buried in four inches of fresh snow. But a snowplow had been through, you could still tell that, probably sometime before dawn, on call at all times from the Aspen Health Club, which opened at six a.m.

He turned and looked at Loren and called, "I'll be back in a few minutes. I'm headed into the health club." He then crossed the lot and took the path down a hill and across a wooden footbridge above the frozen Roaring Fork River, then up the other side past snow-covered outdoor tennis courts and on into the clubhouse.

At the desk he asked the girl, "Is the manager in yet?" He wasn't, but the girl was able to give him the pager number of the man who was contracted to plow the parking lot. It seemed too easy. And Case was beginning to get a feeling that this proceeding wasn't going to be easy at all.

It struck him after calling the man on his pager that he was going to have to contact Heather Kelly's relatives, and do it soon. Funny how he'd forgotten that till now. Well, not funny, Case thought as he headed back into the snowstorm; it was predictable and normal. Who the hell wanted to tell a girl's parents that their daughter had just died? An image of his daughter, Amanda, flashed through his mind, but he quickly blocked it out.

Loren was on the radio when he got back to the parking lot. It seemed there'd been a near miss at the Pitkin County Airport, a small private jet that had skidded off the runway on takeoff. Loren was requesting that the police department help handle it as Bob, the other sheriff's deputy on duty, was busy with a fender bender out on Highway 82.

Case looked at his watch. It was only just past eight. He couldn't help wondering how many more calls his department was going to receive before nightfall in this valley whose population swelled from ten thousand in the off-season to more than eighty thousand during the holidays.

Les Wiggins, the coroner, arrived at nine and insisted that the ambulance personnel wait till he finished his initial examination of the body and scene before they removed the corpse from the automobile. And then, while Case was talking to the snowplow driver, Wiggins suggested the city police department's evidence expert be called to take a fingerprint dusting of the car's interior, door handles, etc.

"I was afraid of this," Case said, taking off his hat, shaking the snow from it. "It's those marks on her neck. You don't think it's a simple overdose."

Wiggins shook his head noncommittally and went back to his work. Case continued his questioning of the plow driver. "Okay, so the car was parked here at three forty-five."

"Well, I can't be exactly sure. . . ."

"Around that time, then. Did you happen to notice the girl in there?"

The driver shook his head. "Maybe if I had . . ."

"I don't think it would have mattered," Case replied. "Anything else? Were there any other cars?"

The man thought for a moment, frowned and then abruptly looked up. "There was this guy. . ."

"Guy?"

"Yeah, I remember now. This guy walking along the driveway toward the highway. I mean, it was so late it seemed strange. Course, in Aspen, you know, there're late parties all the time."

"Sure, I know. Can you describe this man?"

"Well, he was all hunched over in the storm like he was freezing. He was wearing, like, this leather aviator's jacket."

"Interesting," Case said. "Think you'd be able to recognize him again?"

"Well...I...hey, you think this guy might have...you know, hurt the girl?"

"I'm not thinking anything," Case said in his slow, calm manner. "I'm only asking. Could you recognize him?"

The man thought. "I never saw his face or anything. You know, it was dark and snowing like hell."

"Yeah," Case allowed. "Okay, you can go on back to work."

The next hour dragged by. Wiggins took his sweet time while the ambulance driver groused about having to wait out in the cold. The parking lot filled, folks headed to the club getting out of their Range Rovers, four-wheel-drive Toyotas and Subarus, Jeeps and even a couple of Mercedeses that were hell in the ice and snow. They took a look in the direction of the yellow police ribbons and the commotion, then, apparently unconcerned, headed off to work out. Mike, Case's top detective, a former policeman from Denver, went over the scene as well, taking photographs, conferring with Wiggins, filling Case in from time to time.

And all the while, Case knew he had to find out where this poor girl's family was. In the valley, he suspected, because the plates on her car were ZG, those coveted Aspen plates that marked the driver a "local," and the vehicle was registered to a Nancy Kelly, address Lazy Glen Mobile Home Park, a trailer park fourteen miles outside Aspen down the valley. It was nearly ten o'clock.

Heather had been dead for hours and someone had to tell her folks. That someone being him.

At ten-fifteen they finally put Heather's body into a zippered black bag and loaded it into the ambulance. Wiggins blew into his half-frozen hands and stomped his feet. He was wearing tennis shoes. "I'll give you my initial report tonight," he told Case as he got into his car and cranked up the heater. "But right now I think you got more than just a regular OD here, although we'll do her blood."

"She was strangled?"

"Looks like it. And there are marks on her breasts, too, but I'll do that examination in Glenwood Springs."

"And the substance around her nose?"

"Hey, the lady got herself killed in Aspen," Lester Wiggins said smugly and left it at that.

"Yeah, right," Case replied and he closed the coroner's door for him.

It was easy locating Nancy Kelly. Aspen was a small town. It was *not* easy talking to Nancy, not easy at all.

She worked for a local property-management company in the heart of the town, one of those outfits that catered to the megawealthy, right down to filling the refrigerators in their rental houses. She was a receptionist, an attractive woman of about forty, divorced. Case would remember her for a long time. She wore bright colors against her frosted, blond hair, and her clear blue eyes were quite pretty.

Her eyes didn't stay clear for long, though.

After half an hour, her co-workers in shock, comforting her, Case arranged for one of them to drive her to the hospital to identify Heather. Merely a formality, but it had to be done. He told Mrs. Kelly how very sorry he was, and left. In spite of the cold outside and the snow collecting on his dark blue sheriff's department parka, his shirt was sticking to his skin. He remembered something he'd once heard: the Chinese believed there was no worse fate than outliving your own children.

It was an odd day for the sheriff. At times it dragged; at times the minutes flew by. His department answered eight more calls before the skiers descended from the mountain, and the partying wouldn't even hit stride till eleven p.m. Case himself spent half the day tracking down Heather's co-workers at the downtown Antler Club, and each one seemed to think the other had been on shift later than the last, but he did learn one thing— they all agreed on it—Heather Kelly had been last seen at the bar in the company of Terence Connelly, the son of the U.S. senator and known magnet for scandal.

Case left the Antler Club at three-thirty and stood on the busy street for a moment, his brow creased. Hadn't it been just that morning he'd wondered about some well-known celebrity getting messed up in a scandal? Of course, Case realized, the fact that Heather had been seen leaving the Antler Club with Terence Connelly didn't necessarily add up to a hill of beans.

He drove out to the Connelly estate, which was situated in the luxurious east-end subdivision known as the Preserve. As he once again drove toward the entrance to the Aspen Health Club on the edge of town it struck him: the snowplow driver had seen a man walking at an early-morning hour out of the Aspen Club driveway. A slightly unusual occurrence but not seriously suspicious. And yet . . . Case drove on, past the club entrance, and frowned, thinking. The Preserve, where the Connellys lived, was perhaps a mile farther along this same highway, and if someone were to leave a car in the club parking lot and walk to the Preserve, there was only one route he could take—out the club driveway, turn right on the highway... But Case didn't know which way the lone walker had turned, and neither did anyone else. Hell, he didn't even know who the walker was.

It might not mean a thing, but still he logged the information in his mind.

Naturally, when he rang the doorbell of the Connelly house, a maid answered and coolly informed him in a thick Hispanic accent that the Connellys were skiing and not expected back till later. He thanked her, left his card and asked if she'd have Mr. Terence Connelly ring him. He'd be at his office.

At five he called his mother at the ranch, explained the trouble—everyone in town already knew about the girl's death—and asked Dottie if she could keep Nate and Amanda for a few more hours.

At five-thirty Lester Wiggins telephoned him. "The victim was definitely strangled," the coroner said. "She died of suffocation. I'm guessing there was a violent struggle."

"Time of death?"

"Between one a.m. and three a.m."

"Hmm." Case thought a minute. "Was there sex involved?"

"The victim definitely experienced penetration early this morning. I've sent specimens to Denver, but I won't have the results for ten days to two weeks."

"Would you say she'd been raped?"

"I don't want to answer that just yet."

"Your best guess?"

"Yes, but that's not for the record."

"I understand. Oh, that white stuff on her nose?"

"Definitely cocaine. Her blood's been sent for a complete workup, but I expect we'll find her positive for coke, probably alcohol, too. You know Aspen."

After the call Case sat behind his old wooden desk in the basement of the Pitkin County Courthouse and rubbed the blond stubble on his chin. Beverly, who'd stayed late, brought him a cup of coffee and reminded him that he'd had three cups in the past hour. "This isn't like you," she said. "Next thing I know you'll be like the rest of us, uptight and stressed out."

He gave her a weak, lopsided smile that made him appear ten years younger, a handsome college type with a shock of blond hair falling over his brow.

She turned to leave his office. "Oh," she said, "the phone's starting to ring off the hook. I guess someone saw your Cherokee parked up at the Connelly estate today, and everyone knows about that poor girl...."

"Damn," he said quietly. It was beginning.

By 6:45 there'd been a dozen more calls to the sheriff's department but none from Terence Connelly. Case was not one for stewing or impatience, but it stuck in his craw that there was a young woman dead, her body cold and lifeless, and Terence Connelly had gone off for a merry day on the slopes. Of course there wasn't much to tie Connelly to the girl's death, but Case sure wanted to talk to him.

At seven he phoned the Connelly house. The maid answered. Yes, the Connellys were home, and no, Terence Connelly could not come to the phone.

"Is that so," Case said, and he hung up slowly.

At seven-fifteen he was at their door, ringing, his jaw locked. The door finally swung open and, amazingly, taking Case by surprise, he was standing face-to-face with the bulldog figure of Senator Matthew Connelly.

The man wore a sweater and ski pants, not the expensive suits he was usually seen in, but his square face was utterly recognizable and so was the politician's smile on it and the hand he held out with practiced ease.

"Sheriff McCandless? Come in, come in," the senator said affably. "We got the message you'd called. Can I get you something to . . ." He held up his glass.

Case took off his Stetson. "No thank you, sir. I'd like to see your son, Terence."

"Well, I think Terry's in the shower. Why don't we go on into my study and I can . . ."

"It's Terence I came to see," Case repeated, his hat held in his hands. "Could you please tell him I'm waiting."

Matt Connelly's expression didn't waver, though Case was sure the senator didn't like being shunted aside. Matt hadn't once asked what was going on, if there was some sort of problem, but then maybe a cop appearing at the Connelly door was no novelty.

Case did allow the senator to show him inside as far as a sweeping living room that was three times the size of his own house. He stood at the top of the two flag-stone steps that formed a long, elegant curve along the contours of the glass-and-stone room. Snow melted off his cowboy boots and pooled at his feet. There seemed to be Connellys everywhere, a large, formidable group who barely acknowledged Case's existence. They were a boisterous lot, he decided, then he realized they they'd most likely all been out for après ski and were feeling good by now. There were at least four women in the room. One was laughing at something a heavyset man with graying hair was saying by the huge, firelit hearth. Another woman stood near the wet bar and chatted with a man whom Case recognized as the young Edward Crenshaw, purportedly a future presidential hopeful. A very attractive blond woman, perhaps fifty-five or so, looked slightly dazed as she sat on a sofa next to a dark-headed girl with the biggest eyes Case had ever seen and the face of an angel. There were a couple of children romping in and out of the kitchen, and the maid Case had spoken to earlier served fancy-looking crackers to everyone. All in all, there must have been nearly a dozen of them in that big room, and other than an occasional glance in his direction, Case might as well have been a statue.

It must have been ten minutes before Matt Connelly finally reappeared from downstairs with his son, Terence, on his heels. The young man's hair was still wet. A handsome guy, Case thought. Yes, the girls would go for someone with his looks. And an image of Heather Kelly's face rose unbidden in his mind.

"Why don't we step into my—" Matt began, but Case wasn't about to let the senior senator from New York take charge.

In his smooth, slow voice, Case said, "I don't think so, Senator. I'd like to speak to Terence in private."

"Well, then, you can certainly use my—"

"No, sir, thank you," Case persisted. He turned his attention to the man's son. "I'd like you to come on into my office and answer a few questions concerning a young woman named Heather Kelly."

"Heather? Oh, Heather Kelly. Nice girl," Terence said, shrugging. "Met her last night, in fact. What's the trouble, anyway?"

"The young woman is dead," Case stated.

"My God," Matt said. "Dear Lord. Why, she stopped by here." He gazed at his son. "Wasn't that just last night, Terry?"

"It was," Terence said, shaking his head. "She came by for a drink after her shift. I think she left around, let me think . . ."

"Tell you what," Case interrupted. "I'd like to get statements from anyone who saw Miss Kelly last night. We can sure do that in the morning. But being as how Terence here seems to have been the last person to see her, I'd like to get his statement as soon as possible. Tonight, in fact."

"But . . ." Terence began.

It was Matt who said, "Now just a minute here, Sheriff. We want to do all we can to help, of course, but you can't possibly think my son would be . . ."

"I don't think anything, Senator Connelly. I only want to ask Terence a few questions in private. But if you think he needs representation, you can . . ."

"A lawyer?"

Case shrugged. "I never said Terence was being charged with anything. I'm merely collecting information."

"So there's been foul play involved in this girl's death?" Matt finally asked.

"Never said that, either," Case answered pointedly.

"Then what's the trouble?"

"Tell you what," Case said. "If and when there's trouble, Terence here will be the first to know." He switched his gaze to the younger man. "You coming with me or not?" Out of the corner of his eye Case saw the senator give a quick nod.

"Oh, yes, I'm coming," Terence said. "Can I, ah, get my jacket?"

"Sure," Case said.

Matt Connelly was picking up a phone. "Excuse me, Sheriff, but if you don't mind, I'll just call a friend of mine." He smiled, the wide politician's grin that didn't quite reach his eyes. "Harv Burwell. You probably know him."

Case nodded. Burwell was a lawyer. Sure, he knew him.

Matt spoke on the phone, his back to Case, then he hung up and turned around. "Harv will meet you and Terence at your office, Sheriff. Is that all right with you?"

"Sure is," Case said.

"We try to be cooperative," Matt said.

Terence reappeared, shrugging on an aviator-style leather jacket, another fact that Case stowed away in his head.

"All set?" Case asked.

"Harv Burwell will meet you, Terry," Matt told his son.

"Oh, thanks, Dad," Terence said casually. He turned to Case. "This won't take long, will it?"

"Sure hope not," Case replied, and he led the younger man out into the winter night.

THREE

$\Longleftrightarrow$

Billy Jorgenson was everyone's ideal of the picture-perfect ski instructor. Thirty-six years old, six foot two inches tall, with deep golden skin and blue bedroom eyes, Billy had the body of which sculptors dreamed. Around Aspen he was known as someone for the local ladies to avoid—unless they were filthy rich. At night Billy was the star bartender at the Tippler, an après-ski mecca and late-night swinging disco. During the day, of course, he plied his trade on the mountain, though it was said that the perennially youthful Billy was far more interested in what his clients could do for him than the reverse.

The other thing the locals knew about Billy was that he never, ever taught men to ski.

Beth Connelly had met Billy the previous winter, though she'd spent most of that winter in Africa, far away from the clan. She'd taken a private lesson from him, and they'd hit it off, although Beth had been aware from the first that he liked rubbing shoulders with the jet-setters and the wealthy. Still, he was great company, and his ego was so large he never questioned anything she did.

She needed Billy today. She needed to forget, to somehow get that terrible memory out of her head, Terry in the hall, Heather's limp body.... A whole day and night on the town—that would fit the bill.

She met Billy in their usual place in front of the ski school office at the base of Aspen Mountain, Ajax to the locals.

"I was surprised you were free today," she said as she bent over to fasten the buckles on her boots. She could feel Billy's eyes on her bottom, the winter white, one-piece ski suit stretched over her rear.

"I did have a client," Billy said. "But when I heard you'd called, how could I say no?"

"I'm flattered," Beth replied, straightening, giving him a bright smile. He was handsome, and she admired his skiing, the litheness, the grace of his strong body in the moguls. It was no wonder at all that women took Billy on side trips, inviting him to their Caribbean villas or to Switzerland for a week—all expenses paid, naturally.

"Ready to hit the slopes?" he was asking, and Beth nodded, hoisting her skis to her shoulders, following him to the gondola building. For Beth, skiing the Rockies was a powerful kind of drug without the side effects. When she was pushing her body to its limits at eleven thousand feet, euphoria set in, a sense of freedom she could find in no other pursuit. Far below in the real world nothing existed, not her family, not the hungry children so desperately in need. Problems seemed to melt away magically with each perfect turn of her skis, each time she planted a pole and then carved a groove in the snow with her edges. It was pure heaven, the sweetest forgetfulness.

At lunch, still exhilarated, Billy ordered a bottle of wine, and Beth slowly sipped two glasses. God knew she needed it. By two she was exhausted, weak and nauseated, and had to tell him the truth about her medication.

"No problem," he said, standing in the brilliant sunshine on the steep slope of Bell Mountain, his eyes so blue Beth felt her knees go rubbery. "Why don't we go to my place and you can put your feet up."

"I should go home," Beth said, but with no conviction.

Billy's one-bedroom condo was, as always, a monument to himself. Blown-up posters of the daring skier hung everywhere, and there was a trophy shelf dominating the living room. A dozen pairs of skis leaned on walls, and two expensive French racing bikes sat near the door.

The first thing Billy did was check the messages on his machine. There were three. All from women, one an overseas call informing him that she would be in town next week and would love a private lesson. Billy listened to the tape, not even shooting Beth an apologetic smile.

He then made a fire while Beth put her feet up on his once-white couch and leafed through the latest issue of *Ski Magazine*. Out of the corner of her eye, she could see a local newspaper on the far end of the stained coffee table. The headline read: Murder In Aspen. She quickly looked away.

"There," Billy was saying, dusting off his hands as the fire caught and popped behind him. "You want a soda or something?"

Beth closed the magazine, her gaze inadvertently sliding to that headline. She shook her head.

"Sure you're okay?" he asked.

"I'm fine now. It must have been the altitude."

In late December the sun set on the downtown core of Aspen by three. It dipped behind the shoulder of Aspen Mountain and was gone, leaving the old mining town washed in a pale light that faded entirely by five, giving way to night. Beth felt herself waning with the light, slipping into semiconscious oblivion as the pill she'd taken earlier took hold.

They were still in the living room, cuddled together, Billy kissing the pale column of neck exposed as Beth's head lolled on the back of the couch. Her ski suit was off now, and only her silk long underwear stood between his hands and her flesh.

Beth wasn't sure when he carried her into his bedroom. It was dark out. And his room was dark, the bed unmade. A bar of light from the open door fell across the mattress, and when they lay there together she was vaguely aware of her thin, white body against the gold of his well-toned muscles. She recalled him using protection, but that was all.

Awakening later, Beth sat bolt upright and felt her temples pound and the cotton-dryness in her mouth. She padded shakily to the bathroom, drank a full glass of water and promptly threw it up in his toilet. A shower helped, but not much, and somewhere in her fuzzy brain she knew she'd brought this on herself. She belonged home in bed, fighting off the dysentery, getting her strength back. Damn, she thought, stupid.

They shared a frozen TV dinner later, Billy obviously feeling just fine as he moved around his kitchen, pouring himself a drink, offering her one, which she declined. She declined his offer of cocaine, too. Enough was enough.

And then, at eleven, he was ready to paint the town. "Let's head on over to Shooters," he said. "There's a great country and western band in town. Hey, you like that stuff, don't you? It's not too hick or anything?"

"I love good country and western," Beth said, feeling semihuman. "It's just that I don't have anything to wear."

"Your car downtown?"

She shrugged. "Yes. It probably has three tickets on it by now."

"So, we'll run on up to your place. You can change."

"Oh, let's not," she said.

"It would just take a . . . oh," Billy said, "I get it. It's probably a real bummer at the house right now, all the gossip, I mean."

"Who knows, who cares?" she replied. "They have their lives, I have mine."

"I wonder," he said. "I mean, do you think your step-brother really could have . . . you know?"

Beth shook her head at him. "Come on," she said, "let's not spoil our night talking about it. It's such a dreary subject. Let's have a good time, Billy." She caught his hands and teasingly put them around her waist and kissed him soundly then pulled away, purring, feeling suddenly light.

"Okay then. We can skip the dancing. We'll stay in," he said.

"No," she said. "I want to go out. I want to go out and have fun. I'll just wear my ski outfit. No big deal."

"Then let's do it."

"Yes, let's," Beth said, her family totally forgotten.

At dawn she awoke in Billy's bed, her stomach cramping violently. She dressed silently, sick as the devil, and walked out into the frigid dawn, her ski gloves God knew where. She felt like a fool, and unaccustomed shame filled her. Last night she'd taken another pill and she couldn't even remember Billy making love to her, and that meant—oh God—she certainly had been in no shape to fake an orgasm. What must he have thought? And maybe she'd been so hazy she'd let the cat out of the bag and told Billy about her problem. She'd done that once before, and to this day she could still recall the pity written all over the man's face.

Damn it, damn it, damn it, she thought, walking, blowing into her frozen hands. Why couldn't she just have fun without all the extra baggage?

The red Porsche belonging to Matt that she used in Aspen was still parked up Ute Avenue, past the gondola building, a bright, Day-Glo ticket hanging from the door handle, informing her it was going to be towed. She arrived home at the Preserve just as the Mexican cook was being dropped off. No one was awake, and she walked carefully and quietly down the steps and into her room, closing and locking the door.

It was that night, the night before New Year's Eve, that Beth was awakened by a dream she hadn't had in years. It was a vivid dream, in glorious Technicolor, rich in detail. For some the Aspen dream might have been erotic; for Beth it was a horror show. Always it was the same. She was clothed and lying on a red satin quilt, a cone of light above her. There were three men on the quilt with her, and they were all naked. Slowly, piece by piece, they took off her clothes. She could feel her mouth opening to scream but no sound came. And then their hands were on her, stroking, and one of them was spreading her legs.

It was always then that she awakened, sweating, her heart pounding, her stomach heaving. And she'd remember, she'd know why she'd dreamed that, but she was as helpless awake as she was asleep. Often in the past when she'd had the nightmare, Beth hadn't been sure what exactly brought it on. But this time she knew: Terry and that girl... It took the entire morning to shake the nightmare off, to forget, to pretend all was well with the world.

The story broke nationwide on the last day of the year. It was an explosion of media speculation: Had Terence Connelly, son of the prominent United States senator, been involved in the rape and strangulation death of an Aspen woman?

The TV stations and tabloids had an amazing amount of detail considering the "no comments" of the local sheriff's office.

Matt was furious, and the whole house heard his end of the thundering phone conversation with the sheriff.

"What the hell do you mean your office didn't talk to the media? This is going to be the biggest lawsuit you rednecks have ever seen! I won't calm down, goddamn it!" And when Matt wasn't on the phone with the local authorities and Harv Burwell, the lawyer, it was ringing off the hook, the media panting for interviews.

At lunch Matt gave the family orders. "No one, I mean no one, is to talk to anyone about this. It's complete bullshit, and I wouldn't put it past the Republicans to have gotten to that pissant sheriff, what the hell's his name!"

Beth reluctantly shifted her stare to Terry.

It was that day, too, that the police arrived with a search warrant and combed the house. Matt roared at the cops and called Harv Burwell but was told they were within their legal rights as the local judge had issued the warrant. Beth avoided it all by staying in her room, which was also briefly invaded, and from the areas the police searched she could only surmise they were looking for drugs. Of course the men spent a long, long time in Terry's room, emerging with plastic bags of carpet samples, pillowcases, pill bottles, even underwear, despite Terry's sworn statement that he and Heather had remained in the living room.

It was a chaotic day, but Beth managed to steer clear of the confusion, trying on clothes in her room, listening to music, reading, napping. Only once were her thoughts invaded by the image of Terry carrying the girl down the hall, but true to form, Beth was able to blot out the sight, telling herself it would all go away if she just didn't think about it. She'd done that before. In high school and college when the Connelly name had hit the tabloids over one scandal or the other, Beth had learned to bury her humiliation and fear by telling herself that, like Scarlett, she'd think about the whole thing later. Somehow it had always worked.

If Matt was angry that whole day, and Beth's mother took to drinking as a sedative, Terry, much like his stepsister, was doing a good job of pretending nothing had happened. He'd even gone skiing at Snowmass that morning, meeting an old college buddy up at the village twelve miles out of Aspen.

"Maybe you shouldn't show your face around town today," Cynthia had suggested as Terry was collecting his ski gear, but Terry had only shrugged it off, saying he had nothing to hide.

Beth continued to avoid the family, no easy task in the packed house. But the tension was ever present. Every time the phone rang, Matt's booming voice could be heard. "Don't answer the goddamned thing! How in hell did the press get this number, anyway?"

Later she heard him yelling again. "No one's going out tonight, goddamn it! Pull up the frigging drawbridge! I'll kill that Terry, I swear!" Then came her mother's voice, low and pleading.

At five Lee tapped on Beth's bedroom door. "Can I come in, honey?"

Beth let her mother in, but with reservations. Why did Lee always resort to booze every time the going got tough?

The conversation wasn't what Beth wanted to hear, either. "Matt and I have decided the family's going to stay in tonight," she told her daughter as she sat on the edge of the bed, crossing her trim legs awkwardly. "There's no point giving the media anything more to feed on. I'm sorry, dear, I know you were looking forward to Prince Akmet's New Year's party, but—"

"I'm still going," Beth announced. In truth, the glitzy gala at the Saudi Arabian prince's fifty-eight-thousand-square-foot colossus atop lofty Starwood was not Beth's first choice for entertainment. It promised to be a disgusting display of opulence, with every big name in town present. But she was going. Anything to get out of the house.

"I can't understand your attitude," Lee was saying, and she took a long drink from her glass. "You know Matt's feelings about this. And poor Terry, he's . . ."

"Poor Terry?"

Lee lifted a brow.

"Never mind," Beth said. "I'm going. I'm on vacation, it's Aspen, and why should I suffer?"

Lee sighed. "And what should I tell Matt? How am I going to explain?"

"Tell him whatever you want, Mother."

Lee stared at her daughter. "You simply refuse to be a member of this family," she said. "Well, there's one thing you can't turn your back on, Beth. The sheriff's department's been taking statements from all of us. Of course we've cooperated. Tomorrow, I want you to—"

Beth felt her skin crawl. "Why? Why do I have to give a statement?"

"To help your brother. To help—"

"No," Beth said, the blood leaving her face. "I . . . I can't. I didn't . . . see anything."

"That's not the issue. They want to speak to everyone who was here that night. Now, you know what Terry said in his statement. That girl . . ."

"Heather Kelly," Beth said unsteadily.

"That girl was here, and after we all went to bed they had a drink. Then she wanted to use cocaine—" Lee made a ladylike grimace "—and when Terry refused, well, she left."

"I didn't see anything," Beth repeated.

"No, of course not. None of us did, Beth. Just tell them that. Good heavens, it's not as if . . ."

"I don't want to talk about it."

"Then we won't. Just go into the sheriff's tomorrow and—"

"All right, okay," Beth breathed, and she stared out the window at the bleak winter landscape, blinking back tears.

"Promise you won't forget. Do it for Matt if not for Terry, honey."

"For Matt, sure," Beth said. "Let's all bail Matt out. We wouldn't want any more bad publicity. Not this year. It's an election year."

"He's given you everything, Beth, everything. He loves you. He adopted you, he—"

"Yes, he's given me everything. The whole gamut," Beth fired back. "He's given me love and money. But he's also taught me that you can lie and cheat and steal and buy your way out of anything!"

"That's not fair," Lee said.

"Maybe not. But it's true."

She tried calling Billy Jorgenson the minute her mother left the room. She got his machine and left a message, informing her sexy ski instructor that she was going to the prince's party and would love to get together there. Showering, blowing dry her hair, Beth took her stomach medication, promising herself she wasn't going to touch a drop of alcohol and ruin a perfect evening.

But that was before Terry came home and stopped by her bedroom. "Lee says you're going up to the prince's party tonight," he said, standing in her door. "I wish you wouldn't. Matt says—"

"Please just leave me alone."

"Now look," Terry began.

"I mean it," she said. "I don't want to see you or talk to you."

"Jesus," he said. "What's gotten into—"

"You know good and well what the problem is. Don't push me, Terry. I'm warning you."

He left. And she promptly went upstairs to the wet bar and poured herself a stiff drink, lifting the glass in a salute to the Connellys, her eyes brimming with unshed tears.

By ten she felt a little tipsy but relaxed nevertheless. And her stomach was okay, so far. She surveyed herself and smiled at her new outfit that she'd bought at Rita St. John's boutique, a short red satin skirt and matching Western jacket with fringe and big bright appliqués of moons and stars, and red-white-and-blue cowboy boots. The jacket buttoned at a satisfyingly low point and she wore nothing under it. Anywhere else in the world, her outfit would have raised brows. But this was Aspen, after all.

She tried to call a taxi, but there was none available on this, the busiest night of the year. Oh well, Beth thought, and she left the house without a word to anyone, went out through the heated garage and got into the Porsche.

The roads really were terrible. A fine, light snow fell from the inky sky, laying down a thin sheet of ice on the highway as she left Aspen and began to climb the road west of town that led to the private estates in Starwood, the mountainside subdivision made so famous in the John Denver song. The road rose and twisted, a steep ravine on her left, so she hugged the right shoulder in the sporty red car that was utterly ill-suited to winter driving.

Billy, Beth thought, the radio blaring, the car taking the curves, skidding a little here and there. She wondered if he'd gotten her message. Maybe they'd spend the night together again, but this time she'd show a response to his lovemaking. Maybe this would even be *the* night, the first time ever for her. God, what he must think of her, Beth thought, her brain still a bit fuzzy. And that was when she rounded a curve a little too fast, felt the sickening drift of her car on the ice and saw the oncoming headlights.

Beth jammed on the brakes—the wrong move—and the Porsche headed right at those blinding lights. Then the bright beams of the other car swerved, and somehow, miraculously, it passed her, perilously close to the edge of the yawning, dark drop-off.

She slowed, her heart pounding a wild tattoo in her breast. In the rearview mirror she could see the other car, and it was all right—still on the road. For a split second she thought of backing up and saying something, but what? "I'm sorry"? God.

Oh well. She put her car back into gear and headed on, and that was when the image popped into her mind. Had that car had a bar of lights across the top? Oops, she thought, then decided it had only been a ski rack mounted there.

She drove past the silent, snowdrifted fields of manicured ranches and up into mountains again, her tires spinning every time she accelerated. At the gatehouse to the exclusive estates she left Billy Jorgenson's name just in case he'd gotten her message. She couldn't imagine Billy passing up an invitation to the party of the season.

The road grew dark again, the multimillion-dollar homes tucked so deeply into the stands of aspens they were invisible except from the air. Once she took a wrong turn and had to retrace her path, and then she spotted a long, slick limo ahead—a Range Rover limo, no less—and followed it. Of course there had to be dozens of galas in Starwood tonight—maybe she'd end up at the wrong one. She smiled. She'd simply crash it.

The limo led her to the prince's, however, the enormous home appearing like a glittering ocean liner upon a dark sea, commanding the entire valley. For a moment she wished her mother were with her—Lee, with her inborn Philadelphia distaste for ostentatious display, would curl her patrician lip. But then Lee was home, dutifully obeying Matt's wishes and probably drunk as a lord.

Beth shook off the notion as a valet parked her car, and she was whisked inside the huge edifice by a straight-faced doorman who was one hundred percent bodyguard material. There would be fifty bodyguards here, fading into the woodwork but alert. The guest list read like *Who's Who*.

Inside, the mansion was surprisingly tasteful despite the overblown size of the rooms. Most of the house, of course, was bedrooms and bathrooms for the prince's entourage—his family, staff and security people. Beth walked toward the din of 250 of Prince Akmet's closest friends, and she looked around, peeking into lighted rooms, appreciating the splendor of the place. Invaluable Ming dynasty vases and jade artifacts sat atop intricately carved teak sideboards next to plush French settees and Danish modern light oak tables, while handsomely preserved Egyptian relics of gold were enclosed in display cases. The rooms themselves were showcases, and most of what Beth saw was museum quality. Somehow it all fit magnificently. And the artworks—Picasso, Salvador Dali, Modigliani, all lighted and framed beautifully. Ellen would just have drooled, but then most likely Ellen had seen the place. Maybe she'd even sold the prince a painting or two.

The mansion opened up into a space the size of a palace, the ballroom shaped like a ship's prow, the acres of floor-to-ceiling glass affording a commanding view of the Roaring Fork Valley far below, the lights of Aspen twinkling in a snow haze beyond. It was something out of a fairy tale, a true palace set in the heart of the Rockies, the guests' laughter and good cheer filling the immense room, odors of fine food drifting on the air and the sound of champagne corks popping, one after another. At one end of the room people danced to a five-piece band, disco style, and at the other end were tables laden with goodies and gorgeous, carved ice figurines. There was even an enormous Christmas tree, thoughtfully provided ambience from the Muslim prince.

And the crowd of revelers. Every woman was shimmering and sparkling, every man suave and draped with leather and cashmere. This was "Aspen formal," which meant anything went except city-formal clothes, so there were, God forbid, no suits or sport coats or tuxedos.

But despite the lack of formality, the wealth of these people was evident on fingers and wrists and around long, graceful necks. Solid gold Rolex watches were a dime a dozen as were Peretti jewels. Oh yes, the place oozed wealth, and an aura of power zinged in the air.

Beth got her bearings, looked at the masses of humanity for a familiar face and saw a gaggle of movie stars, a diplomat, a famous writer and her host, Prince Akmet, tall and dark and bearded, in a thousand-dollar white cashmere turtleneck sweater, its sleeves casually pushed up, and a heavy gold chain around his neck.

"Would you care for a drink?" a formally attired waiter asked her, and Beth took a glass of champagne. Tonight she'd have fun. To heck with Lee and Matt and the whole clan. To heck with Terry.

She meandered through the crowd, not seeing anyone she really wanted to talk to, sipping at the champagne. She went to stand by the thirty-foot-high windows, and she looked at the town's lights in the distance. She could see Aspen Mountain looming on the south edge of town, an inky, cloud-shrouded mass against the blackness. There was a light crawling straight up the face of a slope, a lonely snowcat on its shift in the clouds, grooming the runs for the hordes that would ski tomorrow. For a moment she lost herself, musing, wondering what that lone soul was thinking. Did he miss family and friends on this holiday night? So lonely up there on that desolate mountainside. But later he'd go home, join his family, sleep a dreamless sleep. A normal life. How bad could that be?

Beth put the glass of champagne down and felt a twinge in her stomach. Damn, she thought, but at least she'd taken her medication before leaving for the party. She'd be okay; she only had to lay off the booze that was flowing like a river around her.

She'd been unaware of a man at her side, studying her. "Hello," she finally heard in her ear and she turned. A young man, dark and as handsome as a young Omar Sharif, stood there.

"Hi," she said, "just admiring the view."

"Quite a view, yes," he said, his voice slightly accented. "I'm Mohammed, the prince's nephew...well, one of his nephews."

"And I'm Beth Connelly," she said, her small, pale hand lost in his. "Very nice to meet you."

"Your father..."

"Yes, Matt Connelly."

"Ah, I see."

"I'm afraid he's not here tonight. He wasn't feeling well," Beth said easily.

"I'm so sorry," Mohammed said. "I do hope..."

"Oh, it's nothing."

"And are you in politics, Beth?"

She laughed, liking this earnest young Arabian prince. "No, not me. I'm . . . well, I work for Children's International. Do you know it?"

"I believe so. A worthy cause. I am being trained to be in the military myself."

Beth raised a brow. "Is that something required of you?"

"Oh, yes. I will be a pilot with our air force. I train here, of course, as do many of my cousins."

"Hmm." She looked at him. "Is that what you want to do?"

He shrugged. "Want has very little to do with it. I do my duty to my family."

"Oh yes, I know that scene," Beth said. "Here's a toast to family. How's that, Mohammed?" she asked, picking up the glass again.

He smiled shyly. "Well, actually, my new friends in your military call me Moe."

"Moe, as in Larry, Curly and . . . ?"

"Yes."

"Great, I love it. So, here's to family, Moe." And she raised the glass to his, which held only soda.

The party was looking up. To tell the truth, most of Akmet's guests were older than she was, Moe being an exception. He took her around, introducing her to various dark-eyed family members, whose names she promptly forgot. Midnight was fast approaching, the party getting noisier with that New Year's intensity: Have a good time or die trying.

Vaguely she wondered where Billy was. Had he found someone else, something better to do? Most likely. What a user he was. "Slam, bam, thank you, ma'am. Someone with more to offer just popped into my life. . . ."

Beth found herself sitting on a soft couch in a dim, cavernous room away from the throng. A new glass of champagne was in her hand, though she didn't remember how it got there. Mohammed—Moe—had his arm around her shoulder and was telling her about his schooling at Harvard. She felt relaxed, her stomach quiet for the moment, and she wondered if Moe was going to ask her to spend the night with him. She wouldn't. Still, he was a sweet young man, kind and gentle. Someday he'd have a harem of adoring wives.

She drifted, sinking into that gorgeously yielding upholstery, listening to Mohammed's lovely accent.

"You like children, Beth?" he was asking, and she had to rouse herself.

"I love them."

"And so your charity work is gratifying?"

"Oh, yes. There are kids all over that need help so badly."

"You have none of your own, then?"

She shrugged. "I'm not married."

"But these children you want to help, they come with many problems."

"We all come with baggage. We overcome it," she began to explain, but they were interrupted.

"Excuse me," a waiter was saying, standing in front of the couch. "Are you the lady who came in the red Porsche?"

Beth straightened a little. "Yes, that's mine. Is . . . ?" It struck her—Billy was here. Oh great, he'd come and he couldn't find her in this mass of people. "Oh," she said, "is someone looking for me?"

"Well, yes. There's a man at the door asking for you."

She turned to the prince. "It's a friend of mine. Excuse me. He's probably lost in this crowd. Okay, Moe?"

She patted his knee and gave him a bright smile. "I'll introduce you to him. Be right back."

She followed the waiter to the front door, smoothing her red satin jacket over her hips and shaking out her hair, running a hand through it. Billy...damn, what was she going to do with Billy and Moe?

It struck Beth, too, as she walked, that despite the fact that she'd only sipped at the champagne, it was still affecting her—or was it those damn pills? Well, maybe she'd just get Billy to drive her home. Sure.

It wasn't Billy waiting for her, though, in the wide, tiled entranceway. It was a perfect stranger, a tall man in the damnedest getup, a dark blue parka over some kind of uniform, cowboy boots, a gray Stetson held in one hand and the lights gleaming on a golden blond shock of hair.

Beth stopped in front of the man and cocked her head. "You're not Billy," she said inanely.

"No, I'm not Billy, whoever he is," the man said in a carefully neutral voice. "I'm Case McCandless, sheriff of Pitkin County. You the lady driving a red Porsche?"

The waiter had slipped away and Beth was alone with the curious character. She tried to bring him into focus. "Yes, how did you—"

"I've been driving up and down Starwood for almost an hour looking for your car."

"Well, you found it," Beth said. "Hey, would you like to come in? It's a terrific party."

He stood there, tall and straight, still smelling like the fresh, cold outdoors, his blue eyes boring into hers. "You happen to recall nearly running someone off the road a short time ago?" he asked, ignoring her invitation.

Beth's heart leapt. "I . . . uh . . . I just skidded a little."

"A little?" he asked. "Had you been drinking at the time, miss?"

"Well, no, I mean I had one drink...."

"So you were driving under the influence."

Her head felt light. This was so silly. "Well, I don't think..."

His handsome, stone-hard face seemed to loom over her suddenly. "Would you please step outside," he said.

"But..."

"I'll need your license and registration."

"You can't possibly—oh, come on, it's New Year's Eve."

"Lady, in this county we take drinking and driving real seriously, especially when you damn near kill somebody."

"What?" she asked like an idiot.

"Please step outside," he repeated dispassionately, and before Beth knew it his parka was around her shoulders—was her coat still inside?—and somehow she'd found her license and registration in the glove box of the Porsche.

Leaning against the car, all too aware of how dizzy she suddenly was, Beth heard his low whistle when he read the name on her license.

"Elizabeth Lee Connelly," he said, his flashlight trained on her New York driver's license. "You're the one I've been trying to get down to the office for a statement." Then, taking her arm, he said, "You're entitled to a roadside sobriety test. If you refuse it your license is automatically revoked—it's the law in Colorado. You forfeit all your rights the minute you admit to drinking and driving."

"Oh, come on. This is so silly. Let's just go on inside. Lighten up."

"The law does allow you to have a breath test at the jail or a blood test at the hospital," he continued.

"No, no. I take this medication . . . I can't take any tests."

"Then I'll just hang on to this license," he said without emotion. "It's the law, lady."

"You can't do that!"

"Why, because you're a Connelly?" he asked.

"No! Good God, no! It's because I take this medicine and it . . . well, you can't drink with it."

She saw him push back the brim of his cowboy hat with a finger and he shook his head. "I'm afraid you'll have to come with me now. Just in case you're not up to speed on the new laws in this state, Miss Connelly, if an officer of the law even suspects you've been drinking and driving, and you refuse any chemical or roadside tests, your license can be automatically revoked on the spot."

"But in New York—" she began.

"This is Colorado, miss."

Beth thought frantically. "But I told you," she said, "the medication I take would show up, and I had a drink at the party, too."

"Do you admit it was you who almost ran me off the road? And you refuse any tests?"

"Yes, I mean no, I . . ."

"Under the circumstances," he went on doggedly, "I'm going to have to place you under arrest for operating a motor vehicle while under the influence."

This isn't happening, Beth thought in a fog as he helped her into the back seat of his car. "The Porsche," she managed to say.

"It'll be fine right where it is," he said, his hand on the top of her head so she didn't bang it.

"Oh, damn," Beth muttered, barely able to right herself in the seat behind the grille, and then they were on their way down the black mountainside, the sheriff driving in silence, his official radio scratching occasionally while her head lolled and her stomach grew queasy.

She barely remembered the ride. It seemed easier to let go and doze than to fight it. She knew she should have been upset, angry, but she couldn't summon up the energy. All she remembered was Lee telling her not to go out. Oh, Matt would be mad as hell, but somehow she didn't care. What did it matter?

She opened her eyes as the Cherokee stopped in Aspen at the light at Mill and Main Street in front of the elegant, century-old Hotel Jerome, lit so prettily for the season, a picture postcard of a long-ago time in a silver-mining boom town. So pretty... She squinted, trying to bring the gay Christmas lights into focus.

And then she was aware of the Cherokee coming to a stop, parking at the Pitkin County Courthouse a block from the old hotel, and of the sheriff helping her out, supporting her as she was led down old stone steps into the basement.

Bright lights assailed her, and people—officers— moved around desks and halls and cubbyhole offices. It was cold in there, and Beth began to tremble, her stomach cramps growing worse by the minute.

Somehow she was charged and booked—a woman was doing it. She managed to ask if she needed a lawyer or something but was told no, not until a court date was set. And then he was there again, asking if she wanted to be picked up by a family member. He'd call for her if she liked.

Beth slumped in her hard chair. Matt would come and get her out of here. Matt . . . She opened her mouth to give the sheriff the phone number, then closed it again. She shook her head. "No," she whispered.

"Look, we don't make people . . ." he began.

"I'll stay here," she got out, the nausea beginning to intensify. She looked up blurrily into that implacable face. "I'm going to be sick," she said, and the next thing Beth knew he was helping her down a hall and opening a door for her. She heard him call out to someone, and then she was in a bathroom, and a lady was helping her and she was miserably, completely sick. Afterward, she splashed cold water on her face, then leaned on her hands over the sink, getting her breath. In the mirror she caught the policewoman's eyes, saw the distaste there and thought, *Oh, what the hell, at least I had some fun tonight.*

It was the sheriff who led Beth across a courtyard, into another building and to her cell, his parka still around her shoulders. "I'll offer you a ride home one more time, Miss Connelly," he said, standing in the door, casually leaning against the bars. "You can come back in the morning when you're feeling better and give that statement."

But she shook her head, handed him his coat and pushed a damp strand of hair off her cheek. "You know," she said, "we could still catch a dance or two somewhere."

"You really are something," he said. "About that ride? This is your last chance, lady."

"No, thank you."

"Okay, but I'm sure the accommodations aren't quite up to your standards."

She gave a weak laugh as she sagged onto a bed. "You haven't a clue about the places I've slept."

"I'll bet," he said, turning, not even closing the barred door. And then he stopped short, his head swiveling back toward her for a moment. "Oh, by the way," he said, "happy New Year."

Beth drew a blanket up to her neck and leaned back against the wall. Happy New Year.

FOUR

Matt Connelly abhorred political correctness. To him it spelled out what was wrong with the country; people were so damned afraid of making a mistake in their places of work, socially, even at home, for God's sake, that this great country was becoming a nation of wimps.

Matt spouted his theory to anyone who'd listen. And when the senior senator spoke, people listened.

A certain type of woman, although sexually attracted to him, shrank with a delicious shiver from his unique brand of political incorrectness. To Matt it was okay if a man and woman took a swing at each other in their own homes, or if a mother hauled off and gave her child a good swat.

Matt hated lawyers. He hated the way they fed on the public. Hell, if you slipped on the ice in front of someone's home and busted your ass, too damn bad. "A bunch of clumsy fools suing everyone in sight," Matt would boom out. "And the goddamn, ambulance-chasing lawyers!"

He hated insurance companies. The powerful lobby of the American Medical Association drove him nuts, and if one more person told him someone wasn't crippled but was "physically impaired," Matt swore he was gonna kill the pussy.

He still drank and drove and thought nothing of two-martini lunches, three if he was in the mood. In the halls of Congress fledgling reporters stalked him, waiting for Matt to say or do something outrageous, rushing back to their editors with a scoop. Nine times out of ten, the editors chuckled. Hell, that was just typical crude Matt Connelly; no one gave a damn, especially the voters. "He gets away with it, kid," an editor would say, "because he achieves what he promises. The public loves the jerk."

Indeed, Matt did produce far-reaching legislation. In dim, smoky hotel rooms, in plush cocktail lounges, on golf courses, ski slopes and on yachts, Matt wheeled and dealed, giving here and taking there, lending an entirely new meaning to the word *compromise*. He got the job done, though. And people voted for him; term after term they shook their heads over the cloud of scandal that enveloped Matt Connelly and they still voted for him. Matt could take the heat, all right, but when it came to his family, when the press went after one of his own, that was another story altogether.

And now they were after not only his son, but Beth, too.

"I have to read about her DUI on the front page of this local rag sheet!" he exploded to Lee. "My own goddamn wife bails her out of jail and can't even tell me!"

Lee sat up in bed, the morning light streaming in the windows, making her head pound. "Stop swearing, Matt," she said. "And what's that terrible noise?"

"A helicopter," he fumed, tugging on the ties of his silk paisley robe. "A news helicopter. They've been circling the house all morning, for God's sake."

"Because of . . . Beth?"

"Jesus," Matt growled, "get a grip, Lee. It's Terry they're trying to photograph. I told him to stay out of sight. If you weren't so damn drunk all the time, you'd know what was going on around here!"

"I am not drunk. Don't be cruel."

"Hungover, then. Does that suit you, dear?"

Lee ignored him and padded to the bathroom, popping a prescription painkiller. Two glasses of water later she was ready to face him. "About Beth," she began.

"Oh, yeah, right. About Beth," he cut her off. "Two days ago she gets her butt tossed in jail—after I told the whole family to stay in, I might add—and now I'm reading about it! Isn't it enough my own son's up to his ears in a mess! What the hell's the matter with Beth?"

"She's upset about Terry," Lee said in a quiet, dignified voice. "I've tried to talk to her, but—"

"So she goes out and gets trashed and it says right here—" Matt stabbed at the headline with a stubby finger "—it says right here she ran that sheriff, what's his name, right off the goddamned road! Is that girl crazy? What's she doing, taking that medication and drinking, too? Is she nuts?"

"Oh, God," Lee whispered, unable to cope with Matt's tirade. "She's oversensitive, that's all."

"To drugs or to life or to what?" Matt thundered. "All that girl does is run off to those Third World countries and make herself sick. Has she ever, once, hung in here when the going got tough! By God, she's a Connelly! I adopted her, raised her, and she chickens out on me every time!"

"She only went to a New Year's party, Matt, she—"

"And got thrown in jail! Drinking and driving!"

Lee glared at her husband. "I wonder who she learned that from."

"Did I ever get thrown in jail? Tell me that!"

"No, of course you didn't. You've been stopped dozens of times, but a well-placed call to the right people got you out of trouble, didn't it? Well, Beth doesn't know how to wheedle her way out of things. She can't pay people off. She wouldn't even think about—"

"Oh, for God's sake, Lee," he said, dismissing her. "Don't start that Philadelphia blue-blooded, holier-than-thou crap on me." He snorted, threw down the paper and went for coffee, leaving her sitting in bed, crying in silence, stifled little sobs welling in her breast— martyr of the year. He hated it.

Matt fumed all day. His entire family was driving him crazy. It was always like this when they congregated on holidays, and he sometimes thought his older sister, Cynthia, was secretly behind it all.

Cynthia was a nitpicker. Like their now deceased mother had, Cynthia believed she was the matriarch of the clan, placed on earth to keep the Connellys on the straight and narrow. And Matt's nephew, Edward, a clone of Cynthia, well, *there* was political correctness if Matt had ever seen it. Oh, Eddy would probably be president someday. But not because of Cynthia's pushing or her well-placed connections, but because, damn it all, Matt had paved the way.

It was on the ski lift that afternoon at Snowmass that Matt swung his gaze onto his sister, a captive audience. "Oh, by the way," he said, "I spoke to the Democratic National Chairman on the phone yesterday, mentioned Eddy getting that Social Security legislation on the books. It was a shrewd move, Cyn. I'm glad I was able to get it through the Senate for him."

Cynthia let out a breath. "Edward did his own leg-work on that bill and you know it."

"Sure he did."

"Don't pat yourself on the back so hard," she said coolly. "It's all we can do to keep our heads above wa-ter these days, Matthew, what with Terry's latest lit-tle . . . escapade."

"Don't worry about Terry," Matt snapped. "It's all media hype."

"Is it?"

"What do you mean, is it ?"

Cynthia shrugged eloquently. "Terry has . . . shall we say, a history of this sort of behavior."

Matt set his jaw. "If you're talking about that little twit at college . . . Date rape," he scoffed. "Hell, he was cleared of all charges. She dropped the whole thing, didn't she?"

"Of course she did, Matthew. After all, you set up a scholarship fund for her, didn't you?"

"Who told you that?"

"My God, Matthew, everyone knew. And she made a mint before dropping charges, too. Didn't she sell the story to some tawdry magazine?"

"Water under the bridge," he grumbled. "And as for this girl, what's her name . . ."

"Kelly. Heather Kelly."

"Yeah. Kelly. The lawyers say she was probably gooned up with cocaine. God knows who she met up with when she left the house that night."

Cynthia sighed, planning her next words carefully. "Matthew," she said, "have you considered the possi-bility that Heather Kelly never left the house that night?"

"Of course she left. They found her at the parking lot of the Aspen Health Club, for Chrissakes."

"I mean...alive, Matthew," she said in an even tone. "I mean that perhaps she was already dead."

"That's enough!" Matt said, aghast. "How could you even think that? Jesus." He fell silent for a minute. "Jesus H. Christ, Cyn," he said finally, "you've gotta quit reading all that crap in the papers. Terry may be lazy. He might be a carouser, Cyn, but he's no killer. I know my son. He likes his women. Who doesn't? But he'd never hurt one. Never."

Cynthia said nothing.

The family met at the base of the Fanny Hill ski lift at four that afternoon. Edward and his father, Buzz, showed up late, as did Edward's wife, Katherine, and their two kids, who'd been in ski school that day. Terry never showed up at all. Matt took off in the Range Rover at four-fifteen, and he stewed about Terry's absence. Where was that kid, at a bar up in Snowmass village? If any newspeople spotted him ... But mostly Matt was fuming over Cynthia's statement: Maybe this Kelly girl had never left the house at all—alive.

Impossible, Matt thought. Terry was a useless kid, but he was not a killer. Terry couldn't have been that stupid!

Beth was home when they all piled out of the car, though she'd been doing a hell of a good job of avoiding Matt for the past couple of days. If she wasn't out skiing on her own, she was locked in her room. Matt stewed about that, too. No one in his family locked themselves away when the heat was turned up. By God, the Connellys stuck together.

By dinnertime Lee was predictably drunk. So was Matt, but he held his liquor better than most. After all, he hadn't survived the past twenty-five years on Capitol Hill by reeling in the halls.

Terry arrived home just as they were all sitting down to dinner. He looked high, but not on booze, and Matt felt a fist tighten in his stomach.

"When the hell do classes at Georgetown start?" he asked his son as he stood at the head of the table, carving a roast.

"Day after tomorrow," Terry replied, reaching for the wine bottle.

"I want you there. No skipping any of them."

"I wasn't going to go back till the weekend," Terry said.

"You'll go back to Washington on time." Matt pinned him with a glare.

A fight erupted then between Edward's two children, who were seated across from each other, and everyone, ignoring the kids, began talking at once—if you could call the conversation at a Connelly meal talking. It was more like a continuous argument.

"Buzz, did you make our reservations for tomorrow morning?" Cynthia asked her husband.

"Now, how in hell could I? I was skiing all day if you'll recall."

Cynthia scowled. "They do have telephones on the mountain, dear."

"Sorry," he said. "I'll call the airlines after dinner."

"You're leaving?" Lee managed to ask, coming out of her stupor momentarily. "Why not wait till we leave on Sunday? Come with us on the Lear?"

"Buzz has work to do," Cynthia said evenly as she gave her husband a look. "A new endorsement for one of the beer companies. We really have to leave."

"Sure you do," Matt put in.

"Now what does that mean, Matthew?" Cynthia asked.

"I think they call it rats deserting a sinking ship," Matt replied. "You can't take the press parked on our doorstep. Might hurt Eddy's image."

"Christ," Edward piped up, but his wife gave his hand a squeeze.

"Do we have to fight?" Buzz asked.

"No one's fighting," Matt said. "We're discussing." He then sat, passing the plate of meat, and turned his attention to Beth. "Where were you all day?"

She looked up, all big, dark innocent eyes. "With a friend."

"Um," Matt said, chewing and talking at the same time. "Care to tell us all about your little stunt the other night?"

She shrugged. "No."

"Um. Don't you think you could have put off your binge until the air clears?"

"Please, Matt," Lee began, but he put up a hand.

"I'm asking Beth. Well? You couldn't do one simple thing for your brother's sake?"

"I wasn't thinking about Terry," she said.

"Now that's real obvious," Matt replied. "And you look like hell, too. Don't you ever eat, get some sun on your face?"

"Her stomach," Lee tried, but it was Beth who interrupted this time.

"Don't worry about me," she told her stepfather.

"Well, I do worry," he said. "They don't take DUIs lightly in this town. It's all the cops have to do. You should know that."

"I do know it. And I was not drunk. I had maybe the equivalent of two drinks all night. It's just that I'd taken my stomach pills...."

"With codeine in them," Matt added.

"Yes. And I guess the law here says if a cop even thinks you're under the influence and you refuse tests, that's it. They can take your license on the spot."

"They took your license?"

"Yes," she said.

"And you're still driving," he stated.

"No, I'm not."

"But you would if you wanted."

"I learned that from you," Beth dared to say.

"Hear, hear!" Cynthia chimed in, raising her wineglass.

But Matt wasn't amused. "It's all a big joke to you, isn't it?" he asked, addressing no one in particular. "Well, goddamn it, it's an election year, and I have enough trouble keeping the press off my butt as it is."

"Every Christmas," Lee said. "Every holiday something seems to happen."

"Don't forget the Fourth of July," Cynthia said. "Wasn't it just two years ago that Matthew was being grilled by the Senate? The savings and loan scandal, wasn't it?"

"A slap on the hand," Buzz said. "Everyone was involved."

"Not everyone," Edward remarked pointedly.

"Your day will come," Matt groused, his mouth still full. "The point is, I want this family to stick together on this trouble here with Terry. I know you've all been in to give statements."

"Beth hasn't," Terry said.

"Beth hasn't what?"

"Given her statement," Terry replied.

"Damn it," Matt said, slamming down his fork. "And why not? If we don't all stick together on this it's going to raise questions. Beth. Beth? Are you listening to me? Why haven't you gone into the sheriff's and—"

"And just what do you want me to say?" she asked tartly.

"For Chrissakes, the same thing we all said! Tell them that this…what's her name?…Kelly, this Heather Kelly left. How goddamn hard is that?"

His stepdaughter was silent.

"Well? I want an answer."

"Maybe you don't," he heard her say.

"Come again?" Matt was aware of an unusual hush at the table, all eyes, even the children's, turned to Beth. He felt a prickling on his skin. "I think you better say what's on your mind, Beth." He heard Terry's voice then, a curse escaping his son's lips, but his attention was still riveted on his stepdaughter. "Let's hear it."

Beth looked at Terry then at her stepfather. "Oh, it's not much, really. I just happened to get up that night, and I saw—"

"Shut up," Terry snarled.

"Well, it could have been that girl, I suppose. I didn't see her face, of course, but she was not exactly conscious."

Suddenly Terry sprang to his feet, his chair falling over backward, his napkin drifting to the floor. "You've really lost it now!" he yelled. "What're you trying to do to me? Goddamn it, Beth!"

Her gaze rose defiantly to his. "I know what I saw," she said quietly.

Terry stormed out, still cursing, while the room seemed to drain of air. Matt felt sweat dot on his brow

and his jowls were shaking. His son. The girl uncon-
scious. Could Beth be telling the truth? Judging by Terry's reaction... Damn, damn. He looked down at his
plate and collected himself—he'd suffered many a blow
below the belt before. He'd always survived. What Beth
was saying, telling the entire family, was only a glitch
in the process. There were always glitches. You ignored
them, brushed them aside, greased palms. In the end
everything turned out just fine.

"We hear what you're saying," Matt finally got out.
"And I'm sure you believe what you saw. But, Beth, keep
in mind that it's only a statement they want. Give it.
Don't rock the boat. You know what to say."

"Beth, honey," Lee began, but Matt shot her a warning look.

"Beth," he said, his tone reasonable, authoritative but
unusually gentle, "you know what you have to do."

"I..." she started to say.

"You're a Connelly," Matt went on. "Period. We stick
together. We survive. That's all you need to remember."

Slowly, Beth rose. She looked him in the eye, and
Matt could see the spots of red on her cheeks. "A Connelly," she said with heavy irony. "Yes, I'm a Connelly,"
and she left the room, heading down the stairs with her
back ramrod straight.

"Goddamn it!" Matt said, his voice hoarse. "Damn it
all to hell."

Cynthia watched Buzz hoist the suitcase onto their
bed in their East Hampton, Long Island, home. She was
frowning. This business with Terry was a ticking bomb;
sooner or later the police were going to get enough on
her nephew to charge him with the murder of that girl.

Terry was stupid. Of course he'd left a trail, and it was just a matter of time....

"Would you like a drink?" Buzz asked her. "I'm going down to get a beer before I unpack."

"Ah, no, thank you. I'll just get my things put away. Tell the cook a light dinner tonight, will you, dear? I must have put on five pounds in Aspen. Matthew always overeats and serves up mountains of food."

"He'll drop dead if he doesn't quit," Buzz added.

I should be so lucky, Cynthia thought, but she caught herself, feeling guilty. She loved her brother, had always loved him despite his overindulgences. It was that son of his. Such a wastrel. Thirty-one years old and he couldn't even manage to get his degree. Why they kept him at Georgetown was a mystery. Probably Matt had fixed it. Matt fixed everything.

And then there was Beth. Cynthia wondered if Matt could fix her, too. If Beth told the truth... But no. Though she wasn't born a Connelly, Matt had control over her in subtle ways. She'd never turn on Terry, not in public. She'd do what she had to and then run off to some remote corner of the world and lose herself in hard work and intermittent bouts of the most god-awful tropical diseases. A sweet, beautiful girl. Overly sensitive, though. And Cynthia wondered if she'd ever escape the family web. No one ever really did.

But that wasn't the problem at hand. Terry was the issue. Damn that boy! He could ruin Edward's chance at the presidency. Public sentiment was evolving; whether or not Matt could see it, the nineties demanded less corruption, more production, and this scandal with Terry could blow up in their faces.

"I won't let it happen," she whispered, shaking out her clothes.

"What, dear?" Buzz asked.

"Oh, nothing, just thinking aloud."

"If that's another reporter, hang up!" Matt bellowed to the cook, who was taking all calls, informing the press that the Connellys were unavailable.

"*Sí*," the young woman called back from the top of the stairs.

But it wasn't another reporter. "Hell," Matt said on the line, "what time is it back there, Cyn? Must be darn near midnight."

"Never mind the time," Cynthia said, brushing aside the chitchat. "I don't want you to blow your stack, Matthew. Just try to listen to reason. I've been giving this business about Terry quite a bit of thought."

"I'll bet."

"Now, Matthew, please just hear me out. That lawyer in Aspen can't possibly handle a delicate situation like this. It's going to take an experienced hand. Someone who knows the ins and outs of the media and can handle the flak. You need a pro. A tough trial lawyer."

"Terry hasn't been charged."

"He will be."

"The hell he—"

"Matthew. I don't mean because of Beth. I know she'd never do anything to hurt her family. It's just that something's bound to turn up."

"Like what?"

"I don't know. So far Terry was the last person to see her alive."

He waved a dismissive hand that his sister couldn't see. "That doesn't mean a thing. They'll find the person who really did see her last."

"I hope so. And that day they searched the house. All the time they spent in Terry's room? What if . . ."

"They found something of this girl's?" Matt snorted. "So what? She left his room."

"It wouldn't take much, Matthew, for them to charge Terry, and—"

"He's not stupid, Cyn!"

"I didn't say he was. He may have overlooked—"

"For Chrissakes!"

"All right, all right, I'm sorry. I'm only trying to help look at this objectively. I think you should have a top-gun lawyer in the wings. That's all I'm—"

"And just who do you have in mind?"

"A woman, naturally."

"Naturally."

"Melinda Feinstein."

"She's, ah . . ."

"A top trial lawyer, Matt. She's based in Washington, too, and she's had a lot of success with delicate situations."

"Delicate."

"Yes. I hear she's one tough cookie. What do you think?"

"Damn it," Matt said.

"I know. I wish none of this was happening, either. But let's be ready."

"Feinstein," he said after a pause.

"She's good."

"You wouldn't happen to have a number?"

It was Cynthia's turn to pause. "She's waiting for your call right now, Matthew."

"Now, how the hell did I know you were going to say that?"

It was three in the morning East Coast time before Matt got off the phone with Melinda Feinstein. He liked her. He liked the way she brushed aside the circumstantial evidence that Cynthia thought could blow up in their faces. What had she said? Something about it not being worth a hill of beans. Feinstein had even gone so far as to tell Matt that the unfortunate incident quite probably could be handled with a few discreet phone calls on her part.

"I'll do some checking on my end if you like, Senator Connelly."

"It's Matt. And if you would, I guess it can't hurt to cover all bases."

"Absolutely, Matt. And why don't we get together and do lunch—" she'd laughed lightly "—when you get back to Washington."

"Sure. You'll do some checking, then?"

"First thing in the morning."

"Good night, then. Sorry about the hour."

"No problem. I rarely sleep."

Oh, yes, she'd made the whole thing sound like a mere nuisance, and one that she could handle quite easily. Matt rose from the couch in the silent house and walked to the wet bar, pouring himself a brandy. He found his cigars—Cuban—in a drawer and lit one, biting off the end, spitting it into the dying embers in the fireplace where it sizzled. He thought fleetingly about Beth. He hadn't mentioned that angle to Ms. Feinstein. But then it was never going to be known outside the immediate family, so why let the lawyer trouble herself over it?

He sat back down on the couch, blowing a wreath of the fine tobacco smoke into the air, and he drank his brandy. God, but life had a way of throwing you curves, he mused. Well, you just swung at the pitches you liked and let the others sail on by.

FIVE

Ellen Connelly often thought that she should have been the son and her brother, Terry, the daughter of the family. She had all the strength of character, all the shrewdness, good judgment and ambition, while Terry had the easy charm and indolent nature of a rich man's wife. Too bad he had to make it in a man's world.

On the other hand, Ellen thought on that cold sunny January morning as she unlocked the door of her art gallery on Cooper Street, if she had been born male, she'd have missed out on Manuel Ortega.

Her generous mouth, so like her father's, curved into an uncharacteristically soft smile as she recalled leaving Manuel just a few minutes ago. He'd been stark naked, his lean brown body lounging on her white, satin-stripe sheets, his long black hair spread on her pillows.

"Come back here," he'd said in that rough, faintly accented voice that raised gooseflesh on her body. "Come back here, Elena, *mi amor*." Oh God, she loved it when he talked like that!

"I can't," she'd replied, putting on lipstick. "I have to go to work." Still the dutiful, older daughter, still the controlled, goal-oriented child.

"Work, work," Manuel had said lazily. "Where does it get you?" He'd stretched, long and lingeringly, like a big, sleek cat. "Come here to me."

She'd sat on the edge of her bed, clipping on an earring, leaned over to kiss him and found herself locked in the embrace of his strong brown arms. He moved like a cat, too, quick and unerring, and he made love— Oh God . . .

"I have to go," she'd protested weakly, drawing in the feel and aroma of him through her skin.

"Yes, go." He'd yawned, letting her loose. "I have work to do as well."

"I'll see you later?" she'd asked, hating herself for her dependency on this mercurial man.

"Yes, I'll be here, working so very hard to make you rich, Elena," he'd said with a mock pout.

"You, too, Manuel," she reminded him, trying to be stern, and then she'd had to leave for the gallery.

Yes, if she were a man she'd have missed Manuel, with his pure, dazzling talent, his crazy moods, his selfishness and drinking and cocaine, his dark beauty, his terrible need and his terrible love.

Ellen flicked on the lights in the gallery, all the specially designed track lights that showed off the artwork to its best advantage. She went into her office in the back and hung up her coat, then checked herself in the mirror. Lipstick smudged, short dark wavy upswept hair out of place, a flush on her cheeks. A girl, she looked like a girl, not the together businesswoman of thirty-four that she really was.

She smoothed her hair, reapplied lipstick, tucked the expensive white shirt into the waistband of the equally expensive beige pleated wool slacks, exchanged heavy snow boots for brown leather flats and went out to check on her gallery.

Mostly Ellen sold Indian and Southwestern art: Earl Biss, Sam English, Nieto and Pena, R. C. Gorman, Dan Bodelson, Frank Howell. She had befriended a few local artists whose work she carried on consignment, but very few, because her standards were high, her taste faultless and her clientele very, very rich. Priceless Navajo rugs and a few pieces of Anasazi and Maria Martinez pottery were in locked cases.

She stood in the middle of her gallery and turned slowly, enjoying all over again the simplicity of the decor: the flagstone floor on which were scattered pastel Southwestern rugs, the white plaster walls, the fine, unobtrusive woodwork around doors and windows. Subtle, a fitting background for her treasures. Her eye scanned the paintings, each one framed with exquisite care, the mats harmonizing, some even scored with designs. Framing was very important. So many clients simply could not visualize a painting's potential until it was framed. She turned slowly, savoring the colors and lines, the composition and brushwork of her children—she thought of all the pieces hung on her walls as her children, the only ones she'd ever have. And how proud she was of them all, every one an original, every one special and cherished and sent off to a loving, appreciative home. Oh, Ellen knew she was a fanatic on the subject of her "children." Once she'd even refused to sell a man a painting he coveted because she knew he wanted it only for an investment and would stack it in a closet somewhere until he could resell it. Oh no, not one of her babies.

Manuel Ortega was one of her discoveries. She'd found him in Durango, a small city in southwestern Colorado nestled deep in the San Juan Mountains. He'd had moderate success selling his paintings there because Durango attracted tourists. But not the kind of success he'd have in Aspen, Ellen had told him. And then she'd named a few of her clients, famous people and celebrities of all sorts and the not-so-famous wealthy ones who made private appointments for showings or whom Ellen phoned with a new acquisition. Manuel's dark, liquid eyes had lit up, and he'd agreed to go to Aspen with her. That had been a year ago, and now . . .

The phone on the counter rang and Ellen picked it up. "The Connelly Gallery," she said briskly.

"Oh, hi, Elly. It's Ginger. Are you too awfully busy?"

"No, what's up?" But Ellen was afraid she knew, and her heart fell. And, of course, she was right.

"Is it true about Terry? I mean, I read the paper, but you know how they get everything wrong. So I thought . . ."

"Is what true?" Ellen asked.

"That he's a suspect in that poor girl's death? They aren't going to arrest him, are they?"

"I don't know, Ginger. Really, you know how I hate that whole family scene. I haven't been around them at all. I don't know any more than you do."

"Oh."

"Sorry, I can't help."

"But, Elly, do you think that . . . well, could it be . . . ?"

"That Terry killed this girl? Absolutely not. He doesn't have the backbone."

That was what she'd been telling everyone, and that was what she believed. Terry was weak and immature. He couldn't kill anyone, not in a million years. Sure, he had a mean streak, a childish selfishness that could be ugly, but Terry killing someone was just not in the realm of possibility.

Oh, her father must be furious, the Connellys in the news again. She was so very thankful that she'd cut her ties to that whole, awful tribe of nuts. Manuel knew about family; he had a large, extended family himself, all over southern Colorado and New Mexico. He disdained them all, talking of them as peasants and dullards. He did call his mother in Durango every week, though, and he sent money to one of his brothers, the one with all the children.

They'd often compared notes on their families, lying in bed together after making love, his skin pressed against hers. The difference was, Ellen had realized, that Manuel's family truly loved its children, while people like the Connellys saw them as a necessary evil.

Terry, the only son, her little brother. She and Terry looked a lot alike, their coloring the same—the thick dark hair and deep blue eyes. Ellen kept herself trim— she'd never be skinny—and her face had good bone structure. She was a handsome woman, not sexy or gorgeous or cute. But Manuel made her feel beautiful. He worshiped her body, he respected her mind. He loved her only one step below his painting, but that was one hell of a big step, because Manuel was first and foremost an artist, a tortured genius who was never satisfied, whose descents into depression and depravity were becoming legend in Aspen—and in the art world at large. But, oh God, how he needed her and how she loved him.

Ellen checked her watch. She had a ten o'clock appointment with a Houston banker who wanted to look at a Corrazar she'd found. Megan would be in then to cover walk-in business. Megan was a good salesperson, attractive and well versed in the art world, but Ellen made a point to take care of her special clients, the ones who could write a check for fifty thousand without blinking.

The phone rang again. Ellen winced. It was probably someone else wanting to know about Terry. It seemed that was all the town was talking about—the season's scandal, served up with all the trimmings: sex, celebrities, murder. How distasteful. And it would, naturally, have to be the Connellys in the thick of it. God, Ellen resented that, the unending trouble her family caused! Manuel told her it was her cross to bear, but, oh, how she'd like to get out from under it! She was continually humiliated by them, and now this, this awful predicament Terry was in.

She picked up the phone. "The Connelly Gallery."

"Miss Connelly?"

"Yes, speaking."

"Oh, hello. I'm Alan Lathrop of the *Aspen News*. I wondered if I could interview you for tomorrow's paper."

"About what?" Ellen asked in a hard voice.

"Oh, things in general. Your gallery, your family."

"I'm sorry, Mr. Lathrop, but I really have nothing to say to you."

"What about your brother? Do you think . . ."

Quietly Ellen put the receiver down, standing there for a second with her eyes tightly shut. Sharks, they were all sharks, circling, smelling blood. Then she mentally shook herself, ran her fingers through her short wavy hair and went into her office to do yesterday's deposit.

The phone rang again as she sat there entering numbers in the computer, and she almost didn't answer it. But she breathed a sigh of relief when she heard the voice. "Hi, Beth," she said. "How're things in the family mausoleum?"

"Terrible," Beth replied.

"I can imagine. You okay?"

"Sure, what else?"

"Your stomach still bothering you?"

"Some. Uh, listen, Ellen, could we get together today? I . . . well, I'd like to talk to you about something."

"About what happened to you New Year's Eve? Listen, that's over and done with and—"

"No," Beth put in quickly, "not about that. Something else."

"Sounds ominous," Ellen said lightly.

But Beth didn't reply to her statement. "I thought we could go skiing, have lunch, you know. Can you get away, Ellen?"

She was going to say no, that she was too busy, but something in Beth's voice stopped her. "Well, I guess so. I have a ten o'clock appointment, but we could go after that."

"I don't want to impose," Beth said, "but this is important."

"Okay. How about I meet you at eleven at the gondola?"

"Oh, that'd be great, Ellen."

"If I'm a few minutes late, don't worry. I've got a client who likes to talk. Okay?"

"Sure, that's fine. See you at eleven," Beth replied. "And thanks, thanks a lot."

Ellen hung up. As she was to think later, she had a presentiment, a nagging anxiety that something was wrong. She loved Beth, and she'd always felt protective of her, a lost, skinny, eleven-year-old when Lee had married Matt. Beth had a good heart, she was smart and pretty. She had everything going for her. But she let herself get caught up in the family stuff, the self-abuse and blaming, the denial, the emotional games Matt played. Beth had her own ways of running away from it all, but she'd never managed to escape, not really. And now—whatever this was that Beth wanted to discuss . . . All Ellen could think was: what now?

Megan came in then, and Ellen had to put her mind on the running of the gallery. There were valuable pieces to be wrapped and shipped, phone calls to be made, plans firmed up for a trip to Santa Fe to an opening for a new potter. And Dave Reed coming at ten to view the Corrazar she'd located for him.

Dave Reed was a small man, but his ego and his wallet were both large. He hated cold weather and snow, detested skiing, but he came to Aspen to shop, and Ellen was always on the lookout for something he'd like.

He arrived promptly at ten, alone, wearing a shearling coat and a suit underneath, cowboy boots and a large-brimmed Stetson. His Texas accent was so strong that Ellen sometimes had to ask him to repeat himself, which made him laugh.

"Howdy, darlin'," he said, "you're lookin' fine, mighty fine. Now let's see what you got for me this time."

She led him to an alcove lined in black velvet and turned on the special spotlight, then carefully set the Corrazar on the easel. Utter silence descended. The painting was a watercolor of a coyote, a large canvas with the animal staring out of it from viciously alive green eyes. His body had been done in a black outline, but there were stabs of bright colors all over, as if to designate the places where his feral energy came through his hide. Ellen waited with patience, admiring the painting. It was a deviation from Corrazar's usual, less representational work, and she thought it was very, very good. If Reed didn't take it, she had in mind another client....

He finally moved, a step closer, his head cocked, then he walked back a few yards and viewed it again. "Uh-huh," he finally said, "yup, it's a good 'un all right."

Ellen smiled. "I knew you'd like it."

"How much, darlin', and don't think you can just name your price," he said, teasing.

"Framed?" she asked.

"Yup, framed with one of them fancy jobs you do."

"I'll give it to you for thirty-five thousand."

"Give!" He chuckled. "Come on, I'm a very good customer, and the banks in Houston're failin' like tired whores. I could be out of bidness tomorrow."

"Thirty-five, firm. That's what the artist wants. Really, I do my best for you, Dave, you know that."

"Damn, woman, but you're hard. Thirty-five?"

"That's it. It'll be worth fifty in six months," Ellen said.

"And you'll buy it back from me then for fifty?"

"I didn't say that." Ellen smiled. "Besides, you'd never be able to let him go, would you?" And she gestured at the coyote in the painting.

Dave Reed laughed. "You know me too well, darlin'. My office will send a check. Ship it the usual way, right?"

"Right." And the sale was consummated.

Ellen even had time to make a call to Manuel before she met Beth.

"I sold the Corrazar," she announced.

"That's good. But, Elena, love, why don't you sell my work to this man?"

"He's not ready for it yet. He likes animals, horses and things. I will, when he's in the mood. Manuel, are you working today?"

"Ay, woman, you press me. Yes, I'll be in the studio this afternoon. I have to work on that landscape, you know the one?"

"Yes, it needed something, didn't it? It'll be wonderful when you're through, though."

"The phone's been ringing, Elena. People calling. You're lucky I answered your call."

"Oh God. Terry," she sighed.

"Yes, yes, Terry, always Terry. He's trouble, that boy."

"Unplug the phone, love," she said. "Listen, I'm going skiing with Beth this afternoon, all right?"

"The family."

"Yes, Manuel, the family. But they'll be gone soon. You work hard, you hear?"

"Yes, my love, I will work till I sweat drops of blood. Will that suit you?"

Ellen laughed lightly. "See you later."

She changed into ski clothes in her office, into a red one-piece Descente ski suit, hat, gloves, ski boots. She kept her equipment in the gallery because it was so convenient to the gondola, only a block away, and from time to time she went up on the mountain to snatch a few hours' skiing. Today, however, she was meeting Beth, and despite the gorgeous day she had that sense of foreboding again.

Beth was standing near the entrance to the gondola line, holding her skis and poles. She wore a fuchsia Nevica ski suit and sunglasses, because it was a sunny day, and when she saw Ellen she smiled and waved. She was very pretty, Ellen thought, with her black hair and white skin and bright suit.

"Hi, Ellen, thanks for coming," she said. "I hope I didn't pull you away from something important."

"Nothing that can't wait."

They got in line, showing their season passes, shuffling in stiff ski boots up the steps to where the gondola took on passengers, six to a car.

"So, what's up?" Ellen asked when they were in a gondola car, but Beth gave a quick little shake of her head because there were four others crammed into the car with them. Uh-oh, Ellen thought.

"It's a nice day, isn't it?" she said, trying for a neutral subject.

"Great," Beth agreed.

"How's everybody?" Ellen asked.

Beth shrugged, both hands holding her ski poles, her sunglasses hiding her expression. "Oh, hanging in there, I guess. As usual."

"Um."

Then Beth smiled and asked in a more animated tone, "How's Manuel?"

A vision of him lying nude in bed that morning flashed in Ellen's head like a strobe light. She couldn't help smiling. "He's fine."

"So you're really crazy about him?" Beth asked wistfully, keeping her voice low.

"I guess you could say that," Ellen replied, a little embarrassed.

"And he's crazy about you?"

"It seems so, hard as it is to believe."

"Now, Ellen, stop that. There's nothing hard to believe about it. It's about time. I'm so happy for you," she whispered.

"Well, Beth, thanks. I am happy."

They smiled at each other, suspended in the car over the white trails of Aspen Mountain, passing above the expert skiers pounding down the moguls of the Ridge of Bell, the classes snaking behind instructors down Copper Bowl, over crowded Deer Park and Silver Bell and up to the summit at 11,300 feet where the original Sundeck restaurant stood. They got out, retrieved their skis and walked into the dazzling sunshine and blue sky and the view of stark white peaks across the deep valleys. They stepped into their bindings and pushed off from the crowded summit where dozens of people were standing around, putting on skis, buckling boots, zipping up parkas, discussing what run to take next. Bright colors stood out against the snow, eight-hundred-dollar ski suits in every shade, every design, in gold and silver and neon colors. Mirrored sunglasses covered every pair of eyes, and there were fur headbands and parkas that matched gold-studded fanny packs for carrying incidentals that wouldn't fit into skintight stretch pants.

And then there were the locals in plain ski suits or dark-colored mountain anoraks. But their equipment was the best, the latest, the most high-tech skis, boots and poles—which they all got at wholesale prices from friends in the business. Hell, locals couldn't afford to pay retail prices for ski equipment!

It was very familiar to Ellen, the colorful, red-cheeked, joyous crowd on Aspen Mountain this Christmas season, and she felt a rush of love for her adopted hometown.

"What should we ski?" she asked Beth.

"Something easy to start with," Beth said. "I'm still out of shape."

"Okay, how about Dipsy?"

And they were off, swishing in big, round turns down the mountainside. Ellen stopped, and Beth pulled up, panting. "The snow's great," she said.

"It is, isn't it?"

Down to the next lift, a fast quad, up again, sharing the chair with a couple from Chicago who had just arrived in Aspen. "Is the weather always this perfect?" the woman asked.

"Sure," Ellen replied, "it only snows at night here."

"It does?" the woman asked, almost believing her, and they all laughed.

They did a couple more runs and then decided to stop for lunch at Bonnie's restaurant at the bottom of the bowl called Tourelotte Park, where a silver-mining town had once existed. Bonnie's was a modest place, but the food was wonderful, freshly baked desserts and bread warm from the oven. Delectable soups and stews and salads and gourmet pizza.

It was jammed. The cafeteria line stretched to the door, the outside decks were full and the inside was the same. Waiting in line, Ellen saw two men near to fighting over a table. "Look at that," she said to Beth.

"God," Beth said, chuckling.

They got their food, clumping along the line in ski boots, carrying trays, looking for a couple of empty seats, a nearly impossible task. They finally found themselves seated next to Aspen resident Jack Nicholson, his hair standing up in outrageous wisps.

After lunch Beth wanted to ski some more, so they left Bonnie's and swept in long graceful turns down the

mountain, into the cleft called Spar Gulch that led to
Little Nell, the run that went all the way back to the
bottom, to the gondola.

This time there was no line and they got their own car,
which swung out on the cable above the snow, leaving
Aspen behind.

"Wasn't Spar wonderful?" Ellen asked happily, pulling off her hat and gloves.

"Um," Beth said.

"It's crowded today, isn't it? But everyone will be
leaving next weekend and things'll die down again.
Now, let's see, what run should we do next? I
thought—"

"Ellen," Beth said quietly.

Ellen was silent for a moment, knowing . . . "I don't
think I'm going to like this," she muttered.

"No, you probably won't," Beth said.

Ellen sighed heavily.

"I've got to tell somebody," Beth said, and she took
off her sunglasses, her brow drawn. "Someone who'll
listen, anyway."

"All right, I'm listening," Ellen said.

"I saw Terry that night," Beth said, then she held Ellen's gaze boldly.

"What night?"

Her eyes flashed. "You know what night. The night
that girl . . ."

"So, you saw Terry . . ."

"I saw him carrying that girl," Beth went on hur-
riedly. "Carrying her down the hall in the middle of the
night. Over his shoulder."

Ellen sat back as if an invisible hand had pushed her.
She felt her blood drain from her cheeks. "Does Terry
know you saw him?" was all she could think of to ask.

"Yes, he saw me. He said she'd passed out and he was taking her home."

"That's probably what he was doing, then," Ellen said, her lips stiff. "Does Dad know?"

"Yes, I told him."

"I see . . ."

"But, Ellen, if what Terry said was true, then why'd he lie to the police? Why'd he say she left by herself? And how'd she end up in the Aspen Health Club parking lot . . . dead?"

"I don't know," Ellen said in a low, hard voice. "And you don't know, either. Terry said she left, and that's what happened."

Beth shook her head. "I don't know . . . I . . ."

"Oh yes, you know. You know damn well. Terry is your brother and he no more . . . killed that girl than I did," Ellen said furiously. "You're one of the family, Beth, like it or not."

"I can't believe that, coming from you."

"I may live apart from them, I may abhor their behavior, but in the clutch I know where my loyalty lies."

"It puts me in one hell of an untenable position," Beth said with a twist of her mouth.

"Position? What position are you in?"

"Ellen, I have to give the sheriff my statement. Everyone else has, and he's been calling for me to come in. Pretty soon it'll start looking suspicious. I mean, I can't put it off forever."

Ellen was quiet a moment, thinking. She refused to consider what Beth had just told her—not now. She could only weigh the problem at hand, that Beth had to give a statement.

"Leave town," she said calmly. "Just leave."

"Where?"

"Take a trip. Far away." Ellen licked her lips. "You're always going somewhere."

"Leave?"

"Yes, just get the hell away from here."

Ellen was sweating by the time she got back to her gallery that afternoon. Damp all over, even though it wasn't that warm out. Her heart was thudding a little too hard and she felt slightly nauseated. With sheer willpower she kept herself from thinking about what Beth had told her.

She let Megan go home and sat at her desk, trying to do some book work, but her mind wouldn't settle on anything. Terry carrying that girl . . . No, she told herself, stopping the thought short.

The phone rang, startling her for a split second. God, she was rattled. Silly. "The Connelly Gallery," she said briskly into the receiver.

"Ellen Connelly?" a strange voice asked.

"Yes, speaking."

"This is Don Limacher, Aspen Police. We have Manuel Ortega here at the station."

"Manuel?" She gripped the phone tighter. "Is he all right?"

"Yes, ma'am. Well, he's a little under the influence, actually."

She put her hand over her brow. Oh God.

"I'm real sorry, ma'am, but the Hotel Jerome bar manager called and asked us to get him out of there before he got in a fight."

"Oh, no," she whispered.

"Now, we don't want to just release him and let him go wandering around. . . ."

"Uh, yes, of course. I'll be down in a few minutes to pick him up. He's not under arrest or anything?"

"No, ma'am, not yet."

"Thank heavens," she said. "Please tell him I'll be right there."

Ellen put on her coat and closed up the shop. Damn, she was thinking as she got her car from its parking place. He had been going to work all afternoon. What had happened to set him off? Damn.

How cruel fate was, Ellen thought as she steered through the après-ski traffic toward Main Street. How ironic and cruel. Her entire family was a bunch of alcoholics, and as hard as she'd tried to leave them behind, she'd ended up true to form, feverishly, hopelessly, in love with one.

SIX

Deirdre VanHagen McCandless was a pretty woman, a fine-boned brunette with very fair skin and dark blue eyes. She'd been brought up to believe looks and clothes were important, a spoiled only child with a sweet but impressionable nature, a southern California girl who typified the "me" generation of the eighties.

It had been cool to play house in Aspen with the best-looking guy in town. It had been cool to be poor and cook and clean, even to get pregnant. But five years of unrelenting responsibility and a husband who Deirdre felt was getting more and more impatient with her own mounting needs had almost done her in.

When she'd fled Aspen and her husband and children to find herself, the only thing that was hard about her new life on the ashram was her spirit's tenacious hold on vanity. But that was a minor sin, David told her often enough.

David was the guru of the ashram and her sometime lover, and he knew Deirdre down to her bones. He was her teacher, her mentor, the one human being whom she depended. She'd once thought Case McCandless was going to be that person, but he'd asked far too much from her, so much she'd had to leave.

She didn't regret her decision, not for a moment. Raised in Los Angeles, she'd always hated the mountain winters. California was much nicer—California and David and her search for self-knowledge.

David was pleased with her progress in every area but one, and that one was a thorny problem: her children.

"Children are blessed. They're the future," David said, sitting cross-legged on his pillow, the way he did for hours when he meditated. "They're precious, DeeDee."

"I know, David." She sat opposite him, cross-legged also, her knees hurting.

"I don't understand how you could have left them."

"I had to," she whispered, feeling that worm of guilt twist inside her. "I couldn't take them, David, I . . ."

"Children belong with their mothers."

She hung her head, seeing her babies, Nate and little Amanda. She'd run from them as if they were devils.

"Wouldn't they be better off here?" David said. "Aspen must be very hard on them, all those drugs and parties and rich people."

"But Case doesn't live like that. He's real straight. And he sure isn't rich."

"DeeDee, honey, they're surrounded. They'll be influenced. Nobody in a place like that can get in touch with their real inner spirit. You have a duty to your kids."

"I gave up custody, David. I don't know if I could get them back now. Case would fight it."

"Mothers almost always get their children if they want them. You do want them, don't you?"

Deirdre thought hard and felt the guilt squirm in her belly. "Of course I want them."

"Well, then, you call that lawyer back."

"Okay, David," she said with more assurance, "I will."

"It never ceases to amaze me," Case muttered to the dispatcher on his way out the door. "Every Christmas holiday it's as if the whole town takes a crazy pill."

"Yeah, well," Beverly replied, "when it rains it pours."

Case hadn't even driven out of his official parking spot when Bev's voice came over the radio: "We've got a fender bender out on 82. Shales Bluffs area. Ah, Glen, can you respond?"

"Sorry, Bev," came Glen's voice, "I'm tied up at the Ritz, that jewelry burglary."

Case frowned and pressed the button on his mike. "I'll take the accident," he said. "On my way right now. Over and out."

Before noon on that early January day the sheriff's department had already responded to three car accidents, two shoplifting incidents, the jewelry theft, a stolen Jaguar report—in winter!—a fistfight between two college kids over a pair of skis at the gondola building and a horse that had gotten out of a paddock in nearby Woody Creek and been hit by a car, blocking the lower valley road for more than an hour while workers were trying to drive into Aspen to their jobs.

At two that afternoon, as Case's stomach growled with hunger, Beverly got him on the radio and reported that the baby-sitter had called and Amanda was sick.

"On my way home," Case radioed back.

By three Amanda had been diagnosed with a strep throat and was on penicillin and safely back in her own bed in their house, but the family dog, Gizmo, a terrier-mix, had run away.

"Should I call the pound?" the baby-sitter, Allison, asked.

"No," Case said, slapping peanut butter onto some bread in his kitchen, "Gizmo splits all the time. He'll be back."

"I hope he doesn't get run over," Allison said just as Nate was coming into the room.

"What?" the seven-year-old asked.

"Nothing," Case said quickly, and Allison stared at her sneakers.

It truly was one of those days. Case arrived back at the Sheriff's Department to find a host of reporters awaiting him. He couldn't even get in the basement door, and a Channel Ten satellite news van from Denver was blocking the entire parking lot.

"Sheriff, is it true Terence Connelly raped that girl?"

"Sheriff, what is this going to do to Edward Crenshaw's chance for the presidency?"

"Is it true, Sheriff, that Beth Connelly got a DUI on New Year's Eve?"

"Is Terence Connelly going to be booked on first- or second-degree murder charges?"

Case put up a hand. He waited for the voices to die down and then, in his inherently calm, quiet voice, said, "No comments, fellas," and he shouldered his way inside.

That afternoon he did telephone the police lab in Denver on the slim chance that one or two results were in from the innumerable tests being run on Heather Kelly's body. There were results expected back from the medical examiner. There were tests being run on hair found in Terence's bedroom, on carpet samples and bedding, even on medicine cabinet items taken from his room despite his sworn statement that he and Heather had remained upstairs while she was in the house. Of course, Case and the D.A. were both hoping for a break on that angle, something, anything found on Heather or anything of hers that came from Terence's bedroom.

It was certain that Heather Kelly had engaged in sexual intercourse, but whether it had been a rape or not was so far unclear. Then there was the newest test— DNA profiling. Labs could now extract DNA from semen and pin down the precise genetic fingerprint of an individual. So, if the seminal fluid found in Heather matched Terence Connelly's DNA, from a blood sample he'd given, then there was no doubt he'd lied, and if he'd lied about having sex with the girl, he'd sure as hell lied about other things.

Case had always wondered about that. Terence had sworn they never had sex, and surely Terence knew it was possible to match up body fluid samples nowadays. Why had he lied? *If* he'd lied, that was. Could the young man be that stupid, or did he think he was so bulletproof because of his powerful father that he could get away with anything?

Case waited a long time on the phone until the police technician came back on the line. God, but it would be great if even one test result was in.

It wasn't.

"Give it another week," Case was told.

The murder of Heather Kelly was getting to him. Combined with the holiday overload, the poor dead girl lying in a sterile examination room in Denver was starting to stick in his craw. Case put his booted feet up on his desk for a minute and thought about that and decided it wasn't just the murder, it was the idea of Terence Connelly up there on those ski slopes enjoying the hell out of himself, very much alive, not giving a damn.

Of course, Case didn't know for certain if Terry was guilty. There was no hard evidence. Yet. But he wasn't sheriff of Pitkin County for nothing, and in his years of police work he'd developed a knack for spotting truth and lies, and something told Case that Terence Connelly had killed Heather. Maybe not on purpose. But somehow things had gotten out of hand and she'd ended up dead, and Terry, panicked, had tried to get out of it.

Case rubbed his fingers over the stubble on his chin and reminded himself that a man was innocent till proved guilty. Still, his money was on Connelly. God, but he hoped the lab people didn't miss anything.

The D.A.'s call came just as Case was heading out at five, praying he could get a night's uninterrupted rest. He was sure it was about the Connelly case. It wasn't.

"I know you've got enough on your mind," Tripp Maddock said, "and I swear to you, Case, I'd bury this on my desk if I could, but I know you'll want to hear this. Well, need to hear it is a better way to put it, I suppose."

"Go on," Case said.

"It's about Deirdre."

"My ex-wife?"

"Yes. She's filed a suit in a California court, Case. She wants custody of Amanda and Nate."

Case was silent for a long moment. "Shit," he whispered.

"I'm really sorry, buddy. I know how you feel about those kids."

It was all Case could do to think. "Look," he began. He cleared his throat. "Tripp, you're a lawyer. I mean, can she do this?"

"Yes."

"Yes? You mean she can just up and decide she wants the kids after all this time and . . . and some lame judge lets her file a suit?"

"She's their mother."

"She's a goddamn wacko! My God, she dropped out like a sixties hippie, Tripp. She's living on an ashram!"

"I know, I know."

"What'll I do?"

"Get yourself a good lawyer, because these cases are touchy as hell."

He thought a moment. "I know this is asking a lot, Tripp, and I . . ."

"Ask away."

"What do you think my chances are?"

"If you can establish her recent history of unconventional behavior, you can beat it. But you'll have to be tough on her, Case, real tough. This could get down and dirty."

"Jesus," Case said. "And you know who the real losers will be? The kids."

"Yeah, I know."

"That guru of hers, you know, Tripp? All he wants my kids for is to have more people under his thumb. He doesn't really want to deal with them, and he doesn't give a damn about their welfare. It's a power trip, that's all!"

"I'm sure you're right."

"I can't give them up, Tripp. You know I can't. They're my kids, my flesh and blood," Case said in a strangled voice.

"Well, it's not a done deal yet, Case. You hang in there."

"Yeah, sure, easy for you to say. They're not your kids, Tripp."

By six-thirty, as he put together a makeshift dinner for himself and Nate—Amanda said her throat hurt too much to eat—Case was feeling rattled. He simply could not believe Deirdre would pull such a stunt. Why did she want the kids after nearly three years, anyway? And the idea that she might just win a court case . . .

"Damn it, Nate, stop feeding the dog under the table," he said. "And when did Gizmo come back? I thought I told you to keep the gate shut."

"Amanda opened it."

"I did not," came her little voice. "Daddy, I'm hungry now. Can I have some ice cream?"

"We don't have any."

"Yes, we do. Allison said we do."

"Good old Allison," Case mumbled.

The next day was equally hectic, though Amanda was much improved and Case's mother was able to take both the kids. Just a little while longer, he thought as he drove from the McCandless ranch back to town, a few more days and the kids will be in school again and the town will settle into the slower season. Just hold on.

He'd worked the holiday season before, ten years in the department, five years as sheriff. He'd get through it, but it sure was stressful. God, he remembered Aspen in its quieter days when he'd been a kid, the days before Aspen's renaissance in the sixties, when it had turned from a sleepy, former mining town into a mecca for intellectuals and artists. Too much of a good thing, Case often thought.

Growth and fame and wealth brought crime. But hell, he thought, he wouldn't have a job if it weren't for crime, now, would he?

The day didn't get any better. The local police and Case's department shared the numerous calls. It began with not one, but two abuse incidents—husband-and-wife battles after a long, boozy night. Then there were the fender benders on Main Street and the countless calls about ski thefts. Beverly had just worked six straight days—as had most of Case's crew—and she lost it on the radio.

"Well, if you can't handle the burger joint call, Glen, then maybe I'll get Ronald McDonald! Jesus!"

"That's enough," Case said, depressing the switch on his mike in the Cherokee. "Cool it, Bev."

There was a scratching as reception broke up. "I'm all right."

"I'm headed in. I'll take over for a couple of hours," Case said.

"You don't have to. Over."

"Yes, I do."

He somehow managed lunch, takeout from a local sub shop, and checked in with Dottie at the ranch. Amanda seemed one hundred percent better, had even eaten soup and a sandwich. And Nate was fine, out helping his Uncle Nick with the snowmobiles.

"Some help," Case said over the phone.

"Oh, Nick doesn't mind. Nate hands him the tools. You know. You sound kinda . . . tired. You all right?"

"I'm fine. It's been a long season."

"We'll be down to fifty percent occupancy in just a few days. Things will quiet down."

"Sure they will," he said. "Always do."

He made a call to a lawyer then, hating to do it, hating to face up to Deirdre's latest stunt. But this mattered. A lot.

"I'll check with Tripp's office this afternoon," the lawyer told him. "And for God's sake, Case, don't go calling her or anything. Let me handle it, okay?"

"Okay," Case replied. "Do you think Deirdre stands a chance?"

"Well, I didn't really know her, Case, but if what you say is true..."

"I don't want to hurt her, but I can't give up my kids."

"Of course you can't," he said with the utmost sincerity. "We'll just do what we have to do."

Case hung up feeling lousy. If he was a quiet man, he was also a bit of a romantic, trying to see the best in people before acknowledging the worst. In most cities that qualification wouldn't cut it for an officer of the law, but in Aspen the liberal population demanded it of its police. You couldn't go around arresting folks for smoking a joint on a park bench or carrying an open can of beer through the mall—half the town's population would have been in the slammer.

Deirdre had called him Victorian, and it was with that old-fashioned outlook that Case had viewed his divorce: Marriage hadn't worked, but Deirdre had wholeheartedly agreed that Case would make the better, more stable parent.

He sat at his desk and mulled that over and wished he could settle this thing with Deirdre, just the two of them and no goddamn lawyers.

There was a bad accident that afternoon not far from the Preserve estate. Case answered the call and was first on the scene, followed by the paramedics and the Colorado Highway Patrol. The victims were air-ambulanced to Denver. One died en route. While the wreckage was cleared and reports filled out, Case found himself staring from time to time across the white fields of snow toward the estate houses, particularly the Connellys'. He wondered if they were all still up skiing, or perhaps they were at the Little Nell Hotel for après ski.

What a group, he mused as the tow truck winched the cars apart. What a useless, overindulged family. There wasn't one of them that he'd interviewed who had a grip on reality. And that Beth Connelly... A real space cadet. A girl gets killed and she goes out to a party, drinking and taking pills, gets herself arrested and can't even bother to come back into the station and give that statement. How, he wondered, could someone be that irresponsible? No doubt she thought her looks could buy her way out of anything. And that crazy outfit she'd been wearing on New Year's Eve. Typical. She'd stood there on a winter night with hardly anything on, shivering, freezing. A fake cowgirl, all gussied up like an idiot. Well, he wasn't impressed. He made a mental note to phone the Connelly estate one last time and tell her to get her butt in and make that statement or he'd have the judge issue a subpoena. Damn right.

What was to become dubbed by the world press as "The Glass Ashtray Incident" occurred at four thirty-six that same afternoon. For the attendees of the after-ski party at the Hollywood producer's Red Mountain home, it had been a splendid day of skiing, of wine and cheese parties on the slopes, of sun and fresh powder and rubbing shoulders with the rich and famous. The après-ski party was the producer's idea, and from the Sundeck on Aspen Mountain he'd phoned the caterer and made the arrangements. In Aspen, on only an hour's notice, it was no problem. But then the cost of such a spontaneous affair was nothing to be sneezed at.

The party-goers, seventy or so of them, took cabs and limos across town and climbed steep Red Mountain, whose cliffside homes were nothing short of splendiferous. Indoor tennis courts and pools were a dime a dozen, but who cared when a building site alone ran two million and change?

By four o'clock champagne corks popped and trays of Russian caviar made the rounds. Everyone was feeling festive, exhilarated from the super skiing and light-headed with wine. Ski boots and glittering parkas littered the entrance, gloves and hats and goggles were tossed in corners. Toasts to old friends and new abounded. Laughter ran up and down the scale in convivial riffs.

And then the lady who was soon to be known as Madame Slasher took offense at something another woman said, broke a glass ashtray and drew the jagged edge across the other woman's cheek.

The cut was deep and long, and the woman bled a flood of crimson on the three-week-old white carpeting. Someone yelled, "Call an ambulance!" Carter John, the caterer, called the police.

"A knifing?" Case said, depressing the button on his mike.

"That's what the man thought. Sounded serious."

"I'll go," Case said. "Which house on Red Mountain is it?" When he heard, he thought, *Oh dear God, spare me the antics of the rich.*

Case arrived at the mansion before the ambulance and was relieved to see that at least one person had taken charge, a man who Case thought had starred in *Dancing with Indians,* or something, a good-looking blond guy who knew some first aid.

The star shook his head. "She'll need a bunch of stitches," he said.

"Looks like it," Case replied, stooping over the victim, who was laid out in a bedroom now. "You did a nice job, ah . . . sorry, I should know your name. Anyway, I'll take it from here."

The movie star rose and handed Case the bloody towel. "Thanks," Case said. "By the way, how did this happen?"

The man was in the doorway. "I'm real glad to say I didn't see a thing," he replied, and left.

The ambulance arrived, the woman was treated and taken to the hospital while two other police cars pulled down the long, steep drive.

"Okay," Case said, "let's go back in and try to get some statements. I have a feeling this is going to be a hot one."

"Who was the victim?" one officer asked.

"Beats the hell out of me," Case said, "but we're about to find out."

As it turned out, the victim was Spanish, a cousin of King Juan Carlos, in fact. And Madame Slasher was none other than the ex-wife and excommunicated former first lady of a small South American country. The minute Case approached her, she said in perfect English, "You cannot arrest me. I have diplomatic immunity."

"Is that a fact," Case replied.

"Yes, it is."

"Well, then," he said, "I guess I'll just let you tell it to the judge."

The beautifully coiffed woman glared at him hotly. "You wouldn't dare."

"Yes, I would," he said, and he took her arm and steered her out while dozens gave damning statements to his deputies.

An hour later, Madame Slasher having been bailed out by a fleet of lawyers, each and every one of whom threatened lawsuits, Case was done in. He sat back in his hard chair, which creaked protestingly, and dialed the ranch's number. "Sorry, I'm running late," he told his mother. "Kids behaving?"

"Perfect little cherubs. They can stay the night, you know."

"I know, and thanks, but I'm about wrapped up for the day here. I'll be out as soon as I can."

"Tough one today?" Dottie asked.

"You'd never believe it," Case said, and then he smiled ruefully. "But, you know, I just had a little bit of faith restored."

"Oh?"

"Yeah. This man helped someone out. Guy's a movie star. I can't for the life of me think of his name, though."

"That's nice."

"Yeah, it sure is for a change."

Stretching, Case rose, took up his hat and parka and snapped off the lights in his office. There was a mountain of paperwork still on his desk, lying there in the dark now. But it would keep. And tomorrow, he knew, the flak was going to fill the air over this ashtray assault. There would be a dozen or more reporters on his doorstep, too, all wanting to scoop the story. That was Aspen, home of the rich and famous and more than its share of eccentrics.

"'Night, Judy," he said to the dispatcher, who was Bev's alternate. "I'll be in at eight in the morning."

"Want to be woken for something out of the ordinary?"

"Only if you have a death wish, Judy."

Case left the building, climbing the old stone steps to street level, taking in a deep breath of the cold evening air. He actually looked forward to the drive out to the ranch, the cold, dark woods bracketing the deserted mountain road, the host of stars above. It never stopped amazing him that such peaceful isolation lay only a few short miles from the madcap heartbeat of Aspen. The smell of pine and wood smoke and crisp air . . .

He drove with the radio turned to its lowest volume, taking the curves expertly, every inch of the road as familiar to him as his own face. After all, he'd been born and raised in this valley.

Case drove and relaxed and smiled at a pair of golden eyes caught in his headlights at the edge of the pine forest. A fox, or maybe a coyote—the deer and elk wintered in the lower valley. Or perhaps it was a cougar watching his passage. There was nothing like the sight of a mountain lion against the backdrop of a black tree trunk.

This is why I live here, this is why I came back after college, he thought. And who said you could never go home again? The hordes could flock to Aspen, fill the tiny mountain mecca to overflowing with their madness, but the wilderness was always going to be there. There was more than a hint of the romantic in Case McCandless.

Another mile and a half and the ranch would appear, the outbuildings resting darkly in silent fields of snow. It would be good to be with family tonight; maybe he and the kids would sit around the fire with the guests and listen to some of his brother Rowdy's foot-stomping music. Yeah, a warm, friendly evening after a day of insanity.

Case was not to get his pleasant evening, though.

Just as the barn came into view he roused himself, remembering one last unfinished chore. No big deal, he thought, reaching for the mike.

He depressed the button. "Judy, this is Case, over."

"I'm here. You're breaking up a little. Over."

"Look," he said, steering with his left hand, "can you give the Connelly house a call and tell Beth Connelly she's expected in before noon tomorrow? Make it very official. Over."

The radio crackled. " . . . funny . . . should mention that," came her voice, punctuated by static. "We . . . call from the airport as . . . fifteen minutes ago. Seems she's . . . the jet fueled for a trip. Over."

Case felt his jaw lock. "Repeat that, please. Over." Judy did, and he felt a fist of anger tighten in his gut. Damn that woman!

He braked hard, the big four-wheel-drive vehicle skidding sideways. When it stopped he did a three-point turn. "Call the airport tower back," he said in clipped tones. "Tell them to hold that plane. You copy? Over."

" . . . copy that, Case. I'll get right . . . it. Over . . . out."

Case tore down the road toward Highway 82, retracing his route. This time, however, there was no sense of inner peace as it all came crashing back: Terence Connelly and the murder, that poor woman's slashed face and Deirdre. Damn that ex-wife of his! And now yet another female was conspiring to pull a fast one on him.

At the intersection of Highway 82 and Maroon Creek Road, Case switched on his flashing lights and sounded the siren as he took the turn quickly and accelerated, speeding toward the Pitkin County Airport and Beth Connelly.

SEVEN

By seven o'clock that evening Beth had decided she really liked Billy Jorgenson a lot. He was absolutely charming and attentive, and he was so damned handsome that every woman in the Pitkin County Airport had given him the once-over. He had on a pair of well-fitting jeans, suitably faded, a pale blue sweater that must have been a present from one of his clients, because he never could have afforded it on a ski instructor's pay, and the most gorgeous butter-soft brown suede jacket.

They sat in Pour La France, the airport café, waiting for the Connellys' Learjet to be fueled, and Beth was feeling better than she had in days. She was leaving Aspen. Ellen had been right; there was nothing to do but avoid the whole, stinking mess, escape. God, she felt relieved!

Outside it was dark, clouds building, threatening another storm, but the weather report had shown it to be clear in Denver, and they'd get out of the mountains before the front hit. It'd be fine. The Lear would drop them at the airport in Denver, then they'd catch the domestic flight to New York, and tomorrow they'd be in Switzerland.

"Listen," Billy was saying, leaning close to Beth, "I'm sorry about not getting to that party New Year's Eve. I tried to, but I got tied up."

"I know," Beth said, "it happens."

"Yeah, it does. And when I heard you got busted, Jesus, I felt bad. That damn McCandless, he didn't need to come down on you so hard."

"Billy, it's over. Forget it." She waved her hand dismissively.

He put his fingers on her neck and stroked her skin, his touch exquisitely gentle. "Yeah, well, it's a bum rap." Then he gave her such a perfect smile it hurt somewhere deep inside her belly. "But you'll forget all about it where we're going. I know this place in St. Moritz where they make the best fondues, one of those cute Swiss places, all dim and cozy. We'll go there, okay?"

"Uh-huh," Beth said, relaxing to his touch. "It sounds wonderful."

"This is going to be a great trip."

She didn't even mind that Billy was making it sound as if *he* was taking *her* to Switzerland. He was so good-looking and such pleasant company. She didn't want to be alone.... No, not alone, and she couldn't go back to her apartment in New York because she'd be too easy to find there. She'd called the director of Children's International yesterday to try for a posting somewhere, but she was still on medical leave, and she'd have to pass a physical to get back on the active list. So she'd decided to call Billy.

"You feeling better?" he asked solicitously, his hand drifting from her neck down her arm.

"I'm fine," she said.

"That's good. You gotta keep your health, you know. You gotta stay in shape. It's all we've got, really," he said soberly. And he meant it, Beth knew. Whatever indulgences he practiced, they were all done in moderation. Billy put a very great value on his body.

Beth sat there in the small café, people eddying in and out, moving through the terminal. Announcements came over the loudspeaker. She looked at her watch: seven-twelve. The Lear would be ready in a few minutes. Their skis, boots and bags had already been loaded, and in a little while Matt's pilot would come to tell her everything was ready. Any minute now.

"I hear the snow's good in Europe this year," Billy said. "It'll be crowded, but what the hey, it always is. Good thing January is quiet in Aspen, or I'd never have been able to get away."

"I can't wait," Beth said, leaning back and closing her eyes. "I love Switzerland."

Billy took her hand, playing with her fingers. "It's a cool place."

"Um." She sat up. "Billy, tell me, seriously, where's your favorite place, your real favorite?"

He thought for a minute. "Oh, Aspen, I guess. But I like Maui, too, windsurfing, you know? Yeah, I sure like Maui. Sun Valley's great, too." He smiled, flashing those white teeth. "Hell, I like it everywhere."

He was so easy to be with. Billy was never in a bad mood, never complained. He was the perfect escort, the perfect, professional escort. She looked at him and smiled again and patted his hand. "Oh, are we going to have fun," she said.

It must have been just about then that she became cognizant of someone striding toward them across the crowded restaurant, a tall figure moving purposefully and quickly, unlike the meandering airport throng. She saw it out of the corner of her eye—until he stopped and stood over her. Then she had to tear her attention from Billy, because the man was saying her name.

"Beth Connelly?"

She looked up, her eyes sliding past the wide leather gun belt, the pressed uniform shirt and dark blue parka, the Pitkin County badge, up over a thrust-out chin and set mouth to a pair of angry blue eyes.

Shit.

"Beth Connelly," he repeated.

She twisted her mouth and stared up at him.

"You were going somewhere, Miss Connelly?" he asked, and Beth could hear the edge in his voice.

"Yes, I'm going to Switzerland," she said lightly, but her heart was pounding inside her chest.

"I think there's something you're forgetting," he said.

"Oh, really?"

"Listen, lady, I called and left a dozen messages for you to come in and give a statement, and you know it. Don't try to bullshit me."

"Now, Case," Billy put in, "take it easy, buddy."

Case McCandless turned his gaze to Billy. "You're not my buddy, Jorgenson, and I guess you'd better stay out of this. Miss Connelly here has a previous engagement."

Billy subsided, holding up a defensive hand, and Case turned back to Beth. "Well?"

"Well, what, Sheriff? Are you arresting me…again?" she asked with bravado.

"Nope, not this time. But you are giving that statement."

"I'm afraid you'll have to wait till I get back. The plane's almost ready."

"That's too bad. The plane can wait. You're coming with me, now."

Beth took a deep breath, stalling for time. There must be a way out of this, there was always a way out. "Look, this is ridiculous," she said. "I don't have a thing to tell you. Nothing."

Case leaned down and looked straight into her eyes. "I don't care what excuses you've got. I'm within my rights and any judge'd agree with me. You are coming with me now. Do you understand, Miss Connelly?"

Billy leaned over and took her hand. "Sounds like you'd better go, babe. I'll wait right here," he said, elaborately casual.

Beth pressed her lips together, furious, outraged, trying desperately to mask the fear that gnawed at her innards. She stood up and pulled her leather coat around her with a jerk. "I resent this," she said, "this . . . treatment."

"And I resent missing my dinner and time with my kids because of your irresponsibility," he said. "You ready?"

She seethed with mortification as they walked through the crowded terminal. Case kept a hand at the small of her back, but it wasn't courtesy, she knew, it was just so she couldn't get away. God! This man, this small-town sheriff, was beginning to feel like her nemesis. Stiff and silent as they walked outside into the darkness, she shivered once in the cold and drew her fur collar closer around her neck. He had some nerve!

His car sat at the curb, a mud-splattered white Cherokee with official emblems on the doors—oh yes, she recalled it well. But this time he opened the passenger door for her and waited while she climbed in.

He closed her door and walked around the car to the driver's side, and all the time she was steeling herself for the inevitable questions. Well, she could handle it. All she had to do was put herself on automatic pilot. It was a handy trick; it got her out of an awful lot of bad situations. And when the sheriff was done, she'd be off to Switzerland, free and clear, with handsome Billy.

He got in his side and turned the car on. "Seat belt," he said curtly, fastening his own, and then he pulled away from the curb and headed toward the highway.

"No sirens?" she asked, her lips stiff, but he only shot her a black look.

It was barely five minutes into Aspen, past the Buttermilk Ski Area, dark and shut down for the night now. A steady line of traffic came toward them from the opposite direction, the worker bees heading home down the valley to their modest homes.

It was an uncomfortable five minutes, neither of them saying a word. The atmosphere inside the car pulsed. Case kept his eyes straight ahead. Beth sat with her arms folded across her chest, her mind racing, not really seeing a thing.

It occurred to her once to offer this man some money, a lot of money—Matt would pay—to turn around and deliver her back to the airport, but she knew without questioning it that Case McCandless would never take a bribe. He had a kind of stalwart honesty that radiated from him. She turned her head slightly and glanced at him—no, this was a genuine, old-fashioned lawman, about as corruptible as John Wayne.

What was she going to say?

A scene flashed in her mind's eye: Terry walking down the hallway carrying a lifeless body over his shoulder, the blond hair cascading down in golden curls and ringlets.... No! She almost shook her head but stopped herself in time. She'd been sick, exhausted. She'd imagined the whole thing, she must have. A chill took her, gooseflesh rising. No, she hadn't imagined it. But could she betray her stepbrother and tell an outsider what she'd seen? It would be the worst thing she'd ever done in her life. Everyone would hate her, despise her. Matt...her mother...Ellen. She'd be guilty of the worst treachery in the world, disowned, absolutely ostracized. It would probably be the end of Terry; it would certainly be the end of her.

The sheriff pulled up in front of the courthouse and came around to open her door. She ignored the cold clammy sweat making her black cashmere sweater cling to her skin. She tried to breathe slowly and calmly; she willed herself to be serene. If Case McCandless saw her vulnerability, he'd attack like a shark smelling blood, and she couldn't let that happen.

The Sheriff's Department was not as busy as she remembered from New Year's Eve. There was a woman on dispatch who gave Case a surprised look. "He's ba-a-ack," she said. "Gosh, Case, I thought—"

"Yeah, so did I, Judy," he said, ushering Beth into his office, flicking on the lights.

"Have a seat," he said, gesturing to a chair in front of his desk. "I've got to make a phone call. I'll be with you in a minute."

He sat down behind his old-fashioned desk and dialed a number. Beth watched, sitting in a hard wooden chair, one leg crossed nonchalantly over the other, an expression of careful unconcern masking her inner turmoil.

"Hi, Mom," she heard him say. "Listen, I'm real sorry. I know, I know. Something came up, yeah, something important. I'll be a while." There was a pause while he listened. "Look, I know, but this is ... Tell the kids I'll see them real soon. Sure, see you, Mom. Hey, thanks."

Mom. He was calling his mother. Apologizing. Tell the kids ... His children? He had said something about missing dinner and his kids. Children. But where was his wife? Beth felt the itch of curiosity even through her anxiety. The sheriff had to call his mother.... She wanted to giggle but she wouldn't. No, she'd be calm, controlled, just like this tall blond man who was backing her into the worst corner she'd ever been in.

"Okay," he was saying, "let me get the tape recorder out and we can start." He was reaching down into a drawer, and she watched him carefully, trying to assess him. What made him tick? What got to him, what mattered to him? He seemed such an unbending type, quiet, exerting authority without effort. He set the machine on his desk and put a cassette into it. A pang struck her heart. Soon he'd ask her questions, very soon, and what would she say?

She sat there, trying to relax. *Think of something else*, she willed herself, *just play it cool*. She thought fleetingly about Billy awaiting her, but then got irritated— he should have come with her, damn it.

She looked up at the sheriff. He was still setting the recorder. A good-looking man, Beth thought anew. As sheriff, she'd have thought he'd have an offensive male strut. But he didn't. He exuded maleness with no affectations whatsoever. Even that "Mom" business on the phone. It was sort of ... endearing.

She took a breath and wished to God she was anywhere but in this office. And then she thought again: maybe Case McCandless had a price. Not money. But a price. Something. Matt said everyone had a price. So what would buy off this upstanding, moralistic sheriff?

Beth's eyes met his and she gave a polite smile, as if to say, "I'm ready."

"It's seven forty-eight p.m., January sixth, 1996. I am taking a statement from Miss Beth Connelly. Miss Connelly, please answer all questions out loud," he said into the machine.

And so it began. He started with the Antler Club. "I understand you were among the party at the Antler Club the evening of December twenty-eighth, is that correct?"

"Yes."

"Can you tell me when you first saw Heather Kelly."

"She was a bartender at the Antler Club. I saw her when I was getting a drink at the bar."

"Did she appear to know Terence Connelly at the time?"

"She was talking to him. You know, at the bar."

"That was approximately what time?"

She thought. "After midnight. I'm not sure."

"And you left the Antler Club with the entire party except for Terence, is that correct?"

"Yes."

"You all went home at that time?"

"Yes."

"About what time was that?"

She rubbed her temples with her fingers. "Oh, I don't know. Around one or two in the morning. I take medication. It's got a relaxant in it. But then you already know that," she said pointedly. "And I did have a drink. Maybe two that night. I was tired, and I don't really remember what time we went home."

"How did Terence get home?"

"He said...uh—" she stumbled over the name "—Heather was giving him a ride."

"And when did he arrive at the Connelly house with Heather Kelly?"

"God, I don't know. It was late. We were all tired. No one was looking at their watches."

"Would you say between one and three a.m.?"

She nodded.

"For the record, Miss Connelly indicated a positive response," Case said tonelessly. "Please tell me what happened next."

"Nothing happened. Some of the family sat around the living room and had drinks and then I went to bed."

"What time?"

"I don't know, I tell you I never noticed. It was late."

"And you left Terence and Miss Kelly alone in the living room at that time?"

"Yes."

"Was Terence inebriated, would you say?"

She shrugged, hoping to appear unconcerned. "He'd had a couple of drinks...."

"A couple...two drinks?"

"I don't know. I wasn't counting."

"Was Heather Kelly inebriated?"

"I have no idea. She wasn't falling-down drunk."

"So, Miss Connelly, that was the last time you saw Heather Kelly?"

"I went to sleep," she said.

"And did you hear anything or see anything out of the ordinary at any time that night?"

Beth uncrossed her legs and crossed them the other way. "I was asleep," she said. "How could I?"

Case pressed a button on the tape recorder, stopping it. "Okay, Miss Connelly, now I want to say a couple of things off the record." He leaned back in his chair, long and lean, his eyes hooded in the harsh overhead light. "We don't have all the test results back, but I'm going to tell you something I probably shouldn't. Heather Kelly had been penetrated sexually, likely forcibly, though we aren't sure yet. And she had marks on her neck."

Beth turned her face away, swallowing.

"Her mother is half out of her mind and, I'll tell you, we're going to be working like hell to find the perpetrator of this crime."

Beth forced herself to meet his eyes. "Why—" she licked her lips "—why are you telling me this?"

"I'm trying to let you know how important your statement is, Miss Connelly."

"I know...I know how important it is," she said hoarsely. "What do you think I am?"

"A Connelly," he said.

She drew in her breath.

"Rape and murder," he said, leaning forward in his chair. "It's not pretty."

Rape. It came to her in raw, hot snatches that seared her brain. She was fourteen and there were those boys, gangly, pimply boys, panting and fumbling. She shut off the picture like a bad TV show.

"Miss Connelly?" McCandless was saying, and she wrenched her attention back to the present.

"You with me?"

"Oh, yes, sure, go on. What did you say?"

But he only watched her curiously for a moment.

"Well, are you through now?" she asked.

He watched her for a minute more, then said in that deliberate, laconic way he had, "Let's go over it once more, just in case you forgot something," and he pressed the start button on the recorder.

From the beginning, all over again. The Antler Club...Heather...Terry...what time...how many drinks...last time you saw her. She answered the questions all over again. Finally, finally, he turned off the machine and pushed his chair back from his desk, regarding her from under drawn brows. She sat very still, waiting, toughing it out.

"Anything more you can tell me?" he asked at last. "Some little detail that you don't even think is important. It might help the investigation."

She shook her head. "Nothing. I was asleep."

"Uh-huh, that's what you said."

"So stop grilling me, for God's sake."

He said nothing, merely stared at her.

"Why are you picking on me?" she said, refusing to look away.

"Am I? Sorry."

"You're making me very nervous."

"Yes, I noticed."

"Anyone would be."

But he didn't look as if he were buying her excuse. "Uh-huh," he said.

Beth felt the tiny hairs on her neck tingle. "Listen," she said quickly, "I really have to go. My plane's waiting."

"That's true, and so is your friend," he said dryly.

She gave him a swift glance. It was a surprising comment coming from the sheriff, pretty darn personal. She wondered how well he knew Billy; if he knew him at all, he knew who was paying for the trip, and he'd think her either stupid or degenerate.

And in a way he was right.

Shouldn't Billy, at least, have offered to go with her to the sheriff's office? For moral support if nothing else. There he was, still sitting at the Pour la France bar most likely, drinking expensive wine on her tab, probably flirting like crazy with other women.

Beth looked up and found the sheriff standing over her. "What?" she said.

"You want to go. You can go."

"Oh," she said, rising, too, aware of the stiffness in her muscles. Nerves. And then there he was, his hand at the small of her back again, ushering her out while he snapped off the lights and shut his door.

"I'll drive you back to the airport," he said.

"Really, don't bother. I can get a cab."

"Hey, it's almost on my way," he said.

"On your way to where?"

"To pick up my kids."

"Are you sure . . . ?"

"I'm so late now it hardly matters. Let's go."

She played with the strap of her bag all the way back to the airport, relieved and unsettled at the same time. It was over. She'd faced the worst and not given in. She hadn't lied, not exactly. And now she was free to leave Aspen, to fly away with Billy and have a ball. . . .

"Sorry if I made you late," she said, trying to defuse the discomfort. She should have taken a taxi.

He shrugged. "It happens all the time. They're used to it."

"Where's their . . . mother?" she heard herself asking.

He glanced at her quickly, then turned back to the road. "In California. We're divorced."

"Oh."

Silence fell again, but it was filled with a gravid tension. Case broke it. "Look, I know you're leaving town and God knows when you'll be back, but if you ever remember anything, anything at all about that night Heather Kelly was killed, I'd like you to call me. Make it collect from wherever you are." He didn't look at her, though; his eyes were gazing straight ahead. All she could see was the angled plane of his cheek, the taillights of the car in front of them glinting red on his skin.

"Sure," she said. "But really, I didn't see anything. I was . . ."

"Asleep. Yeah, I know." He turned to her for a moment. "Put yourself in that poor girl's place. Think about it. The man who did it will do it again sooner or later. Maybe he's done it before."

Put yourself in that poor girl's place. Suddenly Beth was no longer in the sheriff's car on the way to the airport. She was being pulled into that dark bedroom, crying, her skirt being lifted, the boys crowding above her. She screamed but no one heard, and then it was too late. No amount of tears could wash away what had been done to her, but she'd learned to forget, to deny. She ran from her memories, and most of the time she managed to outdistance them. Oh yes, she was a fine sprinter. It was the long haul she wondered about.

"...your address," Case was saying, "in New York or whatever."

"My address?" she asked, tearing herself from her reverie, raising her facade like a drawbridge. "Matt will always know where I am. But why? I've told you everything I know."

"Uh-huh, well, it's routine in an investigation," Case said as he pulled up in front of the terminal. He sat there a minute. "Look, Miss Connelly, about that DUI last week . . ."

"Please," she said.

"You could go before a judge, you know, explain about the medication you were taking. It might get your license back temporarily."

"I'm not even going to be here," she said.

"Well, then you can explain at the formal hearing. I think it's scheduled for late in February."

"I really don't want to deal with it right now," she said. "I just want to get on that plane to Switzerland."

"I can understand that," he said. "Well, you and Jorgenson have a nice trip."

It hadn't struck her as an absolute decision until that moment, but as she reached for the door handle to let herself out, she said, "Thanks, but Billy's not coming with me. I'm going alone." Then she got out of the car and slammed the door behind her. As she walked toward the terminal she wondered if she'd miss her flight in Denver. And she wondered, too, what on earth had made her decide that she couldn't bear to have Billy with her—and why she'd even bothered to mention it to that officious sheriff.

Deirdre was always a little nervous when she called her mother in Malibu. She wanted Leslie—she always called her that—to approve of her, and Leslie rarely did. This time, however, she was pleasantly surprised.

"You are?" Leslie asked. "Well, it's about time."

"So you think it's a good idea?"

"Darling, it's a terrific idea. Your children belong with you, and I've always said that. You'll move now, of course. Will you stay in California or go back to Colorado?"

"Oh no. I'll stay right here. It's a wonderful place to raise kids."

"Good Lord. On an ashram? Deirdre, I swear you've been brainwashed."

"I most certainly have not." Deirdre felt her fingers tighten on the receiver. "This is the most perfect place on earth. You should just see how happy all the children here are."

"My grandchildren . . . on an ashram." Leslie sighed. "First that shack in Aspen and now this."

There was a long pause, and then Deirdre said quietly, "I've found this wonderful lawyer. He says that—"

"Is that what this call's about? Money? Money for a lawyer?"

"Well, I . . ."

"Deirdre," Leslie said, "let's not argue. You just do whatever it takes to get your children back. I'll help however I can. But afterward we need to talk. There's so much room in this house, and we need to talk about you and the children and what's best for them."

"Of course," Deirdre said, agreeing as always when they both knew she'd do exactly as she pleased in the end.

EIGHT

On January eighteenth the full array of test results on Heather Kelly's body were finally back, and they turned out to be exceedingly interesting. Case and Tripp Maddock had a meeting that afternoon and, over coffee and a table piled with computer printouts and reports from the FBI lab in Denver, they discussed the case.

Tripp leaned back in his chair and hooked his thumbs in his suspenders. "Well, Terence Connelly did it," the D.A. said.

"Looks like," Case agreed.

Tripp reached out and tapped his fingers on a sheet of white paper covered with columns of numbers and blue dots. "He definitely had sex with the girl. The DNA profile from his blood matches the semen sample taken from her body."

"He lied," Case said.

"He lied about everything. She was in his room. We've got her hair from the bedding. The carpet fibers found on her boots make a seventy-five-percent match with the bedroom carpet. A snowplow driver saw a man in an aviator jacket walking toward the highway at 3:45 a.m. Could easily have been headed for the Preserve."

"Oh, he did it, all right," Case said. "But everything we have is circumstantial."

"Murderers have been convicted on less," Tripp said. "And look at this—" he flicked another paper "—Heather Kelly had no, repeat *no* cocaine in her bloodstream. Coke on her nose but none in her body? Come on! He put it there to confuse things."

"Sure seems like it."

"And, damn it all, there wasn't a molecule of an illegal substance to be found in his room."

"He was smart enough to dump it," Case said, shrugging.

"Yeah, a real brain we got here."

"This case had better be airtight before we arrest him," Case said, "or we're up the creek. He gets off and the town'll lynch us, not to mention the press...."

"And the goddamn Connellys," the D.A. reminded him.

"Yeah, the Connellys. Be careful, Tripp, real careful."

"He did it, though. The medical examiner put it down in black and white: 'What killed her was pressure on her neck, which reduced blood flow to her brain and heart, leading to death.' A classic choke hold, in other words."

"You think you can nail him?" Case asked.

Tripp pursed his lips. "I'd like to be able to use that tip you got about him being in trouble before."

"The dropped rape charges?"

Tripp nodded. "The trouble is, I'm sure the judge would never allow it."

"Um," Case said. "But what we do have is the timing—when she died and the snowplow driver's sworn statement of when he saw the car in the club parking lot. Heather didn't have time to leave the Connellys', meet up with someone else, have sex and get dumped at the Aspen Health Club before she died."

"I wish the time of death was more precise," Tripp said.

"They nailed it to within a couple of hours," Case reminded him. "It's close enough."

"But will a jury see it that way?" Tripp frowned. "I sure wish we had a witness."

"Well, we don't," the sheriff said mildly. "But we do have Terence's sworn statement that's blown all to hell now."

"Then we go on circumstantial evidence. He lied. He swore he didn't have sex with her, but we know he did. That's significant. If we can get him on the stand, we'll cross-examine him till he pukes. He's a coward and dumb to boot. He should've known about DNA profiling."

"So," Case asked, "do we go ahead and arrest him or not?"

Tripp pursed his lips again and looked upward. "Tell you what. Let me contact an old law professor of mine. Then I'll decide."

"It's your call, Tripp."

"Yeah," the D.A. said glumly, "the goddamn buck stops right here."

On January twenty-fifth, on a warm, sunny afternoon, Case McCandless and his deputy Loren in one car, and Tripp Maddock and his assistant D.A. in another, set out for the Pitkin County Airport. As prearranged, they drove straight onto the runway to the far east end and sat there for a few minutes until the sun glinted off a trim white Learjet that banked and came in for a landing, taxiing up to the two waiting cars. From the doorway of the Lear emerged three people: the solid, squat figure of Matt Connelly, his handsome son, Terence, and a woman with shoulder-length dark hair, dark eyes and a superb figure not quite hidden under a Savile Row trenchcoat.

Matt and the woman ducked quickly into the D.A.'s car, which pulled away instantly; Terence was handcuffed and put into the back seat of the sheriff's car. At the jail Terence Connelly was read his rights, booked and offered a phone call, which he declined, as his lawyer, Melinda Feinstein, was present. The arraignment hearing was held next door at the courthouse in front of Judge Snyder. Terence Connelly was advised of the severity of his alleged crime, murder in the second degree, and what type of punishment he might expect if he were found guilty. Bond was then set at fifty thousand dollars, for which Matt Connelly wrote a check on the spot. The party of three walked out into the warm sunshine of a January thaw and went on to the bar of the Hotel Jerome to have a drink before reboarding their Lear to fly back to Washington.

The next day, January twenty-sixth, the news hit the headlines: Terence Connelly Charged In Murder Of Aspen Woman.

And all hell broke loose.

It started to snow heavily at the end of January. By mid-February even the old-time locals couldn't recall a winter this bad—not for thirty years, anyway. Around the big joiners table at the workingman's breakfast spot, the Hickory House, it was all anyone could talk about.

"Snow's up over my toolshed," Larry the plumber said.

Harold, a city snowplow driver, agreed. Forking up a mouthful of sausage and hash browns, he said, "The snow dump at the Rio Grande lot is full. Don't know where we're gonna put another drop."

And outside it just kept snowing, big fat wet flakes, day after day.

The danger of avalanches in the backcountry surrounding Aspen was severe. Already a slide in the Ashcroft area had possibly buried three cross-country skiers, and roads and mountain passes were closed throughout the Rockies.

The media had another field day. With shots of cars buried in avalanches flashing across television screens nationwide, and camera crews interviewing the rescue teams searching for the missing skiers, Aspen was once again in the headlines. Of course, every reporter had to finish an interview with the inevitable question: "And how does the local community feel about the Terence Connelly affair?"

Sheriff McCandless gave the same answer each and every time. "I'm afraid we're too busy digging out of the worst storms in recent memory to be dealing with a trial that hasn't even been scheduled yet." He was becoming quite a politician.

A Denver anchorman stated that the only safe place to be in Colorado was in your living room.

And it kept on snowing.

The McCandless ranch was hit hard by the huge storms. Situated in the narrow Maroon Creek Valley, the avalanche danger was high every winter, but this year it would have been suicide for Nick McCandless to take folks up into the wilderness for the backcountry skiing tour. The guests didn't complain, though, because no one wanted to risk their lives, and besides, people reveled in the massive piles of snow, the super downhill skiing and warm cozy fires at night. It was a real Rocky Mountain winter no one would forget.

But that was before the avalanche south of the ranch.

The snow broke six hundred feet above the road in the early afternoon of February twenty-first. It thundered down the mountainside, snapping trees like matchsticks, careering through gullies and uplifting boulders until it reached Maroon Creek, crossed the road and forged its way to the base of the opposite mountain.

The Lazy M Ranch was cut off from civilization. Even the water supply to Aspen was blocked, and no one knew for sure whether a car or two had been in the path of the slide. By early evening helicopters were able to fly over and evaluate the damage, but it would be morning before the road crews could come in and dynamite, hopefully opening the creek and the road.

Case was one of the first to call Dottie after the avalanche. "You all right out there?" he asked.

Dottie breathed a sigh of relief. "Yes. We're fine. But we didn't know if anyone had reported the slide yet. Rowdy was in his truck when it went. I guess he saw it."

"He's okay?"

"Okay, but stuck here along with the rest of us."

"We won't be able to get in till tomorrow," Case said.

"We'll survive. There's lots of food and wood. We'll be fine." Dottie found the isolation refreshing. Like most old-timers in the vicinity of Aspen, she couldn't remember a winter this snowy. The drifts piled up against the main lodge and behind the guest cabins, and the fences in the fields disappeared. The folks who were supposed to fly out that day resigned themselves to staying. You couldn't fight Mother Nature, after all.

That night they all stuffed themselves, barbecuing their own steaks and chicken in the open hearth at the center of the great room, a cathedrallike expanse of giant timbered walls reaching up fifty feet. Rowdy struck up the music early, and some of the guests danced, redcheeked and exhausted from the thin air and a day in the snow.

Dottie finished up in the kitchen and joined the throng in the great room. It was hot despite the massive space. Guests were dancing, the fire blazed; every bench and chair was full. Rowdy, on his guitar, was working up a full sweat while the guests took to the wooden floor and danced the Texas two-step.

"Come and sit, Mom," Nick said, moving over on a bench. "Take a breather. It's been a long day."

Dottie sat gratefully. Though she'd never tell a soul, lately her bones were weary by evening. "I wonder if they'll get the road open tomorrow," she said, lifting her hair off her neck.

"I'm sure they will. Can you imagine letting Aspen run out of its water supply in the middle of the ski season?"

Unconcerned, Nick shook his blond head and tapped a foot to his brother's music.

Dottie patted his knee and smiled. They were good boys, she thought, as she'd thought so many thousands of times before. Good, strong, handsome sons. But all so different. Whereas Rowdy, the oldest of the three, lived up to his name, and Nick, the youngest, was the ladies' man, Case was perhaps her favorite—if Dottie really had one. It was Case who reminded her so much of her late husband with his quiet strength and instinctive knowledge of right and wrong. It was Case who could so easily take charge of a difficult situation. Somehow her middle boy always knew what to do. Rowdy got angry as a means of coping and even now occasionally got involved in a barroom brawl. Nick, on the other hand, was more for turning his cheek and heading off into his beloved wilderness. But Case always stood his ground, and he got the job done with a calm sort of authority. It was Case who was the only one truly cut out for marriage. If only he'd chosen someone with a little more sense . . . But Deirdre, my Lord. Of course, Deirdre had pursued Case, and naturally, being an old-fashioned gentleman, Case had proposed.

Dottie wouldn't have traded her grandchildren for anything. At least Deirdre had given him those two angels. But Case still needed a good woman. He *deserved* a good woman.

"Hey," Nick was saying by her side, "you look about a million miles away. You aren't worried about the road crews getting through to us, are you?"

"No . . . no, I was just thinking." She sighed. "I wish Case and the kids were with us tonight. Knowing him, he's probably trying to dig the slide out with his own hands. He just does too much all the time."

"You worry too much."

"With your children," she said, "you can never worry enough."

If the unusually heavy snow was a problem to many Rocky Mountain inhabitants, it was a blessing to Billy Jörgenson. No one who worked on Aspen Mountain could remember a snow year like this, and the powder hounds lined up by the hundreds each morning an hour before the lifts even opened. To make fresh tracks down the face of Bell Mountain, or to be the first to glide through the trees on Last Dollar was nothing short of heaven. And Billy had been living in this wonder-world since he'd been just out of high school in Denver. He'd live the lush life of Aspen all his life, or so he planned. Hell, he could keep this up till he was eighty if he chose to.

As the big snowflakes drifted endlessly from the sky, Billy's plate got fuller and fuller. Bookings for private lessons piled in from all over the globe, and the only thing stopping the private jets from landing was the terrible weather. Still, limos could be hired in Denver, and the true powder devotees would make the hairy road trip over the twelve-thousand-foot passes just to get in a day of exquisite pleasure on the slopes.

Billy, of course, was booked solid by female clients. The day before the avalanche blocked the Maroon Creek road, he'd not only made his regular pay on a six-hour private lesson with the latest French film sensation, Claudette Beauchamp, but she'd tipped him five hundred U.S. dollars as well.

And then there was the evening.

Billy had had his share of women. There were some he was truly fond of. There were some with bitchy personalities or drug problems, but their perfectly kept female bodies made up for those shortcomings. And then there were the "special clients," as he thought of them— Claudette was one. Beth Connelly was another, though Beth had her share of problems, such as her inability to have a climax. But Billy figured he'd cure that for her one day. He'd planned on curing Beth in Switzerland, in fact.

But now it was Claudette who consumed his days and mental energies, and he was determined to make their time together memorable—to keep those big tips coming in, among other things. And so the night before the big avalanche Billy was with Claudette in her fifteen-hundred-dollar-a-night Ritz-Carlton suite, dining on gourmet delicacies and fine wine, sliding into the en-suite Jacuzzi and kissing away the soreness in her muscles from the heavy day of skiing.

"French women taste different," he told her, his mouth trailing across a nipple as his hand sought the hotness of her inner thighs and water swirled around them.

"Mon Dieu," she moaned. And the starlet opened her body like a flower to greet him. "You think we taste better?"

"No," Billy said, sliding a finger into her, "just different."

And outside the snow kept falling.

The Maroon Creek road was open by the following morning. The guests at the McCandless ranch who'd missed flights the previous day piled their suitcases high in the entrance of the main lodge, and both Nick and Rowdy made several runs to the airport in the big Suburban with its Lazy M logo on the side. More guests arrived, though, greeting old friends, all anxious to hear about the avalanche. And had those poor cross-country skiers been found yet?

And then, of course, the inevitable questions to Dottie from those who knew Case: "Say, isn't your son the sheriff? What's he think about Terence Connelly's chance in court?"

"My Lord," Dottie told them, having learned from her son, "the trial date isn't even set."

By dinnertime the main lodge was crowded, the usual stories of the day's skiing being batted back and forth, talk still coming around to the missing skiers. Dottie worked in the kitchen, glad to be away from the chatter—it had been a strange winter, Aspen in the headlines day after day. Sometimes she wished she could turn the calendar back forty years to a slower, easier time when Aspen was just a sleepy little mining town and she and her husband had just moved to the valley. In those days it had been hard to make ends meet. Old mining shacks had occupied the same lots that now held modern replicas of Victorian houses. The downtown area had been minuscule, a few old brick buildings and a lot of vacant, unkempt land.

In those days the sheriff had had a simple job. Crime was nonexistent. Save for the boys getting rowdy on the Fourth of July and putting cherry bombs in mailboxes, there had been little to distract the sheriff from his business as a plumber or store owner.

Things sure had changed. And you had to change with them, Dottie told herself sternly.

Case arrived at six-thirty. He came through the back door, Nate and Amanda in tow, his hat and shoulders white with snow.

"Hi," he said, shooting Dottie a weary smile. "Sorry I couldn't make it out sooner."

Dottie gave the kids their usual hugs then sent them off to the cookie jar. "I knew you'd be swamped today," she said, wiping her hands on her apron while her son poured himself a mug of fresh, strong coffee. "Was the slide awful?"

"It wasn't the slide," he said, sitting at the old, scarred wooden table. "Mountain Rescue found those missing skiers."

Dottie turned from the sink and looked at his face. "Oh God," she said.

"We're still notifying relatives."

"Were they locals?"

He shook his head. "From Colorado Springs."

"What a shame."

"They didn't belong back there," he said as if to himself. "Hell, why would anyone risk it?"

"It's not your fault," Dottie put in carefully. "There're signs on all the roads...the radio and TV have been full of warnings."

"I guess," Case said. "It's just that you always think that maybe if you'd issued one more warning..." And his blue eyes, so like his father's, lifted to the window and the falling snow beyond.

That night they all ate dinner together at a long wooden table. Case was seated across from a doctor and his wife from Georgia, who'd been coming to the ranch for years.

The doctor, Craig Whitcomb, kept his counsel, but his wife couldn't resist. "Oh, Case," she began, "you must be so tired of this Connelly scandal. How do you stand it? I can't even go to my grocery without those headlines staring me in the face. You know, Rape and Murder in Aspen. My God, it's ridiculous. Why, Terence Connelly hasn't even gone to trial yet, has he? It's awful. It gives Aspen such a terrible name."

"Terrible," her husband concurred.

"But I suppose you can't really say anything about the Connellys. I mean, your office must have a lot on him or you wouldn't have charged him with murder."

"It wasn't my office," Case explained patiently. "It was up to the D.A."

"But you must know what's going on. I mean..."

"Now, Laura," her husband cautioned her, "I'm sure Case here must be sick of all these questions."

The conversation slowed then but soon took a new tack—the fate of the cross-country skiers and how crazy it was to risk your life for a walk in the woods. Patiently Case answered everyone's questions, explaining how a helicopter had spotted a pair of skis sticking up from a snow slide not a hundred yards from shelter, a cross-country hut.

"Isn't that always the way," Rowdy said, and he rose, picking up his guitar. "Well, gotta get to work. I'll let my brother here off the hook and do some entertainin'."

Indeed, Case seemed glad to escape the throng, to leave the kids to play on the dance floor, and join his mother in the kitchen, where she and a helper cleaned up. He leaned against a wall, stifled a yawn and looked like a man with a whole lot of weight on his shoulders.

"You know," Dottie said while she scraped plates, "you can leave Nate and Amanda here this weekend."

"Allison's sitting for them."

"Well, if she has a problem or anything, I'm happy to have them."

"I know. And thanks."

"Anytime," Dottie said, and she went back to work, leaving her son to stand there, staring out at the falling snow.

Rowdy's music, which grew louder as everyone finished dinner and took to the dance floor, flowed through the lodge, good old country and western songs about drinking and loneliness and unrequited love: "'Cause I've got friends in low places where the whiskey drowns and the beer chases my blues away and I'll be okay..."

People clapped and sang along, and a few guests even formed their own line dance, strutting, bending, kicking, thumbs hooked in jeans pockets. Usually Dottie finished up in the kitchen and rejoined the group around the big hearth, but tonight she stayed behind, quietly keeping her son company.

She poured them both coffee, laced it with brandy and sat at the table. "Come have a drink," she said. "You look as if you need one."

He gave her a tired half smile and sat. "I guess I do at that. It's been a hell of a winter and it's not over yet."

"Are you getting any sleep at all?" she began, but then caught herself. "Now don't I sound just like a mother?"

Case reached across the table and squeezed her hand. "You can be a mom if you want."

Dottie laughed. "Not me. Not any longer. I'll stick with being a grandmother, thank you."

"You do that okay, too." He looked past her shoulders and frowned, sitting back in his chair, holding his mug with both hands. "There's something I haven't told you," he said. "I've been meaning to, but I didn't want to worry you."

Dottie nodded slowly.

"It's Deirdre. She's gotten it into her head to sue for custody of the kids."

"Oh, my Lord."

"Now don't go off in a panic, Mom, but I guess I'm going to have to put up a fight."

"Can she . . . ?"

Case gave her a reassuring smile. "Not if I can help it."

"You're going to fight it? You have a lawyer?"

"Yes. You know Deirdre doesn't really want the kids. She's the one who left them. It's that David, that nut, who's pushing her. He just wants to add to his flock. It's prestige for him, that's all."

"And Leslie," Dottie said.

"My sweet mother-in-law, yeah. I wouldn't be surprised if she had her spoon in the pot."

"Oh, Case."

"I wouldn't mind if I thought that was better for them. You know that, Mom. But she can't handle it. She can't settle down. She can't stand being responsible for other human beings."

"I know, Case."

"Don't worry, Mom."

"Do Nate and Amanda know?"

He shook his head. "And I don't want them to."

"When did this happen?"

He sighed. "Right after Christmas."

"Oh, God. Why didn't you tell me?"

"If you'll recall, I had a lot on my mind."

"Oh, damn," Dottie said, biting her lower lip. "If only you were remarried, Case."

"And who do you suggest I marry? Come on, Mom, haven't I been through enough?"

"Just because you made a mistake once... Listen, Case, you'll find the right woman. A good woman. You're the marrying kind."

"Oh? You know that for sure, do you?"

"Darn tootin'. Now your brothers...I wouldn't wish either of them on a decent woman, but you...you're your dad all over again."

"I guess that's a compliment."

"It certainly is. I love your brothers to death, and I don't know how I'd manage this place without them, but neither is down-to-earth. Not like you."

"Well, I'll find someone to propose to tomorrow and the judge will see that I'm a real steady sort."

"Don't be sarcastic."

"I'm only being half-sarcastic."

"Um," Dottie said. "You just put up a good fight. Don't you let that woman take those babies."

"I'm doing my damnedest."

It was Case who rose and poured them both another coffee, carefully changing the subject. "How's your Forest Service permit coming along?" he asked.

She shook her head at him.

"I'm serious. You never know what can hang up a federal land-use permit these days. And if Nick can't use the access roads to get guests into the backcountry, well, they might just go elsewhere."

"It's a standard renewal," Dottie said, shrugging. "I fill out the papers every seven years like clockwork. We've had permission to use those access roads for forty years. There won't be a problem."

"Didn't the Forest Service shut down that logging operation last summer? Deny them access?"

Dottie bristled. "They were logging. You know how the environmentalists are nowadays."

"Yeah, well, maybe Nick and his snowmobiles are disturbing the ecosystem or something."

She made a dismissive gesture with her hand. "So we'll just use the sleigh. The snowmobiles break down every day as it is."

"I was only asking," Case said.

"Well, I sent in the papers and the check, and the permit will be along any day now."

"I'm sure it will," Case said agreeably, despite the fact that he and his brothers had all tried to talk their mother into hiring a lawyer last fall to reapply for the permit. There truly were so many environmental groups with concerns over wilderness use, it couldn't hurt to take every precaution. The backcountry tours were a big draw for the ranch, the reason a lot of the guests stayed so far out of town in the winter. Of course, Dottie made money in the summer, too, running horseback tours, teaching Western riding—but the big bucks came in the winter. Without that wilderness-use permit . . .

But Dottie was a stubborn woman, saying she'd be damned if she was going to pay some highfalutin lawyer to file a simple application when she'd been doing it herself for decades. They'd get the renewal and the guests would keep coming and that was that.

She looked her son in the eye. "Nice try," she said.

"What?" Case said.

"Trying to get me off the subject."

"Subject?"

"Deirdre."

"Forget it," he said. "I've got it covered."

"Then I guess," Dottie said, "we both have everything under control. Right?"

Case had to give a tired laugh. "Right."

It rained a lot in northern California that February. Deirdre knew that meant Colorado was getting snow, which was good. Colorado depended on snow for business. And whenever she thought of Colorado she thought of Case and her babies. She lay there in bed with David, listening to his gentle snoring, his smell still on her, and conjured up her ex-husband in her mind. Oh, how handsome he'd been. The blond good looks, the well-honed body of an athlete. Deirdre had been in Aspen after college, ski-bumming for a season, working at a ski shop, when she'd met Case. She'd taken one look at the handsome young deputy, and for the first time in her life she'd known exactly what she wanted and had gone about getting it. She'd chased him unabashedly, seduced him and married him. And then he'd turned out to be so straight, so serious, impossible to live with.

She saw Nate in her mind's eye, the darling boy. And Amanda, who'd only been a baby. Amanda wouldn't even recognize her, she supposed, and she felt sad. Guilty and sad. David made her feel guilty, but the sadness was all her own.

Yet Deirdre knew, somewhere deep inside her, that Case was a better father than she was a mother. She had growing misgivings about the custody suit, but she didn't dare tell David. And she knew she'd follow through on the lawsuit because David wanted her to, because he was always right, always sure, always balanced.

The lawyer in Point Reyes seemed to think she had an excellent chance to recover the children. So did David. They belonged with her, everyone agreed. Her very wealthy, twice-divorced mother had even come through with the mounting legal fees. Everyone was on Deirdre's side, so it must be right.

Deirdre lay there and tried to sleep, saying the peace mantra over and over.

Sleep was slow in coming to Dottie that night. But then she often lay awake and went over things in her head when the lodge was utterly silent save for the occasional groan of a ceiling beam under the weight of the snow. The eiderdown quilt tucked under her chin, she stared up at the high, timbered ceiling and thought about everything, making decisions, forming plans, thanking the good Lord for her blessings. Tonight, as the snow still drifted against the panes of her bedroom window and wood smoke scented the air, she thought about Case and she worried. He was under too much pressure. If people weren't off getting themselves killed in the high country, then they were conspiring to drive her son crazy with their antics—cutting each other up, suing each other, murdering each other. Case could fool the public and all those awful newspeople who hounded him daily, but he couldn't fool his mother. The strain was around his eyes and in the set of his jaw. It wasn't going to end soon, either, because the Connelly trial wouldn't be for months yet.

Darn those people! Dottie thought. Users, snobs, the worst sort. Why, in the thirty-odd years that the Connelly family had been visiting Aspen, not once had they set foot on the McCandless ranch. City folk. Noses stuck up in the air. It was bad enough they came to Aspen at all, but why couldn't they leave their sick behavior back east and act like decent folk out here?

She turned her head and felt her heart beating too quickly and told herself to calm down. Case was a grown man, utterly independent and capable, and he'd handle the reporters and Connellys and Deirdre just fine, as he handled everything. And soon, in six weeks or so, the town would empty for off-season and they'd all get a much needed rest. Sure, Dottie mused, comforted, her eyes closing, a few more weeks . . .

Outside the snow fell steadily, the moisture coming from the Pacific and freezing over the mountains as it rose. By morning ten more inches of the white stuff cloaked the valley, and in town, Larry the plumber awoke to find that the roof of his toolshed had collapsed.

At the joiners table he put a wad of tobacco in his mouth and said, "Damn. Betsy told me to shovel the thing. I sure hate it when she's right. Damn."

NINE

The lobbyist for Smith-Brown Laboratories possessed a two-thousand-dollar suit and a mellifluous voice. He was full of statistics and had an answer for every question the senators asked him. Matt Connelly had known him for years. John Klingemann was his name, and last year he'd represented the tobacco industry; the year before it had been the airlines. This year Klingemann was working for the huge research lab. They had a promising treatment for cancer, but it was too soon to go public with it, the usual story.

What Klingemann wanted for his client, Smith-Brown, was more federal funding for research.

The senator from Montana was asking just what this new treatment was, and Matt tuned in.

"Well, Senator Dodge, it's actually a combination of drugs. Now, we don't want to raise false hopes again, but this new conversion combination therapy stopped the growth of cancer cells in a test tube. We have great expectations," Klingemann answered.

"Don't you make enough on your regular drug sales to fund your research?" Senator Mendenhall asked.

"Drug companies have been price-gouging the public for years."

Klingemann smiled indulgently. "The government's new policy on cheap immunizations for children has cut our profits drastically. We need help, Senator. I have here charts to show where we stand, and of course we will provide you with a financial report if you want."

And on it went. Matt played with a pen, doodling on a pad of paper in front of him. Meetings, meetings. He'd developed the knack, over the twenty-five years he'd been in the Senate, of putting his mind in neutral, but it never ceased to amaze him how much he actually remembered of what went on in the meetings he chaired.

There were more questions, more give and take. Klingemann was persuasive, regardless of whom he was lobbying for. He had all the facts at his fingertips, and he never got flustered.

Surreptitiously, Matt glanced at his watch. Six twenty-five. Jesus. Lee's dinner party started in a half hour. He waited until Klingemann finished an explanation of how research funding would result in "incremental progress," and how, for each dollar appropriated by the federal government, the return in better health would save Medicare millions.

"Okay," Matt said, "I think we all get the picture, John. We have the report here. I know I speak for every member of this committee when I thank you for your input. Now, gentlemen, I believe the meeting is adjourned."

They all milled around in the room, the power-mongers, winding down.

Matt approached Klingemann, shook his hand. "Good to see you again, John. Say, do you need a ride?

I'm on my way home for a dinner party, but I'll have my driver drop you...."

"Oh, there's no need, Senator."

"I insist. The traffic's hell this time of day." He gave Klingemann a blunt look.

The lobbyist gathered up his papers rapidly and stuffed them into his briefcase. "Well then, I accept your kind offer."

In the basement garage of the Capitol building, Matt's driver was waiting, the engine of the black Cadillac sedan ticking over silently, all warmed up.

"Where you staying?" Matt asked Klingemann.

"The Harrington."

"Perfect. Right on the way."

Inside the car Matt directed his driver, then settled back against the leather seat and sighed. "Well, John, I think we can work together on Smith-Brown's request."

"Excellent," Klingemann said.

"Now, I believe strongly in medical research, always have, although sometimes with the budget constraints—" he shook his head sadly "—it's very, very hard to juggle appropriations."

"I am well aware of the problems."

"I can put pressure on people, certain key people, who'll come through for me when it gets down to a vote but, you know, John, it uses up a lot of my political currency."

The car drove smoothly out of the garage and onto Pennsylvania Avenue toward the White House. Traffic was heavy, the sky a low, grainy pewter color that pressed upon the great solid buildings lining The Mall. February in Washington. Neither man wasted a glance at these monuments to representative government; they were too busy making decisions that affected millions of people.

"Smith-Brown would certainly appreciate greatly any help from you, Senator Connelly," Klingemann said.

"Um."

The question lay on the air unspoken: If I scratch your back, will you scratch mine?

Matt sighed again. "I'll tell you, John, it's hard. I have to juggle priorities. You know how it is. Everyone wants a piece of me."

"I truly do believe Smith-Brown is a worthy cause," Klingemann said, managing to sound sympathetic but not obsequious.

"Oh, I know, I know, but there're so *many* worthy ones."

"You know, if there is a breakthrough announcement on this new drug, our stock will skyrocket. Anyone who holds Smith-Brown will stand to make a fortune."

"Absolutely," Matt said, nodding.

"I'm sure it can be arranged so that you're the first to know of any such announcement, Senator."

"Um," Matt said, his mind working. Smith-Brown stock was presently selling for about sixty-six-and-a-half. An announcement could push it to seventy-five or better before the programmer traders scooped up a tidy profit. "Um," he repeated. He'd have Buzz Crenshaw snatch up a few hundred thousand shares quietly over the next six weeks in their dummy corporation.... "Now, you're sure this drug is a winner?" he asked. "You wouldn't bullshit me and screw the taxpayers?"

"Absolutely not."

Matt's driver dropped John Klingemann in front of the Harrington on E Street. Matt and John shook hands, their eyes met. It was a deal.

And then Matt told his driver to hurry because he was going to be late as hell, and Lee would have a fit if she had to entertain Ambassador Creighton alone. All the way north to M Street, Matt felt a nice, warm glow of satisfaction. He'd done well. Funding for cancer research, a worthy cause, no doubt about it. And a simple little phone call that'd net him a few hundred thou. Not a bad bargain.

Along M Street, then a turn onto a narrower street in Georgetown, leafless trees along brick sidewalks, fine old brick houses elbowing one another for space, each as understated and sturdy as the next. Lights glowed like molten gold from windows. The sedan stopped in front of a three-story brick that was painted dark gray with white shutters and a white Georgian doorway. Home. Well, Matt thought, one of his homes.

He just had time to change and grab a quick Scotch before the guests arrived, stylishly late. They crowded into the narrow hall where the girl provided by the caterer took their coats, then pressed on into the white-paneled living room with its Latrobe mantelpiece, Aubusson rug, rosewood and mahogany furniture, dark oil paintings on the walls and silver ice bucket and bottles on the Queen Anne sideboard. Lee was quite sober this evening, a marvel. She was such a lady, so delicate and lovely, in a pale rose Valentino dress and pearls. God, it made her look as young and beautiful as when Matt had met her. He leaned toward her and whispered in her ear, "You look wonderful, hon," and she bestowed a gracious smile on him. Oh yes, Lee could still get it together.

Todd Weldon, the junior senator from New York, Matt's protégé, came first, accompanied by his cute, dark wife, Mindy. He'd been a Rhodes scholar at Oxford, so he'd fit in well with Ambassador Creighton from England. Todd had been given express instructions to charm Creighton's rather formidable wife, Jane.

Then Terry arrived, towing a gorgeous young thing—Angela was her name—who towered over Matt and had lots of wild dark hair. Then Julian Creighton and his wife, an impressive couple, he portly and awfully British, she horse faced and unlovely in burgundy velvet, but smart and worldly and dripping with jewels. Last to arrive was Beth, in town for the night on her way to the Connelly beach house on the Outer Banks. She had a date, too, Andrew Detrick, a good-looking fellow who worked for the United Nations. They'd met in New York, Beth said.

Everyone stood around the living room and talked, sipped drinks, ate canapés served by the caterer's girl—translucent smoked salmon and moist caviar and miniature spring rolls. Lee had a glass of soda, Matt noted.

Todd was dutifully talking to Jane Creighton. Smart kid, Todd. Young but willing to learn. He came from some hick town in upstate New York, but he'd managed just fine in Washington. A little too idealistic still, but he'd get over that. Ideals only got in the way of effective governing, Matt kept telling him. You want to get something *done*, you work it out. Negotiate, compromise.

"Dad, you've met Angela," Terry was saying. "She's a model."

Matt looked up at the tall beauty. "Goddamn, woman, why are you so *tall*?" And she laughed coyly, showing a dimple, tossed her hair, and Matt could feel the vibes pass between them like electricity. He looked her up and down, from those long, long legs to the short tight leather skirt to her red silk blouse, then he winked at her.

"So," he said to his son, "how's school going?"

"Fine, the usual," Terry said.

"Good, good. Now, you remember our lunch date tomorrow?"

"Sure, Dad."

Matt moved on to Creighton's side, where Mindy Weldon had him laughing. He chucked Mindy under the chin and gave her one of his smiles then said to Creighton, "Don't hog her, Julian." God, he loved pretty women.

Beth sat in the corner with Andrew. She was looking a little better these days, put on some weight, the dark circles gone. She wore a black silk pantsuit and gold hoop earrings. Very sophisticated. The young man was saying something, gesturing with his hand. He seemed very intense.

"Hi, Dad," Beth said. "Thanks for having us."

"Glad to, anytime, you know that sweetheart. You're looking lovely this evening."

"You say that to everybody," she said, teasing.

"Yup, it's true, and I mean it."

"Senator Connelly, I want you to know how thrilled I am to finally meet you. You've been a hero of mine for years," the young Mr. Detrick said.

Liar, thought Matt, but he smiled and said, "I do my best for my state and my country."

"I appreciate being here. What a beautiful house you have," Andrew said.

"Thanks. Now tell me, what is it you do for the U.N.?"

"I work for UNICEF, the children's fund, you know. It's a great opportunity for me. Travel, contacts, all that."

"That's how I met Andrew, Dad," Beth put in. "I was volunteering in the office and we started working on a project together. Bangladesh."

Matt knew that Beth hadn't been able to get another overseas posting yet, so she'd been volunteering at the main office of Children's International in New York. "Uh-huh, love the U.N. You keep up the good work there, Andrew."

"Oh, I'll try, Senator Connelly."

Matt swallowed the rest of his drink and got another. He grabbed two caviar canapés off the serving girl's tray and ate one in a bite. "You make these?" he asked her.

"No, the chef did. Are they good?" she asked.

"Great. Here, try one," and Matt stuck one out toward her. "No, go on, go ahead, take it."

She looked around guiltily and popped it in her mouth.

"See? Good, huh?" Cute girl, he thought, even if her hair was all pulled back under that little white tiara thing.

Lee was still on soda water. She was talking to Jane Creighton and Todd Weldon, behaving absolutely perfectly. God, Matt loved Lee when she was in her Main Line Socialite mode.

Mindy and the ambassador had hit it off, and Angela and Terry had joined them. They were all laughing about something. Then he saw that Beth and Andrew had attached themselves to the group around Lee, and for a minute Matt took a breather before he had to rejoin the group, summing up the day's events in his head while he stared at Terry's date, his eyes riveted to those long, long legs.

"My," Julian said to him, "I do so like those young people. What a nice change from all the old men we deal with every day."

"You know me," Matt said jovially, "I never give in to old age, Julian."

"Admirable trait, Matthew," the ambassador said, chuckling.

The dinner went well. The table was lovely, with all of Lee's best Royal Doulton china, her Waterford crystal, the heavy old Gorham silver and linen tablecloth that she'd inherited. The menu was chicken Kiev, sautéed vegetables, wild rice pilaf. The wine flowed freely and the decibel level rose accordingly.

Matt had seated Angela next to him, and he flirted with her outrageously. Terence, on her other side, was being immature, sulking when Angela didn't pay enough attention to him. Matt suppressed a surge of annoyance at his son.

Lee talked to Beth's date on one side and Julian Creighton on the other. Lee did so well when she tried; she was a wife to be proud of.

Andrew Detrick was telling a story. Lee and Beth listened politely, but Matt thought it was dumb, something about his posting to New Guinea and how bad the insects were there. Yeah, the guy was a jerk. Well, Beth usually saw through them sooner or later.

"I am just so glad Terry brought me along," Angela was saying. "This is so much fun."

"Where'd you meet Terry?" Matt asked.

"At Georgetown. I take a class there."

"Um. But you're a model?"

"Well, the money's good. I'm lucky. I'm trying to save up, but you know . . ."

"Boy, do I ever," Matt said.

Terry was leaning on the table, over his sulk, talking to Julian. "I love England. I was there one whole summer, you know. Great place. Tradition and all."

Matt could see Terry had been downing the wine, and now he wanted to show off for Angela.

"Funny place," Terry went on. "You drive on the wrong side of the road." He laughed. "Having a hell of a time with the EEC, aren't you?"

Julian smiled politely. "Well, actually, that's not my area."

"The pound's in trouble again, I read that somewhere. I say dump those wogs in Europe."

Matt rolled his eyes. Terry had a way of putting his foot in his mouth. No matter how many damn courses he took, he just didn't get it. "Terry, hey, Julian doesn't want to talk shop tonight. Lay off."

"What you need," Terry went on, "is Maggie Thatcher back."

"I daresay she'd agree with you," Julian said coolly.

There was a sudden lapse in the conversation. Jane Creighton filled it in like the old hand she was. "Now, Lee, dear, you must give me your caterer's number. This is wonderful. Would you mind?"

"Not at all. I'll phone you tomorrow," Lee said. "He's very dependable. Tipper uses him."

Dessert was chocolate mousse, the old standby. Todd Weldon praised it to the skies. He was being awfully nice to Lee, who tapped him affectionately with her fingers, then said to his wife, "Mindy, I hope you see that Todd gets his exercise, the way he eats."

"Oh, I do," Mindy replied with a wicked grin.

"Makes me go out for a jog every morning," Todd said, his timing perfect.

"Mom, Dad," Beth said then, "we're really going to have to be going now. We're driving on through to the beach."

"Oh," Lee said, "you'll get there so late. You could stay here, you know, and go in the morning."

"Thank you, Mrs. Connelly," Andrew said, "but we'll be fine. I'm so anxious to see the Outer Banks, I hate to waste a minute. I've never been there."

Beth rose and excused herself, while Andrew babbled on much too long. Boring. Lee raised her face for her daughter's quick kiss. "Drive carefully, Andrew," she said.

They made a good-looking couple, Matt admitted grudgingly. Slight, dark-haired Beth and the clean-cut Yale type, Detrick. Matt stood and excused himself to follow them out into the narrow entrance hall. He took Beth aside while Andrew got their coats. "Listen, Beth, you change your phone number yet?"

"I will when I get back."

"They bothering you?" Both of them knew who "they" were.

"Not too much. I leave the phone off the hook."

"Okay. You're looking better, kid, but you're still too damn skinny."

Beth gave him a look.

"Stay in the good old U.S. of A. for a while. Listen to me. And remember, you're always a Connelly. The family is here for you. If that pushy D.A. in Aspen bothers you, or that holier-than-thou cohort of his, McCandless, tries to put any pressure on you, well, you let me know right away, okay?"

"Okay."

"I mean it, Beth."

"I said okay."

"So, you need any money?" Matt stuck his thick fingers in his rear trouser pocket.

"No, I have plenty, Dad."

"Never enough," he said gruffly. "Here." He thrust some bills at her, hundred-dollar bills. "Buy some groceries for the house down there."

"Thanks."

"The thing is, Beth," he said, "you just can't let the bastards get to you." Then, ignoring Detrick's protestations of eternal thanks, he turned on his heel and went back to his dinner party.

Everyone had left by twelve. Lee started upstairs to bed, saying she was exhausted. She stopped on the third step up and resting her hand on the graceful trench balustrade, said, "It went well, didn't it, dear?"

"Just fine, hon. You did a great job."

"Coming to bed?"

"In a minute. I've got to wind down some, okay?"

"Don't stay up too late."

Matt watched his wife's slender form mount the staircase, then poured himself a double brandy, lit a cigar and wandered around the littered living room. He stood for a moment by the glass door that led out into the small walled garden at the back of the house. It was dark out there, the magnolia tree a black shadow, the dogwood and lilacs bare, everything in cold winter sleep. He looked out into the garden and thought. Tomorrow he and Terry would meet with Ms. Feinstein. An important meeting. The legal stuff was moving along slowly but relentlessly. Poor Terry. He'd get off, of course, but this whole mess was ugly, damn ugly. Maybe Ms. Feinstein should talk to Beth, yeah, tell her what she'd be expected to say in the depositions, if the damn thing ever went that far. Ridiculous. But it was bothering Beth. And that baloney she'd come up with about Terry carrying the girl out of the house in the middle of the night . . . He gulped some brandy. Hogwash. Too much imagination, but, shit, she couldn't say that to anyone else, God forbid. Yeah, he'd have Ms. Feinstein give Beth a call. What in hell was he paying that smart lawyer chick for, anyway?

The swinging door to the pantry opened and the caterer's girl came into the room. "Oh," she said, "I thought everyone was gone. Excuse me."

"You still here?" Matt asked.

"I'm cleaning up. The kitchen crew's gone, though."

"So, you're a jack-of-all-trades, huh? Coat check girl, waitress, cleanup."

"Tonight I am. We were shorthanded," she said, picking up empty glasses. "Well, I'll just put this stuff in the dishwasher and go."

"Wait a minute," Matt said, walking up to her. "You worked hard tonight." He reached into his back pocket and pulled out the wad of bills. "Here, have a tip." He peeled off a hundred dollar bill and pressed it into the girl's hand. "What's your name?"

"Kathy."

"Listen, Kathy, you did a good job tonight. I appreciate it." He still held her hand.

"Well, uh, thanks. I mean, you don't have to . . ." The girl stared at Matt's meaty fingers on hers.

"My pleasure. You're a cute girl, Kathy." He leaned forward and planted a kiss on her cheek, then patted her fanny.

"Yeah, a real cute girl." God, Matt thought, he did enjoy a good dinner party.

* * *

Case McCandless looked Tripp Maddock in the eye and pressed the Play button on the recorder. "Right here," he said, "listen to this."

The D.A. leaned forward and put his elbows on his desktop, his expression intent as the taped interview began.

"And did you hear anything or see anything out of the ordinary at any time that night?" Case said on the tape.

There was a noticeable pause, then Beth Connelly's reply. "I was asleep. How could I?"

Case pushed the Stop button and then Rewind. "I'm telling you, Tripp," he said, "if we had this on video, you'd be able to see her face."

"So what are you saying?" Maddock asked.

"She was lying. I'd bet my last dollar on it. Keep in mind that Beth Connelly's room is right next to Terence's. She had to have heard something."

"She said she'd had a few drinks. Maybe..."

"Maybe nothing," Case said, pushing Play again. "Catch how long she hesitated, and then her voice was strange."

The taped interview began again. "...any time that night?" The long pause. Then, "I was asleep..." Over and over the sheriff played it.

"Okay," Tripp said, sitting back after another twenty minutes, "I get it. She won't crack at the depositions, though. They're too innocuous. No oath, no audience."

"How about the trial?" Case asked.

Tripp thought that over. His fingers steepled beneath his chin, he finally said, "If the judge allows me some leeway, I can break her. You bet. I'll grill little Miss Beth Connelly until she cracks at the seams."

Case sat there frowning. "It's a pretty nasty stunt," he said.

"Yeah, but so is murder. So is perjury. Listen, Case, it's the only possibility we've got."

"This girl—" Case hesitated "—well, she's a little...odd."

"How?"

"Sort of free-spirited, you know? Doesn't seem to ever stay in one place. Drinks while she's on medication, takes risks."

"Unstable?"

"I don't know...maybe...delicate, somehow."

"Good. She'll break easier, then," Tripp said.

"What if I'm wrong about her statement?" Case asked.

Tripp shrugged. "Then Terence Connelly may very well get off and do it again to some other girl."

The Hill Club on Louisiana Street was old, by Washington standards, and a revered institution: absolutely private, absolutely privileged and absolutely discreet.

Matt had picked Terence up, to make sure his son didn't conveniently forget the luncheon appointment, and they were now seated at the senator's own special table in the corner, the one with walls on two sides and a waiter's station on the third. They sipped water from heavy crystal and didn't say much; they were awaiting Melinda Feinstein. She was right on time, one o'clock, striding briskly across the carpeted dining room with her briefcase at her side and her trenchcoat open, flaring as she went.

She nodded, a quick, masculine movement, threw her coat over a chair and slid into the empty one before Matt could stand and play the gentleman.

"Mr. Connelly," she said to Terence. "Senator."

"Please, none of that. It's Matt and Terry," Matt said, and then he waited for her to say, "Call me Melinda," but she didn't. She only said, "All right."

The gaunt old waiter arrived with menus, handed them around and glided away before anyone even remembered he'd been there. Ms. Feinstein looked at the menu for perhaps twenty seconds, then put it down in the decisive way she did everything. Matt was impressed; the women he generally liked were more conventionally feminine, but this Feinstein woman was really something. Not beautiful except for that superb figure, but a good face, strong features emphasized by blunt-cut dark hair to her shoulders. She obviously didn't fuss with her hair or nails or makeup. She was wearing a tailored suit of gray gabardine and a silk blouse in burgundy. A thin gold chain hung around her neck. Tasteful, sober, effective.

"So," Terry asked, "anything new happening?"

"Nothing unexpected. We won't really find out what they have until the preliminary hearing next week," she said in a level tone.

"That's important?" Matt grumbled.

Ms. Feinstein turned her dark, weighty gaze on him. "Senator, it is very important. Terry should be there, of course. I'll go before the judge and try to show him that there is not sufficient cause to bind Terry over for trial. The other side, the D.A.—that's Maddock—will try his damnedest to demonstrate that there is indeed a strong case against Terry."

Terry was staring across the room, tapping a fork on the linen tablecloth. He might not have heard a word she'd said.

"Um," Matt said.

The waiter returned and they ordered. Terry asked for a double Scotch on the rocks.

"I might point out, as your lawyer," Ms. Feinstein said to him, "that it would be best for you to behave very circumspectly until this matter is taken care of."

"Sure," Terry said.

"What she means," Matt put in, "is no boozing it up, son. No wine, women and song. Stick to the old straight and narrow. No double Scotch on the rocks for lunch."

"Sure. This is my last one," he said easily.

Matt turned to the lawyer. "Now, listen, what I want to know is why in hell the whole thing has gone this far. I asked you that when Terry was charged. You said the D.A. had to do it for political reasons, protect the public and all that bullshit. Okay, fine. But I want it ended at this hearing that's coming up. I want that judge to find insufficient cause for a trial. Goddamn it, there isn't a shred of evidence that proves Terry did anything!"

"I'll do my best, Matt. And my best is pretty good. Unfortunately, there is quite a lot of circumstantial evidence to implicate Terry. With enough circumstantial evidence no judge can dismiss the charges. You do understand that." She leaned forward while she said this, resting on an elbow, pushing her hair behind one ear. Matt noted that her ear was pale and very nicely shaped, a lovely ear, with a small gold pierced earring. "And there is the fact that Terry stated he had not had intercourse with the victim when DNA profiling of the semen in her vagina showed that he had."

"I'd had a few drinks," Terry said. "I was confused."

"And you forgot that you had sex with Heather Kelly," Ms. Feinstein said without inflection.

Terry squirmed in his chair. "I thought it didn't matter, you know, like I didn't want to advertise the fact.

What's the big deal? So I screwed her, that's not murder."

"No, it isn't," Feinstein said, "but the very fact that you didn't disclose the whole truth puts your entire testimony in doubt. Do you understand that?"

Terry mumbled something and took a long swallow of his drink.

"Shit!" Matt burst out. "This whole thing is ridiculous! Someone's out to get me, I swear."

"Dad, I'm the one on trial," Terry pointed out peevishly.

"Yeah, right," Matt said bitterly.

Feinstein put up a hand as if their male bickering were a waste of her valuable time. "There are some promising angles. There are no witnesses and, of course, no weapons to tie Terry to the girl. As I said, all the evidence is circumstantial, and that can work two ways. It depends on the jury. In cases like this the jury has to go with gut instinct, make a judgment call. The prosecution has the entire burden of proving guilt. All we have to do is present reasonable doubt."

"Sounds easy," Matt said, "when you put it like that."

"It isn't," she said flatly.

"What kind of chance do you think I have?" Terry asked. "I mean, especially since I'm innocent."

"An excellent chance," she said. "But I'm afraid it'll go beyond next week's hearing. There will be a trial."

"Son of a bitch," Matt said. "It's a...a travesty, that's what it is! I tell you, that D.A. and that damn McCandless have a personal grudge against us. Just because we're not locals, not born in that inbred valley!"

"Tripp Maddock and Judge Snyder aren't locals," she reminded him.

"Then it's McCandless behind it all. Jesus, he arrested poor Beth when she was sick. Arrested her and made her spend the night in jail. He's got it in for us!" Matt growled. "God save us all from pitifully provincial, self-righteous idiots like that ass of a sheriff."

Terry perked up. "Hey, what about paying them off?" he asked bluntly. "The D.A. or the judge, even McCandless. Hell, Dad, you've always told me everyone has his price. Buy them."

"Christ, Terry!" Matt said.

Ms. Feinstein never batted an eye. "It's risky. Forget McCandless. He's probably untouchable. The others, I don't know. I could do some research. I have to tell you, though, it's not a good bet."

Matt looked at her with admiration and not a little bit of awe. "But you can look into it?" he asked.

She shrugged. "I look into all possibilities. If you have the resources, then that is a possibility. Touchy, but a possibility."

The waiter brought their food then. Rare roast beef for Matt, a club sandwich for Terry and a salad for Ms. Feinstein. Matt gazed down at the bloodred meat lovingly as he picked up his knife and fork. He cut a piece and popped it into his mouth, then said while chewing, "Okay, so the sheriff's a good guy. But do me a favor, have the McCandless family checked out. They run this ranch. It borders on Forest Service land, I hear. I wonder if they run horses or cows or some damn shit on federal land. If they do, I want to know about it, permits, the whole nine yards. And check out that damn sheriff. I know he's supposed to be lily-white, but there may be something...."

"He's divorced and has custody of his two kids," Melinda said.

"That's interesting," Matt replied thoughtfully. And then he swallowed his mouthful and went for another.

Terence Connelly knocked on the pebbled glass of the door.

"Come in," came a strong contralto voice.

Giving a quick glance, an automatic gesture, up and down the corridor, Terry opened the door and slipped inside. "Professor Reigel," he said respectfully, "I'm Terry Connelly. I'm in your Political Systems Analysis class."

The woman took her large, tortoiseshell glasses off and peered at him through nearsighted green eyes. "Yes, well, Mr. Connelly, what can I do for you?"

"I wanted to tell you how much I like your lectures. The way you analyzed British and American systems was really excellent."

"Thank you, Mr. Connelly," she said dryly, crossing her shapely legs.

"Well, actually, I'm having some trouble with the paper you assigned. The one due tomorrow."

"The one on communism."

"Yeah, that one."

"What's the trouble?"

Terry moved around the small office, ostensibly reading book titles on the professor's shelves. "I can't find enough research items."

"Oh, really, I'd have thought they'd be in every journal ever put out. What about Hedrich's *The Fall of Communism*? And Mantena's *Communist Manifesto Revisited*?"

"Yes, well, sure, I looked at them. . . ."

"And?"

He shrugged and sat down in the chair by her desk. "Nothing new."

"New? Mr. Connelly..."

"I wanted to talk to you about my thesis," he put in quickly.

"Yes, go on." Professor Reigel sat politely, holding her glasses by an earpiece.

"Actually, it's complicated. Could we discuss it later?"

"Later? Mr. Connelly, my office hours are over in half an hour."

"I meant ... much later." Terry smiled at his professor, his white, roguish smile that never failed to attract women.

"Excuse me?" Professor Reigel sat upright.

"Over dinner. Someplace nice. My treat, naturally."

The woman looked at Terry steadily, then a corner of her mouth quirked. "Let me get this straight. You are asking me out to dinner?"

"Sure."

"To discuss your paper."

"Right."

She put on her glasses again and turned her back to him, saying over her shoulder. "You are truly full of crap, Mr. Connelly."

"Now, wait a minute..."

"You're excused. I'm busy, Mr. Connelly. Don't waste my time."

He stood staring at her back for a long moment, his dark eyebrows meeting, his hands clenching. Then abruptly he turned to go.

"Oh, Mr. Connelly," Professor Reigel said coolly without looking up, "that paper better be in on time, and it better be good."

TEN

"Two more skiers found buried in an avalanche south of Aspen," the "Today Show" anchorwoman said. "That story and others next . . ."

Beth pointed the remote control at the TV and clicked it off.

She rose from the wicker couch, pushed up the sleeves of her Irish knit sweater and padded to the kitchen for another cup of coffee. Outside the window, the ocean off the North Carolina coast pounded the beach and tossed seafoam into the surprisingly mild air. She could see Andy just down the beach, his hair windblown as he stooped, picking up shells, filling his trouser pockets. Everyone who'd ever visited the Connelly beach house collected shells. Outside was, after all, one of the few pristine beaches left on the East Coast. Beth knew Andy would deposit the sandy shells on the driftwood coffee table—everyone did—and when they left he'd forget them—everyone did.

She fixed two cups of coffee, intending to walk over the dune and down to the beach to join him. There was nothing like a mild February day on the coast. Somehow it made your heart sing.

And then the phone rang. It was Lee. "Oh, I'm glad I caught you," Beth's mother said. "I was checking my calendar, and it says here that your court hearing is this Friday."

"My court . . . ?"

"Oh, Beth," Lee said. "You can't have forgotten your DUI hearing in Aspen. If you miss it, Matt will have such a fit."

"Damn," Beth muttered.

"The family has been in the papers all too often this winter. We can't have another incident."

"I know," Beth said lightly. "You don't have to remind me. It's an election year."

"You needn't be like that, dear. It was you, after all, who got the DUI."

Beth sighed. "Friday?"

"This Friday. In Aspen. The notice said two p.m. at the courthouse."

"I'll be there."

"You don't sound too . . ."

"I said I'll be there."

"Would you like me to fly out with you?"

"No," Beth said. "I'll be fine."

It had been a pleasant couple of days with Andy at the deserted beach house, days in which Beth had been able to relax, to forget. And now this . . . Schemes formed in her mind: she'd call her boss in New York and ask for the first posting he had—anywhere—and she'd just pick up and go. She'd had her physical and was fine now. Unfortunately, she couldn't. Damn it. The lawyer Matt had gotten for Terry had told everyone in the family to be available for depositions at any time. They had to present a united front, and above all, they had to cooperate. Absolutely no jaunts out of the country.

Damn Terry. He was a lousy excuse for a human being. God, how she hated his self-satisfied expression. The other night in Washington he'd been so puffed up, mouthing stupid remarks to the ambassador. It made her sick.

But, still, no matter what a rat he was, she couldn't turn him in. Even Ellen, levelheaded Ellen, who'd done something with her life, knew that Beth couldn't betray the family. She would be blamed, ostracized, pegged as a traitor. And as much as it hurt to admit it, Beth knew she couldn't go it completely alone.

Aspen, she thought again. There was no way to avoid it, she'd have to fly in and make that court date. Well, she'd just have to pray no one noticed her, asked her anything about Terry. She'd go and she'd simply hide out in the house. No parties, no discos. In and out.

"Anything wrong?" Andy asked when she handed him the mug of coffee down on the beach.

She told him, saying that he'd have to drive her back to New York that afternoon. He seemed awfully disappointed until Beth locked her arms around his neck and kissed him, setting aside all thoughts but one.

The landing gear thumped beneath Beth's feet as the commuter flight from Denver to Aspen made its final approach, banking steeply, squeezing itself into the narrow air traffic corridor of the Roaring Fork Valley. Big gray clouds clung to the mountainsides—it was going to snow.

She took a cab to the Preserve, thankful that the house was empty now; no one was expected until World Cup week in the beginning of March. She thought about

Andy and then Billy and decided she was like a sailor, with someone waiting in every port. Snatches of her last day on the Outer Banks with Andy came back to her. Andy's disappointment . . . the kiss on the beach, and then he'd wanted to have sex, his hand reaching up under her sweater in the rustic living room, caressing her breasts, his lips on her neck and her mouth, tasting of sea salt. But she couldn't; suddenly she hadn't wanted to make love, to go through the ordeal of trying and trying to reach that elusive sweet spot and then having to fake it.

Beth squeezed her eyes shut and erased Andy from her mind. He was a nice enough man, but Andy, like all of the men in her life, was a fortune hunter. What had he said when he'd dropped her at her New York apartment? Something like, "I hope I can meet your family again, Beth. Matt is really a super person. I'd like to talk to him, you know, person to person sometime."

The snow began to fall again late that day, and Beth couldn't believe the size of the drifts piled up around the house. It was kind of welcoming, though, the big house all tucked into mountains of the white stuff, all safe and secure and warm.

She built a fire and called the maid who came in daily and told her to take the next couple of days off—with pay, of course. What the heck? It was Matt's bill. She tried Ellen's house, but her stepsister was still at the gallery, Manuel told her. She got Ellen finally and told her about the hearing on Friday.

"There won't be any more questions at the hearing about Terry, will there?" Ellen asked.

"This has nothing to do with him," Beth said.

"I heard about the sheriff stopping you at the airport. You didn't have any... problems with giving the statement?"

"God, Ellen, no. I did my duty."

"I'm sorry, Beth," Ellen relented. "I know it's... difficult. Look, you want to have lunch tomorrow? Maybe Manuel could join us."

"Sure," Beth said. "You know, he has the sexiest voice. I really do envy you."

"He is wonderful."

"And not all botched up like the rest of the family."

There was a pause. "Yes, isn't that refreshing," Ellen said.

After the call to Ellen she snuggled up on the couch in front of the fire and watched night settle over the fields outside the big window, and the snow came down more heavily.

Reality returned with morning and daylight as Beth showered and remembered why she'd come to Aspen in the first place. The court hearing. She thought about calling a lawyer to be there with her. What was the old adage? A person who represents himself has a fool for a lawyer. Still, she thought the judge would somehow be impressed if she, a Connelly, faced the music alone. He would fine her, of course, because the laws in Colorado had taken away all her rights the minute she'd refused any tests. And Billy had told her everyone had to put in community service hours and go to "drunk school." But surely the judge would let her have her driver's license back. They couldn't just keep it because she'd refused sobriety tests. She'd explain about her stomach medication. Sure. And the arresting officer... McCandless, right, Sheriff McCandless, would have to testify that she'd told him about the medication and had not wanted to take the tests.

She put on a black oversize turtleneck sweater and black tights and boots and thought about that. Sheriff Case McCandless. If he'd go to bat for her with the judge, at the very least corroborate her medication story...

She dialed the sheriff's department from the kitchen, stretching the long cord behind her as she fixed coffee and toast. But he wasn't in, the dispatcher told her, and no, she didn't know when he'd be back.

At noon she tried again. "But he has to come in sometime today, doesn't he?" Beth asked.

"Sometime. I'll leave him a message to call you. All right?"

"Ah, sure. You wouldn't know if he's scheduled to be in court Friday? Does he testify about arrests he's made?"

"I really don't know," the woman said.

Beth tried his office again at three. It seemed he'd run in for a few minutes but had left almost immediately. "Did he get my message?" she asked.

"I don't know," Beth was told, and she hung up, exasperated. If she knew where he lived, she'd park herself on his doorstep and...

It came to her like one of those light bulbs turning on in a cartoon. The phone book. She'd get his home address and she would park herself on his doorstep. She'd explain how much she needed her license, and he'd be a real jerk if he didn't tell the judge how bogus the arrest had been. Just because she'd skidded on an icy road and been stupid enough, hours later, to admit she'd had a drink! He simply had to help her out.

She leafed through the local phone book. Mac...Mc. There it was! McCandless, C., 17 Park Circle East. Why, that was on the way into town from the Preserve, not very far at all.

She thought of walking, but then remembered the huge snowdrifts on either side of the road, forcing cars into a single lane. Bad idea. She'd get run over.

A cab, then. But it would cost an arm and a leg to have a taxi wait outside his house. What if he didn't come home at all?

She could drive herself. Take the Porsche and park it nearby—where he wouldn't spot it—and at least keep the heater going. It really wasn't that big a deal.

Beth threw on her leather jacket, scarf and dark wool beret and found the car keys in a kitchen drawer. Park Circle East was easy to find. Skirting the edge of town, it curved along the Roaring Fork River and ended up at the trailer park, the workingman's employee housing. The homes on Park Circle were below Aspen standards, simple houses, functional, belonging to locals.

The addresses were hard to read, though. Some were on mailboxes, mostly covered by snow now. And the numbers were weird—102 was right next to 113. Beth drove the snow-rutted road, her wipers going, and searched for addresses. Across a side street she saw number 26. Then number 17 must be just a few...

They came out of nowhere. Two dogs playing. And then there was a thump against her tire and Beth knew she'd hit one of them. A terrible sickness swept over her as she yanked on the parking brake and threw open the door.

Please God, let him be all right . . . Oh, please!

The little black-and-white terrier was not all right. He wasn't dead, but he was injured and in pain, and Beth felt panic rise inside her.

Carefully, carefully, she took off her leather jacket and put it over the poor little whimpering thing and began to lift him into her arms, desperate to get him into the car and find a vet.

The voice came from behind her, a little agonized voice all mixed with tears and horror. "That's my dog! That's my dog!"

Beth tried to calm the little boy, telling him it was going to be okay but they had to get him to the veterinarian right away. "Do you know where there's a vet, honey?" she asked, her voice controlled.

"At the business center," the boy told her between sniffles. "Can I go with you?"

Without thinking it through, still holding the whimpering dog, whose big brown eyes implored her, Beth said, "Sure. Sure you can. But first tell someone where we're going. Hurry."

The little boy was gone for less than a minute while Beth put the injured dog carefully in between the two bucket seats of the Porsche, her jacket a pillow. And then they were off, taking Main Street out toward the highway and the business center.

Keeping her voice even as she drove, she said, "He's going to be all right. What's his name, anyway?"

"Gizmo."

"And what's your name?"

"Nate."

"How old are you, Nate?"

"Seven."

"That puts you in . . . second grade?"

"Uh-huh." He kept patting Gizmo's wiry head and sniffling. "It's okay, boy, it's okay."

"Do I take this turn?" Beth asked him, hoping he really did know the way. But Nate was an intelligent little boy and directed her straight to the vet's, who, thank God, was there.

"Looks like a broken leg," the vet said over the stainless steel examining table while he gave the dog—Gizmo—a shot that made his big brown eyes flutter and roll back. "We'll have him patched up real soon."

"Phew," Beth got out, and she realized her knees were rubbery. "I'm afraid he ran out into the street. I never saw him until it was too late." She looked at Nate and put a hand on the back of his blond head. "Guess old Gizmo here lucked out, huh?"

Nate gave a small, shaky smile.

"Okay," the vet was saying, "I need to know if we've seen Gizmo before. I'll have to check on his shots." He looked at Beth.

"Oh," she said. "He's not mine. He's Nate's. Nate, honey?"

The boy looked up, confused, and the vet said, "If you'll tell me your last name I'll see if I can find your dog's records."

She should have known. He really did look a lot like his father. But she could only stare, shocked, at his cute little face and those calm blue eyes.

Nate McCandless. And then they were sitting out in the waiting room, Beth utterly silent, Nate sucking on a lollipop given him by the nurse. "Dad's gonna be so mad," Nate told her. "Gizmo gets out all the time, and I'm supposed to keep him on a leash."

"Um," Beth said. "Your dad."

"My dad's sheriff."

"Uh-huh. Right. I know that."

"You know my dad?"

"Ah, yes. Sort of." Oh God, she thought, Case McCandless was going to be so furious. She'd been *driving*. And his dog! He'd kill her. It struck her all of a sudden then. Who'd been watching Nate at the house? Case McCandless? But if he had been home, surely he would have . . .

"Nate," she said abruptly, "who did you tell about going out here to the vet's?"

"The baby-sitter."

"Who is?"

"Allison. She lives next door."

"And she *knew* you were coming out here for sure?"

"I yelled at her."

"Right," Beth said. "What's your telephone number?" She got the number, stood and asked to use the phone, her fingers crossed that he wasn't home yet. No such luck.

The whole way back into town Beth bit her lower lip, recalling the tight fury in Case McCandless's voice. Of course he was right to be mad. She'd run over his dog, his seven-year-old had yelled something incoherent to a fourteen-year-old sitter—who'd panicked when she couldn't find the boy and then called his father with the garbled message. And then for nearly an hour the sheriff had combed the neighborhood, baffled, worried, unable to understand what his son had meant by yelling, "We're taking Gizmo in the car!"

It occurred to Beth to drop Nate at home, make sure he got safely inside and then run. Get the hell out of Dodge. But she wouldn't. It had been a series of accidents, after all, and surely he'd see that when he calmed down.

She pulled up in front of the house and sighed, turning off the motor.

"I wish Gizmo could have come home with us," Nate told her as he got out.

"Well, he'll be better off tonight at the doctor's," Beth said, and she saw the painted wooden door of the old frame house swing open and there he was, uniform and all, his expression utterly implacable.

Somehow Nate got by his father with just a few words, and disappeared inside. Beth sat in the car a moment longer, then swung her legs out, reaching back inside for her jacket, trying to stall. Damn, she thought. Damn.

He asked her to come in in a voice surprisingly calm yet firm. He held the door open for her, then stood there, partially blocking the entrance so that she had to twist sideways to get past him. The door closed behind her with a distinct thump.

She took a breath and turned around and faced him. "I'd like to explain," she began, but her voice was threatening to quiver. *My God*, she thought, *it isn't the end of the world.* "I'm sorry the dog couldn't come home yet," she said. "The vet thought he'd rest better at the clinic. I'm, ah, sure he'll be fine. I'll certainly pay all the bills."

He said nothing. He only stood there, his arms folded as he leaned against the door, staring at her with those very blue eyes against golden, weathered skin.

She started again. "I told you on the phone, Sheriff, I honestly thought Nate had gone inside and explained that we were—"

"That's not the problem," he said.

Beth felt herself grow rigid. "Then what the . . . what *is* the problem?"

"You don't know?"

She shook her head slowly.

"You were driving, Miss . . ."

"It's Beth. If we're going to argue about this, let's do it on a first-name basis, Case. It is Case, isn't it?"

He regarded her for a long moment, then nodded, and she couldn't believe she'd stood up to him.

"That's better," Beth breathed. "Look, I know it was stupid . . . driving. But it isn't as if I'm the only person who's driven without a license. And besides, this is the first time."

He lifted a sandy brow.

"Honest," she said, giving him a tentative smile. "Cross my heart."

Beth was aware of the two children in the room behind her. She turned and looked at them, and at the room. Two adorable little blondes in the warmest, most cluttered little room she'd ever seen. It was right out of a Norman Rockwell painting!

"I'm Amanda," the little girl said. "Nate's my brother. I'm five." She held up five fingers. "Nate's seven." She held up six.

"How do you do, Amanda?" Beth said, smiling, still clutching her purse. "I'm Beth."

Amanda's cheeks colored and she hid her face.

"Okay," Case said, "upstairs and put your toys away and dinner'll be ready soon. Go on."

The children gave Beth a last look and ran up the old staircase, Nate pushing Amanda until she hit him.

"They're cute," Beth said, meeting his eyes again. "They really are cute."

"I take it you don't have any," he replied after a pause.

She shook her head. "Someday," she was saying when a noise came from the next room, the kitchen. Something had boiled over on the stove.

"Damn it," Case muttered. He went past her, and she followed him into the kitchen, a room half again as large as the cluttered living room. "Well, that does it." Case angrily threw a smoking pot into the sink. "Ruined it."

"Dinner?" she asked.

"Canned stew. It wasn't much, but it's something they'll both eat."

Beth looked around. A crooked table against a wallpapered wall, four unmatched chairs. Gingham curtains at a six-paned window over an old enamel sink. A sixties fridge, but an iron gas stove that decorators would drool over. The floor was wooden and scarred, the countertops cracked Formica—red. Awful, Beth was thinking, but somehow she'd never seen a more welcoming room.

Case was opening and closing cupboards, pushing cans and boxes aside. "Great," he muttered.

Beth cleared her throat. "I, ah, could drive on over to the store . . . walk, I mean. I could get you something, more stew." She shrugged.

"I'll go myself," he grumbled, still searching a cupboard. But then he caught himself. He turned. "Sorry, that was nice of you, Miss . . . Beth. But I . . ."

"Then go," she found herself suggesting, "and I'll stay here with the kids."

"I couldn't ask . . ."

"I offered." Beth shrugged off her jacket and pulled off her hat. "Go on. We'll be fine. It's the least I can do."

He seemed hesitant.

"When you get back," Beth said, "I'll tell you all about how I can baby-sit forty kids at once. Now go on. Go."

And he did.

Beth's time with Nate and Amanda began with Bert and Ernie of "Sesame Street" on TV. But by the time Case returned she'd shut off the tube and sat with them on the stained carpet and begun to tell them a fairy tale, an African myth about two little black twins who'd been raised by Shitako, a wise old elephant who was sometimes a medicine man, sometimes a great chief and wore many beads and much paint and owned a dozen cows. The twins were lost in the bush when Case was putting the two grocery bags on the kitchen counter. Beth felt a little uneasy, because he was obviously listening, but she went on, remembering the story she'd learned four years ago in Somalia.

"And so Shitako found them, and he came down onto his front haunches, and using his big ears, they climbed onto his back...."

They loved the story and begged for more, and even Case came to the door and applauded.

Beth unfolded herself and stood, making a mock bow, blowing the kids a kiss. "That's it," she said, "you've worn me out. And besides, you're going to have dinner now, so I'll just—"

"There's plenty," he said.

"What?" she asked.

"If you can handle canned stew, there's more than enough."

"I've never had it," she said.

"Well, then it's time you did."

Dinner at the old kitchen table was a unique affair for Beth. The children did most of the talking, everything from how Gizmo was going to walk with a cast to what they'd done at school that day to ski school on weekends.

Beth swallowed a mushy carrot. "It's all so... normal," she said. "I mean, Beaver Cleaver and 'Father Knows Best' all rolled into one."

Case lifted his gaze to her. "You probably don't have too many meals sitting in a kitchen like this," he said, his tone carefully neutral.

"Where do you eat?" Amanda asked, wide-eyed.

Beth laughed. "At tables, but very fancy ones, usually. Sometimes, though, I eat out of a bowl with my fingers, sitting in the dust."

Case raised one sandy brow.

"Really," she said. "I work for Children's International. It's..."

"The relief organization?"

"Yes."

"No kidding," he said, and suddenly Beth was struck by how incredibly, boyishly handsome he could be. "I remember something you said once," he went on, "something about me being surprised at the places you'd slept, and I thought you meant..." He stopped abruptly and got very busy with his stew.

"Oh," she said, "that night at the jail."

"What?" Nate asked.

"Nothing," Case said.

The kids talked about the ranch then, telling Beth all about their Uncle Nick and Uncle Rowdy, who was as big as a bear and played a guitar.

"It must be fun living on a ranch," Beth said.

"I like summer," Amanda said. "Grandma makes more cookies in summer."

"Well," Beth said, aware of Case watching her now, "she must be awfully busy in the winter."

Something had shifted, she realized as Case continued to study her. A moment ago she'd been merely sitting at a table having a meal because circumstances had led to the invitation, but now . . . His look had changed somehow, and he was studying her, not as a sheriff would study a suspect, but as one human being would regard another.

A singular discomfort began to enfold her as they cleared the table and the kids headed off to the television. Case put on a pot of coffee and Beth stacked the dishes in the dishwasher.

"Does their mom live nearby?" she found herself asking as she wiped her hands on a towel stuck on the handle of the fridge.

"California."

"Remarried?" It was curious, Case raising the children.

He shook his head. "She lives with some guy on an ashram."

"Really?"

"Really."

"No wonder you have custody," Beth said, but caught herself. "I'm sorry, that was none of my business."

"It's no secret," he told her, and he shrugged. "You want some coffee?"

"Ah, sure," she said, and they sat back down at his table, and she wondered how on earth she'd come to be sitting in this tacky kitchen with this man. Was he wondering the same thing?

She looked up from her hands and gave him an uncertain smile.

"Tell me," Case asked her, "just why were you driving along my road, anyway? I had a message earlier that you'd called."

"Called and called," she pointed out. "And I was going to park myself on your doorstep." She laughed, pushing a dark veil of hair behind an ear. "I guess I did better than sitting on your steps, though—except for Gizmo, that is."

"Damn dog is always running off," he said. "You're not to blame."

"That's a relief."

"So what was it you wanted?"

"Oh," Beth said. "Right. I'm in town because this Friday I have that court date. The DUI."

"Uh-huh."

"Well, I was wondering...I really do need my license back. It's a real pain without it. And I thought if you'd put in a word with the judge..."

Up went that brow.

"Maybe he'd take under consideration that I was on stomach medication. I swear, Case, when I skidded on that road I wasn't loaded. I really don't drink all that much. Well, in Aspen...the family does kind of let it all hang out...." Suddenly she stopped, a knife in her chest. My God, she thought, let it all hang out? Terry murders a girl and Beth wants her license back.

She felt his gaze on her. "I...I didn't mean that. Not the way it sounded."

Thank God he let it pass. But not her request. "I'll be in court," he told her, "but you're going to have to face up to the fact that no matter how you got intoxicated it's still against the law to get behind the wheel of a car."

"Even on prescription drugs?"

"Especially on medication," he said. "And I haven't forgotten that you were driving your car today, either."

"You wouldn't say anything in court?"

But he didn't answer that. He only asked, "Don't you have a lawyer?"

She shook her head.

"Well, get one before Friday."

"But if you'd just tell the judge, explain . . ."

"I can't go to bat for you, Beth."

"Why not? Because I'm a Connelly?"

He let that pass.

Beth shrugged. "Are you really this straitlaced? My God," she said, "you are a rare breed."

He let that pass, too, but his eyes rested on her, weighing, assessing, trying to figure her out. *Well, good luck*, she thought.

Beth allowed her gaze to lift to his. Sipping her coffee, she studied him until he stood up and went to pour himself another cup. Still she stared at him, trying to convince herself that he couldn't be so damn Victorian. No one was. It was just too . . . old-fashioned.

He even *looked* wholesome—a Robert Redford type. She couldn't picture him anywhere except in the West, right where he was. She watched him put sugar in his coffee. He wore well-worn blue jeans, not designer ones, and his clothes fit his lithe but muscular body just right. When he came back to the table she averted her gaze and found herself asking, "How did you become the sheriff here?"

"Well, I really got into it by accident," he said. "A friend of mine from high school was with the department, and he talked me into filling a vacancy. Thought I'd try it for a while. Anyway, I ran for sheriff, oh, about five years ago, got elected. So, here I am," he told her easily, without bragging, without false modesty. He was a man who had nothing to hide, no secrets, no dark corners. She'd never met anyone so . . . simple and unassailable.

She found out that he'd never been west of California or east of St. Louis. Amazing. He liked Mexico, though, and every fall he and his old friends from the University of Colorado drove to Canada and went bird hunting.

"You really are a Westerner," Beth said.

"Dyed-in-the-wool. I'm not much for big cities and fancy clothes. But you," he said, "I take it you're a stone who gathers no moss."

She smiled without humor. "If you had to put up with my family," she said, "you'd do a lot of traveling, too."

"I see," he said, but she thought, *no, you don't, not really.*

At eight he put the kids to bed, though they did pretty darn well on their own. With no mom around, Beth decided, she supposed the kids would have to do for themselves a lot.

While Case was upstairs, she snooped around idly, looking, not touching. On the fridge were notes, mostly appointments for Nate and Amanda. Nate played ice hockey, it seemed, and Amanda was in a beginner's gymnastics class three afternoons a week. There were elementary school schedules: dates of plays and parent-teacher conferences, outdoor education events. There were notes on the door for Case, too, but it was all work related.

In the living room there were pictures hung helter-skelter on the walls. Most of them were crooked. There were old photos of Case from high school and college days, that shock of blond hair that fell over his brow making him stand out in the groups. It was clear he loved sports: football, basketball, rock climbing, hiking, hunting.

There were pictures of his wedding, too, obviously a small affair, an outdoor service somewhere in the mountains, a reception in front of a huge lodge, a log building . . . Of course, that must have been the ranch.

How young and handsome he was. And his wife, ex-wife now, a very pretty girl, slender, dark-haired, a lot paler than Case. It struck Beth that the woman's coloring was not unlike her own.

"Pretty dusty," he said behind her, and Beth jumped. "I should clean more, huh?"

"Well, I imagine you're awfully busy."

"Busy, yeah."

"Well," Beth said, taking a breath, "I'd better get going. I'll drive the car back home, put it in the garage and it'll stay there."

"No," he said, and she couldn't take in what he was saying for a minute. "I'm serious, Beth. I can't sit here and let you break the law."

"You're putting me on."

"I'm afraid I'm not."

"So if I walk out your door and drive off you'll... you'll do what?"

"Why are you pushing this?"

"Because," she breathed, "I know in my heart that if I were anyone but a Connelly you'd turn your head this once."

He looked at her hard then, and she knew she'd gotten to him. Oh yes. If she were anyone else, anyone... She felt the blood rise to her cheeks.

"I am an officer of the law, and I can't willingly stand by while someone breaks it," he finally said.

"Fine, so drive me home yourself."

"Damn it, you know I can't leave the kids here alone," he said, an edge to his voice.

Beth put a hand to her forehead in exasperation. "You know what you are? You're an uptight ass."

"I resent that," he said stiffly.

"I'll bet you do, Sheriff, but it's true. Now, I've had a lovely evening and your kids are real cute, but I think it's over now. I'm leaving. I live about a mile up the road, and I'm going to go out, get in my car and drive home. If you want to arrest me, go ahead." And she glared at him, arms folded.

"You have no right . . ." he began.

"You know what? I'm real tired of being told what to do by you. You're picking on me because I'm a Connelly and I'm sick and tired of being judged by people like you. You don't know the first thing about me, but you've already made up your mind. Okay, fine, but I'm driving home. Do what you have to do." She gathered up her jacket and her purse, put on her beret and stalked toward the door. Then she stopped and turned on her heel.

"Oh, I forgot." She reached into her wallet and pulled out a couple of the hundred-dollar bills Matt had given her in Washington. She dropped them on a table. "Here, for the vet bill. I'm sure you'd drag me to court over that, too." She turned away, walked to the door and went out into the night, reaching into her pocket for the car keys, feeling free and alive and a little wild.

Heather Kelly's mother, Nancy, sat on the edge of her bed in the trailer home near Woody Creek and succumbed to her grief and rage, reaching for the phone— as she'd done a hundred times before. But this time she dialed the unlisted number she'd begged from a friend in the sheriff's department. She sucked in a deep, ragged breath and listened to the rings: one . . . two . . . each was a knife twisting in her stomach.

The phone was answered on the fifth ring. "Hello . . . hello?" A woman's voice, a young woman. The maid?

"Is this the Connelly residence?" Nancy asked, her voice breaking.

"Yes. Who is this?"

"Is this . . . a Connelly?"

"Who is this?" came the girl's guarded voice.

"It's . . . Nancy Kelly. Heather Kelly's mother." *Please, dear God,* the woman prayed, don't let me fall apart now.

There was a long silence on the line. "I'm . . . I'm afraid this is inappropriate," the girl said finally. "I'm going to hang up."

"No!" Nancy cried, frantic. "Please, dear God, please just listen to me!"

"I really . . ."

Nancy fought with all her strength to go on. "I have to know what happened to my Heather. Someone knows. Please . . . I'm begging you . . . Please . . ." she choked out. "Please tell the truth," she got out before the line went dead.

The following day at work at the property management office Nancy read in the daily paper that Beth Connelly was in town, scheduled to go to court on Friday. She closed the paper and felt tears press hotly behind her eyelids. Beth Connelly. The stepdaughter—not a blood Connelly. She felt a terrible burst of hope in her breast. What if . . . what if this girl had seen something? What if she was a decent human being . . . ?

In a daze Nancy picked up the phone and dialed the number again. She wasn't herself, and if anyone in the office had been watching, he would have been concerned. But no one was watching.

The phone rang and rang, but no one answered this time, and finally Nancy had to hang up. She couldn't have spoken in any case, as she was sitting at her desk, sobbing uncontrollably.

ELEVEN

Friday started out well. Ellen had planned it that way. Manuel was an absolute dream, double-checking with the caterer to make certain the trays of hors d'oeuvres were delivered to the gallery an hour before the show, stopping by the liquor store and purchasing the wine, even finding plastic glasses that weren't utterly tacky. And all before eleven.

At noon Ellen hurried to the frame shop to check on two matting changes she'd made to Manuel's latest creations—and even they were ready, looking absolutely perfect.

She grabbed a bite of lunch at the tiny In and Out House on Main Street and then headed up to the gallery on foot, glancing at the current issue of the daily paper as she hurried along. The advertisement for Manuel's latest showing was to be in this issue, a full-page ad inviting the general public to stop in between five and eight p.m. for refreshments and a first look at Manuel Ortega's newest creations.

Ah, there was the ad. Ellen stopped in the middle of the brick-paved mall and just stared at it, her heart swelling with pride. Manuel was the centerpiece of the ad. He was leaning against a plain white wall in the gallery, one of his paintings on an easel just behind him. He wore his bolero jacket and his arms were folded across his chest; he had a little half smile on his lips. He was absolutely...beautiful, and Ellen couldn't believe he was hers, all hers. At that moment she felt as if she were the luckiest woman on earth.

And then the adjacent article caught her eye: A review of Manuel's work by a local critic, Dale Willey. It was not very flattering.

"Ho-hum," was the bold-print lead-in. Then, "Another day, another dollar, another display of Southwest art. Manuel Ortega's show at the Connelly Gallery Friday evening promises the same old tired themes: Indians, adobes, horses, cacti, dry mountains ad infinitum."

Ellen stopped reading and caught her breath. How dare they print this, and on the day of his showing! Dear God, she thought, if Manuel saw this ... Calm down, she told herself, she'd simply have to keep him so busy he wouldn't have time to read the paper. And no one would mention the review to him. No one who knew him, anyway.

Fuming, she hurried on toward the gallery, plotting, thinking up errands that would keep him busy until five. Oh damn, she thought, there was always a fly in the soup.

She did manage to keep Manuel occupied. Ellen even dragged him to Beth's DUI court appearance, telling him that her stepsister needed the moral support. At the hearing, as Beth was being told by the judge that she wouldn't get her license back till next Christmas, Manuel shook his head, muttering under his breath in Spanish.

"What?" she whispered.

"Alcohol," he said, "always causing trouble, so much trouble. My Latin blood makes me weak, Elena, but this girl Beth, she has no excuse."

She said nothing, only putting her hand on his knee. After a short time she dared to bring it up. "Manuel," she said, not turning her head, "let's neither of us even have a wine at the showing. Wouldn't that be wise?"

"I'll just have soda water if it pleases you, my love."

"Well," Ellen began, not certain if he was being sarcastic or not, but she let it drop, focusing on Beth's ordeal again, thinking about how very much alcohol abuse had damaged the people closest to her. It never seemed quite fair.

After the hearing she spoke to Beth briefly, reminding her about the show and urging her to come.

"I saw the ad in today's paper," her stepsister said. "I wouldn't miss it."

"I'm sorry," Ellen said, nodding back toward the courthouse from where they stood on the street. "That was rough."

"And they didn't do you any favors," Manuel put in.

"It was my fault," Beth said, "I blew it. By refusing tests I gave up all my rights."

"Still," Manuel said, "maybe if you'd brought a lawyer along today..."

But she shook her head. "The end result would have been the same in this state. No tests, no license for twelve months."

"Life is very unfair sometimes," Manuel said, and he gave her a heart-stopping smile of sympathy.

The afternoon soared by, and Ellen forgot about the critical review of Manuel's work. The gallery was all set, his work displayed with the most advantageous angles and lighting, virtually filling the large room. At four-fifteen they both went home to change, Manuel into his silver-studded jacket and trousers, Ellen into a tailored, pearl-gray jumpsuit and a fine silver-and-turquoise squash-blossom necklace. Understated but very, very Santa Fe.

"You look beautiful," Manuel told her, and her heart squeezed with pure love.

At five, the early arrivals began to wander into the gallery, greeting Ellen and Manuel, heading straight to the hors d'oeuvres and wine before mingling.

By six the crowd had become eclectically mixed. There were the megawealthy and the worker bees, who appreciated Manuel's work as much as anyone but would never be able to afford even one of the paintings. Two Hollywood celebrities showed up, one of whom Ellen had sold several paintings to in the past. City council members stopped by. Tourists roamed the rooms, gawking as much at the prices as at the celebrities. And of course there were the local business people, gauging the crowd, the other gallery owners positively green with envy that Manuel's work was exclusive to Ellen. God, she felt proud.

At six-thirty Beth arrived by taxi, stunning in a black crushed-velvet Navajo dress. She wore absolutely no jewelry and her makeup was subtle, her pure white skin standing out against that shining cropped curtain of dark hair. Ellen observed her for a moment and decided she truly was the most attractive person in the crowded room. A little too thin, perhaps, but so gracefully poised with that deceptively sweet, innocent face.

Beth took a glass of wine and made her way over to Ellen. "Quite a success," Beth said. "And Manuel looks so . . . stunning. He's quite the figure, Ellen."

"That he is," Ellen agreed and she found him through the throng, saw him heading toward one of the rough, wooden easels, where . . .

"Oh, no," Ellen breathed. "Damn it!"

"What is it?" Beth asked.

"He's headed for Dale. Dale Willey."

"And who is he?"

"A local critic. He wrote a terrible critique of Manuel's paintings in today's paper."

"Did Manuel read it?"

"I don't think so."

But Ellen was wrong. In fact, Manuel had seen the article just after lunch. At the time he'd shrugged off the article as the ranting of a moron, an ill-bred northern cretin. After all, the man had originated in Chicago; what could he possibly know about art?

But for all Manuel's efforts to ignore Willey's review, the words had kindled an ember inside him.

Manuel made his way over to the table of hors d'oeuvres and wine and drank three glasses in the space of a minute. He picked up a fourth and headed back into the throng, aware of Ellen's eyes following him from across the room. He didn't give a damn.

Later, Manuel would not recall grabbing Willey's arm, though dozens saw him do it. He'd always swear to Ellen that Willey had approached him first and begun the fight.

"You low-class Anglo," Manuel snarled as he spun Willey around, knocking the man's plate of hors d'oeuvres to the floor. "I demand you retract your insults right here and now!"

Silence pulsed outward in a circle from the two men until the entire gallery was hushed. "Go to hell, Ortega," Willey said as tension crackled in the air.

Manuel swore in Spanish, his eyes bloodshot as he shoved the critic backward into several people, knocking over one of the easels in the process.

Someone gasped, and someone else let out a stifled scream while Ellen quickly tried to get to Manuel.

Furious, humiliated, Willey was righting himself and telling the inebriated artist that his paintings belonged in the garbage. And then Manuel really exploded, picking up a hundred-thousand-dollar oil and smashing it over his knee, the frame shattering, the canvas ripping.

A mad frenzy ensued. Several men tried to restrain Manuel while one of Ellen's employees dialed 911. By the time the sheriff's Cherokee pulled up out front there were two more broken frames and the fragments of a priceless black-on-black Maria Martinez bowl littering the gallery floor.

"Okay, move aside," Sheriff McCandless said as he made his way into the room and saw three men trying to hold Manuel down. "The show's over, folks," he said. "Let's clear the place out now."

Ellen didn't know what to do. Instinct was pushing her toward Manuel; logic told her to walk away from him and never go back. And all around her people were finding their coats, whispering things like, "Disgusting," or "Wouldn't you just know he lives with a Connelly." Oh, Ellen heard snatches of praise, too. "I think it's terribly exciting, so . . . sexy, so artistic." Someone even pressed a business card into her hand, whispering, "I want that torn canvas. I don't care what it costs. Call me."

Manuel was on his feet by now, Case handling him without too much difficulty. The gallery was almost cleared, and Ellen took a hesitant step toward them, torn, her heart breaking.

"Don't," said a voice at her ear. It was Beth. "Let the sheriff handle it, Ellen," and her stepsister took her hand and gave it a squeeze.

"I want to press charges," she heard then, and she turned, seeing Dale Willey standing there, straightening his clothes.

Manuel appeared to bristle again until Case said, "One more wrong move, Manuel, and I'll toss you in jail so fast your head'll spin. As for you, Willey, I'd rethink that."

"I have every right to press charges, McCandless, and you damn well know it. Why, this drunken Mexican attacked me!"

"Yeah, well," Case said, "it seems to me you took the first shot with that article of yours. Everyone in town read it. I doubt you'll get a lot of sympathy."

"So Ortega here just gets away with it?"

"I wouldn't put it that way," Case said. "When he wakes up in the morning he's going to have one hell of a headache."

Willey contemplated that for a moment. "All right," he finally said. "But I'm not about to keep this out of the paper."

"Never thought you would," Case replied in an even tone. "Now, why don't you go on home."

Muttering threats, Willey did leave, no doubt heading straight for his typewriter.

"Okay," Case said when he was gone, "one down, one to go." He looked at Ellen. "My inclination is to let Manuel sleep this off at the jail."

"No," Ellen said, straightening. "Please. Can't he just go home and rest? He isn't going to cause any more trouble, Sheriff. Case. Please. I'll call a taxi for him."

"And I can go with him to make sure he's okay," Beth offered, still holding Ellen's hand. "Ellen can clean up in here, and I'll stay with him until she gets home."

He looked from one woman to the other. "Okay," he said after a moment. "But I really insist that Manuel come into the office tomorrow for a talk."

"I promise he will, Case," Ellen said.

"I'll what?" Manuel chimed in.

"I'll tell you on the way home," Beth said. "Ellen, where's the phone? I'll have to get a cab."

"Look," Case broke in, "tell you what. Ellen's place is in the west end, and I have to head out to the ranch, anyway. I'll drop you two on my way."

Beth gave him an uncertain look.

"I doubt if you can handle him alone," Case said, nodding toward the swaying artist. "And besides, there's a matter concerning your hearing this afternoon I'd like to discuss."

She got her coat and Case helped Manuel out to the car. When he had the man safely slumped over in the back seat, he turned to see Beth giving Ellen a quick hug and a reassuring smile. It was a damn shame, Case thought. Ellen Connelly was a decent woman who apparently had jumped from the frying pan into the fire.

He held the front passenger door open for Beth and then rounded to his own side, putting the still-running car in gear. He found himself wondering about Beth then—did she get herself tied up with drunks, too? Of course, Billy Jorgenson wasn't much of a drinker. No. But he was a user, all right. Then again, Case had only seen her with Jorgenson that one time, and hadn't she flown off without the guy?

"That was good of you," he heard Beth saying, and he had to bring himself back to the present. "Not allowing that jerk to press charges, I mean."

"It wasn't my decision," Case said.

"Oh, I think you made it very clear to Dale Willey that he'd look like an ass if he pursued the matter."

"Well, that was my intention," he allowed, turning at the corner of Eighth Street and then onto Bleeker. "That Ellen's house?" he asked, slowing.

"Yes, that's it," she said.

He pulled up in front of the multicolored Victorian and turned off the engine. In the back seat Manuel stirred. "So," Beth said, "what was it you wanted to discuss?"

"It's not a big deal," he said. "I only wanted to say that I'm sorry I couldn't be of much help in court today." It seemed to him that his statement had been a perfectly decent gesture, but Beth was laughing, pushing a lock of hair behind an ear and laughing. "What?" he asked.

"That's the first time I've ever heard you lie," she replied lightly.

"Hey, come on," he said.

"It's the truth, isn't it? You aren't sorry one bit, you're just trying to be nice."

"Well, that's better than nothing," he muttered.

"You're the only honest man I've ever met in my life," she said.

"That's ridiculous."

"No, it's not. It's a fact."

"Well, I gotta say, I'm real sorry about that."

"You know, I believe you are," she said, amused, looking straight ahead, her profile backlit by the streetlight at the corner. "Shall we get Manuel out?" she asked.

"Ah, right," he said, "let's do that."

They got Manuel Ortega inside Ellen's house and up the stairs to the bedroom. Beth yanked off his boots with surprising strength, while Case lingered in the doorway, looking around. It was a charming house, a lot of pastel colors blending in with dark woods and antiques. Tasteful, he supposed was the word. He switched his attention back to Beth and saw that she was having trouble getting Manuel to lie down. "Here," he said, crossing to the bed, and he gave Ortega a hard lecture while Beth put her hands on her hips and sighed.

They were on their way downstairs when Ellen came in, breathless, looking as if she'd aged ten years.

"God, what a day!" she said, throwing her purse on a Navajo-patterned couch.

"You can't have cleaned up the gallery already," Beth said.

"A little. I just couldn't...oh, look at me," Ellen said, "I'm a wreck."

"Things will be better in the morning," Beth said.

Ellen gave a weary smile. "Sure they will."

"Well," Case said, looking at his watch, uncomfortable with Ellen's obvious distress. "I guess I'd better head on out to the ranch and get the kids."

"Thank you," Ellen said. "If this weren't a small town, I'm sure Manuel would have been locked up."

"Well, he might be if he pulls a stunt like that again," Case said. "I figure he had cause—this time."

"Thank you, really," Ellen said.

"Okay then, I'd better be going."

"Uh, just a sec," he heard Beth say, and he stopped, his hand on the brass knob. "I wonder...do you think, if you don't mind, you could drop me back in town? I can get a cab home then. Is that all right with you, Ellen? I mean, I could stay if you . . ."

"Oh, no, go on. I'm fine. We'll both be fine."

"Well, if you're sure."

"Go on."

"Okay," Beth said, taking up her coat, giving Case a look. "You don't mind, do you?"

"No, no, of course not," he said, and by the time they were outside again he was damn glad for the blast of fresh air. What a family.

Beth got into the car. "You don't have to go all the way back to town. You can drop me at the next corner," she said. "I'm sorry, I didn't mean to put you on the spot back there. It's just that...well, that scene was too much like . . . oh, never mind. I just couldn't stay and watch Ellen fall apart."

Case pulled out onto Bleeker Street. "She doesn't strike me as the type to fall apart."

"Usually she's not," Beth said.

Case never was sure what happened next. He'd offered to drop her at the taxi stand downtown, and she'd said it was a shame he had to go so far out of his way. He guessed out of politeness he'd said something like, "Then ride out to the ranch with me. The kids would enjoy seeing you again." Or had it been Beth who'd said, "Why don't you just drive on out to the ranch and drop me downtown on your way home?"

Oh, hell, Case thought as he turned onto the dark road that led up the Maroon Creek Valley. The outcome was the same—he was stuck with Beth Connelly.

The ride, which was supposed to have been a turnaround, somehow became an invitation to dinner, though that was Dottie's doing.

"A Connelly at the ranch?" she said, cocking her head at Beth. "Well, you'll just have to stay for dinner and see how the other half lives."

"Thank you," Beth said, standing right up to her. "If it's all right with Case, that is."

Trying to keep his irritation in check, he could only shrug.

If the ride to the ranch had been awkward, dinner turned out to be relaxing, but then a loud, cheery meal at the ranch usually was. Case and Beth sat across from Nate and Amanda, who regaled her with stories about Gizmo's cast and how he hardly knew he was wearing one.

"I don't ever let him out anymore," Nate told her.

"Not even to . . . you know?" Beth asked, teasing.

"Well," Nate said.

And Amanda piped up with, "Gizmo pees yellow snow cones in our yard."

"Guys," Case said.

Dottie joined them halfway through the meal, and Case felt that tension again, but this time it was between the two women. He could just read his mother's thoughts. Well, she was dead wrong. He'd like to tell her that, too, but it really was none of her damn business.

Brother Nick, after finishing up with the sleigh horses for the day, spotted Beth the instant he entered the crowded room. Blond and ruddy and devilishly handsome, the youngest McCandless strode right up to their table and thrust out his hand. "I'm Nick McCandless," he said, smiling with unabashed charm. "And just who would you be?"

Beth couldn't help smiling. "I'm Beth Connelly," she said, giving Case a glance as her hand was lost in Nick's.

"Connelly," he said. "Uh-huh. Maybe when Rowdy starts playing we'd better dance."

"Oh?" she said. "And why should we do that?"

"A Connelly? Somebody's gotta rescue you from the sheriff here."

"Knock it off," Case said. But when Rowdy's music kicked in and everyone took to the floor, Nick was right there again, pulling an unprotesting Beth to her feet.

Case watched them, his expression impassive. Dottie, while helping the busboy clear the table, said, "They make a nice-looking couple." Her son nodded and then turned to check on the kids, who were dashing in and out of the swinging kitchen doors, completely underfoot.

Nick and Beth took a breather in between dances, plumping themselves down at the table, laughing.

"I can't believe it," Nick said to his brother, "she does the two-step better than I do! Don't tell me they teach that back East."

"Actually," Beth said, "there are places for country dancing right in New York City. But I picked it up here."

"You ought to try it, Case," he said. "She really can dance."

"Yeah, later," Case said, and Nick shrugged, taking Beth's hand and leading her back to the dance floor.

They did make a nice-looking couple, Case noticed; handsome Nick with his laid-back cowboy strut and beautiful Beth with her silky black hair swinging and her dark velvet skirt swirling as she turned.

He sat there watching the dancers, enjoying the music despite his irritation at the fix he'd gotten himself into. Well, Nick sure came in handy at times—he'd taken Miss Connelly right off his hands.

Case remembered other nights like this, lots of them. Deirdre had been a great dancer, and they'd really stepped out when they were younger—the Cotton Eye Joe, the swing. They'd been good.

It occurred to him that he should stand up, tap Nick on the shoulder and do a round with Beth Connelly, show her all the fancy steps. Course, she'd just get the wrong idea. Better not.

Instead he found himself wandering into the kitchen, where Nate and Amanda were still running wild and Dottie was threatening to put them to bed right then and there. And then Amanda fell down, bumping her head on the corner of a table and bawling loudly.

Dottie picked her up. "These little Indians here belong in bed," she admonished Case over Amanda's sobs. "Tomorrow's Saturday. You can just pick them up in the morning."

"I'll get them home right now," Case said.

"Oh, sure. And just how are you going to drag Miss Connelly out of here?" And with that, Dottie ushered the two kids toward the guest rooms in the main lodge. Great.

The evening didn't turn out all that badly, though. Even though Case felt like a dope for not dropping Beth in town in the first place, he managed to put aside his irritation, chat with Kip, the bartender, and relax with a beer.

"Hey," Kip said, leaning toward Case, "is that really a Connelly out there with Nick?"

"Uh-huh." Case pivoted, put an elbow on the bar and found the two of them in the crowd.

"No shit?" Kip said.

"Have I ever lied to you?" Case asked.

Soon afterward, Rowdy took a break from the guitar while everyone found their seats, fanning themselves and ordering fresh drinks. Still laughing and breathing hard, Nick and Beth walked up to the bar.

"Phew!" Beth said, lifting her hair from the back of her neck. "That's work out there."

Nick ordered a beer. "Work, but fun," he said. "You should try it, big brother." He gave Case a hard slap on the back.

Case tipped the long-necked beer bottle to his lips. "I'll wait for some better competition," he said dryly.

"Well," Beth said, sitting on a bar stool between them, "I never imagined the ranch to be like this. It's so . . . friendly. I'll bet your mom has to turn away reservations right and left."

"She wishes," Nick said.

Beth cocked her head. "Really?"

"People who stay this far from town," Case explained, "do it for specific reasons. Some like snowmobiling, others want to do the backcountry sleigh trip. Some just want the peaceful setting."

"What's the backcountry trip?" she asked.

Nick told her about it, and Case was surprised she was interested.

"You mean, you take skis or a snowmobile all the way to the base of the Maroon Bells in the winter?"

"Yep," Nick said, and then abruptly he stopped, his eye catching someone—a lady—who'd just come in. "Excuse me," he said, "I'll be back in a sec."

"Uh-huh," Case said.

And Nick never did rejoin them.

Nine o'clock came and went, and with it so did some of the weary guests. Out of sheer courtesy Case did ask Beth if she wanted to dance, but she declined, looking down at her high-heeled boots. "I don't think these were made for dancing," she said, giving him an easy out.

And so they talked, or were forced to talk. She was a curious woman, he was learning, lively and unconventional one minute, guarded the next, soft and brazen all at once. She'd been a lot of places and seen a lot of things, and yet in many ways she had been incredibly sheltered.

Case listened politely when she told him how she'd begun working with children. He listened without saying much; they were, after all, as different as day and night. Whereas Beth was capable of speaking her mind with that uncanny blend of worldliness and whimsy, he felt restrained and uptight. How could she put aside the fact that he'd arrested her not so long ago. And that little stunt the other night—driving herself home without a license right under his nose. Well, he'd give her one thing, she sure had guts.

At ten Rowdy hung up his guitar and had a shot of whiskey with them before heading off to his cabin. By ten-fifteen only Case and Beth and two other couples remained. The fire was burning down, the lights dimmed, casting long shadows on the vaulted log ceiling.

"Well," Case began, ready to give her a ride home at last, but Dottie—good old Dottie—appeared a minute later and changed all that.

"Now look, the kids are already asleep, so they might as well stay put. There's no point in driving all the way to town and then coming straight back out in the morning. You can stay right here," Dottie said.

"Beth needs a ride," Case said, reaching for his hat.

"Fiddlesticks. She can sleep in the spare room. You use the room right next to mine, Case."

He looked at Beth. She looked at him and shrugged. "I guess I could stay, if it's easier for you, that is."

"Done," Dottie said, and then she asked Case to help her with something in the kitchen. The something didn't surprise him. "Okay," she said when they were out of earshot, "what's going on with you two?"

Case was taken aback. Dottie was outspoken, but she almost never interfered in her sons' lives. "You really think this is your business?" he asked. She nodded. "Nothing is going on. Does that suit you?"

"I asked because that girl . . . that Connelly woman isn't for you, Case."

"Jesus," he muttered.

Dottie folded her arms and sighed. "She's rich folk. She's never dirtied her hands in her entire life. My God, Case, she doesn't even look as if she eats, and her head's in the clouds!"

"Tell me something," he said. "If you think that badly of her, why did you invite her to dinner and then to spend the night?"

Dottie let out a huffing sound. "Never let it be said that the McCandlesses aren't hospitable."

Dottie turned to leave, but not before saying, "Now don't you go telling that woman that I disapprove of her."

"Maybe I will and maybe I won't," he said.

As it turned out, he didn't have to tell Beth a thing.

"Your mother doesn't approve of me," she said from her bar stool. "I know she asked me to stay to save you the drive, but I can always call a cab."

"All the way out here? It'll cost you a fortune." And then he caught himself.

"You know," Beth said, shaking her head, "everyone always assumes I'm loaded. That's what you're thinking, isn't it? Well, I'm not, Case McCandless. I have some money of my own but I still draw a paycheck."

"I thought you volunteered . . ."

"I do. I also get paid when I'm doing office work in New York."

"So Matt Connelly doesn't support you?"

She laughed. "Matt doles out pocket money as if it were confetti. This is true."

"And you take it."

Her lips turned up impishly. "Sure, I take it. Remember the money I gave you for the vet bill? That was Matt's."

"Jesus," he said. "You're putting me on. You wouldn't have . . ."

"You'll never know, will you?" she said.

"Beth."

"Oh, lighten up, Case. Life's too short."

"Is that on the family coat of arms?"

She seemed to sober. "Everyone loves judging the Connellys. I don't know what the scandal sheets would do without us. And you're just as bad."

"Now look—"

"How about the first time we met, Case? Talk about judging someone."

He chewed that over. "Listen," he said after a moment, "if I judged you too quickly, I'm . . ."

"If?"

"Yeah, if I did, I'm sorry. It was unprofessional. But the truth is, I don't get you at all."

"Get me?"

"Know you. Hell, you don't know me, either."

"Then maybe we should start from scratch."

He raised a sandy brow. "Start what from scratch?"

She shrugged and gave him a smile. "An acquaintance," she said archly. "Unless, of course, you really don't want to get to know me."

"I never said . . ."

"You don't have to say anything. Maybe Connellys and McCandlesses really can't mix."

"Look, Beth," he began, but her expression silenced him.

"We are bad news," she said, suddenly deflated, and he felt like a heel. All she'd asked for was an acquaintance. Hell, he was acting as if she'd come on to him. "You know," she was saying, "I feel like a real ass. I've ruined your night, you've got to be really tired. . . ."

"I had a good time tonight," he found himself admitting. "You're . . . you're ah . . . not like anyone I've met before."

Beth shot him a smile. "You put that very politely." Then she sighed and folded her hands on the bar, looking into the middle distance. "There are things," she said, "things about me that maybe you don't want to know."

"Hey," he said, "we all have things in our lives."

"I'll bet you don't."

"Of course I do."

"So tell me one."

"Well," he said, "I really screwed up on the woman I married."

"What is she, an ogre? Come on, Case, she gave you two lovely children."

"That she wants back."

"You'll handle it."

"Let's hope so."

"The bottom line is, there're no dirty little secrets in your closets."

He said nothing.

"Well, mine are full of them."

"Are they yours or your family's?"

"They're all mixed up together."

"So you're a real bad person. Is that it?"

She gave a short laugh. "Compared to you, I'm pretty bad."

"Christ," he said, "you make me sound like a saint."

"You are a pretty nice guy. I can't even be mad at you about the DUI. Even when you came out to the airport and dragged me back into town to give that statement, I..." She faltered.

"What is it?" he asked.

"Nothing, really," she said.

But he wondered, he sure did wonder, and later, lying in bed that night, Case kept remembering how she'd hesitated when she'd spoken about giving that statement. How many times had he called and left messages for her? And she'd been running off to Switzerland. Running. He tossed for a long time that night and knew in his heart she was hiding something. He could press her, but he knew he wouldn't.

Despite his restless night, when morning came, dawning without a cloud, Case felt oddly rested, ready to tackle a new day. He showered and put on the same clothes he'd worn yesterday, then headed to the kitchen.

"Good morning," Dottie said, holding up the pot of coffee. "Sleep well?"

"Not bad."

"Oh, I thought you might have stayed up late," she said casually.

"Why would I do that?" he asked, deadpan.

Dottie looked at him askance. "Okay, I'll mind my own business. What I really want to know is what's going on with Deirdre's suit."

"I wish you hadn't reminded me," he said, his face hardening.

"Why? Is she going to win? Oh, Case . . ."

"It's not that far along yet, Mom. It just drags on and on. Hanging over my head."

"Darn that woman."

"She's got a good lawyer."

"Well, so do you."

"Um," he said. "Kids up yet?"

"Still sleeping."

"You know," Case said, "I was thinking that it's been a long time since I took a full Saturday off. Maybe if Nick's got a couple of extra snowmobiles available, Beth and the kids might like to go for a ride today." He took a long swallow of coffee. "I'll bet she's never even been in the high country."

"Nice idea," Dottie said. "There's just one problem. Your little Miss Connelly left about twenty minutes ago."

Case looked up.

"She called a taxi and waited outside and took off."

"Well, I could pick her up in town, later, I guess. I've gotta change clothes, anyway."

"I guess you could do that," Dottie said, "but she mentioned catching the early flight to Denver and then on to New York."

"Oh," Case said. "Well, I suppose I can just ride both kids with me on one snowmobile."

Dottie looked at him. "Is that all you have to say?"

"What else is there to say?" he replied, pouring himself a second mug of coffee.

TWELVE

It was World Cup Week in Aspen, the annual celebration of the only FIS-recognized World Cup downhill race in the United States. There were coaches and downhill racers from Europe and Japan, Canada and the States—even one from Puerto Rico, seeded eighty-second out of eighty-two racers. The big names were all there, spouting ski jargon in many languages: edges and tuning and snow conditions, wax and gates and lines. Every morning at ten there was a practice run, and people lined the course on Aspen Mountain to watch the heavily muscled downhillers, those paragons of pure speed, streak by, their bright skintight suits flashing, their skis making a hissing roar on the hard snow.

The town was decked out with American flags; hundreds of volunteers worked to organize the event. On Friday night there would be the annual torchlight descent and fireworks display that shook the ground and lit up the night sky and mountains with explosions of red and green and white. Then on Saturday the race would take place. An exciting time for Aspen.

Television crews from all over the world roamed the streets, interviewing their hometown heroes in French and German and Italian, and on the mountain there was a deadly serious group of security men, and people working endless hours to prepare the course.

If the slopes were jammed with racers during the day, the streets of Aspen were packed with party lovers at night. Most discos were filled to capacity after eleven, and cover charges were sky-high. Naturally, there were other less-glitzy bars, almost eighty of them, between Aspen and the village of Snowmass twelve miles away. And these, too, were full from five in the afternoon until closing time.

Those who weren't partying roamed the quaint downtown brick malls after skiing, their arms loaded with designer bags and pretty packages. The shopping, though expensive, was irresistible.

It was at the close of World Cup Week that Lee Connelly made an appointment at Les Dames—facial, manicure, pedicure and a quarter-inch trim from her frosted-blond hair. Sitting in the plush, expensively appointed waiting room, Lee pondered the possibilities of having a dinner party in Aspen before the season's end. Nothing extravagant, as the family was keeping a low profile until this dreadful business with Terry was over, but fifty acquaintances or so who were in town for World Cup... Surely Matt couldn't object now that the preliminary hearing was over. After all, Terry's trial wouldn't be until August. And, she thought, life had to go on. She took out a pen and notepad from her purse and began a list. The Scotts, the Freemans—if they were in town—the...

"Oh, Mrs. Connelly," came Mona's voice from the door to the salon, "I'm so sorry you had to wait."

Mona had been giving Lee facials and manicures for years. In fact, the girl had worked at two other salons in Aspen, but when she changed "opportunities," so did her elite clientele. She had magic hands, and Lee let herself go, utterly relaxed, under the expert ministrations of Mona. It was pure, sensual pleasure, the stroking and prodding and smoothing, the soaking and rubbing and trimming. Delightful.

All Lee had to do was listen to Mona's cheerful chatter, especially when the facial mask was drying, and she couldn't talk anyway.

"You know I speak French, Mrs. Connelly?" Mona was asking as she filed and polished. "I'm sure I told you. My mother and father spoke it at home, you know? So I always sign up as a translator for World Cup Week in case one of the team doesn't speak English."

"Um," Lee murmured under her mask.

"So anyway, this year they sent me to Guy LeComte, you know, the French Bomb?"

"Um."

"Oh, is he gorgeous! Those buns! Well, the downhillers all have them, you know. It's from that crouch. So, Guy, well, he is something. We had a ball. I took him here, I took him there. He wanted to see everything. He wanted to see cowboys, so I drove him down to the Relay Station in Carbondale, the country and western bar? He had to try dancing. What a riot! He was sweating and trying to do the steps, and yelling in French."

"Um."

"Now, do you want this pink or the geranium, Mrs. Connelly? Oh, okay, this one." Mona unscrewed the top of the nail polish with an expert twist. "But I have to tell you—" Mona leaned close "—this Guy is, well, I couldn't believe it myself, with the reputation he has. We went to a party, real late at the Austrian team's hotel. All the teams were there—and women. I tell you!" Mona rolled her eyes.

"Now, I was sticking with Guy, who was really coming on to me. I was in love, I tell you. There was booze, there was a bowlful of cocaine on a table. Like sugar! The skiers didn't use it, but all the coaches did."

"Um," Lee managed.

"Well, you know Aspen. I mean, what're you going to do? But, wait, I have to tell you. So Guy starts coming on to this blond Norwegian downhiller. A man, yes! And he dumped me. He and this Norwegian left together. I was so ticked off. Can you believe it?" Mona sprayed fixative on Lee's nails. "There," she said, "nails done." Then she felt the hardening mask. "So Guy LeComte is bisexual, I guess. He can't be gay. I know he liked me, you know, Mrs. Connelly?"

"Um," Lee said, trying very hard not to smile.

"I don't know what language they were speaking," Mona reflected.

Lee couldn't help laughing. Her mask cracked and flaked off, but Mona only got out a hot scented towel and picked a last flake off Lee's face. "Well, it was almost done anyway," she said, unconcerned. Then, more seriously, "And I even did his nails for him. Clear polish, you know?"

Lee left Les Dames shaking her head over Mona's stories and deciding on the date and menu for the dinner party. Those adorable cards she'd seen earlier today at Just Paper would be perfect for the invitations.

There was a problem, though. The maid at the estate was not doing the job she used to, not to mention the fact that food had been missing from the garage freezer and two of Matt's best bottles of brandy were gone. It was going to be distasteful talking to the property management company that provided domestic help, but it had to be done.

Lee headed along Cooper Street toward the management company's offices, stopping to window-shop, popping into Ellen's gallery to say hello.

"Lee!" Ellen said. "What brings you in?" She gave her stepmother a peck on the cheek. "You look . . . great."

"Thank you, dear, I just left Les Dames. Mona does wonders."

"So you're out shopping?"

"Shopping and errands. Matt's supposed to meet me at the Ritz after skiing."

"And how is Dad? We didn't even get to talk at the hearing. And Terry. He was in and out of town so quickly. . . ."

"Oh, they're both fine. You'll have to come up to the house and see Matt soon, though, because he's due back in Washington in a couple of days."

"You aren't going?"

"Oh, I don't know. The weather's so wonderful right now. And Matt's going to be busy in Washington. We'll see. But how are you, dear, and that talented young artist of yours?"

Ellen laughed. "Young?"

"Younger than I am," Lee said.

"Oh, he's fine."

"And everything's well between you?"

"Perfectly marvelous," Ellen said. But Lee wondered. She'd heard things through the gossip network; evidently Manuel could get quite out of hand. But then, there was no one more capable of handling the errant artist than Ellen. Even though Lee had married into the family just as Ellen was headed off to Vassar, she had pegged her stepdaughter immediately—Ellen was a controller, a difficult young woman with whom to share a home. It had been somewhat of a battle, in fact, between the two women in Matt's house, and to this day Lee knew she'd have lost the war had Ellen not gone off to college. Terry, on the other hand, had been a typical teenage boy. Off at boarding school in upstate New York, he'd visited on weekends with friends. A raucous, high-spirited bunch, sowing their wild oats, though harmlessly.

Lee browsed in the gallery, impressed as always. Oh, the new Santa Fe look wasn't for her, but she certainly could appreciate the lightness of it, the pastels and sunlit desert colors, subdued, peaceful, the lines unfolding in perfect simplicity.

"My Lord," Lee said, stopping at a ceramic jar sitting atop a lighted glass table. "Sixty thousand dollars?" she gasped. "Isn't this rather . . . pricey? It's not even an antique."

"Actually," Ellen said, smiling at Lee's horror, "it's quite a bargain."

"Um," Lee said, moving on, hiding her distaste for anything under 150 years old that commanded such extravagant prices. "Oh," she said, stopping. "Is this one of Manuel's paintings?"

"Yes."

"It's . . . lovely. Really it is," Lee said, careful not to mention the price tag.

"Thank you."

"Um," Lee said, "so many exquisite pieces." She paused, "Oh, I'm planning a dinner party in a couple of weeks, a small get-together. I hope you and Manuel will come."

"We'll try, just let me know when."

Lee left the gallery shortly, checking her watch as she headed to the management company. She got there just before closing and hurried in, catching her breath. Her mind was on a dozen things: the chore of breaking in a new maid, Matt waiting for her at the Ritz bar, the party, invitations, menus, flowers from the florist. She paid no attention to the nameplate on the receptionist's desk.

"Hello," she began, "I'm Lee Connelly, and your company manages my property here in town. I'm afraid I'm having some trouble with . . ."

"Excuse me," the receptionist interrupted in a strange voice. "What did you say your name was?"

"Lee Connelly. As I was telling you . . ." But the receptionist was staring at her. *How rude*, Lee thought.

"Connelly," the woman behind the desk whispered.

"Yes, we have a house at the Preserve, and I'm having trouble with the maid you sent over. Do you suppose I could speak to someone about it?" The woman was pale, still staring as if mesmerized by something awful. *Is my mascara running?* Lee wondered. *My lipstick smeared? Did Mona leave some mask on my face?*

But the woman's answer had nothing to do with any of that. "You're Mrs. Connelly," she said in a hollow voice.

"Yes . . ."

"Oh, my God."

"I really don't know what the problem is, Miss . . ." Lee glanced down quickly at the receptionist's nameplate, "Mrs. Kelly."

"Nancy Kelly," the woman said tonelessly.

"*Mrs.* Kelly. I don't really . . ." Lee's throat closed. *Kelly. Nancy Kelly. Heather.* Inadvertently she backed up a step, transfixed by a knowledge so stark she had no defense against it.

"Yes," the woman hissed.

Lee tried to back away, to turn and leave, but she was frozen to the spot. A terrible heat pricked her skin, and the room tilted. She tried to say something, but her mouth was dry as ashes.

The woman stood up behind the desk, and her face was haggard, ugly, a sickly gray. "My daughter," she breathed, "is dead."

Lee shrank, trembling.

"Terence Connelly killed her." The woman's words were like nails, and Lee was pierced by each one of them, each one hammered home. "He killed her, and now he thinks he's going to get away with it."

"No," Lee managed to croak. "He didn't...."

"You know he did it. All you Connellys know he did it." The words were torn like raw flesh from the woman's throat.

Lee opened her mouth, but nothing came. Nausea rose in her.

"Tell the truth," Nancy Kelly said in that terrible hollow voice. "Tell the truth." She spoke louder now. "Don't let him get away with it! You have to tell the truth!" And then she was wailing, her face crumpled, and Lee's paralysis broke as if a dam had given way, and she rushed out of the office, away from that horrible place, Nancy Kelly's cries ringing in her ears.

Oh God, oh God, she kept repeating. *No.* The next thing she knew she was pushing open another door—the Ute City Banque's—and standing at a crowded après-ski bar.

"Excuse me," someone said sarcastically as she elbowed her way toward the bartender.

"A brandy," she said, leaning across the bar. "You, over there, I want a brandy."

"Okay, hold on, lady, I'm coming."

"Make it a double," she managed to say before giving in completely to her misery.

The taxi ride to the Preserve was a blur. Lee sat in the back seat with her shoulders straight and her eyes glazed over.

She never recalled paying the driver or exactly how she got inside. It seemed that one minute she'd been sitting at the venerable old Aspen bar talking to a young man, and the next she was on the side of her bed, the lights blindingly bright. Matt was there, too, standing near the door, still in his ski clothes, a glass in his hands.

"I need a drink," Lee said. "Get me a drink."

"Like hell I will. Where were you, anyway? Jesus Christ, Lee, you're a mess!"

"As the children like to say . . . screw you, Matthew. Now, I want a drink."

"You're a real thing of beauty," he said, disgust dripping from his voice. "What in hell set you off? I thought you'd cut back."

She waved a hand airily. "I want a drink!"

"Get it yourself," he said and left, slamming the bedroom door.

The next time Lee stirred it was past midnight. She awakened fully clothed, the light still on, and her head was pounding with pain. She managed to get into her nightgown and swallow her pills, but nothing seemed to help. A drink, the hair of the dog . . . She drew on a silk robe, found her satin mules and went up to the living room and the wet bar.

"So you're alive," came Matt's voice from near the fireplace.

Lee ignored him and poured herself a stiff drink, downing it in a single gulp. "Oh God," she whispered, her head thrown back as the liquor burned all the way to her stomach.

"So," Matt said, "care to tell me what happened now? You know you left me waiting at the Ritz for two hours before I figured you weren't coming."

Lee turned slowly to face him. "I ran into Nancy Kelly this afternoon," she said.

"Who?"

"Kelly. Nancy Kelly. She's the mother of the girl that Terry..."

"What in hell are you talking about?" Matt demanded.

"The woman begged me, Matthew, she begged me to tell the truth!"

"What are you talking about?"

"The truth about Terry, for God's sake, to tell the truth at the trial."

"We've told the truth," he said in a hard voice. "Have you lost your mind, Lee?"

"I think I've just come to my senses," she said, and she gave a pained laugh. "You know the truth, everyone knows the truth, Matt, and we just keep covering it up, pretending Terry is a nice young man...."

Matt strode across the room and grabbed the silk lapels of her robe. The veins in his neck protruded alarmingly. "I don't want to hear another word about this," he said harshly. "Not another word. You've forgotten who you are, who *we* are."

"I may be drunk," Lee said, shaking off his grasp, "but at least I can open my eyes and see what you refuse to face."

"Damn you," Matt snarled.

"And you, too, my darling," she shot back. "And by the way, Matthew, I won't be flying to Washington with you. I'm staying right here and I'm calling a lawyer."

He looked at her for a moment and then laughed. "Sure you are, honey, just like the last time, and the time before that."

"I mean it, Matt. I'm divorcing you."

"Right," he said, turning away, "and just where do you think you'll go? You're one of us ill-bred Connellys now, babe, and there ain't no escapin' it."

It was three-thirty in New York when the phone rang at Beth's bedside, startling her out of a sound sleep. "What?" she said, trying to rouse herself. "What did you say, Mom?"

"I need you here. I need your support. I'm divorcing Matt." Her mother broke into tears.

"Look," Beth said after a minute, "things will look better in the morning. They always do. Why don't we talk then and . . ."

But it was no use.

"Okay," Beth said, "all right. It's really slow in the office, anyway. I could take a couple of days, I guess. There's the deposition, though, day after tomorrow. I'm doing mine here in New York. But then I can fly out. Okay?"

"Oh, thank you, darling, thank you." Lee wept.

"It's all right. If you need me, I'll be there," Beth said, and she hung up. Divorcing Matt, she thought. Not again.

Matt was pissed. He sat in the Washington club awaiting Melinda Feinstein and Terry and downed two double Scotches. Damn that Lee! he fumed. She had a way of pushing his buttons that made him seethe inside. My God, he thought, accusing Terry of hurting that girl. No matter what the hell Beth thought she'd seen, it was bullshit. Terry had finally admitted having sex with the girl, but he'd only been helping her down the hall and back to her car. Shit, he mused, Lee was as crazy as Beth.

He looked at his watch. It was ten past one. Feinstein and Terry were late. Sure, it was snowing in Washington, a bear of a spring storm, but he'd flown in from Aspen—you'd think they could make it a few blocks and be on time.

Feinstein arrived first, and at least she made no excuses. And then Terry got there, full of explanations. "Boy, the city falls apart when we get an inch of snow," he said. "Traffic's hell."

"You're never gonna make it in this world," Matt grumbled, "if you can't keep appointments, kid." He eyed his son, the perpetual student. Terry still wore casual, college-boy clothes—baggy trousers, a bulky, suitably worn Shetland sweater and a ski parka. Most men his age were out in the business community and sported at least five-hundred-dollar suits. When was this kid going to get his shit together?

But Ms. Feinstein. Only a few years older than Terry, this lady definitely had her act together. Today she was wearing a tailored puce suit, the skirt showing off her good legs, an off-white silk blouse and no jewelry whatsoever except a plain, functional watch. No furs for Ms. Feinstein, either. He'd only seen her in a really nice-looking trenchcoat, one of those English jobs, plain scarf and gloves. Matt liked that. At least she wasn't spending his hard-earned money on clothes and jewelry. This woman would tuck it all into triple A, tax-exempt bonds. Safe, secure. Oh yeah, he certainly was liking Melinda Feinstein better and better.

They ordered lunch with the usual efficiency. Matt had coffee—he wasn't about to order another drink while Terry was there. Terry drank designer water and Melinda had hot tea.

"You understand," she said to Terry, "that the media hype is going to gain momentum all over again as the trial nears."

"It hasn't even died down from the preliminary hearing," Matt groused. "Isn't it time for the Royal Family to get into a fix again? Hell, you'd think my family was all those asses have to write about."

Melinda gave him a rare sympathetic smile. "It might not die down till August, Matt, after the trial is over. I only hope Terry's life isn't too disrupted. Are things terrible at school?" she asked the younger Connelly.

Terry shrugged. "Not really," he said, as if the subject were of no significance.

She nodded, giving nothing away, neither approval nor disgust, and Matt just shook his head.

"Now, let's talk about the depositions," she said. "We'll—"

But Terry interrupted. "Can I ask something? I mean, how many hearings and depositions are there, anyway? I really wanted to take this trip to Europe with—"

"What?" Matt said. "You can't leave the country. Are you nuts, boy?"

"Your father's right, of course, Terry. And not only that, it's important you seem one-hundred-percent focused on the trial. I hope you didn't make any plans through a travel agent or anything."

"Not yet," Terry said, disappointed.

"Good. It really is vital that these charges appear to mean something to you."

"That's right," Matt agreed.

"You might even speak to a reporter or two at this stage and say that you're anxious for the trial to begin, that you want to be vindicated and the truth to come out."

"Good," Matt said. "I like that." Every time Ms. Feinstein spoke, he realized, his admiration for her grew. Damn smart lady. Savvy.

"So how are your grades, Terry?" she was asking.

"Could be better, I guess."

Melinda dabbed at her lips with the linen napkin.

"Um," she said, her eyes lifting to his slowly. "It would behoove you to carry a good grade-point average this semester. It's important that the public perceive you as a diligent student, a man of good character. Do you understand what I'm saying?"

Terry looked at her, confused.

She sighed. "We want the public to sympathize, Terry, to see you working really hard while under great duress. We don't want any idle gossip, even on campus, that you're folding under pressure."

"I guess I understand."

"You're a Connelly," she said. "That in itself, unfortunately, is a strike against you. It's the haves against the have-nots."

Matt folded his arms across his barrel chest. "Now, I know the media is ready to fry Terry here, but I can't believe the general public would go for it, too."

Melinda's eyes pivoted to the senator. "There's a lot of circumstantial evidence, as you know. I think I can combat the vast majority of it, but we want Terry to look lily white, an innocent victim of these circumstances. We want a sympathetic jury."

"Speaking of which," Matt said, "what about a change of venue? Is it a good idea to have the trial in Aspen?"

"It can work both ways," she said. "I asked about changing the venue because of pretrial publicity, but the judge refused. I could fight for it, but I don't think it's worth it. Aspen has a very sophisticated populace, and I think the jury will be fair."

"Okay," Matt said. "I trust your judgment, lady."

"Good. Now, let's go over exactly what you need to do and say for the upcoming depositions. They are very, very important, and I want every family member to be in harmony on these."

"We did pretty good on the initial statements," Matt said, but then he shot Terry a look. "All except this kid here, of course, who really blew it."

"I told you—" Terry began.

But Melinda interrupted. "Water under the bridge. What we do is repair the damage now. Terry will be well versed on exactly why he . . . got confused when he first talked with the sheriff. There's nothing that can't be explained."

"Except that he lied," Matt said under his breath.

"I was scared," Terry said defensively.

"Exactly," she said. "Anyone would have been. We'll use it to our advantage, in fact, when the time arrives."

Terry looked pleased, but then abruptly he frowned. "What about Beth?" he asked, staring at his father, and Matt's stomach knotted.

"Beth?" Melinda said.

"It's nothing," Matt put in quickly.

"Are you sure there's . . ."

"You've got all the facts, Ms . . . Melinda," Matt said in a hard voice. Then, "Terry's just concerned because his stepsister was really the only one who saw him with Heather Kelly earlier at the bar. He's worried it will look like he picked the girl up and not the other way around. Right, Terry?"

"Ah, yeah. That's right."

Melinda looked from one to the other. "If that's all you're worried about . . ."

"It is," Matt said.

"Well, then, to be blunt, it's Terry's word on that. Obviously, the girl can't testify. And what jury won't believe a poor college girl working two jobs wouldn't try to hit on a Connelly? We'll certainly make sure Terry appears to be the victim on that angle."

"Sounds good to me," Matt said.

They talked at some length about the depositions, Melinda assuring Matt that she'd go over everything with the individual family members in great detail before they were deposed. Matt listened carefully, his respect for Ms. Feinstein growing and growing—this woman had it all down to a science. Mildly, he wondered if Terry was as appreciative of her professionalism. All his son seemed truly aware of were her very shapely crossed legs. Oh well, Matt thought, at least Terry was a true Connelly in that respect.

At three Terry left for a four o'clock class. Matt himself had a committee meeting to attend, though he'd missed a few during World Cup Week already. But it was no big deal; all senators took breaks from the day-to-day boredom of meetings. The trick was to be there for the ones that received TV coverage, make sure the voters at home got the right impression.

"A drink?" he asked Melinda, allowing himself a little sexual fantasy as his eyes fixed on that pretty, shell-like ear of hers.

But she declined. "I would have one," she said, "but I've got an appointment myself."

"Cancel it."

She raised a brow and then smiled, inflaming Matt further. "And why should I do that?" she asked.

He leaned forward and whispered, "Because I enjoy your company."

Melinda regarded him soberly for a long moment. "All right," she said. "I'll cancel my appointment, Senator. Now all we have to decide is your place or mine."

"Well . . . well I'll be damned," Matt said, whistling between his teeth. "You really are a woman who knows what she wants."

"So they tell me, Matt, so they tell me."

It was an afternoon Matt would not soon forget. His driver let them out in front of the Georgetown brick with instructions to wait. And then Matt led the way to the door, Melinda following him as if they were merely going to duck inside and collect papers or something.

He unlocked the door and swung it open for her and actually experienced a moment of regret for asking her back to the empty house. Too cold, he was thinking; he'd wear himself out trying to arouse her.

The door closed, and Matt barely had his overcoat off when Ms. Feinstein snaked her arms around his neck. "Oh God," she breathed, "I do love a powerful man." The next thing he knew her lips were on his, opening his mouth, and her tongue was thrusting against the back of his throat. Desire exploded in his loins and he grabbed her to him right there in the narrow hall, half tearing their coats off, his suit jacket, hers, as his mouth found the hot pulse beat on her throat and his meaty hands fumbled with the tiny, covered buttons on her blouse.

They fell against the papered wall, Matt pulling aside the silky blouse, freeing her breasts from the lacy bra. They sprang at him, the peaks rock-hard and brown, and he buried his head between them as her hands tore at his zipper.

For a fleeting moment Matt thought that they ought to at least make it up to the bedroom, but then her capable fingers began to squeeze him and knead him and that was the last rational thought he was capable of.

Matt spun her around hard against the wall, his teeth on a nipple. She moaned loudly, and together they got her skirt bunched up, the garter belt pushed aside. Jesus H. Christ, Matt realized, his brain on fire, she wasn't wearing another damn thing! He put his strong hands beneath her buttocks and lifted her, her legs going around his back until he found the sweet spot and drove himself into her.

Her head forward now, she clung to him and sank her teeth into his neck as he pumped away into that hot wetness, banging her back against the wall. He was only slightly aware of the Lalique vase next to them on the tabletop, rocking, too. On and on Matt pumped himself into her, lifting her higher, his mouth sucking on a breast as little cries of delight escaped her. And then he felt himself about to climax, and he told her, "It's coming, oh God, it's coming," and she seemed to open up even farther, drinking him in until she, too, was gasping and twisting and crying aloud. And then, along with his rocketing climax, came a loud crash that resonated through his body, heightening the sharp pleasure, and when he could focus again he saw the Lalique vase shattered on the hall floor.

Shit, Lee would kill him, he thought fleetingly.

How long they sagged against the wall, still locked together, Matt wasn't sure. When they got their breath back, he unwrapped her legs from his torso and tried to straighten his clothes. He felt singularly embarrassed all of a sudden—fornicating like a first-time teenager right in his goddamn hallway! But Ms. Feinstein was unperturbed.

"May I use your powder room?" she asked, buttoning her blouse as if nothing had happened.

"Ah, sure," Matt said. "It's down the hall. To the right."

"Thank you," she said, and disappeared. Five minutes later she returned, went to the door and thanked him for lunch, assuring him that the depositions were going to go just fine.

"Sorry about the vase," she said, and she left.

Matt just stood there utterly spent and knew he'd finally met women's lib face-to-face. What he didn't know was who had screwed whom.

THIRTEEN

Aspen, CO

Deposition of Darrell Skaggs

Tripp Maddock: On the night of December twenty-eighth of last year, where were you, Mr. Skaggs?

Skaggs: I was working my shift at the Antler Club, that's the private downtown bar. You know. Me and Heather...Heather Kelly.

Maddock: What time did Miss Kelly get off?

Skaggs: She was done at one. I worked till closing, at two.

Maddock: Tell us what she said when she left that night or, rather, that morning. The morning of December twenty-ninth.

Skaggs: Well, she was real excited. She'd met Terence Connelly, and he'd invited her to his house for a drink after work. She said he was real nice and real cute.

Melinda Feinstein: Mr. Skaggs, was Heather Kelly in the habit of going home with men she met at the Antler Club?

Skaggs: Habit? Well, gee, I mean, sometimes. I guess.

Feinstein: And she'd just met Mr. Connelly that night?

Skaggs: Yes, I think so.

Feinstein: Thank you, Mr. Skaggs.

Deposition of Walter Shandler

Maddock: Mr. Shandler, please tell us what occurred the morning of December twenty-ninth of last year regarding the discovery of Heather Kelly's body.

Shandler: Well, I was jogging like I usually do. It was about seven o'clock, I guess. Snowing out. I was on my way home and took my usual route up the Aspen Health Club driveway. There was this car in the parking lot, an old VW, yellow, I think. It was pretty covered with snow, but I could see through the side window there was someone inside, looked like they were asleep. I figured they'd freeze to death, sleeping in a car like that, so I rapped on the window. It was this blond girl in there, and I thought it was sort of odd. I opened the door and shook her, and, man, she was cold. I knew then. I knew she was dead. I ran up to the Aspen Club and used their phone to call the sheriff. And, well, you know the rest.

Maddock: Thank you, Mr. Shandler. Ms. Feinstein, any questions?

Feinstein: No, Mr. Maddock.

Deposition of Brian Evanick

Maddock: Now, Mr. Evanick, relate what you saw the morning of December twenty-ninth of last year when you were plowing the Aspen Health Club driveway and parking lot.

Evanick: It was snowing pretty heavy that night, so I got up early. See, I have these regular customers who need to be plowed early. So I started, oh, maybe three-thirty, maybe three forty-five, I started down the driveway of the health club. It was really coming down by then. I saw a man walking toward me, up the driveway, all hunched over against the snow.

Maddock: For the record, the man was walking toward the highway, is that correct, Mr. Evanick?

Evanick: Yes.

Maddock: Describe the man, please.

Evanick: I couldn't see too well. It was dark and snowing. I'd say he was medium height, dark hair, wearing an aviator jacket.

Feinstein: Did you see the man's face, Mr. Evanick?

Evanick: No.

Maddock: Then, Mr. Evanick, what did you see in the parking lot?

Evanick: There was a car there, an old VW. Just sitting. I figured somebody left it there overnight. People do that at times. Makes it a pain to plow, though.

Maddock: Now, Mr. Evanick, can you recall how much snow there was on this car, and if there were tire marks, like someone had recently driven it there?

Evanick: Gosh, I couldn't see well. My plow throws up spray all over the place. I don't know if there were tire tracks. I think there was snow on the car, on the top.

Maddock: And on the windshield?

Evanick: I don't know.

Deposition of Mike Sabbatino

Maddock: Deputy Sabbatino, please explain to us your connection with this case.

Sabbatino: I work for the Pitkin County Sheriff's Department. In this case I was asked to lift prints from the car in question, the yellow VW that Heather Kelly's body was found in, license plate number ZG440.

Maddock: What were the results?

Sabbatino: There were the girl's prints all over the car. Also her mother's, Nancy Kelly. Walter Shandler's prints were on the door handle.

Maddock: Nothing else?

Sabbatino: No other prints that we could use.

Deposition of Loren Stevenson

Maddock: Deputy Stevenson, relate to us what happened on the morning of December twenty-ninth.

Stevenson: I responded to a call from the Aspen Health Club—a dead body in a car in their parking lot. I went over there, about seven-thirty, saw the girl's body and called the dispatcher to get hold of Case McCandless, the sheriff. That's about it.

Maddock: Thank you, Deputy.

Deposition of Case McCandless

Maddock: Okay, Sheriff McCandless, tell us about that morning of December twenty-ninth.

McCandless: I got a call from Beverly, the dispatcher, about seven-thirty. I arrived at the Aspen Club parking lot about eight. There was a yellow VW with local plates and a body in the driver's seat, whom we identified as Heather Kelly, twenty-two years old, resident of the Woody Creek Trailer Park.

Maddock: Anything unusual about the body, Sheriff?

Feinstein: Excuse me, Mr. Maddock, that is a leading question.

Maddock: Describe the body, Sheriff.

McCandless: Her head was resting back against the seat. She was dressed in jeans and a sweater and a dark-colored parka and boots. There was a white substance smeared around her nose. I also noticed some marks on her neck. Like bruises.

Feinstein: Are you a forensic expert, Sheriff?

McCandless: No, ma'am, I'm not.

Feinstein: Then let's leave conclusions like that to the experts.

Maddock: Thanks, Case.

Feinstein: Oh, Sheriff, one last question, please. During the search of the Connelly house by the Pitkin County Sheriff's Department, were any illegal drugs found?

McCandless: No, ma'am.

Feinstein: No cocaine, nothing whatsoever?

McCandless: No, ma'am, nothing.

Deposition of Lester Wiggins

Maddock: Dr. Wiggins, you are the medical examiner called in on this case, is that correct?

Wiggins: Yes, I am.

Maddock: Describe the state of the victim's body, please.

Wiggins: It was the body of a healthy white female in her early twenties. Some lividity on her neck. A white substance on her nose, later tested out to be cocaine. Rigor mortis had fully set in.

Maddock: Please tell us the results of the forensic tests on Heather Kelly, Dr. Wiggins.

Wiggins: The girl had had sexual intercourse within the past six hours. The DNA profile showed the DNA of the sperm in her vagina matched that of the blood sample taken from Terence Connelly. The marks on her neck were made prior to her death, which we can tell by the lividity. After death the skin no longer bruises—unless the victim was lying facedown, that is. This girl spent hours after death in an upright position. She died from strangulation, a classic choke hold, cutting off blood and air. The heart stops. Blood tests showed point-zero-six alcohol in the blood and no cocaine.

Maddock: No cocaine.

Wiggins: Nope.

Maddock: How do you explain coke on her nose but none in her blood?

Wiggins: I can only surmise that someone put it there, but after she was dead, which is why she never inhaled it.

Feinstein: That is conjecture, is it not, Dr. Wiggins?

Wiggins: Sure is, ma'am. But I defy you to come up with a better story.

Maddock: Okay, let's go on. The time of death?

Wiggins: Well, with the cold and all, it was a little harder to tell than usual. We pinned it down to between one and three a.m.

Maddock: And the other tests?

Wiggins: Carpet fibers found on her boots made a seventy-five-percent match with the carpet in Terence Connelly's bedroom. Strands of her hair were found on his pillow.

Feinstein: Was there cocaine found in Mr. Connelly's room or on his person?

Wiggins: No, ma'am.

Maddock: I believe, Ms. Feinstein, that you're belaboring the point.

Feinstein: Quite right, Mr. Maddock.

Maddock: Okay, Doctor . . . please tell us if Heather Kelly was forcibly penetrated, sexually, that is.

Wiggins: I can't give a positive answer, but with the bruises and a small amount of vaginal tearing—

Feinstein: Conjecture.

Wiggins: As I was saying, it's very possible there was a rape.

Feinstein: The bruises on the victim's neck, Doctor, occurred some time before her death, is that right?

Wiggins: Yes.

Feinstein: Can you pinpoint the time?

Wiggins: No, not exactly.

Feinstein: She could have received those bruises two days before she died, then?

Wiggins: Possibly, not likely.

Feinstein: But she could have?

Wiggins: Yes.

New York, NY
Deposition of Beth Connelly

Beth: I met her, yes. Terry introduced me to her at the Antler Club. Then she came home with him later. The time. Oh? One or two, about then. Then I went to bed, like everyone else.

Maddock: And you never heard or saw Heather Kelly again.

Beth: I went to sleep. I'd had a couple of drinks and I fell asleep.

Maddock: Thank you, Miss Connelly.

Deposition of Roland (Buzz) Crenshaw

Buzz: Yeah, sure, I saw her when Terry brought her in. He introduced her. That's all. I went to bed then.

Maddock: What time was that, Mr. Crenshaw?

Buzz: Oh, God, I don't know for sure. After one sometime.

Maddock: Can you pin the time down any closer?

Buzz: With the load I had on?

Maddock: Thank you, Mr. Crenshaw.

Deposition of Cynthia Crenshaw

Cynthia: I saw her for five minutes, maybe ten. Pretty girl. She was hanging on to Terry. Then I went to bed. Around one or one-thirty.

Washington, DC
Deposition of Lee Connelly

Maddock: Mrs. Connelly, when did you first see the victim, Heather Kelly?

Lee: Well, I might have seen her in the Antler Club that night, although I don't recall her at all. And when we got home, I . . . well, I was very tired, and I went straight to bed. Before she and Terry came in. I never saw her.

Deposition of Matthew Connelly

Matt: Yes, I met her. For a few minutes. She seemed high, excited. She was a pretty girl. I went to bed then.

Deposition of Terence Connelly

Maddock: Now, Mr. Connelly, tell us what happened between you and Heather Kelly that early morning of December twenty-ninth.

Terence: I met her at the Antler Club and invited her home. She seemed very nice, although she'd had a little to drink. Well, so had I. Not much, just a couple. Anyway, she said she'd give me a ride home. I took it because the Range Rover was really going to be crowded. So we got to the house and everyone was going off to bed.

Maddock: What time was this, Mr. Connelly?

Terence: Oh, about one-thirty, two. I'm not exactly sure.

Maddock: Then what happened?

Terence: We had a drink.

Maddock: Just the two of you?

Terence: Yes, everyone else went to bed.

Maddock: Continue, please.

Terence: She was getting real friendly by then. We went down to my room and we . . . uh . . . had sex.

Maddock: In your original statement, Mr. Connelly, you said you had not had sex with Miss Kelly, that she had never been in your room.

Terence: I . . . yeah, well, you know, I was scared. I mean, this girl was dead. I didn't want anyone to think . . . I guess I sort of panicked.

Maddock: So now you're telling the truth.

Terence: Absolutely. Yes.

Maddock: Heather Kelly willingly had sex with you.

Terence: Yes.

Maddock: Then what happened?

Terence: She, well, she wanted to do cocaine. I don't do that. I told her so. She insisted, and she got mad when I wouldn't. Then she left.

Maddock: She left by herself, under her own steam?

Terence: She walked out. I assume she drove her car away. I didn't watch.

Maddock: Then you are saying that when Heather Kelly left the Connelly house that morning, the last time you saw her, she was alive.

Terence: Yes.

Feinstein: That's what Mr. Connelly already said, Mr. Maddock.

Maddock: You did not go with her?

Terence: No, she was angry, as I said. She left in a huff.

Feinstein: This is not a trial, Counselor. Don't belabor the question, please.

Maddock: All right, Mr. Connelly, I have another question. Do you own an aviator jacket?

Terence: Yes, I do.

Maddock: And were you walking up the Aspen Health Club driveway at around three forty-five the morning of December twenty-ninth?

Terence: No, of course not.

Feinstein: Mr. Maddock . . .

Maddock: You had not just driven Heather Kelly's car with her body in it and left it in the Aspen Club parking lot?

Feinstein: You are badgering the witness, Mr. Maddock.

Maddock: Please answer the question, Mr. Connelly.

Terence: I never drove her car. She left, like I said. She got mad and walked out and drove her own car.

Maddock: She left alone, drove her car to the Aspen Health Club parking lot, somehow got bruises on her neck, cocaine on her nose and died!

Feinstein: Mr. Maddock!

Terence: She must have met someone else. . . .

Feinstein: Don't say another word, Terry.

Maddock: All right, Mr. Connelly, that'll be all.

FOURTEEN

At the Preserve the March sun was hot on the deck of the Connelly house, where Beth and her mother were sitting.

"I shouldn't have called you like that," Lee was saying. "I can manage on my own. I don't know what got into me."

"You were upset."

"I was. Matt and I had just...quarreled. But I shouldn't have called you." Lee stretched her legs, resting her feet on the cushioned lounge.

"Well, I'm here now. No use crying over spilt milk," Beth said.

"I know, I know. And I was upset. I was going to leave Matt right then," Lee said, her eyes covered by large octagonal sunglasses.

"Well, are you still leaving him?"

Lee turned her face away to stare across the valley. "I don't know. After he got back from Washington he apologized so sweetly, you know how he can be, and I...well, I've been here, just relaxing, and somehow it seems so terribly much trouble to go to over a quarrel."

"Um."

"It's this thing with Terry, you know. This awful trial. It has everyone so on edge. I couldn't possibly desert Matt now, not with the trial and all." Lee took off her glasses and looked at her daughter. "I hope the deposition wasn't too awful for you, Beth. I know how terrible it all is. Mine was mercifully short."

It was Beth's turn to look away, out over the mountains. "It was okay. Didn't take long."

"Good, good. Matt tells me that the D.A. has a very weak case, so I'm sure it will all end up just fine, but meanwhile . . ."

"Yes, meanwhile," Beth said dryly.

"This family," Lee said. "They're so . . . so rambunctious. Always getting into trouble. It's so tacky, sometimes I think I can't bear it."

"I know, Mom."

"But then I think, Matt is a good man. He takes care of me. He adopted you. He loves everyone in the family so much. He really does." She sighed and put her glasses back on. "He does his best."

"So you're not leaving him this time, either," Beth said.

"No, I suppose not. I can't figure out whether I'm too weak to leave or too strong to leave, I really can't."

"Maybe it doesn't matter."

"Maybe it doesn't at that."

They sat in companionable silence. Beth saw a tiny bird hop from branch to branch in a bare aspen tree by the deck. It sang, over and over, the same notes: chick-a-dee-dee-dee! Overhead the sky was as blue as a painting, and two hawks circled lazily, looking for some small animal to come out into the warmth of the day. A perfect day.

But Beth's thoughts were far from idyllic. She'd never say it, but she knew that her mother was a helpless and ineffectual human being. Lee would never leave Matt. Her first divorce had been her husband's doing, and it had totally devastated Lee. Then there was her drinking and denial of her own complicity in her dysfunctional marriage, the screwed-up children that had resulted from that marriage, the inability of even one Connelly to live a normal life. It occurred to Beth to wonder if she'd end up like her mother, buying into a giant lie, never really knowing what life might hold outside of the family.

Sometimes she knew what she should do: just leave. She'd done it back in college. She'd been destined for Bryn Mawr or Radcliffe or Vassar, but instead she'd stuck to her guns and gone to the University of Arizona in Tucson, an easygoing school that disdained East Coast rigidity. She'd done well and she'd loved it. Then she'd stayed away from the clan, bumming around Europe and the Mideast, sucking up experiences like a sponge. She'd loved that, too, the traveling, the new cultures, the food, languages and scenery.

Then she'd ended up in Morocco and been recruited by Children's International. Life had taken on meaning. Yes, it had been a good time.

"I think I'll go back to Washington with Matt next week," Lee was saying, stretching out on the lounge, her face to the sun.

"You may as well," Beth murmured.

"Yes, I suppose."

The family. An insidious, grasping entity that demanded utter loyalty and allowed no questions. And Beth had never been one to stop asking questions. Neither had she been able to stay away from the clan, because every time she returned to visit, she found herself following the same old patterns, saying the same old things. She sometimes felt as if she were on a merry-go-round, one moment up, the next down, all of it out of her control, and the machine went around and around, never stopping, yet somehow seductive.

"How long are you staying this time?" Lee was asking.

"Oh, I don't know. I feel like a yo-yo, Mom. Maybe I'll hang around a few days."

Lee looked at her daughter, her fingers playing with the end of her silk scarf. "A terrible thing happened to me the other day, Beth."

"What was it?"

"I wasn't going to tell anyone, but I have to . . . unburden myself."

Beth braced herself.

"I met that girl's mother the other day. By accident."

"What girl?"

"You know, that girl that . . . died."

"Heather Kelly? You met her mother?"

"It was horrible. She heard my name and . . . oh, I can hardly bear to talk about it." She held a hand to her brow. "She got hysterical, accused me . . . us . . . of lying. She . . . well, it was too ugly."

"Oh, Mom, it must have been awful."

Her hand still on her forehead, Lee went on. "You know, Beth, I don't often make judgments. I feel it's not my place. Others are better suited for decision making. But I think . . ." She drew in a quavering breath. "I think that maybe Terry . . ."

"Mom . . ."

"I would never tell anyone else. I don't know, really. I have no proof, of course, but I just . . ."

Beth got up from her own lounge and walked to the railing, nervously picking at a sliver of wood. She badly wanted to confess to Lee what she'd seen that night, but she'd disclosed it once and look what had happened. Even Ellen . . .

"I'm sick to death of worrying about Terry," she said. "I don't even like him."

"He's your brother, Beth."

"No, he's not."

"You wouldn't . . ." Lee said nervously, "you wouldn't tell anyone . . . ?"

They stared away from each other, eschewing guilt, denying the lies, in collusion to deceive the rest of the world.

"You're a good girl," Lee finally said, and the bitter irony of it made laughter well up in Beth's throat. She thought of telling her mother then about her own encounter with Nancy Kelly—the telephone call—but Lee was already so distressed. And then the doorbell sounded and the moment was lost.

The bell sounded again. "Do you want me to get it?" Beth asked, but Lee was already on her feet, complaining about the new maid and—where was Matt?

Alone on the sun-drenched deck, Beth continued to stare out across the blindingly white fields of snow, wondering why she'd ended up back in Aspen when she'd sworn she'd never set foot in the place again.

"It's that sheriff," came Lee's voice from behind her. "He's here to see Matt. I just don't know why they can't leave us alone."

Beth straightened. "The sheriff? What does he want with Matt?"

"I can't imagine. I stay out of it whenever I can."

Beth went and stood by the still-open sliding glass doors.

"Beth, honey," her mother began.

"Shh," Beth said.

"But, really, you can't—"

"Mom, please."

She heard most of it, standing there, listening, an absurd caricature of a spy.

"I don't know what you're talking about," Matt was saying.

"For thirty years the Forest Service has issued us an access permit," Case began, "and you—"

"That's federal land, buster," Matt interrupted.

"And you put one goddamn word in and it's turned down. You can't do that!"

"I just did," Matt said.

"Beth," Lee said behind her. "Let's go. Into my room. Beth . . ."

She hardly heard her mother. She stood frozen where she was, listening. A Forest Service permit . . . federal land . . . Oh, God, Matt . . .

"Hey, you redneck jerk, you're the one who started meddling in my family's life," Matt said.

"I'm doing my job."

"So am I, Sheriff. So am I."

There was a taut silence, then the thump of boot heels across the flagstone floor, the opening of the front door and a loud slam that made Lee emit a muffled exclamation.

Beth's heart pounded with a sick anger. Behind her she heard her mother. "Beth, please, let it go. It's not worth it, Beth." But she kept on going, right into the living room, where Matt looked up at her, surprised, a brandy snifter in one hand, a fat cigar in the other.

"Beth?" he said. "I didn't know you were—"

She slashed across his words. "What have you done now?"

"What the hell?"

"You did something to the McCandlesses. What was it?"

"Hey, just a minute. That was business, Beth."

"Business! You deliberately used your influence to hurt decent people, and you think that's business! My God," Beth said. "Their entire livelihood depends on that permit!"

"Hey, what is this crap, kid? And what the hell do you know about their livelihood?" He drew his thick brows together.

But Beth ignored his question. "What did you do? Pull some strings?"

"Oh, come on, it's nothing. A little pressure. Jesus, you'd think I bought an election."

"Pressure. You think Case McCandless is going to give in to that?"

Matt shrugged. "Can't hurt, and it's worth a try."

"Oh, my God." She was trembling with anger and shame for her family, and the awful feeling that she couldn't forget this, couldn't run away from it. "You haven't got an ounce of integrity," she breathed. "You're rotten. You don't even—"

"Integrity? Jesus, what in hell did integrity ever accomplish?" Matt yelled, finally stung.

After that, Beth didn't care about anything. It gave her a kind of free-flying sensation, not to care. So she didn't even bother calling a cab—she took the Porsche. And she drove like a maniac, too, racing toward town, taking the corners dangerously fast. She was going to go straight to Case and tell him the truth about Terry and

Heather and what she'd seen that night. Because if nothing mattered anymore, then it didn't make any difference if she told him.

She felt drunk, although she hadn't had a thing, but there was an odd distance between herself and the world, a numbness that set her apart from everything. She shifted gears, her feet worked the pedals, her eyes judged distances, but none of it was real.

Case was real, though, and she'd tell him, yes, she'd go to him and tell him....

It occurred to her as she passed the street his house was on that he'd be at work, so she drove straight there, slamming on the brakes in front of the courthouse, leaving the Porsche parked illegally.

Her heart still beat in sickening lurches and her mouth was dry. But it didn't matter. She pounded down the stairs to the department, the words piling up in her throat.

He wasn't there.

"Gosh, Case went to Redstone, won't be back till late. It's sixty miles one way and—"

"When? When will he be back?"

"Oh, late. But he'll probably go straight home. I won't see him again. Do you want to leave a message?" the dispatcher asked.

A message. Beth shook her head. "No, no message."

"He'll be in tomorrow," the woman offered helpfully.

She went to the Tippler Bar after that. She couldn't go home. Matt would be there. And Lee. She walked right into the crowded bar, filled with skiers relaxing after a day on the slopes, and singles on the prowl. The vibes were powerful: alcohol, sex, tossing hair, sleek-fitting suits, suntanned skin and knowing looks.

There was noise and music and anonymity. Beth ordered a glass of wine, sat at the bar and drank it down, ordered another. There was something important she'd been going to do, but now that was all over. Fate had thwarted her.

"Well, hello, babe," someone said behind her. "How you doing?"

It was Billy Jorgenson. More tanned than ever, gorgeous, smiling like the Cheshire cat. Lovely.

"Billy," she said with a husky catch in her voice. "Billy, I've had the most awful day."

"Poor thing. Tell me what I can do to cheer you up," he said, his hand on her shoulder.

"Do I have to tell you?"

Billy grinned.

They drank, they danced. There were friends of Billy's who kept coming by, introducing themselves, all tan and fit and full of compliments. None of it mattered, but it filled the time and it was fun.

It had somehow gotten dark outside, and they weren't in the Tippler anymore. Billy had decided they had to go to Shooter's, his favorite place. "The Blues in Black and White" was playing in the background, and Billy was on a bar stool, facing her, his hands on her knees, his turquoise-blue eyes resting on her soulfully.

"Why'd you dump me like that back in January?" he asked.

"Oh, I don't know. Things."

"Damn, babe, it really messed me up. I lost a whole week of private lessons."

"Hey, I'm sorry."

"Okay, just never do it again."

Beth crossed herself mock soberly. "Cross my heart and hope to die."

They danced some more, and Billy ordered food, which Beth didn't touch. And beer, which she did touch. It got later, and Beth knew she was drunk, but she didn't care. At least everything didn't seem so awful and far-away, and there was always Billy. . . .

"Let's go to my place," he said after a while. "Listen, I gotta get some shut-eye, babe, I got lessons tomorrow."

So they left Shooter's, and all the way to Beth's car she held on to his arm, staggering a little, giggling, the people in the streets a colorful blur. Billy drove the car to his condo, stopped and came around to let her out. She reached up, put her arms around his neck, laughing, nuzzling him, and he pulled her upright. "Hey, take it easy there," Billy said, laughing, as she teetered, off-balance.

An arm around her waist, he steered her to his door. Inside there were the same dirty dishes and bicycles and skis. Beth half fell onto his couch, while Billy went into his bedroom to listen to the messages on his machine. She heard the voices, all women's, the messages, in a foggy haze. Déjà vu. Quietly, she got up, walked to his door and let herself out. It didn't really matter anyway. It wasn't Billy she wanted.

The red Porsche gleamed like fire under a streetlight. Pretty car, Beth thought, walking toward it with exaggerated care, lifting each foot too high. She could drive, sure she could. Carefully. Nice and slow.

She got in, put the keys in the ignition, brought the engine to life. Sure, why not? Only. . . where was she going? Home? God, no, not home. Downtown to party.

But there was somewhere she needed to go. A flicker of unpleasantness ran through her brain. Case. Oh, yes,

Case. Matt and Case. Only Case hadn't been there, damn him, and then . . .

She revved the engine and took off too fast, jerking through the gears. Parked in a No Parking zone, and walked into a liquor store.

"Champagne," she said. "A nice big bottle of champagne."

"Lady, you got proof?" the clerk asked.

"Of course I do," she said haughtily, and showed him her Children's International ID.

"Glasses," she said. "Two glasses."

She left the store with two plastic wineglasses and a bottle of Veuve Cliquot. Back to the Porsche, driving very, very carefully, shutting her eyes then opening them to get the road into focus, squinting in the glare of other headlights. She drove straight to the house, pulled up in front and shut the engine off. The house was dark.

She got out and cradled the glasses and bottle in her arm, walked up to the front door. She raised her hand to knock and almost dropped the bottle. "Oops," she said, then giggled, transferring the bottle to the other hand, the glasses in her coat pocket.

She knocked at the door. There was no answer. She knocked again, louder. Nothing. A minute went by. She banged with her fist. "Case," she yelled, "wake up!" He wasn't going to evade her so easily this time.

She raised her hand again to pound on the door and thumped the flat of her hand on the hard wood, getting mad.

The door opened abruptly, almost causing her to pitch forward onto her face.

"What the . . . ?" a sleepy voice said. A light switched on inside.

"Case," she said with a degree of satisfaction. "It's about time."

"Who?"

"It's me. I'm here."

"Beth?"

"That's right."

"Jesus." He ran his hand through his hair.

"Well, aren't you going to ask me in? Some gentleman you are."

"Uh . . . Beth, do you know what time it is?"

"Late."

"Yeah, it's late."

"I'm coming in anyway." She pushed past him, setting the glasses and bottle on a table. She turned to face him and smiled broadly. "I brought you a present."

"So I see." He stood there, arms folded across his naked chest, wearing only pajama bottoms, his feet bare. "You're drunk."

"You're so clever," she said. "But I came for a reason. I have a good reason."

"You'd better tell me in the morning," he said.

"No, can't wait. I know what Matt did. See, I heard this afternoon."

He frowned.

"So I'm apologizing. For Matt. For the Connellys."

"Beth, you don't have to do that. Now, look, why don't you . . . ?"

But she was working at uncorking the champagne, and it opened with a pop and fizzed over. "Oops." She giggled.

"Shh, the kids," he said.

Exaggerating, she held a finger to her lips. "Shh. Don't wake up the kids."

"God, Beth."

"What?" she asked. "You're disapproving of me again, aren't you?"

"I'm making some coffee is what I'm doing. You need sobering up."

"I don't want to sober up. It's no fun," she said. "Come on, Case, have some bubbly with me."

But he turned his bare back, padding into the kitchen and filling the coffee machine. It was a nice back, though, smooth and golden and . . .

"Here," he said, thrusting a cup at her. "Drink it."

Three cups later Beth was sitting at the kitchen table across from him and feeling ill. "I can't drink coffee anymore," she said.

"You want to go home now?"

She shuddered. "No."

"What's going on?" he asked.

"I told you. Matt and the Forest Service thing. I remember you telling me about the backcountry trips. I'm so embarrassed that Matt's putting the screws to you. Damn him."

"I'll take care of Matt Connelly," he said.

It occurred to her then that there was another thing she'd been going to do—tell Case about Terry, the whole horrible truth.

"Case?" she began, and she licked dry lips.

"Go on."

"Ah," she said, but somehow the words got all clogged in her throat.

"Well?"

"Ah, it's nothing, really," and she gave him a bright smile.

"Uh-huh. So you get drunk and come here in the middle of the night?"

"Dumb," she mumbled. "I feel sick."

"Not again. Do you want . . . ?"

"Just let me lie down for a while, okay?"

He helped her to the couch, and she half fell onto it.

"Thanks," she whispered, and she closed her eyes. "God, I'm dizzy."

Case went to a closet for a spare blanket, and when he returned she was already asleep. He stood there for a moment, looking down at her. She was awfully pretty, even passed out—her skin so smooth and white, strands of fine black hair lying on her cheek. She wore a long black sweater with a wide leather belt around her waist and black jeans. She was slight and small boned, perfectly formed, with the elegance of good breeding. She had problems, though, this pretty lady. Big problems.

He laid the blanket over her carefully and sat down in the old stuffed chair next to her. Now, what was he going to do about this fey creature who'd passed out on his couch?

He watched her for a while, saw that her chest rose and fell steadily. She'd be okay in the morning, he thought. Jesus, coming to his house in the middle of the night! He didn't know whether to be insulted or flattered. He knew one thing, though. He felt protective of this girl, and that was a real big mistake. Case laid his head on the back of the chair and closed his eyes for a minute, trying to figure out what to do with her.

Beth was having the nightmare again. The cone of light, the red satin quilt, the three men. Their hands were on her, undressing her, and she was helpless. She tried with a mighty, wrenching effort to get away, and she cried out and woke up with a jerk. Eyes wide, she stared around, horribly disoriented. She was in a strange place, on a lumpy couch, her head spinning, and Case Mc-

Candless was sitting in a chair, half-asleep, staring at her. Then she remembered.

"You okay?" he asked, running a hand over his face.

She shook her head, unable to talk. Tears burned in her eyes. Oh God, what a fool she was. "I'm sorry," she said. "I shouldn't have come here."

"Look, it's okay, but . . ."

"I'll go now."

"No, you're in no shape to go anywhere, Beth."

"I'm fine, I'm okay."

"The hell you are."

"Why do we always argue?" she asked, getting up shakily, the blanket falling to the floor. A blanket . . . he must have gotten it for her.

"I don't know."

"I'm going."

"Look," he said, rising, and there was an odd tone in his voice. "Why did you . . . run that morning?"

She bit her lip.

"All the way to New York. Why?"

"I . . . I didn't think I'd, ah, like you so much," she got out.

"Really," he said, his face cast in half-light from the kitchen, his eyes on her, as if he were deciding something. And then he said, "Stay."

Beth felt her body go still all over, but her heart pounded in a slow, heavy cadence. "You don't really want me to stay, Case."

"Don't tell me what I want."

They stood there looking at each other. Then he took a step toward her, and she was in his arms, fitting as if she'd always belonged there, melting against him, her face in the hollow of his neck. He smelled fresh and sweet, his flesh like warm satin.

"Beth."

She turned her face up, searched his eyes wordlessly, and his mouth came down over hers, banishing all thought. His lips were gentle, and they felt so familiar, so good. She put her arms around his neck, sliding her hands across his bare skin.

They broke apart, staring at each other in a kind of wary fascination.

"Are you sure about this?" he asked.

"No, are you?"

He smiled wryly, touching her face with gentle fingers, until she put a hand over his, closed her eyes and leaned toward him.

"This is crazy," she breathed.

"Yeah."

They kissed, savoring each other's taste. She couldn't get close enough, and she pressed herself against him. His hands were under her sweater, on her hot skin, and in her belly a sweet ache kindled. A warning flashed in Beth's mind. It would be no good; he'd be disappointed, puzzled, disgusted. But the feel of Case's hands on her was heaven, and she pushed the thought away. She'd faked it before.

"Wait," she said breathlessly, unbuckling her belt, pulling her sweater over her head. His glance swept over her, hot and desirous, crackling the air between them. She felt a heaviness in her limbs.

"Damn it," Case said then. "Not here. The kids."

Together they went up the stairs to his bedroom, his bed rumpled, the sheets fragrant with his scent. Her pants fell to the floor, his pajamas. A long quavering breath came from Case. He buried his face between her small breasts. "Oh, Jesus, Beth . . ."

Making love to Case was like being engulfed in a big warm blanket. She didn't have to do anything, because Case took care of it all with such ease. She couldn't hold back anything; he demanded of her body the same absolute honesty he demanded of himself. She wasn't self-conscious or hesitant. She knew his body as if she'd been with him for years, not minutes.

There was too much heat at first; they came together with a clash that allowed no tenderness, all passion and murmurs and his body driving into hers as if he'd waited a long, long time to do this thing.

He shuddered into her, too soon, and Beth felt the letdown, the shame. God, she'd ruined even this beautiful thing between them.

"I'm sorry," Case said into her ear. "It's been...a while."

He...apologizing to her? Beth's mind spun. "It's okay," she said wonderingly.

"It's not okay," He kissed her, long and sweet. "I want you to have it, too."

"Case..."

He quieted her with his lips and began once again, only slower this time. His hands, his mouth and then the slow stirring in his loins. She felt herself relax utterly, going all warm and silky inside, turning to liquid all over as if he'd given her a narcotic. He kissed her hand, finger by finger, her earlobes and her nipples. The warmth grew in her, an orb in her middle. Her breath came fast, her body writhed as his hands found her secrets, found them and made them his.

She moaned, uncontrolled now, but he still went slowly, touching and teasing, his fingers burning on her flesh. Then he was inside her again, hard and powerful, agonizingly slow. Whispering in her ear. She trembled to her soul, filled with him, and the orb grew inside her, hot and hard and aching. Grew and grew, and he plunged into her and the orb exploded, her body bucking, cries of surprise and passion in her throat, and still he pressed into her, opening her more and more, her body convulsing with the strength of it.

She was limp with wonder afterward, and tears squeezed from between her eyelids, tears of joy. He breathed heavily, lying on her, then his heart and his breath slowed and he rose on an elbow and bent to kiss her once more.

"Better?" he asked.

"The best," she managed.

They lay together for a time, his leg over hers, the fingers of his free hand entwined in hers.

"I have to tell you something," she said after a while.

"You don't have to tell me anything."

"I want to." She hid her face in his shoulder, embarrassed. "That was the first time I ever . . ."

He was silent. She felt the beat of his heart and smelled the scent of his skin.

"Case?"

"I'm just a little surprised," he said carefully.

"I know." She drew her fingers through his thick golden hair. "You're a very special man."

"You're a very special lady."

She ran her fingers down his cheek and neck, trailed them across his chest. His skin shivered under her touch.

"Go to sleep, Beth," he said.

"Hold me," she murmured, closing her eyes. "Hold me, Case."

FIFTEEN

If Ellen Connelly had believed in biorhythms, she would have said that Manuel's were completely out of kilter that morning. He lay on top of her, his hips grinding against hers, his beautiful dark face twisted in pain as he tried to reach his climax.

"It's all right," she whispered soothingly, her own pleasure come and gone.

He made a throaty sound of frustration and pressed into her more fiercely, trying, trying so hard.

"Manuel," she whispered again, "it's all right, my love, your mind's elsewhere."

Abruptly he withdrew himself and rolled off her, their slick bodies parting. He flung an arm over his eyes. "Never has this happened to me," he said harshly.

"I think it happens to all men," she said, "eventually. You can't be perfect all the time. No one can, love. You're just worried about that canvas."

"Don't patronize me, Elena," he said, and suddenly he was atop her again, and she opened to him as his hand kneaded her breast and his mouth took hers in a hard kiss.

He did finally reach his climax, but he was spent, panting and drenched and angry. Ellen lay there naked and sore and said nothing. It was because of his temperament, the great passion with which he tackled everything in life; nothing short of absolute perfection would do.

But then, that was why she loved him so desperately.

Ellen showered first, her mood a little dark. She knew that her lover's frustration lay deeper than his failure to perform with perfection in bed. He was troubled about his painting, the demands being placed upon him to produce at a speed much greater than he was used to. Only last night he'd spoken of the price of success being perhaps too great, but she'd eased his worries by telling him that all artists suffered doubts from time to time.

"My work is not good," he'd said. "I painted with more passion before all this success."

"No, you didn't," Ellen had assured him. "You're doing the finest work you've ever done. Trust me."

"Trust me," he'd repeated, shaking his head.

At breakfast that morning she again broached the touchy subject. "Why not take the day off?" she said. "You deserve a rest, Manuel. You've been working too hard lately."

"I need inspiration," he shot back, "not a rest."

It was best to let it go. And, Ellen knew, he'd finish his canvas and in a few days they'd celebrate and all his frustration would be forgotten.

She left for the gallery quietly, going out to warm her car without a word, having merely squeezed his hand to let him know she understood. But as she sat in the car he appeared, his shirt unbuttoned in the cold morning air, his feet bare.

"You'll catch your death," Ellen said, laughing at him as she rolled down the window.

"Forget that," he said, leaning over and kissing her. "I'm a fool, Elena. How can you bear me?"

"Because I love you."

"Then I will think only of that as I paint today."

She laughed again. "If you can paint with pneumonia."

Ellen unlocked the gallery and turned on the office lights, ready to tackle the tedious book work. Her mind was elsewhere, though, still back at the house with Manuel. She worried so much about him, too much, and she couldn't imagine how women with children managed. Didn't they go out of their minds, always wondering, worrying, desperate to ensure their loved ones' happiness? It was such a burden.

She was still pondering that when a knock at the front door made her frown more deeply. What now? she thought in irritation. The gallery didn't even open for another hour. But it was only Beth standing outside, hugging herself in the cold morning air.

Ellen unlocked the door. "Well, good morning," she said. "Isn't this awfully early for you?"

Her stepsister smiled sheepishly. "I don't really have a clue what time it is. If I'm bothering you . . ."

"No, certainly not, come on in," Ellen said, noting that Beth's clothes were rumpled, as if she'd slept in them.

Beth saw her perusal. "That bad?"

"Well . . ."

"I haven't been home."

"I never would have guessed," Ellen remarked dryly. "So what's this all about?"

"Lots," Beth said in an odd tone.

"Well, let's go sit down and you can tell me. I'll make some coffee."

"Ugh, no thanks," Beth said. "Got any tea?"

Ellen's office was small and cozy and crowded; bright art posters overlapped on the walls. She sat in her desk chair, and Beth sat in the clients' chair, and they looked at each other while the water heated.

"How's Manuel?" Beth asked.

"That's not what you came to talk about."

"No." She pulled up her legs and crossed them Indian fashion in the big chair, just as she'd done as a kid. "God, I'm not sure what happened."

"Then why not just start at the beginning."

"Well, yesterday Case McCandless was at the house. He and Dad had a fight. It seems that Dad, in his own inimitable fashion, pulled some dirty deal so that the McCandlesses Forest Service use permit has been turned down."

"Typical," Ellen said.

"Yes, nice stuff. And you know why, of course?"

"Terry."

"Right again."

Ellen busied herself with hot water and tea bags, her back turned. She wasn't sure she was going to like Beth's story. In fact, she knew she wasn't.

"Okay, so Case left in a fit, and I took up the fight with Dad."

"Beth, for God's sake—"

"Well, things went downhill from there. I left, I had a few drinks." She ducked her head, looking a lot like the skinny kid she'd been all those years ago. "And then I got this bright idea to go over to Case's house to apologize. Only I was loaded and I woke him up."

"Lovely."

"I know, I know, one of my classier stunts. Anyway, he fed me coffee and I passed out for a while and..." She looked up at Ellen, and her eyes were shining like dark lanterns. "When I woke up we, well, somehow we made love and, God, Ellen, I'm scared stiff."

"Consorting with the enemy?" Ellen asked, handing her a mug of tea, sitting back down.

Beth took a deep breath. "I've never felt this way with a man, about a man. He's..."

"Spare me," Ellen said.

"No, really." Beth's voice pleaded for understanding. "I don't know... For God's sake, I'm—" her voice lowered "—I really like him."

"Oh, Beth, you can't be falling in love with a redneck, small-town sheriff!"

"Ellen, that's why I'm scared!"

"Hey, he's a handsome guy, and then there's that uniform. I don't blame you for taking advantage."

"No, it wasn't like that. It was..."

Ellen got up and went to her younger stepsister. She leaned down and hugged her, then, with her hands on Beth's shoulders, she gave her the best advice she could think of. "Honey, you're lonely, he's a handsome man. Fine. It's natural, but you can't be serious about him. He hasn't got any money. He's got two little kids. Not only that, but he's trying to put your brother in jail!"

Beth's eyes flew to Ellen's. "Oh, no, that has nothing to do with it. He'd never bring that up, he'd never—"

"Don't be too sure. He's got a job to do, and I bet he wants to nail Terry badly enough to use some... unorthodox methods."

"No, Ellen." Beth shook her head. "He's not like that. He's the most honest human being I've ever known."

"Wow, has he got you snowed."

"God, Ellen, nobody says 'snowed' anymore. And it's not true. I went to his house, remember? He never would have . . . come on to me. I'm not his type."

"No, you're not," Ellen said emphatically.

"But, we were, oh, Ellen, we were good together. He was so perfect."

"I may just be ill."

Beth smiled then. "Sickening, aren't I? But it's new to me, the first time in my life. Oh, Ellen, you can understand, can't you? It's like you and Manuel. You're different, but you're together. You love each other."

"Manuel and I are hardly comparable to a one-night stand you had with Case McCandless," Ellen said imperiously.

"But it might work. It might."

"You be careful. He could be using you," Ellen said.

"No, not Case. I know that." Beth sipped at her tea, her face suffused with a glow of color, that smug aftermath of passion. "But what are we going to do about that Forest Service permit thing?"

"Do? We can't do a thing. What's there to do?" Ellen asked, surprised.

"I don't know. Something. It's not right. It's got to be illegal. Can't we go to a lawyer or something and . . . ?"

Ellen cut her off. "I refuse to discuss it. That's Dad's business. I don't blame him, frankly. He'll use every bit of influence he has to help Terry, and he's right to do it."

"Ellen."

"I mean that, Beth. Terry's our brother. This is our family we're talking about. If you were in trouble, Dad would pull every string he could to help you, and you know it."

Beth regarded her with pain. "It's not right. Innocent people are being hurt. You can't—"

"There are no innocent people, Beth."

"I don't believe you're saying these things."

"Look, this isn't some passing tabloid scandal, Beth. There're times, no matter what, that we have to put aside our reservations and do what's best for the family."

"You always went your own way," Beth pointed out. "I'm really surprised—"

"I *do* go my own way. But this is different. This is Terry's life we're discussing."

Beth put down her mug, shaking her head thoughtfully.

"Don't be mad at me. I'm only telling you the truth."

"Your truth, Ellen." She unfolded her legs and stood. "I'll see you," she said vaguely. "Thanks for listening."

"Anytime. Hey, don't forget tonight. Dad's birthday."

"Right." She walked away, waving her hand a little, her head down so that her hair hid her face, and that was the last time Ellen ever really talked to her stepsister.

That was the morning. The afternoon held its own knotty relationship problems. Right after lunch Manuel called; he was coming apart at the seams.

"Ellen, get over here," he ordered.

"What is it, Manuel?" she asked, but she was afraid she already knew.

"I am having trouble with this painting. It doesn't work. I can't do it!" His voice was as petulant as a child's.

"I can't come right now. Why don't you just leave it, darling, and I'll take a look when I get home."

"I can't do that, you know I can't. I'm going crazy with this thing. I tell you, I need help!"

"Oh Lord, Manuel..."

"Please," he wheedled, trying a new tack, "Elena, I can't do it without you."

Ellen sighed. "I'll be there as soon as I can."

Manuel's studio was in an upstairs room of Ellen's house, where she'd had skylights installed when he'd moved in. It was an austere place, no carpet, bare walls, no radio or telephone, only easels and paint and turpentine and brushes and rags. And canvases. In her mind's eye she could see Manuel in his usual painting garb—a paint-stained blue work shirt, old jeans and tennis shoes.

Ellen had been steeling herself all the way home. This morning she could have predicted this and she felt torn: on the one hand she couldn't abide Manuel's clinging, but on the other, she secretly craved his dependency.

Poking her head in the studio, Ellen put on a brave smile. "Here I am."

"Come here," he ordered, scowling. "Look at this. Look!"

She approached. The canvas he was working on was of an adobe house against a background of dry mesas. It was half-done, the background only sketched in. "I think it's very good," she said carefully.

"It stinks! It reeks! Nothing is right!"

"Almost everything is right. Maybe...maybe the perspective is off a little. That corner of the house..." She pointed.

"That's not it!" Manuel whirled on her. "Help me! Why can't I do anything right!"

"Listen, Manuel, calm down and really look. Fix the perspective and the shadows. See, there. Make them extend farther. Is it morning? Where's the sun? See, if you did it, there, like that, with burnt umber."

He turned back to the painting. "No, no, no!" he shouted.

"Yes, Manuel, look," she insisted, knowing him so well, his outbursts, his panics, the pattern of his rages. "Stop yelling and look."

"I can't, it's hideous." But he was quieter now, moving from anger to apathy. Then it would be up to Ellen to spark his interest, to light his flame once again.

"No, my darling, nothing of yours is hideous. You just need a critical eye sometimes. It's so hard, I know, to judge your own work. You need someone who's objective."

He was shaking his head sadly. "Useless, futile."

"No, Manuel, look at it. Change the corner. Fix the shadows—the vigas, you see, they need defining, and the roof, it's not in shadow yet. You can do it."

"I can't," he muttered, but he was looking at the canvas.

"You can—you've done it before. You know you can."

Manuel sighed, and then Ellen knew it would be all right.

He worked feverishly for an hour while Ellen read some art magazines downstairs. She was afraid to leave until he'd done what he needed to. She couldn't watch him because he got nervous, so she waited, calling Megan at the gallery to tell her she was tied up. As she leafed through *Southwest Art*, Ellen wondered if she enjoyed being a martyr.

He came downstairs finally, smiling.

"Is it all right?" she asked.

"Very much better. I can work on it tomorrow. Thank you, my love, I couldn't have seen that corner, not in a thousand years. You have an eye," he said fervently. "And I love you."

"For my eye?" she dared to tease.

"For that...and other things." He held his paint-stained hands out. "Come here, Elena."

She rose and went to him. He took her in his arms, and she could smell paint and turpentine, so familiar to her now.

"I couldn't do it without you, you know that," he said into her ear. "I am hard on you. Forgive me, my love."

"You're hard on yourself."

"Yes, but that's my destiny."

She nestled closer against his chest. "Your problems are my problems, Manuel. I always want to help you."

He kissed her, his unshaved face scratchy, his lips warm and sweet as honey, his hands kneading her back. Her bones melted in her skin, and she could have cried with relief and adoration. He drew back, a half smile on his mouth. "Return to work, now. I'm fine. You give me new life, over and over."

"You'll be all right?"

"Absolutely."

"Oh, Manuel, don't forget. Tonight is Dad's party at Piñons. It's his sixty-first birthday. Lee made me promise to go. You, too."

"*La familia*. Yes, yes, I know. We'll go, my love."

"I know, I hate it. There'll probably be some awful scene—or a row. But we'll leave early." She got up her nerve to suggest something. "And, you know, I think I won't have a drop to drink. And you shouldn't, either. I don't want us to buy into their terrible behavior."

"I agree. Nothing to drink. A pact, my love." And he drew her close and kissed her again, long and lingeringly until a hot ball of passion burned in her belly.

* * *

Matthew Connelly's birthdays were always grand affairs. He never let one pass without a celebration, and he loved his family to be gathered around him. He demanded presents and a cake and candles, the more the better, and there had to be a big dinner. For his party in Aspen he chose Piñons, a very expensive, very tasteful, very excellent restaurant done in the kind of Southwest style that would have impressed even Dale Willey's jaded eye. Pastels, desert motifs, a menu of the most delectable dishes: game from the open range, home-baked bread, seafood such as ahi sautéed in crushed macadamia nuts. During the ski season reservations were needed weeks in advance.

Of Matt's family, only Lee, Beth, Ellen and Manuel were in town. But there were two other couples invited, a former vice president and his wife, and a local writer and his mistress *du jour*.

Ellen had chosen to wear an oatmeal cashmere turtleneck and matching leggings, one of her understated Aspen outfits, played up with Indian-style dangling earrings in coral and turquoise and gold. Manuel was terribly handsome in a plain blue shirt with no tie and a tweed sport coat that she'd bought him at Ralph Lauren's Polo Shop in Aspen.

When they arrived, Matt was already in an expansive mood, having been drinking in the bar for nearly an hour. Lee was halfway comatose, and the others were feeling no pain.

"Ah, there they are!" Matt bellowed. "My gorgeous daughter and her great spick artist!"

Ellen and Manuel looked at each other. She laughed it off, but Manuel frowned. When he was sober he despised scenes. She knew that, and her inner alarm bell sounded. Introductions were made. Ellen knew the writer's girlfriend, so they made small talk. The former vice president, a good-looking nonentity, and his shrewd wife were pleasant enough, Ellen supposed, even though they were Republicans. *Just don't get into politics*, she thought.

"Where the hell's Beth?" Matt was asking. "Ellen, you know? Damn that kid, she's such an airhead. You think she forgot?"

"I saw her this morning, Dad. She said she'd be here."

He subsided, grumbling, and ordered another round of drinks. An obsequious maître d' came by to say the table would be ready in five minutes. "Great, great," Matt said, slapping a hundred-dollar bill in the man's palm. "I hope it's a nice big table, lots of room," he said meaningfully.

"Oh, it is, Senator. Our best."

Beth still wasn't there by the time they were seated. Matt was pretending not to notice, but he was angry. Ellen knew that look. Menus were passed around and people began talking about this dish or that, and the waiter intoned the specials of the evening.

Still no Beth.

Manuel was talking easily to the former vice president's wife. He'd ordered soda water. Ellen let herself relax, read the menu and decided she'd have the free-range chicken Rochambeau.

Beth arrived then, very late, a predatory gleam in her eye that Ellen recognized. She looked very stylish in a dark sweater tucked into a wraparound, calf-length suede skirt with diagonal fringe running up the front. She might have had a couple of drinks to fortify herself for the evening's events, because she didn't remotely resemble the girl who'd sat cross-legged in Ellen's office and spoken about things that mattered to her. No, she looked like a blasé swinging single out for an evening of fun and games—and maybe a little danger thrown in to spice things up.

"Hello, everybody," Beth said. "Sorry I'm late, sorry, sorry. Happy birthday, Dad."

"It's about time," Matt grumbled. "What happened to you?"

"The crosstown traffic was hell," she threw out insouciantly.

Everybody laughed.

Dinner progressed quite smoothly. Lee roused herself to be charming, as she'd been trained. Beth sat next to Matt and spoke mostly to the writer, whose books she appeared to have read. The food was marvelous. Two waiters were required to pour the wine that Matt kept ordering. No one talked politics.

The writer's girlfriend was very interested in redecorating her lover's house. She and Ellen set up a tentative appointment for her to look at some paintings. "Please, call me tomorrow, will you?" Ellen said. "I don't have my appointment book here, and I'll forget . . ."

"You bastard," came a voice, not very loud, but very clear.

Ellen's eyes flicked up.

"Beth," Lee was saying. "You apologize right this instant."

But Beth ignored her mother. "You won't do anything about it, then?" she was asking Matt, and it hit Ellen like a thunderbolt that Beth hadn't been drinking at all. She was high, all right, but with anger over that permit thing with the McCandlesses.

"Christ, Beth, shut the hell up," Matt growled. "You're making a spectacle of yourself."

"Since when have you cared about that?"

Oh God, Beth was on a roll. Ellen sat there frozen, and all she could think was, *I should have known.*

"Ellen, stop her," Manuel said in her ear.

"I can't," Ellen whispered. "She won't listen. I can't do anything."

Manuel swore in Spanish under his breath, and Ellen saw him pour himself a glass of wine. Her heart lurched and she put her hand on his, her gaze pleading silently. Cold, flashing ebony eyes met hers. He shook her hand off and raised the glass to his lips. Oh God, Ellen thought helplessly.

Beth had risen and was standing over Matt. Everyone in the restaurant could see her. The writer was sitting back in his chair enjoying the scene, the former vice president's wife looked as if she wanted to cry.

"I can't handle you anymore," Beth was saying. "You're no good. You're a crook!"

"I'm warning you, Beth . . ." Matt said harshly.

"Oh, really? What're you going to do—ground me?"

"Beth, please," Lee bleated.

"Listen to me, Dad. I will not spend one more night under your roof. Ever. You hear me?" She looked around the packed restaurant, swinging her hair, arms akimbo. "Everyone hear that?"

By the time they got home Ellen was shaking and wrung out. Manuel had downed half a bottle of Matt's wine, then unceremoniously dragged Ellen home without a word. Once there he got out a bottle of tequila and upended it, legs splayed out as he reclined on the couch, brooding.

"Let's go to bed," Ellen tried. "Please, Manuel."

"You go. I can't sleep. Your family of *pendejos* disgusts me."

"I'm sorry. I'm so sorry. I had no idea. Manuel, never again, I swear. I'll never see them again."

"Sure, right. Your family and you'll never see them! What have I gotten myself into?"

"They don't matter to me. Only you matter, you know that. Come with me, please. Don't sit here and poison yourself."

"Leave me," he said, waving an arm.

"No, I won't. I love you. Come to bed," she cried.

He drank more from the bottle, then held it loosely, resting it on his stomach. His eyes were unfocused, the way they got when he was drunk. She knew that look, oh God, she knew it.

She tried again. "I'm sorry about tonight, but it'll never happen again, Manuel. You know I keep my promises." She went over to him and took the bottle from his flaccid hand. In one split second he turned from a morose drunk into a madman. He lunged for the bottle, knocking Ellen backward, so that she fell on her hands as she stretched them out behind her to catch herself. She felt a sudden searing pain in her left wrist and lay there trying to catch her breath, waves of nausea assailing her.

Then she became aware that Manuel was standing over her, weaving, legs spread, staring down at her.

"Please help me up," Ellen said icily. "I think you've broken my arm."

SIXTEEN

Dottie dried her hands on her apron and made a decision. If her son wasn't going to voluntarily tell her what was going on in his life, then she'd march herself into his office and wheedle it out of him. She'd bet her bottom dollar, though, that she already knew why he was so darn preoccupied these days.

Her morning chores done, she fired up the Suburban, grocery list in her pocket, and headed into town. Case might not be in the office, but she had till three or so to get back to the ranch and start preparing dinner. She'd sit herself down in front of his desk and wait.

As it turned out, Dottie didn't have to wait at all. She bumped straight into him on the street in front of the courthouse.

"Well, hello," Case said. "You have jury duty or something?"

She shook her head and clutched the straps of her worn leather purse. "No. Actually," she said, "I was heading down to your office."

"Something wrong?" He frowned. "You hear anything more from the Forest Service?"

"No, not yet. But I called Scott Nordin—you remember him, he's our representative in Congress—and anyway, he told me he'd get to the bottom of the permit being rejected."

"You think he has the clout to handle Matt Connelly?"

"Now that Connelly has played his hand? Sure, why not? If this gets out, Senator Connelly is going to look like a real ass."

"He is a real ass," Case muttered. "So, why the visit? Is there something else . . . ?"

"No, no, I just thought we could have a chat."

"A chat," Case said. "Uh-huh."

The Sheriff's Department was busy, uniformed officers milling around, the dispatcher trying to eat a sweet roll in between calls, a couple of lawyers carrying briefcases and pacing in the outer waiting room, checking their watches and looking annoyed.

Case opened the door to his office and stood aside for his mother to enter. "Have a seat," he said, "I'll get you a cup of coffee. Two sugars?"

"Ah, sure. Look," she said, "if you're too busy . . ."

"I've got a few minutes." He disappeared to get the coffee, and Dottie glanced around, eyeing the clutter on his desk and stacked on top of a filing cabinet in the corner. The computer behind his desk was on, gibberish scrolling down the screen. In a corner were two pairs of skis—as if Case ever had time to go skiing anymore. For a minute Dottie crawled with guilt, plumping herself down like this, ready to nag her son. But then she squelched the emotion. Other than his brothers and a few male friends with whom he hunted and fished, Case kept his life completely private. He needed an ear sometimes, a woman's ear. And as for any advice Dottie might offer, he could take it or leave it. He usually left it, anyway.

"Here we go," he said, kicking his door closed behind him, handing her a mug. He sat down, his wooden swivel chair creaking while he pushed a few files aside on the desktop.

"Well," Dottie said.

"Well," he repeated. "Let's hear it, Mom. And please don't start by making excuses and saying I'm not going to like it."

She bristled but shrugged it off. "I was wondering about Deirdre," she began. "Have you heard anything more about the custody suit?"

"That's not why you're here," he said. "But to answer your question, yes. My lawyer says he's going to require that Deirdre take a battery of psychological tests."

"Can he do that?"

Case shrugged. "Apparently, if the judge agrees."

"Case, Deirdre isn't crazy."

"No, she isn't, but she lacks a sense of responsibility, and the lawyer says it'll show up in the tests."

"What if it doesn't?" Dottie asked.

"Then we try something else," Case said.

"It's ugly."

"Yes. Scares the bejesus out of me."

"You do what you have to, Case. It's for the kids, those innocent babies."

"Yeah, I know that." He took a long drink of coffee, put the mug down and clasped his hands on top of the desk, pinning his mother with a direct stare not unlike her own. "Okay. Now let's hear it."

Dottie cleared her throat. "I suspect," she said, "that you've gotten involved with that Connelly woman."

"That's certainly not your business," he said tightly.

"I know that, Case."

He gave a humorless laugh. "You're a great one to talk to," he said. "You don't even like her."

"I don't know her. Why don't you tell me about her?"

"Why should I?"

"Because I care about you and the kids, and if you're upset, they will be, too." She took a breath and looked at her hands. "Case. Are you involved?"

He was silent for a long moment and then shook his head. "Up to my ears. Now, are you happy?"

"The girl's an accident waiting to happen," Dottie declared.

"She certainly is," he said glumly.

"Are you . . . in love?"

"Hell, no."

"Then do you think this situation is wise?"

"Wise?" he said bitterly. "What does that have to do with it?"

"Then . . ."

"I want to help her," he said. "I don't know how to deal with her, though. It's that family of hers. I just don't know."

"Look, Beth Connelly has to deal with her own problems. You can't do it for her."

"If she could just get away from them," he said. "But every time she does, she runs off to some disease-ridden country and gets sick as hell."

"What are you talking about?"

And he explained about Children's International, taking Dottie totally by surprise. Sure, she thought acerbically. With the size of her checkbook.

"I never thought she had that in her," Dottie reflected.

"Yeah, well, like you said, you don't know her at all. And she's never gonna know herself if she doesn't make a clean break from that clan."

It came to Dottie slowly, a way out for her son, for little Miss Connelly, a solution that she herself could live with. For only a second did guilt rise up and nip her, when she realized she was about to set the girl up and watch her fall flat on her face in front of her son. She was doing this for him, she told herself, for Case and her grandchildren.

She looked him in the eye. "Offer her a job at the ranch," Dottie said.

"What?"

"Tell her she can come and live in the maid's quarters. Room and board and pay. It's busy now, and you know I always take on extra help at the end of the season to get the cabins cleaned. It's honest work, and she won't get sick like you say she does with the children's organization. It's a way out for her."

"That's crazy," he said.

"Why? You said you wanted to help her. So help."

And then Case cocked his head. "Why are you doing this?"

"Does it matter?"

"Yes."

She shrugged.

"Come on," he said. "I know you've got an ulterior motive."

Dottie thought a moment. She rose to leave. "Let's just say I'm trying to give you two a chance to really know each other."

"Sure." He snorted. "And you're hoping that familiarity will breed contempt."

"Ask her, Case. The worst she can say is no."

"We'll see," he said as Dottie opened the door and closed it behind her.

Deirdre McCandless sat across from the lawyer with a fixed smile on her face, David next to her. They'd both dressed for the occasion—he in a respectable dark suit and she in a white silk blouse, gray skirt and navy wool blazer. She knew she looked good and tried to focus on that.

The lawyer, Ben Ritchie, was studying some papers, pulling on the loose skin under his ear. Finally he looked up and smiled. "Yes," he said.

"Yes...what?"

"Yes, you're going to win."

"Even if I voluntarily gave up custody when we were divorced?"

"Circumstances change, right? You're the mother. You're not a criminal or anything like that?"

"No, no," she said swiftly. "Not even a traffic ticket."

"No history of mental problems?"

"No." She didn't mention the months with a shrink after her divorce. She and David had discussed that, telling Ritchie, and decided against it.

"Of course, it would be better if you were remarried. You two aren't...?" And he looked from one to the other of them.

"No," David said, "we're just friends. I'm her spiritual adviser."

"I see." Ritchie turned to Deirdre. "I have to ask how you'd support the children. The judge will definitely consider that."

"Oh." Deirdre swallowed. "My mother is going to help. And I do work."

"She gets free room and board for her work," David offered. "And wouldn't she get child support?"

"Some," Ritchie said. "Although this McCandless fellow isn't exactly rolling in dough."

Deirdre looked down at her hands.

"So that's it?" Ritchie asked. "No extenuating circumstances, nothing else I need to know? Your ex isn't going to pull one of these child-abuse complaints against you?"

"Case?" Deirdre said, aghast. "Oh no."

Ritchie shrugged. "Lots of people doing it these days."

"Case would never . . ."

"You'd be surprised what people do," Ritchie said, then he smiled broadly. "But not to worry, we've got this sewed up."

"You're sure?"

"It's my job, Mrs. McCandless, and I'm good at it."

"Wonderful," David said, rising. "We . . . Deirdre, that is, is so very anxious to have her children with her, where they belong."

The next day flew by and Case kept busy, busy enough so that he could tell himself there was no time to deal with Beth, even though she was constantly on the edge of his thoughts.

He was uncertain about what course of action to pursue, a new concept for the normally cocksure sheriff of Pitkin County. He knew he was purposely keeping busy, needing the time to sort things out in his head. His heart kept getting in the way, though. For the life of him, Case McCandless couldn't figure how he'd let that thing happen between them. Christ, he kept thinking, she was Terence Connelly's sister, and if the press were laying off the Connellys at present, as soon as the trial date neared, all hell was going to break loose again. What if he and Beth were seeing each other? The media would have a field day.

And then his thoughts flip-flopped. Screw the media. He'd never compromise himself and discuss Terry with Beth. Never. And yet . . .

Oh, he recalled the night Beth had arrived on his doorstep, bottle in hand, apologizing for Matt. But he'd kept thinking there must be something else on her mind to make her act that way, something else . . . And Case couldn't help but wonder if it didn't concern Terry. He'd wondered all along about that, ever since.

A strange, strange lady, Beth Connelly, a mixture of bright lights and dark shadows. My God, he often thought, her confession that she'd never had a climax before . . . Had that been true? And then he'd think hard on that aspect of Beth, and he'd wonder some more— why? She'd spoken of secrets in her life. Was there some sexual secret? Abuse? Rape? At night alone in his bed Case itched to find some answers; he swore to himself he was going to call her first thing in the morning, sit her down and get it all sorted out.

But in the morning he didn't make that call.

It was several days after they'd made love that it all came to a head. At least he'd reached a decision. He'd call her. Okay, a call didn't mean a commitment, after all. And a gentleman didn't just drop a lady cold after they'd been . . . well, intimate.

He picked up the phone at midday on his break at home. The kids were at school and only Gizmo sat there staring at him, tail thumping on the rug. Case dialed the Preserve estate number and stared back at the dog. "What's your problem?" he said, listening to the rings.

But Beth wasn't there, hadn't been there for days, the maid told him, though she believed Miss Connelly was still in town.

He tried Ellen Connelly's gallery. "I really couldn't say, Case," Ellen told him. "Beth could be staying anywhere."

He thought about calling Billy Jorgenson, but as he reached for the phone book Case couldn't make himself go through with it. If she was staying with that pumped-up ass of a gigolo . . .

Case stewed the rest of the day, and after he picked up the kids at school, he ended up driving them out to the ranch, asking Dottie if she'd keep them for the night.

"You going out?" Dottie asked casually.

"Yes," Case said, distracted.

"With Beth?"

He only shot her a look.

The first thing Case did after showering and donning civilian clothes was to head over to the Ritz Hotel to see if Beth was staying there. She wasn't. Nor was she at the Little Nell, the Christmas Inn, the Aspen Club Lodge or the Hotel Jerome.

By ten his only option was to check the bars and discos, which, Case realized as he walked the downtown malls, he should have done in the first place.

He wondered why she'd moved out. But the other, far more important question plaguing the sheriff was what, exactly, was he going to do when he found her?

She wasn't at the Red Onion Saloon, nor was she at the Downtown Sports Center. No Beth at Cooper Street Pier or the trendy Mezzaluna bar. At eleven he strode into the Ute City Banque, where he ran into two of his off-duty officers and had a beer. At eleven-thirty he tried two other spots: Bentley's and the bar at the Mother

Lode. At midnight he tried one last place, Shooter's Saloon, the country and western disco.

Bingo.

But she wasn't alone.

He spotted her instantly across the smoky, crowded room. She was dancing, wearing a black Stetson with a silver band, a real short black skirt and a black, fringed jacket that formed a low V over her breasts. She was whooping it up with a city slicker, also dressed in pseudo-Western getup, dancing up a storm.

Case gritted his teeth.

Okay, he told himself, it was no big deal. So she was dancing, having a good time. So the big-shouldered blond guy was a hunk. Case and Beth had had sex, that's all. Men and women slept together every day. It didn't mean a thing.

Case tapped the man on the shoulder. "Mind if I cut in?" he asked mildly.

The guy turned abruptly. "Get lost, buddy," he said.

"I'm cutting in," Case said, and it struck him: How was it going to look in the headlines? Sheriff Fights Tourist Over Connelly Woman In Saloon.

Holy shit, he thought.

It did almost turn into a scene. Case wasn't about to give ground, nor was the big blond guy. It was Beth who kept the tension from descending to fisticuffs. "Hey," she said to her pal, smiling that innocent smile, "he's an old friend. Just one dance, and I'll see you back at our table. Okay?"

"Well," the man said reluctantly, "I suppose." He let go of Beth's hand, shot Case a hard glance and finally made his way across the dance floor, disappearing into the crowd.

Case took hold of her arm above the elbow. "Are you drunk?" he asked, his anger barely in control.

She shook her head. "Haven't had time yet."

"We're leaving," he said, and a couple bumped into them and danced on past.

"I don't want to."

He swore, then said, "Where the hell's your coat?"

"At the table. But, Case—"

"Get it," he said. "I'll be at the door. Don't keep me waiting."

"But . . ."

Case gave her arm a hard squeeze, making her dark eyes flash at him. "Get your damn coat!"

She didn't keep him waiting long. He was actually surprised when he saw her coming, her slender frame moving through the throng, that dark curtain of hair hiding half her face.

"Give me that," he said, taking her leather jacket from her and helping her into it. "You ready?"

But she just stood there. "You hurt me back there, Case McCandless," she said.

"Your pride?"

"No, you ass, my arm! Don't you ever, ever handle me like that again!"

He was completely taken aback. He'd seen a hundred sides to this woman, but never this one. "I'm sorry," he said. "I didn't . . ."

"Apology not accepted," she said. "Men think they can do anything to you, anything, and then afterward say, 'Gee, I'm real sorry.' Well, it doesn't work. Just don't ever hurt me again."

"Okay," he said. And he knew—he knew as sure as he was standing there that Beth had been badly abused, maybe even raped. Suddenly it all fit: her flighty behavior with men, the way she'd let them use her until she dumped them. And her response in bed—she sure hadn't faked that. Oh yeah, those little secrets of hers . . . The only question left was who? Who had hurt her?

Case looked down into her eyes. They were still sparking, moist and glistening with anger and pain. He put his arm around her, pulling her close, bundling her out the door onto the street, away from the heat and smoke and clamor of the bar.

"Okay," he said again, stopping on the sidewalk and holding her at arm's length, trying to read her expression. "I said I was sorry, but that isn't enough, you're right. Tell me what I can do."

"Oh, Case, forget it. It doesn't matter."

"It matters," he said.

She turned her face away. "Why do you care, anyway?"

"I don't know why. Believe me, though, I care a lot."

She was searching his face, and in the half-light of the Victorian street lamps, he saw a tear slide down her cheek. "Damn you, Case," she said brokenly.

He pulled her close, bent his head and kissed her with an aching gentleness, tasting her tears. "My God, Beth, why didn't you tell me?" he whispered.

He drove her to his empty house, the silence in the dark car seeming to pulse in the air. There were so many questions, too many. He had no idea where to begin. He glanced at her profile as she sat there shrouded in silence, unwilling to abandon its familiarity. He couldn't think of a damn thing to say to her right now.

He pulled up in front of his small, dark house, turned off the engine and took a long, ragged breath, his gloved hands gripping the steering wheel. Jesus, he thought, what was he getting into?

It was Beth who finally spoke. But what she said was hardly what he'd expected. In a very small voice, she said, "I want you, Case, I want you so damn bad." And then somehow he was pulling her to him and their mouths were fused, tongues plunging, searching, probing, his hands reaching beneath her jacket, pushing aside the fabric, grasping the firmness of her warm flesh. For only a fleeting moment did it occur to him that they should go inside, but the notion fled with the cold night wind, and his zipper was down and she was lying beneath him on the car seat, ready, and suddenly they were one.

It was over quickly. And after the groans and throes of passion, they both subsided into silence again as they readjusted their clothing. His arm around her shoulder, Case led Beth through his front door, past the cluttered kitchen, up to his bedroom. And then she was in his arms again, her head resting on his parka.

"Oh, Case," she said in a forlorn voice, "my life's so screwed up I don't know what to do or where to turn."

"What happened?" he asked.

"I had a fight with Matt."

"Uh-huh," he said, his hand pushing her hair from her brow. "What about?"

"It was over you. Well, not you, but your family. The permit thing."

"I see. And where are you staying?"

"The Lenado Hotel. I was going to leave, but . . ."

"Why didn't you?"

"I . . . I wanted to call you. I couldn't leave without talking to you, seeing you."

"So why didn't you?"

"I don't know. I guess it was too heavy, you know." She turned her face up to his. "Is what we're doing crazy?"

"Yes," he said, and then he kissed her, slowly and gently and he felt her melting against him and he knew he was lost.

They made love again, only this time there was no rush. He couldn't believe her response, her joy, the incredible tenderness between them. And afterward she laughed and asked him if it was as good for him, and Case laughed, too.

They slept for a while. At dawn they awakened and listened to the birds outside his window. It was then that Case told her about Dottie's offer.

"But if I stay at the ranch, Case," she said, "you know the press is going to find out. It will look...awful. I don't care about myself. But for you..."

"Screw them," he said.

"You really mean that? You'd put up with them for me?"

"I told you. I don't care about them. If you think you can stand to work out there, then the job's yours."

"Oh, Case."

"What about your other work?"

"I'll call my boss."

"So you want to do this."

"Yes, oh God, yes!"

"Then we'll get your things this morning from the hotel."

She snuggled close to his bare skin. "You in the habit of rescuing people?" she asked playfully.

"Yeah, actually I am. It's what I do for a living," he said. "I'm pretty good at it, too."

She ran a hand through his hair and kissed him lightly on the lips. Her dark eyes were very serious now. "Sometimes a person can't be rescued, though. It's too late."

"It's never too late, but it's always up to the individual. I'm only a . . . well, a catalyst, but maybe I can help a little."

"I've never met anyone like you," Beth said quietly.

Case chuckled a little, deep in his chest. "Same here, lady."

The phone rang and Ellen answered it awkwardly with her left arm. "Connelly Gallery."

"Ellen, is that you? It's Aunt Cynthia."

"Aunt Cynthia, how nice of you to call."

"Darling, I heard you broke your arm. How is it?"

"It's all right. It wasn't a bad break," Ellen said.

"What a pain," Cynthia remarked. "Did you do it skiing?"

"No, no, I fell on the ice. You know how slippery it gets around here."

"You've got to be careful, Ellen. Do you have boots with good soles?"

"Yes, Aunt Cynthia, I do, really. I was just clumsy."

"Do you think you should fly to New York and see a specialist?"

"Oh, for goodness' sake, it's a simple fracture. I'll be fine," Ellen protested.

"So, how's everybody out there?"

"Oh, we're fine."

"Good, wonderful. And the weather's good?"

"Well, it's snowing on and off, but that's what a ski resort needs."

"I hear Beth's disappeared, crazy kid."

"Beth? Oh, she's working here now. I thought you knew."

"Beth working in Aspen? Where?"

"Well, she's working out at the McCandless ranch, for Dottie McCandless," Ellen said, glad to be off the subject of her arm.

"McCandless? The sheriff out there, the one who arrested her, that one?" Cynthia asked, aghast.

"Beth's working for his mother, but I think she and Case are seeing each other. Pretty strange, isn't it? But, really, he's a nice guy."

"A nice guy? Ellen, darling, he's the enemy, that's what he is," Cynthia declared. "By the way, where's your father? Is he still in Aspen?"

"I think he flew back to Washington," Ellen said. "Something about having to see Terry's lawyer. Why?"

"Oh, no reason, just wondering," Cynthia replied.

The next morning, Cynthia boarded the train at Penn Station for the trip to Washington, D.C. She could have phoned, she could have taken the air shuttle, but she preferred the train. It was so much more civilized. And this particular visit had to be face-to-face.

She got a cab to Georgetown, hating the way the houses were all squeezed together here. Her own place in East Hampton had two acres of lawn and half a mile of beachfront. As she straightened, getting out of the cab, she saw a young woman closing Matt's front door behind her and coming down the steps. A nice-looking woman in a dark brown business suit, carrying a briefcase. She nodded to the woman as she climbed the steps; the woman nodded back and walked briskly away.

Matt was indeed there. "Is Lee here, too?" Cynthia asked.

Matt stood at the door, obviously surprised to see his sister in Washington. "Ah, no," he said. "Lee's still in Aspen. Come on in."

"Good," Cynthia said, pulling off her kid gloves a finger at a time. "We have to talk."

"Sit down, Cyn. A drink?"

"A double, Matthew. Better pour yourself one, too."

He sat down in a tapestry wing chair next to hers with a snifter, handed his sister a matching one and began to unwrap one of his Cuban cigars.

"Good God," she said, "must you smoke that revolting thing?"

Matt looked wounded but dutifully laid it aside. "Okay," he said. "I'm sure you didn't make the trip just to bitch about my smoking. Let's hear it."

"Are you aware that Beth is not only working for the McCandless family, but is seeing the sheriff, Case McCandless?"

"Seeing? What in hell does that mean?" he asked.

"Sleeping with him, you old fool, what do you think? Sweet, innocent Beth."

"Jesus H. Christ."

"Yes, I agree." Cynthia took a long swallow of her brandy. "What are you going to do about it, Matthew?"

"What *can* I do about it? Beth's over twenty-one. Shit." He peered at Cynthia. "You sure about this?"

"Ellen told me."

"Damn, what a hell of a situation. What's wrong with that girl?"

"You indulged her, Matthew, spoiled her rotten. She has no moral fiber. Now, the way I raised Eddy, that was different...."

Matt held up his hand. "Spare me, Cyn."

"Well, I thought you should know," Cynthia said.

"Yeah, I'll figure something out. I have a few tricks up my sleeve yet. The McCandlesses don't crap roses, you know."

"Do you think she'd . . ."

"Hell, no," Matt said quickly. "Don't worry."

"You'd better be right." Cynthia narrowed her eyes at her brother. "By the way, who was that young woman leaving when I got here?"

She could have sworn her brother flushed. "Oh, her? It must have been Melinda, uh, Feinstein."

"Feinstein, the lawyer I got you?"

"Yeah, Terry's lawyer, you know."

"Oh, so that's her. Is she any good?"

"Oh, boy, is she good," Matt said, and he quickly rose to freshen their drinks.

SEVENTEEN

"Don't move," Case whispered.

She said, "I want to move."

"Don't move," he said again.

He hovered over her, deep inside her, still and quivering, and Beth thought she might pass out from the sharp delight building inside her.

"Please," she said faintly.

He held himself above her on his arms, one second, two, then his face changed and he began the rhythm again, and she cried out with the sensations. He went slowly, with absolute control, and she went with him, climbing and climbing until she knew there was no place left to go because her body was so engorged with stark pleasure. And yet he went on. She felt him reach the top, his breath coming hard, and then her body took over and annihilated all thought.

Afterward they lay together in his bed. It was snowing outside, a heavy wet spring storm. Nate and Amanda were at school and Beth had the afternoon off.

"Do you have to go back soon?" she asked.

"Yeah. This is my lunch break," he said.

Beth giggled, hiding her face in his bare chest.

"Cut it out," he said affectionately. "I'm hungry, by the way."

"I'll make you a sandwich," she said.

"I think all there is is peanut butter."

"Um."

Case kissed her, then swung his legs over the side of the bed and sat there. She watched the play of muscles in his back, admiring them.

"God, I feel like a teenager," he said. "This is ridiculous."

"Ridiculous but nice," she replied.

"I'd like to spend the night with you, all night, and get up in the morning and have coffee and . . ."

She put her hand flat on his back. It was warm and smooth. "I know."

"I hate sneaking around."

"We're not sneaking. Everybody knows about us, Case. It's not as if you were still married."

"But you're out at that damn ranch working for Mom. . . ."

"Would you really want me to move in with you? With the kids here? Come on, Case. And then there's my brother. . . ."

He was quiet for a time. "Yeah, it's a problem."

There wasn't anything else to be said about it. There wasn't any solution, not right away. They'd have to just take what they had and cherish it for now—and not get impatient for too much more. How wise and philosophical, Beth thought.

"Whatever we do, Case, and whatever happens, I just don't want to hurt the kids, or you."

"You couldn't hurt me," he said, turning to face her.

Her expression darkened. "The Connellys have a way of hurting people."

"You're not a Connelly, not anymore," he said softly.

He drove her back out to the ranch after that, and they kissed goodbye before she went in. She worked cheerfully that evening, and Dottie bustled in and out, her sharp eye on Beth's work, but she found nothing to complain about. It was getting better between them after the first difficult week, and Dottie was beginning to reveal her sharp-witted, funny side.

Oh, Beth knew Dottie couldn't bear the thought of her and Case being involved. She disapproved ferociously, but she wouldn't meddle in her son's life, well, not overtly, anyway.

Truth be told, Beth figured that Dottie was absolutely right to disapprove; if she had a son like Case she'd disapprove, too. But what Dottie didn't know was how happy she and Case were together, how crazy they were about each other, how sweet and utterly fulfilling was their lovemaking. No, Dottie didn't know about that.

"All right," Dottie said, "when you finish that stuff, you could vacuum up the main room. Here, I'll do that. You're putting too much in that container."

"Sorry," Beth said.

"It's okay. No big deal. You're doing okay, Beth," Dottie offered.

"Thanks," Beth said, flushing. Dottie was not big on compliments.

"Listen, I'm grateful for any help around here. It's so hard to keep anyone in this town."

"I'm not going anywhere, Mrs. McCandless. Not till the end of the season, anyway. Funding is really tight at the children's organization I work for, and my boss said I was doing him a favor right now by not drawing a paycheck. So you're stuck with me for a while, Mrs. McCandless."

"For heaven's sake, I told you to call me Dottie. Everyone calls me Dottie."

"Right...Dottie."

Dottie sank down in a chair, sighing. "Thank God the season's almost over. I'm too old for this."

"It does seem like a lot of hard work, but you've got such a great place here. It's a real tradition."

"Well, it is, but the reason I do it is to make a living, not for any old ideals."

Beth turned back to washing potatoes and laying them out on trays. When the talk turned to finances, she got very uncomfortable, knowing the Forest Service permit thing was a big issue with Dottie. It jeopardized the whole operation. Damn Matt, she thought.

"Is Case coming out tonight?" Dottie asked.

"I'm not sure. He was going to call."

"Uh-huh," Dottie said.

Beth turned around, still holding a wet Idaho potato. "Dottie...I, uh, well, I really like Case a lot. He's very special to me. I would never do anything to hurt him. I know you don't...approve of me, but I care about Case, I really do."

Dottie squinted up at her, her hands resting on her jeans-clad legs. "It's none of my business."

"He's your son."

"He's got his own life to lead."

"Yes, but I'd like everything out in the open. No secrets. I'm tired of secrets. I'm not going to live like that anymore," Beth said earnestly.

"Sounds like a good idea to me," Dottie said. "Not always so easy, though."

Case called that night. He couldn't make it. He'd forgotten that Amanda was in a play at school he had to go to.

"I'm sorry," he said. "I want to see you."

"Me, too."

"I'd take you to the play, but I have to work late, and I don't have time to drive out to pick you up. You wouldn't want to sit through it anyway."

"A school play," Beth mused.

"Yeah, silly stuff. Amanda's a bunny or something."

"I'll miss you." She twisted the phone wire around her fingers. "If I had my license back I'd drive in and see it with you."

"You'd be bored."

"No, I wouldn't."

"How's Mom treating you?" he asked, changing the subject.

"Fairly," she said.

"That's something."

"It's all I can expect."

"Listen, Beth, I have to go. I'll see you tomorrow."

"I don't have a break tomorrow," she said.

"After work. I'll bring the kids out for dinner."

"Okay."

"See you then."

"See you, Case."

She hung up smiling, feeling like a giddy teenager with her first boyfriend. It *was* her first, though, her very first, and she was half-delirious with happiness. She felt whole for the first time in her life, whole and normal.

She went back to work, setting the rustic old wooden tables for the dinner crowd. It was routine work, easy once you knew the setup. And while Beth worked she thought about herself and Case and what was happening in her life.

All these years she'd punished herself with sex and alcohol and men who used her. She knew a psychiatrist would say she was punishing herself because of the dysfunctional family she came from, following patterns of behavior that were familiar to her. And beating herself up with ugly relationships because of a poor self-image—the aftermath of her rape.

Oh, sure, she knew all that psychological jargon, but knowing something intellectually didn't help the emotional pain, which was untouched by logic. What had been done to her was bad, yes, but if she'd been able to confide in her mother, get support from her family, she would have gotten over it much better than she had.

Only she hadn't been able to tell anyone—the secret, the dirty, guilty secret had been locked up inside her. No one in her family could have dealt with it, and somehow, even at fourteen she'd known that. And so it had festered in her, a suppurating wound that had never grown protective scar tissue. She knew all that, but it hadn't helped her in the past.

She was going to fight it now, though. Now that she had a man like Case on her side, she was going to live a normal life. She was going to be happy.

She vacuumed the towering, timbered main room, around the central hearth, all alone in the empty place. The machine hummed, a soothing mechanical sound. She'd never vacuumed before; there'd always been a maid to do it.

Oh, God, how everything had changed! It was still an uphill battle, though. Even in the midst of her new-found joy, there were small dissonances: the Forest Service permit; her old feelings of unworthiness and guilt that made her ask herself why she deserved this happiness, why she deserved Case's goodness and love. And then there was the one she still couldn't quite face.

She pushed the vacuum harder, faster, feeling her heart squeeze in that awful, familiar way. She'd told Dottie she wasn't going to lie anymore, she'd convinced herself she wasn't going to. She even forgot, sometimes, for a little while, the upcoming trial and her testimony. Oh yes, there were heavenly moments when all that was forgotten so easily, but the stark reality always came back—with a vengeance.

Well, she'd figure it out. There was time yet. Something would happen to solve the problem, something. She put the thought away from her, shoving it behind all those carefully wrought barriers. She couldn't deal with it now, not yet.

Case came out with the kids the next evening. He watched with a smile as she kissed Amanda's cheek and hugged Nate, and they chattered at her about school and the play Amanda had been in and how Billy Haverstock was a jerk and stole Nate's lunch money.

Over Nate's and Amanda's heads, Case gave her a quick kiss, a little embarrassed, but the kids didn't seem to notice or to mind.

"Okay, kids, leave Beth alone. Go find Grandma and tell her we're here," Case said.

"Can I sit by you at dinner?" Amanda asked Beth.

"Gee, I'd love to, sweetheart, but I can't eat with you. I'm working."

"Oh."

It was exquisite torture to see Case, to be so close to him. There was no privacy at the ranch. They couldn't be alone—there were Dottie and Nick and Rowdy, his children. She could look but not touch, and she wanted him so badly.

He found her in the kitchen after dinner, where she was stacking dishes in the big commercial dishwasher.

"Beth."

She turned and smiled at him, pushing her hair back from her damp forehead with a wrist.

"I hate to see you working like this while I'm just . . . hanging around," he said.

"You put in your day's work."

"Yeah, but . . ."

"I'm fine. I just miss you, that's all."

"I've got to get the kids home soon. It's late and they have school. I wish I could stay. Or you could come with me."

"You're sweet."

"The hell I am."

"I'm off Sunday and Monday," she said.

"I know. We'll figure something out." He moved close to her and pushed her hair behind her ear, then leaned forward and kissed her.

She put her wet soapy hands around him. "Someone'll come in and see us," she whispered.

"Let 'em." He released her reluctantly. "Sunday," he said.

Deirdre had to wait until David was through with his yoga before she could talk to him. When he was done he slowly untangled himself and stood up, taking a deep, cleansing breath. God, she envied him. So calm, so centered. Always knowing what to do or say.

"What's wrong, DeeDee?" he asked. "You're very tense. Your aura is absolutely a mess."

She clutched a letter, then held it out to him. "It's from Case's lawyer in Aspen. They want me to take some psychological tests. Oh, David, I told you . . ."

"Well, take them."

"It scares me. What if they show I'm crazy or something?"

"You're not crazy. You're a wonderful individual. You're halfway to Nirvana, DeeDee, and that's the most important thing."

"Oh, David, maybe I should drop the suit."

"You could do that, of course," he said carefully. "But you need to think about it first. Meditate. The truth will come to you."

The truth came to Deirdre McCandless in the form of a telephone call to the office of the ashram.

"Who?" Deirdre asked the girl who conveyed the message.

"Melinda Feinstein. I wrote it down with the number. She said to call back collect. It's very important."

"But I don't know any Melinda Feinstein," Deirdre said, puzzled.

"Call her. It's free, isn't it?"

David agreed that she should call this Feinstein woman back. It could be important, maybe related to her custody suit. So Deirdre did, finally, getting the woman after the ashram's communal lunch. When she hung up she was smiling and feeling very much better. She went straight to David, who was on duty in the chicken house that afternoon. Amid the rank, hot smell of poultry, she told him what Melinda Feinstein had wanted.

"She said Case is going out with a woman named Beth Connelly, the daughter of that senator from New York. I can't believe it. *Case*. I mean, he's not like that at all.

He's so small town, really." Deirdre took a breath. "Anyway, she thinks they're living together, and if I can prove that he's got this woman living in the house with my kids, well, I have a good chance to win."

David took her hands. "See, DeeDee, I told you something would come up."

Deirdre phoned Case that night, driving into Point Reyes so that the call would be more private than the common phone in the office. He got even more angry than she expected.

"Damn it, Deirdre, who gave you that information?"

"It doesn't matter," she said, knowing she had to stand up to him. "But it's true, isn't it?"

"I like Beth, yes. We've gone out. She is *not* living with me."

"That's not what I hear, Case."

"Then you hear wrong," he said in a hard voice.

"I want my children back," she said staunchly.

"The hell you do. This is just one of your whims. It'll pass. You know you don't really want the kids. It's that guru of yours pushing you, and all he wants is more lost souls under his power. Well, he's not getting Nate and Amanda and that's final, Deirdre. Just go back to your ashram and meditate some more. But you leave me and the kids alone. You're not supposed to be contacting me, anyway."

"You're mean."

"Just truthful. Now, goodbye, Deirdre, I'm going to hang up."

Case and Beth took Nate and Amanda skiing at Tiehack Buttermilk on Sunday. It wasn't often that Case got to ski anymore, he'd told Beth, even though he'd practically been raised on skis, so this was a treat for all of them.

It was a warm spring day, a perfect day. They loaded skis, boots, poles, hats, gloves, goggles in the car, along with the kids, red-cheeked with excitement.

"I'll show you the Bear Jump," Nate told Beth.

"Me, too!" Amanda cried.

"Kids, take it easy on Beth," Case put in, "or she'll never go skiing with you again."

"I will so," Beth said. "I'll go anytime you want."

"See, Daddy!"

It was fun, watching the two children show off for their father. Amanda was only five, but she could do a sturdy snowplow anywhere she wanted to go. Nate was good, aggressive, doing parallel turns already. And they knew the mountain, every nook and cranny and path through the woods, every hump of snow they could get some air off, the nickname for every run, the names of all the instructors and lift operators.

Case skied expertly, effortlessly. He complained that his legs were getting tired and that he wasn't in shape anymore, but to Beth he seemed to skim down the slopes with the grace of a World Cup racer.

They each went up the lifts with a child, and there was one place where the drop under the chair was considerable.

"Oh, that's the Toilet Bowl," Amanda explained to Beth matter-of-factly.

"Don't lean forward!" Beth said in alarm, and Amanda looked at her, puzzled.

"You could fall off."

"No, I couldn't," Amanda said.

At lunch the kids had hot dogs and fries. Nate got mustard on his red parka.

"It'll come off," Beth said. "We'll wash it at home."

"Slob," Amanda said scornfully.

"Shut up, Fatface."

They could have been a family, Beth dared to think as she dabbed more sunscreen on both the children's noses. A nice, ordinary middle-class family. It was a new situation for her, splendidly new. She could live like this, she thought, she really could.

Of course, it was all a fantasy.

"Are they bugging you?" Case asked, worried.

"Oh no, Case, they're darling. They love skiing with you. You should take them more often."

"Sure, when I have all that free time," he said.

"It's hard, isn't it?"

He looked out the window of the mountaintop restaurant, his eyes distant and, for the first time, a little bitter. "Yeah, but nobody ever said it was going to be easy. I worry about them, you know. Are they being deprived of something important, so that later they'll be all screwed up?"

"No, Case."

"Well, I can't help wondering. They're my kids, and I want the best for them. I would have stayed with Deirdre, you know, for their sakes, but she left. I'd do anything for them."

"They'll be fine," Beth said. "They have a wonderful family, all the love and security they need. You've done a great job, Case."

"They need a mother," he said in a hard voice, and they were both quiet for a time.

After a while Beth said, "Something's happened. Is it about your ex-wife trying to get the kids back?"

"Deirdre called the other day," he said after a long pause. "She knows about us. She threatened..." He turned his gaze out the window again.

"Oh, Case," Beth said, her heart sinking. "But it's not as if we're doing anything wrong. I mean, I'm not living with you."

"She'd heard you were."

Beth bristled. "From who?"

He shrugged. "She wouldn't say."

"Oh damn, it's just not fair. You don't think she can win her case, do you?"

He shook his head wearily. "I don't know anymore, I swear I don't."

Afterward they all went home to Case's house. The kids were tired from the sun and skiing. They watched TV while Beth tried to find something to cook.

"You'll stay tonight?" Case asked, sitting at the tilted kitchen table with a can of beer.

"What about...?"

He smiled. "Nate's going to Nicky Kern's house and Amanda's going to Katy Kluchko's. All set."

"You do good work, mister," she said, rummaging through the cupboards.

"This must be an awful pain for you," he said.

"What?"

"Skiing with kids, cooking, getting mustard stains off parkas."

"Why?"

"Well, you're used to maids and jet-setting, stuff like that."

She laughed. "You think that's fun?"

"Sounds like it to the rest of us."

"It's boring and empty. This is better. This is real life."

"It sure is that," Case said.

That night they were alone in his small, ramshackle house. They made slow, leisurely love, used to each other now. She knew every inch of Case, every dip and hollow, the swell of his muscles, the way his hands felt on her, his unique scent, the squeaks of the old brass bed.

She'd never been so happy.

Her head fit into his shoulder perfectly, and she lay there, sated, her heart slowing, her skin damp with perspiration. The words were on her lips, and she almost said them: "I love you." But it was too soon, and she wasn't even sure if this euphoria she felt was love. She sensed, too, that Case didn't want to hear something like that, not with his kids, his problems. He had a life, and she couldn't intrude on it with her newfound passion. So she held her tongue.

She did talk to him about something else, though, something as close to her heart, as difficult. But he needed to know, she thought, so that he'd understand.

"Case?" she murmured.

"Um." Idly, his fingers stroked her arm.

"I have to tell you something."

"Um."

It took all her courage, but she got the words out. "I was . . . uh, a long time ago . . ."

"You don't have to tell me," he said quietly.

"I do have to. Case, listen . . ."

"I'm listening."

"I was raped."

He was silent for a time, and she was afraid he'd think she was unclean now. She hid her head in the hollow between his neck and shoulder and held on to him for dear life.

"I figured," was all he said.

"You couldn't . . . how could you?" she asked, raising her head.

He shrugged. "Some things you said. The way you . . . acted."

"Am I that transparent?" she asked, ashamed.

"No, Beth. It's just that I've had a lot of training in that kind of thing, what to look for, you know."

"Oh God, I'm a case history."

"No, no. Look, it doesn't matter."

"It matters to me. I'm not through. There's more." She swallowed and went on. "I was fourteen. It was some friends of Terry's . . ." She felt Case tense. "School friends. He . . . he let them. He . . ."

"Terry," Case said in an odd voice.

"He watched."

He took her in his arms and held her, kissed her fore-head, her nose, her lips. "It's over," he said.

"I felt so dirty, so used, for years. I imagined every man looked at me and knew. I couldn't believe any man could like me. I know it sounds crazy, but that's how I felt. Case, does it . . . bother you?"

He pushed her hair off her forehead. "No. It doesn't mean anything."

"You're not lying to make me feel better?"

"I don't lie, Beth. You know me well enough by now to realize that, don't you?"

"Yes," she whispered, but she clung to him. Then she went on in a small voice, "If I'd had a family like yours, a mother like Dottie, I could have talked to somebody, gotten some help, but my mother . . ." She sighed. "I never, ever told anyone. Until you."

He held her protectively, and she almost cried with relief and love and need.

"Do you want to talk about it any more?" he asked carefully.

She shook her head.

"Okay, that's fine. But if you ever do . . ."

"I will."

"Just remember, it's over," he said again.

"It's never over."

"Yes, it is. It doesn't matter. You can handle it, Beth."

"I can?" she asked with a little laugh.

"Yes," he said firmly, then he muttered, "That son of a bitch."

"He's not my favorite person," she said with false insouciance.

"You never have to see him again," Case said. "He's out of your life."

And then Beth knew he was thinking of the trial, the testimony she would have to give, and she was afraid, feeling her body grow cold all over, chilled. She shivered.

But Case's arms were around her; his strength enfolded her. He kissed the top of her head. "You don't ever have to worry about Terry again," he said. "You hear?"

"Uh-huh," she said, but she knew it was a lie and so did Case.

The weeks went by so quickly, Beth was dumbfounded. She worked, she saw Case, talked to him on the phone every day, spent every moment she could with him, worried about Amanda's ear infection and Nate's homework. And she worried about Deirdre.

The ski season was almost over. Aspen was emptier each day, and parking places were a dime a dozen. Restaurants were half-vacant, and there were no lift lines on the mountains. The locals began to relax, to let down. On the streets, rivulets of melting snow made pathways in the mud, and every day the piles of dirty snow shrank. Often you could see knots of locals on street corners and in the malls, stopping to chat, which they hadn't been able to do since November. It was becoming a small, friendly town again.

Magpies flew to last year's nests, carrying branches for repairs. Robins ventured back to the valley, and Beth saw raccoons and porcupines, skunks and foxes out on the ranch. A foal was born to one of the McCandless' big sleigh horses, and Beth thought it was the cutest thing she'd ever seen, except maybe for the kittens the barn cat had. All around her the world was coming back to life, renewing itself in the age-old cycle. It was just that Beth had never noticed it before.

She felt renewed herself, living in a kind of exhilarating limbo. She hadn't spoken to anyone in her family except for a short phone call to Lee. She studiously avoided Ellen. Her world was focused on the ranch, her chores, Dottie and Nick and Rowdy. And Case and his kids. She didn't read the newspapers, except for the daily rag sheets that Aspenites delighted in, and didn't even watch television. New York was farther away than the African villages where she'd worked. She refused to think about those things.

She and Dottie engaged in an elaborate game, the point of which was to spare Case any grief. They both worked at it so hard that one day Beth realized she liked Dottie, and, to tell the truth, Dottie got along fine with her. They gossiped in the kitchen and laughed over Nate and Amanda's antics. They talked about Case, and Dottie told Beth more about Deirdre.

"What a nut," Dottie said, shaking her head. "Nice girl and all, but some strange ideas. Had to find herself. Lord save me from the introspective ones."

It was then that Beth asked, "How did they break up?"

"Oh, my gosh," Dottie said, "let's see. I think Case was in Canada, goose hunting with his friends. You know, he does that every autumn. He and a couple of college buddies pile a mountain of camping stuff in their Jeeps, and the dogs, of course . . . Anyway, when Case got back, Deirdre had packed up all her stuff and announced she was going to California."

"Poor Case."

"He was pretty shook up. But he had the kids, and that helped. He's always said he'd have had a couple more." Dottie shrugged. Then, casually, she asked, "How about you, Beth? Do you ever want children?"

"Yes. I love children. And I'll always want to work with kids, too. I've just seen too many helpless ones in the world."

"That's nice of you."

Beth looked away. "Not really."

At the very end of the ski season, on a warm, overcast Easter Sunday, Beth went to the top of Aspen Mountain with Case and the children for the annual Easter sunrise service. A sincere young minister gave a sermon while people dressed in ski clothes stood and listened in the midst of the vast white peaks of the Rocky Mountains. Then they all had breakfast at the Sundeck Restaurant and took the gondola back down.

"That's the nicest church service I've ever been to," Beth said as they walked along the street to Case's car.

"I try to do it every year," he said. "The kids like it, you know. They'd never sit still in church."

"What great memories your kids are growing up with," she mused. "Lucky little brats."

"You think so?"

"Oh, Case, I know it."

He took her hand and they walked along, Nate and Amanda running ahead.

"You've made me very happy," Beth said. "You know that, don't you?"

"Hasn't been real hard," he said gruffly.

Dottie had cooked a ham for dinner, a private family dinner at last, now that the lodge was closed for the season. Beth wore a skirt for the first time in weeks and felt overdressed, but it was an occasion, after all. She was treated as one of the family now, teased by Nick and Rowdy, clung to by Nate and Amanda, gossiped to by Dottie. A family. A real-live family, whose members loved one another.

The McCandlesses laughed and joshed, recalled hysterical incidents from their childhoods, even spoke of their father and one of his practical jokes that had backfired.

"And there Dad was, all covered in horseshit," Rowdy said, "and Ma was mad as hell. I'll tell you . . ."

They all ate too much and groaned in mock suffering. After the meal Nate and Amanda ran outside to see the foal they'd named Star and the kittens and the big nest the magpies were making in the tall cottonwood tree by the barn.

"Come on, Beth," Dottie said. "A woman's work is never done."

But the three men cleared the table and brought everything into the kitchen, so it really wasn't bad.

Then Dottie shooed them out of her way while she and Beth did the dishes.

"Why don't you wrap up the rest of the ham for Case to take home. He can't cook worth beans. Sometimes I think those kids are going to get beriberi or something," Dottie said.

"I'm not much of a cook myself," Beth said, rinsing dishes to put in the dishwasher.

"You can always learn."

"I lack motivation. Living alone, you know . . ."

"Well, you won't always live alone, Beth."

"Um."

Dottie leaned on her hands over the counter she was sponging off, then she turned to face Beth. "Now, hold on there a minute, Beth, I really gotta say something."

Beth shut off the water and glanced at the older woman. A faint trepidation fluttered her heart at Dottie's tone of voice. "Uh-huh?"

"Look here, I gotta confess something. Darn it all, I'm not real proud of what I've done, asking you to work here like I did." She shook her head, and her gray pageboy swung. "I had an ulterior motive and it didn't work out."

Beth dried her hands on a towel nervously. "Dottie, it's okay, I understand. . . ."

"No, now you listen." Dottie held up a hand. "I disapproved of you, I admit. Wasn't too subtle about it, either. I wanted you to . . . I never thought you'd make it, but you have. You've done real well, and I'm ashamed of myself. I'm just a prejudiced old redneck, and I hate people like that."

"Really, Dottie . . ."

"You've been good for my boy and my grandchildren. I hadn't seen Case happy in a long time, but he is with you. I appreciate that."

"He's made me happy, too. I can't tell you how much," Beth said sincerely.

"I guess I learned something," Dottie said. "And at my age, too. Goes to show you."

Beth smiled. "I'm glad. I'd like to be your friend."

Dottie went to her and gave her a quick hug. "Friends," she said, and Beth hugged her back and repeated, "Friends," and they both wiped surreptitiously at the embarrassing moisture in their eyes.

Dottie kept the children that night. "Go on home, you two," she said gruffly.

"You sure, Mom?" Case asked.

"Yes, I'm sure. Just bring Beth back in the morning so we can get to work cleaning the cabins."

"I'll pick up the kids before eight," he said.

"Fine, fine, just get going. I'll have them ready, school lunches and all."

"Thanks, Mom."

"Thanks, Dottie."

"Get outta here," she said.

It was another night of love, of stirrings and murmurings in the darkness, of bare satiny skin and body heat and deep, deep slumber that refreshed utterly.

They had to get up early to drive out to the ranch. But there was time for a few lazy minutes in bed, no urgency, no need even to make love, just tickling and kisses and affection and the deep enjoyment of the other's closeness.

"We have to get up," Beth said.

"Yeah."

"Lazybones."

"I had a tough workout," Case said, running a hand over her hip.

"Dottie will be mad."

"Oh, well then, we'd better get a move on. Dottie'll be mad. Hot damn."

On the ride out to the ranch Beth got philosophical. "This isn't going to last, you know," she said.

"What isn't?"

She put a hand on his knee. "This. The way things are."

"Why not?"

"Something will come up. It always does."

"You're superstitious."

"No, realistic."

"I don't know what's going to happen," he said, "unless you decide to leave or something. Me and the kids aren't going anywhere."

"I don't want to leave," she said.

"Then don't. It's simple."

"Nothing's ever simple," she said thoughtfully.

"Look, Beth, I've been real happy lately. I . . . well, I don't want . . . I mean, it's kind of hard for me to make a commitment, you know?"

She smiled at his squirming. "You don't have to make me an honest woman, if that's what you mean. It's too soon. We don't know each other well enough. I'm content to leave things the way they are." She was lying, but it was okay—Case needed the room. "And maybe things'll work out and maybe they won't," she said cautiously.

"You're not trying to tell me something, are you?" he asked suspiciously.

"Now look who's paranoid."

"I'd like you to stick around, you know."

"I'm not going anywhere, Case."

In mid-April the town emptied out almost overnight. Most of the seasonal workers either went home or to Mexico until the summer jobs opened up in June. The weather was lousy; winter hung on tenaciously. There would be a nice day, then a few blustery, snowy ones. The trees weren't out yet and mud prevailed. A lot of businesses were closed until summer, and the pace slowed and slowed some more. Locals could breathe again.

Dottie went to Denver for a few days, and Beth and the guys ran the ranch, but it was easy—no guests. She could have spent a lot of time with Case, except his job was keeping him tied up. The ashtray incident was up for trial, and Case had to spend time in court. There had also been a series of burglaries at the end of the ski season, and a cocaine ring run by illegal immigrants had been discovered in one of the bars in town. The county was having financial problems, and Case had to come up with a new budget, and the new paid parking plan was raising everyone's hackles. But worst of all, Case's lawyer called and told him things were looking sticky with the suit for the kids—Deirdre had agreed to take the test and go to court. Also, the lawyer said, he sure hoped Case was being careful with the new lady he was seeing. "No live-in stuff," he warned Case. "Deirdre knows about her, and she could make trouble over it."

Oh yes, Case had his hands full.

The few stolen hours they had were good, though. Sometimes Case was so tired that he'd pick Beth up at the ranch and when they got home he'd fall asleep in the living room while she put the kids to bed.

The one thing they both had decided without even discussing it was that Nate and Amanda would never see Beth spending the night in their father's bed.

At the end of April there were still old piles of snow on the north sides of buildings and in shaded spots. The weather was horribly erratic, a battle between summer and winter. But the buds were beginning to swell on trees and flocks of migrating birds wheeled in the sky.

It was a Friday night, and Dottie had cooked a big meal for the whole family. They sat around talking after dinner, the kids running around, hollering, stuck inside because there was a wet snowstorm blowing outside. Case was weary, Beth knew, having been in court all day, badgered by the South American defendant's high-priced New York lawyer. He was preoccupied, sitting in a chair that was pushed back from the table, legs stretched out in front of him, thumbs hooked in his pockets. He wasn't talking much.

"Will you kids keep it down?" he finally said, roused by one of Amanda's screeches.

"Leave 'em alone, Case," Dottie said. "They're bored."

"Listen, Mom, they have to learn to behave. They're too wild."

"You should have tried to raise you three boys," she said. "Wild wasn't the word for it."

Beth started to clear the table.

"Leave it for now," Dottie said. "We'll do it later. I feel lazy."

They sat there at the table, easy with one another. Amanda finally got tired of chasing her brother and climbed onto Beth's lap.

"You sleepy, kiddo?" Beth asked.

"No. Tell me a story."

"Leave Beth alone," Case said.

"It's okay," Beth replied. "I'll tell you one later, I promise."

"Okay."

Rowdy was the one who brought up the subject. "I thought I might take some time off, Ma. Go down to the desert. Moab, Sedona. I wouldn't mind getting away for a spell."

"When?"

"End of May, when it's good and hot down there."

"Wouldn't it be better to go earlier? I mean, you're usually so busy getting the hut ready and all in May," Dottie said.

Rowdy stood up and walked to the fire in the big hearth, prodding at it with the poker. "It's real uncertain about the hut this summer," he said carefully.

"Come on, Rowdy," Dottie said, "that'll be cleared up soon."

"Maybe. Maybe not."

Beth felt that chill on her skin. The Forest Service permit. The present one was up in a matter of weeks now. She closed her eyes and rested her cheek on Amanda's blond head. Why did she feel personally responsible for this thing Matt Connelly had done?

She gathered her courage and asked the question that had been on her mind for weeks. "Has Matt really stopped you from getting that permit? I mean, for good?"

Dottie gave her a thin-lipped smile. "Over my dead body."

Nick spoke up. "What Ma means is we've got some clout of our own. We've got our state senator working on it."

"Do you think he can stand up to Matt Connelly?" Beth asked. "I know how ruthless he is."

Rowdy answered her. "Now, don't you worry about it, Beth. The McCandlesses have been here for a long time and they'll still be here after Matt Connelly is long gone. We can hold our own."

"I hope so," Beth whispered into Amanda's fragrant hair.

"Okay," Dottie said, heaving herself up from her chair, "time to do the dishes."

That night Case stayed at the ranch. Beth held him close and ran her hand through his shock of blond hair. "Tired?" she asked softly.

"Yeah."

"Too tired to . . . ?"

He stirred, pressing against her, and she felt his hardness.

"I guess not," she breathed.

They made slow, unhurried love, until the end, when the liquid heat filled their veins and they came together with a clash, with surges of pleasure like waves against a shore. To Beth it was always new, every time, the sensations, the absolute pleasure, the wild, leaping surprise that Case could bring her to such abandon.

In the end they lay there together, breathing hard in each other's arms. She wanted to say those forbidden words so badly. Her heart cried out to unburden itself. Three simple words: "I love you." But she was afraid. He'd never said he loved her, and she didn't want to push him, to burden him. They needed more time. What was between them was wonderful, special, so very sweet and good, but it was undefined. Complicated. Small fragments of guilt curled on the edges of Beth's conscience. Case was so honorable; she didn't deserve what he gave her. She didn't deserve him and his family and his loving children, and so she didn't dare press him.

She lay there in his arms, awash with happiness that was tinged with a fateful kind of sadness. The Connellys always came to a bad end, one way or another, Beth thought, but then she felt her resolve harden. She'd fight that destiny. She wasn't a Connelly and she'd fight it with everything she had in her.

Outside, the cloud-tossed moon filtered down onto glistening white peaks, and the coyotes howled, keening, warbling, yipping, welcoming spring, while Beth held her man in her arms and watched him sleep.

EIGHTEEN

Springtime in the Rockies was a dismal, drawn-out time of gray skies and cold battling for domination over the coming of summer. Snow would stay on the highest peaks until July, but Independence Pass would open, the high, twisting road that was the only other exit from the Roaring Fork Valley. Once the pass was plowed open, the inhabitants of Aspen felt that their long winter imprisonment was over, Denver a mere three hours' jaunt, and the most perfect summer in the world imminent.

Grudgingly, the brown, muddy slopes and high meadows turned green, and by the beginning of June the gray skies were blue, a pellucid blue devoid of humidity. Out came the hikers and campers, the fishermen; out came cameras and artists' palettes, dabbed with unbelievable, vivid colors. The high, twisting mountain roads were abruptly lined with bicyclists, and the early-morning skies blossomed with brilliantly colored hot-air balloons. In the old, sleepy mountain towns the streets began to fill with tourists seeking that idyllic Rocky Mountain weather: warm, dry days and cool, crisp nights under a black bowl of star-filled skies. The thick forests were scented with pine and an earthy, fecund odor peculiar to the high country of the Continental Divide.

If the streets of the lesser known, smaller mountain towns were filled with tourists, the streets and flower-lined malls of Aspen were nothing short of jammed. Every annual summer event, every festival and conference was grand, drawing celebrities and artists and intellectuals from all over the world. There was the International Design Conference; the beloved Aspen Music Festival, a summer-long event; and the Aspen Institute of Humanistic Studies, a think-tank get-together of great minds. In Aspen the Physics Institute brought a gathering of cerebral greats from Boston, London, Paris, Tokyo. The town became a giant melting pot of humanity, while quiet and untouched, the slopes of the mountains were blanketed with bright wildflowers. Iridescent rainbow trout leapt from the splashing rivers. Deer, bear, elk, mountain lions and sheep roamed the pristine forests right up to the tundra country and higher still, where nothing grew and the air was too rare to breathe and year-round snow held fast to the peaks, where only the furry marmot and mountain goats and golden eagle thrived.

Far below all this unspoiled beauty Aspen hummed beneath the benevolent summer sun. The off-season was over, the jets lined the airport tarmac once again, and those who'd escaped the seemingly endless long cold spring were back in town, roller-blading, golfing, hiking, fishing, camping, hang-gliding, ballooning, bicycling, jogging and working. "Hell," the locals were saying of the gathering crowds, "it's like there was no off-season at all."

Ellen's gallery, which had been closed for eight weeks now, was reopened, as were all the downtown shops and galleries and restaurants—open and doing a booming business.

"God," Ellen said with a sigh to Megan, who'd just returned from sunning in Mexico, "I can't keep paintings on the wall."

"Business sure is good," Megan agreed, dusting the glass countertop by the register. "I was wondering," she said, "if I could get a raise, you know. My friend over at the Santa Fe Trails gets ten dollars an hour, and . . ."

"Megan," Ellen said, "this sounds like blackmail."

"Oh, no, I'd never ask you for a raise if . . . Well, you know, I'm not going to leave you or anything, it's just that my rent went up."

"You can have your raise," Ellen said. "I only hope that if you're planning to leave, you give me two weeks' notice."

"Oh, I'm not quitting, I really am happy here."

But it wasn't three days later that Megan did indeed leave, going to work just down the block for twelve dollars an hour.

It was a lousy day for Ellen. The International Design Conference was in full swing and the shop was busy. She had an eleven o'clock appointment for physical therapy for her arm, but missed it, thanks to Megan's one-hour notice. And then Manuel telephoned, informing her that he'd torn up a canvas. "It's impossible!" he cried. "I need a rest, Elena! My work is indecent. I can no longer paint!"

"But, darling," she said, whispering into the phone in the crowded gallery, "we just had a lovely trip to Madrid. Surely you can't be overworked. Just try to . . ." But he hung up.

And then the bank called. The officer was so sorry, but a stop-payment order had been put on a check for $120,000 that Ellen had deposited just last week.

"No," Ellen said. "That can't be. The customer was delighted with the piece. You simply have to check your records."

"We've double-checked, of course, Miss Connelly. There's no mistake."

"But the client has the painting—in Miami!"

"Well, that's a shame, but we really can't, ah, help you on that end."

"Of course not," Ellen said.

At two that afternoon, Ellen looked up to see a familiar-looking woman in her shop, someone, she thought, who did news spots for one of those hour shows like "60 Minutes." She guessed the reporter was just another famous face browsing the shops of Aspen.

She was wrong.

Before she could collect herself, a cameraman had also entered the shop, and the reporter was approaching the counter.

"I wonder, Miss Connelly, if you'd care to comment on your brother's upcoming trial," the woman said, and she nodded at the cameraman, who turned on a bright light that instantly blinded Ellen.

"Miss Connelly," the reporter went on, "were you at the Connelly estate on the night that Heather Kelly was found strangled and brutalized . . ."

"Turn those lights off!" Ellen choked out. "How dare you come in here!" It was another ten minutes before Ellen could convince the news team to leave, and only after picking up the phone to call the police. A crowd had collected in the shop, but now they were eyeing Ellen rather than the fabulous artwork. "Oh, she's one of *those* Connellys," people whispered.

By five Ellen was exhausted. She called Manuel, praying his mood was brighter, and told him about her day. Thank God he was calm, even apologetic, offering to cook them a wonderful seafood pasta dish.

"Oh, Manuel," she said, "I'd love that. It's been such a dreadful day. I'll be home at six. I love you."

At a quarter to six Patti MacPhersen strolled into the shop and casually looked around. Ellen wondered about that as she closed out the credit card sales for the day. Patti, a local woman who did a lot of charity work, had never been in before. Oh well, Ellen thought, greeting her politely.

Later, Ellen would think that she should have known, made the connection and been better prepared. She should have realized that among myriad other volunteer jobs, Patti was the head of the local group known as Response—women who helped women in trouble. Rape, abandonment, abuse.

Yes, Ellen should have put it together.

"Oh my," Patti said after browsing for a time, "I heard you'd broken your arm, Ellen. It must have been a terrible inconvenience."

"Oh, this thing." Ellen held up her Ace bandage-wrapped forearm and grimaced properly. "It was a pain."

"Broken bones always are. Was it a skiing accident?"

"No," Ellen said, "I slipped on some ice in front of my..." And suddenly the alarm sounded in her head. Response...abuse. Oh God, she thought.

"You know," Patti said, smiling, "sometimes we all do the most embarrassing things. Or something happens, and it's just too painful to think about it and—"

"Excuse me," Ellen broke in, her voice cooler than she'd intended. "It's six, and I really do have to close up the shop."

"Oh," Patti said, "I'm keeping you."

"Yes. I have an engagement." Ellen walked toward the door and flipped the sign to Closed.

"Well," Patti said, following, "if there's ever anything, anything at all we can do." She reached out and laid a gentle hand on Ellen's uninjured arm. "We're here for each other, Ellen. I want you to know that."

Ellen showed her through the door and felt her body begin to quiver. "I appreciate your visit," she said, "but you've made a mistake. Now, good night." And she closed the door firmly.

At six-twenty the phone in the back office rang. It rang and rang and Ellen knew it was Manuel. She couldn't pick it up. She'd think of something to tell him when she got home, if she went home. When the ringing stopped she blew her nose a last time and thought: *Everyone knows.* The whole town knew Manuel had broken her arm! Oh God, God, she thought. And he'd never stop drinking. She knew that. She knew just as surely as she knew Lee and Matt and Terry and the rest of the Connellys would never stop. She couldn't live with that for the rest of her life. She wouldn't. There were other men out there, functioning men—there had to be someone who could love her, who needed her as desperately as Manuel, someone sober. She could get out of this—she'd gotten away from her family, hadn't she?

Tonight, Ellen thought, she'd tell Manuel to pack and leave. She wasn't going to live in shame like this.

At six forty-five she picked up her keys and her purse and snapped off the lights, heading out to her parking spot in the alley. She'd tell him as soon as she got home.

Manuel was cooking dinner, the scent of seafood bubbling in a rich marinara sauce assailing Ellen when she entered the kitchen. "Ah," he said, glancing up, his dark eyes resting on her, "here you are. I was worried, Elena. What kept you?"

Ellen swallowed. "Did you call?" she managed to ask.

"Yes. The phone rang and rang. You were there?" He turned toward her, the white, open V of his shirt displaying deeply tanned skin and crisp black hairs. "Elena?"

"Oh," she said.

"What is it?"

Her eyes met and locked with his. She felt her stomach twist.

"A client," she whispered.

"What?"

"A client. I was tied up with a client in the front. I'm sorry," she lied, pasting on a smile, "I didn't mean to worry you. Um, that smells wonderful. What a darling you are."

And with those words she knew she was irretrievably lost, she'd never give him up, any more than Lee would give up Matt, in their own sick ways, they were exactly the same.

The third rejection of the Forest Service use permit arrived at the McCandless ranch in early July. Dottie just stared at it in disbelief, and neither Rowdy nor Nick could believe it, either. One thing was for sure, the Colorado senator Scott Nordin didn't have the clout to put the brakes on Matt Connelly.

"We've gotta have access to the wilderness," Nick said, picking up a chair and slamming it down. "Without that permit we can just kiss the winter business off!"

"I'm gonna kill that asshole Connelly," Rowdy said, the veins in his neck swelling.

Dottie took a ragged breath. "I'll call Case," she said. "There's got to be some law Matt Connelly's broken. I won't lose this ranch. I won't."

Beth overheard it all from the kitchen and steeled herself—Matt and Lee were reportedly in town for the Fourth of July events. She'd go and see Matt. She'd beg if she had to; she'd swear that she'd back Terry up on the witness stand no matter what. And it occurred to her that this pressure Matt was putting on the Mc-Candlesses might be a smoke screen to ensure her loyalty in court. She wouldn't put it past Matt. There was no level he wouldn't stoop to if cornered.

As it turned out, Beth didn't have to go to Matt at all. Dottie's call to Case pushed the sheriff of Pitkin County right over the line.

"Goddamn that man!" Case snarled over the line.

"Isn't there some law he's broken?" Dottie asked.

"Law? You think that jerk gives a damn about laws?"

"Stop swearing," she said. "It's not going to help."

"Sorry," he muttered. "Look, just hold tight, I've got an idea."

"Oh, Case . . ."

"Don't get your hopes up, but maybe I can put the screws to the esteemed senator myself."

"Oh, thank God."

"Yeah, well, we'll see," he said.

With the holiday at hand and the town filled to overflowing—not to mention the trial of the decade coming up in a few weeks—reporters covering the Aspen beat were numerous. Even the President was due for a stop in town just after the holiday to give a short speech at the Aspen Institute on national health care. Oh yeah, Case thought, there were plenty of newspeople around, and that might just come in real handy.

Case called the Connelly Preserve house and was put through to Matt after a short wait.

"I don't think we have anything more to say to each other," Matt said coolly over the line.

"Well, now," Case said, "there is one thing, Senator, but I'd rather we meet somewhere private to discuss it."

There was a long pause. "This better be good," Matt grumbled.

They agreed to meet that evening on neutral ground, a campground, in fact, several miles east of the Preserve, up toward Independence Pass. Case drove into the crowded camping area first, parked his car and went on foot toward the river, crossing it on a narrow bridge and taking a path posted as a nature walk. A quarter of a mile in he stopped by a picnic table and sat down, awaiting Matt Connelly, wondering if the senator would actually show up.

It was a beautiful summer evening, warm and soft, the aspen leaves quaking gently in the mild breeze. Case settled his Stetson on his head, picked up a few pebbles and tossed them into the rushing water while he planned his speech. He sure as hell hoped it worked.

Five minutes later Matt Connelly showed up, puffing only a little. He was dressed in jeans and boots and an expensive plaid shirt and looked as if he would be right at home hiking. "Nice spot," he said. "Always liked this area," and he sat down across from Case. "Too bad we didn't bring our fishing poles, huh?" His words were congenial, but his stare was glacial.

"I'm glad you came," Case began, "because, depending on what you decide right here and now, I'm prepared to do something that's completely against my nature."

"Oh?" Matt raised a thick brow.

"I'm prepared," Case went on, "to go to the press with the whole story about your blackmail attempt."

Matt studied him for a moment, digesting this, then laughed. "So what? Do I give a shit? You think I left a trail, kid? Get serious."

Case had expected something like this. "Oh, I'm sure you covered your tracks, Senator. But even if the media can't come up with a damn thing, there'll be plenty of flak."

"I'm used to it."

"In an election year?"

Matt waved a hand in the air. "I've weathered a lot worse."

Case sighed as if bored and began to rise. "Well," he said, "I guess we'll both be losers, then. I'm going to the press, Senator. This whole thing was a waste of time because, despite what you think, I have absolutely no influence over the D.A.'s office or anything that happens at Terry's trial. And if I *could* influence it, I wouldn't, not one way or the other." Case gave a lopsided grin. "So you gain nothing but a lot of bad press."

Matt still seemed unruffled. "Yeah, well," he said, "I may just do a little yapping to the press myself. Tell them about how you're fucking my stepdaughter."

Case grimaced at the senator's crudity. "You'd do that to her?"

"To you, Sheriff. She'll look like an innocent victim."

"Guess it's a Mexican standoff then. My family loses, Beth loses." Case shrugged.

"Oh," Matt said, "I don't think you'll go to the press. Not you, McCandless, you're too damn honorable."

"Don't underestimate me, Senator," Case said coldly. "There's a hell of a lot at stake here."

"You're bluffing."

"Uh-huh," Case said, pushing his Stetson back with a finger. "And you go right on believing that."

Case wasn't back in his house ten minutes that night when Senator Connelly was on the phone. "I've been thinking," he said, "and I don't want Beth hurt."

Right, Case thought. "So I'll tell you what, Mc-Candless. I'll see to it that you get that stinking permit of yours, and we'll let your affair with Beth go."

"That's real good of you, sir," Case said.

"No point hurting innocent people," Matt declared in a pious tone.

"I couldn't agree with you more."

The very next morning Dottie McCandless got a call from the U.S. Forest Service headquarters in Denver — they were so awfully sorry about the delay, consider the permit renewed.

It was a hot, bone-dry July day when Laura Curtis smiled to herself as she walked down the old stone steps and entered the Pitkin County Sheriff's Department. She was a reporter for ABC's "Breaking Stories" news show, and she'd been in Aspen covering the President's visit. He'd come and gone and there hadn't been much of a story, but then something always cropped up when you needed it.

"I'd like to see the sheriff," Laura told the dispatcher.

Beverly looked up. "Aren't you...ah, that reporter?"

"Yes, I'm a reporter."

"Well, the sheriff isn't giving interviews," Bev said smugly.

"He'll want to see me."

"I doubt..."

"Look," Laura said, "believe me, he'll want to hear this. Now, why not just page him?"

Case showed the reporter into the seat across from him and turned the stand-up fan on High. "Sorry about the heat in here," he said, sitting down himself. "No air-conditioning. Don't much need it. Now, what's so important that it can't wait, Miss Curtis?" But the sheriff was afraid he already knew.

Laura gave him a pleasant smile. "I've been doing some digging around town," she said, "on the upcoming Connelly trial, in fact, and I'd like to get your comment on something."

"Really."

"We strive to be fair on my show."

"I'm sure."

"So let me just begin by telling you that anything you say right now will be on the record."

"I see," Case said evenly.

"Good. Then let's get to it. Word around town has it that you're living with Beth Connelly. Is this true?"

He'd known it was coming; he'd known for a long time that someone was going to get wind of it, but still he felt his gut clench. Shit, he thought.

"Sheriff?"

"No," he said, "it is not true."

"Oh? But isn't Miss Connelly living at your ranch?"

"First, it's not my ranch. And second, Beth Connelly is working there."

"And you don't live there?"

"No, I do not." He could feel his back sticking to the chair.

"Okay," the reporter said. "Then let me ask you this — are you having an affair with Miss Connelly?"

Case was silent for a long moment.

"Sheriff?"

"I have no comment on that," he said.

"I see. Then let me ask you a hypothetical question. If you were involved with Beth Connelly, wouldn't that compromise the prosecution's case in the Terence Connelly trial? She is a material witness for the defense."

"Look," Case said, "my private life has nothing to do with the trial. I wouldn't allow it, nor would Miss Connelly."

"Okay," she said. "I'd like to send in our affiliate news team from Denver and do an on-screen interview. Can I get a time set up?"

He considered it, all the ramifications. "I think I'll pass," he said.

"Are you sure about that? The questions aren't going to stop, Sheriff. By refusing to answer you're opening a pretty wide door for speculation."

"I'll risk it," he said and told her goodbye, knowing what had to be done.

The last time Case made love to Beth was bittersweet. It was as if she knew something was going to happen, the something she'd spoken of that day in the car. She'd been right, damn it, she'd been absolutely right. And he'd been naive. Worse, he'd known for months that Tripp Maddock planned to break her on the witness stand. Hell, it had been his idea. And what had he done about it? Nothing. Yeah, he'd been a selfish ass to boot.

That morning in late July Case lay with Beth in his arms and felt like a heel. It had to end between them; it was just too complicated to let it go on. And when Beth got on that witness stand she'd know why he'd had to break it off. Jesus, he thought, Jesus. She'd never forgive him.

He kissed her forehead and hated himself. "Beth . . ."

"Um?" She sighed.

"We've got a problem," he said.

"Tell me."

"They know about us."

He felt her stiffen. "Who do you mean? Is it Deirdre? Is she . . . ?"

"The media. I got asked some real personal questions."

"Shit," she said, and she pulled away from him.

"It's bad." He couldn't look at her. He lay there staring straight up at the ceiling, an arm behind his head.

She was silent.

He swallowed. "I've got to be honest with you. It's not just the press snooping around."

"Then they don't know about us for sure?"

"Not yet. But it's more."

"I think you'd better tell me."

"I can't."

"Case . . ."

"I can't, Beth. You'll find out soon enough."

"It's about the trial."

He said nothing.

"I guess that's an answer," she said.

He mustered his courage. "I think it's best if we don't see each other till it's over. I just can't let you...be hurt."

"So this is all for my benefit?" she asked in a voice he barely recognized. She pulled the sheet around her. "I should have known."

"It's only for a little while," he managed to say. "Please, try to understand. It's not just the media thing, Beth. I wish I could . . ."

"Of course, I understand," she said.

Case sat up, swung his legs over the side of the bed and gazed out the window toward the corrals. "How the hell do you think this makes me feel?" he asked.

"I said I understand," Beth repeated, the catch in her voice unmistakable.

"It's only until the trial's over. After you've testified we'll talk, figure things out. Maybe I was wrong about your not living at the house in town with me. I don't know, Beth. I can't think straight."

"It's hard on everyone," she said. "You should try to be more like Matt, just shrug it off and go out and do something even worse."

"It's not funny."

"I'm not laughing."

She took it bravely, he thought that whole day. Beth took the news that they couldn't be together anymore like a real trouper. He was right to have done it. There couldn't be any questions about loyalties at the trial.

He stopped back out at the ranch that evening, just to reassure Beth one last time. In the kitchen he said to her, "You okay with all this?"

"Sure, I'm fine. I wouldn't expect anything else from you, Case McCandless."

"Are you being sarcastic?"

She flipped that dark curtain of hair back and said, "Me? Certainly not. See you around, Sheriff."

He drove back into town and tucked the kids into bed and brushed aside Amanda's question: "Daddy? Can Beth go on our Jeep ride tomorrow?"

Alone in his own bed he justified his actions. Beth would surely understand when Tripp put the screws to her—she'd know why Case had ended it. By ending their affair, he was also making sure the Terence Connelly trial would be fair. No one would believe that Beth could give unbiased testimony if they were still sleeping together. Hell, he never should have let their relationship go on this long. Beth would understand, then, she'd know he was right.

He flung an arm across the cool, empty space next to him and was forced to ask himself a question: Just who in hell had appointed him God?

NINETEEN

Melinda Feinstein tapped a pen on her knee and leaned forward, glancing at Beth Connelly's deposition, which lay on her desk. "Okay, Terry," she said, her gaze rising to meet his, "I don't see anything in your stepsister's statement that in any way differs from anyone else's."

Terry clasped his hands behind his head, seemingly a man without a care in the world. "Yeah, well," he said, "I just thought you ought to know that she's screwing that sheriff and . . ."

"*Was* screwing him, Terry. My sources in Aspen tell me it's over and done with. What I want you to explain is why you're concerned about her testimony all of a sudden."

"No particular reason," he said calmly, shrugging. "I just thought you might somehow use the sheriff's involvement with Beth in the trial."

"And just how?" she asked.

"You know, say that the sheriff influenced her testimony. It'll look bad for the prosecution, won't it?"

"Yes, it will look bad for the prosecution and, don't worry, it'll all come out. Believe me, we won't have to do a thing. The press will pounce on it. The problem is, your stepsister has absolutely nothing of importance to say, so it doesn't really matter except in terms of psyching out the other side."

"Right," Terry said, "but what if she . . ."

"What?"

"I don't know," he said diffidently.

"Listen," she said, "I just want you to focus on one thing. Now, remember, I'm not sure yet whether I'm going to let you testify on your own behalf. You don't have to—the law is clear on that. But if I decide it's in your best interests to testify, you must be ready. I want you to be one-hundred-percent prepared when you're on the witness stand, and the district attorney brings up your initial statement that you and Heather Kelly never engaged in sex, nor did you go to your bedroom. You've got to focus on convincing the jury that you only stated that because you were scared. You've got to look the jury members in the eye and convince them it was a stupid mistake. Show them you're sincere, create that doubt, that shadow of a doubt, Terry. Period."

"We've been over this a dozen times," he said. "I get it."

"We'll go over it a dozen more, too, until you can do it in your sleep. It could be the crux of the trial."

"All right, all right," he said.

"Now let's begin again." She leaned back. "From the top, Terry, every last detail from the moment you met Heather at the Antler."

"Jesus."

"Let's just begin," she said in a cool, professional tone.

Beth ached inside. This time it wasn't an unfocused ache but a sharp, specific one that she'd never felt before. This time she couldn't run from it, she couldn't party away her blues and she couldn't drink them away, although she was sure contemplating it....

She loved a man, a wonderful, honorable man, and they'd made each other happy, and he'd dumped her.

Beth walked across the green lawn between the main lodge and her cabin and felt the tears pricking behind her eyes. God, she hated feeling this way. There was nothing to fall back on, and no guideposts to tell her where to go, what to do next. Her whole body mourned Case's loss as if he were dead.

Sure, he'd said this was just until after the trial. But if he really loved her, he wouldn't have let some newspaper stories or the trial stand between them. If he loved her, he would have chosen her over his damn job. They could have worked it out somehow. What a cop-out, Beth thought, all that bull about right and wrong and ethics!

Well, at least she knew where she stood. Connellys and McCandlesses didn't mix, and in his own way Case had proved he was just as prejudiced as the next guy.

Beth had somehow managed to function that day after Case dropped the bombshell. But she knew she couldn't stay—it was simply too humiliating. Dottie would understand. Hell, Case's mother had twice the common sense that her son possessed!

The morning dragged by, and the afternoon crawled. Beth asked herself a hundred times what a person did when suddenly tossed aside like a used shoe.

If she searched her soul dozens of times for an answer that miserable day, she cursed Case McCandless a thousand times. It killed her to realize how very far she'd come, how close she'd been to being a normal, functioning person. Case had guided her every step, and now, here she was, unwilling to jump back into that abyss, yet not knowing how to stay out of it.

What did people do?

It was just before dinner that she made a decision. She was going to leave in the morning, go somewhere, anywhere, and get her head straight. Maybe to the Outer Banks of North Carolina. The beach house was deserted because everyone was in Aspen for the . . . trial.

Oh God, the trial! She'd been so tied up with Case that she'd relaxed into believing that she'd somehow get through her testimony—somehow.

The worst irony of the whole thing was that she'd been contemplating telling Case the truth about Terry. For so many months and days and hours she'd been living with the knowledge that her stepbrother had murdered that poor, innocent girl, and Beth had been nearing the moment of truth. Each day she'd awakened and thought, today, today she'd tell Case and he'd know what was right to do and he'd support her.

Beth told Dottie in the kitchen that evening that she had to leave.

"I see," Dottie said after a moment. "I guess I understand."

"I'm so sorry," Beth managed.

"It isn't your fault," Dottie muttered, and she never said another word until Beth was out in front of the main lodge the next morning, suitcases sitting on the grass, awaiting the taxi. Dottie walked up to her in the early-morning sun and smiled, taking Beth's hands in hers. "You'll always have a home here," she said, and Beth couldn't help crying.

The flight to Norfolk, Virginia, was a nightmare. She was running again, all sick and twisted inside, and Beth knew it wasn't just her love for Case that hurt so damn bad, it was also the constant, stinging knowledge that she was fleeing the trial, too. Over and over she kept seeing Terry carrying that girl down the darkened hall...and hearing Nancy Kelly's pleading voice on the telephone.

It was over Kansas that the drink cart sat next to Beth's aisle seat, all those little bottles of sweet oblivion jingling. God, how she wanted a drink! And she realized with a sudden, stark knowledge what her mother went through, day in and day out, battling the urge, finally giving in, always giving in.

Beth averted her gaze from the bottles and ordered a juice, sweat breaking out on her upper lip. She wouldn't give in. She wasn't going to end up like Lee.

From Norfolk she took an airport limo south to the beaches. She tipped the driver too much but never noticed. The August heat was hideous, bludgeoning her, so wet and still that her limbs felt leaden as she dragged her suitcases along the sandy walk and up the steps. Even inside it was unbearably hot and stuffy. She opened all the windows and the four sets of double doors that led onto the deck facing the ocean. The sea air smote her, the hot, salty August air that was utterly breathless. Even the sea oats on the dune stood stock-still, and below her a lazy ocean moved gently in and out, in and out, almost soundless in the summer evening.

Beth went back inside, stood in the spacious wood-paneled living room and looked around, a sense of panic welling up inside her. She was crazy to be there, surrounded by memories, Connelly memories of huge beach parties, Matt's booming, drunken voice coming from the deck, "Hey, somebody fill up the goddamn ice bucket out here!" And loud music, playing so late into the night that Cynthia would always come storming out of her and Buzz's room, furious.

So many memories. Lee tanning herself on the beach, Terence and his college buddies learning to surf. The smell of suntan lotions and the inevitable sunburns, bright red cheeks and noses and blistered backs. Barbecues, houseguests coming and going—so much laughter and commotion and noise, the Connelly clan at its best.

What was she doing here?

She took a cool shower and then, with only a towel wrapped around her, sat on a lounge outside and watched the colors of the summer evening tint the sky, the ocean turning lavender and then slate.

She wanted a drink. She sat with the hot night air enfolding her and desperately wanted to forget. She saw Case in her mind's eye. Case...the feel of him, the smell of him. His smile, the way his hair flopped boyishly over his forehead, making him seem so very young even in his sheriff's uniform. And that serious look he got when he felt something strongly. His forearms, muscular and sinewy below rolled-up sleeves. His feet, his ankles, his knees, the blond curling hairs that covered his legs and chest and arms.

And the children. Nate, with his earnest, freckled face and blue eyes so like his father's. Amanda, cuddled up on Beth's lap, asleep, her pudgy, sturdy arms and legs relaxed and warm.

Love. Beth had known love for a short time and now, without it, there were only the stabs of panic and a terrible emptiness. What did people do, how did they live with such pain?

Darkness gathered around her, a thick, moist darkness that caught the lights from neighboring beach houses, diffusing them. The ocean was now only a muffled sound below Beth, a gentle lapping.

She slept, and then she awakened with a start and had to orient herself. The beach. She was at the beach. Alone.

She ate something, a can of fruit, and drank two glasses of water, thinking she'd have to go into Nag's Head tomorrow and buy some food. Tomorrow, Beth mused; she didn't want to think about tomorrow. She walked back out onto the deck, too tense to sleep again. Case, the trial... She couldn't do anything about Case, but her testimony... She could do something about that.

A haze had gathered over the ocean, rolling in to the shore in thick, hot breaths. The graveyard of the Atlantic, Beth remembered, the name given this desolate stretch of ocean and shoals. Hundreds of years ago it had indeed earned its name, the once-uncharted waters claiming pirate ships and commercial vessels alike, tossing their wooden hulls against the sandy shoals like bits of flotsam.

The Graveyard, she mused, recalling suddenly her first summer here with Lee and Matt and Terry, and a disturbance down the beach. Yes. Someone, a very wealthy widow who'd owned a house nearby, had just walked right into the ocean and never returned. A suicide. And now Beth sat in the darkness with her feet curled beneath her and thought that no matter how bad it got, no matter how deep the pain, there was always a way out. She thought a lot about that. Last winter she hadn't known that, but now she did. Case had left her with a gift, then.

Case and the trial, she thought again. They were somehow all jumbled up in her head. And Terry. How could she forget Terry, the man who twelve years ago had stood by and watched his friends ruin her life? Terry. And then later, that college girl who'd claimed Terry had raped her but had dropped the charges. Matt had paid her off. And why not? Beth thought grimly. The violation had been committed and could never be erased. Why not get something out of it?

But Heather Kelly. No one was going to offer her a payoff. She was dead, murdered…and her family—all the money in the world wasn't going to make a dent in their pain. Something would, though, Beth thought with sudden, stark clarity. Justice would.

TWENTY

Case knew when the phone rang that morning that it wasn't going to be good news. But then, there hadn't been much good news lately.

"McCandless," he answered.

"She left," his brother Nick said.

"Who . . . ?"

"Beth, who'd you think, you jerk?"

"Left? Where?"

"How the hell do we know? She told Mom last night and now she's gone."

"Jesus," Case said.

"Thought you'd want to know," Nick said sarcastically.

"You don't know where she went?" Case asked again.

"Nope. She called a taxi this morning and just split, outta here, gone, lock, stock and barrel."

Case leaned his elbows on his desk and lowered his voice. "Was she . . . I mean . . . how did she . . . seem?"

"Jesus H. Christ," Nick muttered and hung up.

He didn't have much time to consider the news, though, because he was already late for a meeting with

Tripp about the Connelly trial, which was less than a week away now. As he climbed the stairs to the D.A.'s office there was a heaviness in his gut, but he tried to ignore it for the time being.

"She what?" Tripp yelled when Case told him.

"She left town."

"Goddamn it, first you screw my only possible witness, then you chase her out of town!"

Case felt an angry flush rising from under his shirt collar. "Now, look, none of this was exactly planned."

Tripp pushed himself back from his desk in an angry gesture and glared at Case. "You being paid off by the other side or something, McCandless?"

"Very funny."

"I don't believe this."

"You don't even know that you could get anything out of her," Case said, feeling like a heel.

"She was my only shot and you know it!"

"I'm not real happy about it myself."

"Yeah, I can understand that. You blew it big time, pal." Tripp leaned forward, forearms on his desk. "What'd you do, Case? Did you two engage in some pillow talk that scared her off?"

The sheriff drew himself upright. "Listen, Maddock, cut that crap right now. You know me better than that. Yeah, I had a relationship with Beth Connelly, but I never discussed the trial with her, I never compromised her or myself in any way."

Tripp pursed his lips and sighed noisily. "Okay, okay, I believe you."

"She probably left because she got sick of Aspen. She moves around a lot," Case lied.

"Sure." Tripp grimaced. "The chick was unstable. I know."

Unstable. Case remembered thinking that a lifetime ago, but he couldn't fit the notion with the Beth he'd held in his arms. A sudden flare of anxiety hit him. "I'll find her," he said grimly.

"Oh, you will, huh?"

"Yeah, I'll find her. I'll make sure she testifies."

"Christ, Superman to the rescue," Tripp said disgustedly.

"Trust me, Maddock."

"What else can I do?" Tripp asked.

It was hot that day, eighty-two degrees. Not a cloud in the sky. But Case wasn't paying attention to the weather as he drove out to the Connelly estate. It was all mixed up in his mind—loving Beth, the trial, her testimony, his worry, her abrupt flight. All tumbling around like clothes in a dryer, a sodden lump of tangled pieces. Somehow he'd have to find Beth and bring her back. She'd run away because of him, he knew that, and he felt guilty as the devil. Even worse, this business about her testimony—he'd been real good at avoiding that subject for the past few months. It was pretty ugly, all right, and he'd done everything wrong, everything.

He rang the doorbell at the Connelly place, remembering another time he'd been there. It had been winter, piles of snow, and a girl had just been murdered. . . .

A different Mexican maid answered the door.

"Is the senator in?" Case asked.

"Yes, he is."

"Tell him the sheriff is here to see him, please."

Matt Connelly had lost none of his bulldog pugnaciousness. "What now, McCandless?" he asked.

"I'm trying to locate Beth," Case said, controlling his temper.

"You'd know where she is better than I would," Matt said, leering.

"She left the ranch. Is she here?"

"No."

Case was aware of Beth's mother hovering in the background. He tried again. "Do you know where she went?"

"No."

"Look, Senator, this is an official visit. I'm here in my capacity as an officer of the court."

"Oh yeah? Well, I can't help you." Matt looked Case up and down. "Of course, in your official capacity you might want to stop this three-ring circus and settle the whole thing out of court."

Case didn't bother answering. "Maybe someone else in your house knows where Beth is," he said pointedly.

"No one's heard from her since she took up with you. Go ahead, subpoena us all. We don't know where she is," Matt said. "What's the matter, McCandless, did she dump you?"

Case ignored the barb and kept his face expressionless. "If you hear from her, the district attorney is trying . . ."

"Sheriff," said a voice from behind Matt, "please, wait."

Matt pivoted. "Goddamn it, Lee," he said, but she was standing right behind him now. "Lee, stay out of this," he warned.

Lee Connelly stood her ground. "Go away, Matthew," she said. "I'm going to talk to this young man."

"That 'young man' happens to be the sheriff," Matt growled.

"Leave us," Lee said, and she addressed herself to Case. "I'm Beth's mother."

"I know, ma'am. Do you have any idea where your daughter is?" Case asked hopefully.

"No, I don't."

He felt deflated. This lady wasn't lying.

"Beth called me once," she said, "last spring. She seemed very happy."

"Yes, ma'am," Case said tonelessly.

Lee Connelly, so delicate, her short hair perfect, her nails polished, her clothes immaculate, stood there and studied Case for so long he felt like squirming.

"Well, thank you, Mrs. Connelly," he finally said, "I really have to be going now."

Lee put her small, delicate hand on Case's arm. "Try the beach house in North Carolina. It's in Ocean Sands," she said quietly, and then she fled.

Once Case learned that Beth was no longer in town, it was easy to follow her trail. She'd taken the taxi to the airport and gotten on a United Express flight to Denver, then Norfolk, Virginia. The ticket agent, who'd bowed to his authority, said, "That's right, Beth Connelly, it's on the screen. Flight 632 out of Denver."

"But to Virginia?" Case had to ask.

"It's the nearest airport to the beaches."

"Can you get me on a flight in the morning?"

She began to punch the information into the computer. "First class or coach, Sheriff?"

But Case wasn't listening. Unstable, he was thinking, and unless there were more Connellys he'd yet to have the pleasure of meeting, they were all in Aspen. And that meant Beth was alone. Alone on a deserted beach.

Case was utterly preoccupied packing and trying to get the kids fed when the call came that night. It was Deirdre. And she was crying.

"Deirdre," Case said carefully, putting the phone to his other ear, sitting down, "take it easy. I can't understand you."

It seemed she'd taken the court-ordered psychological tests and—in a word—failed. The examiner had suggested to the Marin County judge that Mrs. Deirdre McCandless seek professional help.

"Oh God, Case," she wept, "I'm not screwed up, I'm not!"

And for the next thirty minutes he had to sit there and agree with her, feeling guilty as hell for having put her through this, while at the same time elated—the kids were going to stay with him. It was practically over.

"Can I come visit this winter?" she asked once she'd calmed down.

"Of course," Case said. "You should start to see them again."

"Will you send pictures?"

"Yes. This week, I promise."

There was a pause. "I hear you and that woman, that Connelly woman, aren't together anymore."

Case laughed humorlessly. "You've got good sources, Deirdre."

"Well?" she asked, "Are you or aren't you?"

"It's all up in the air," he said, the understatement of the year.

The next morning, the children safely at the ranch, Case caught the first flight on his way to the East Coast. He hated to fly. His hunting trips to Canada, even vacations in Mexico, he took by car, seeing the country, taking in the sights and smells and new faces. Flying, he believed, was for stressed-out businessmen, and politicians who, naturally, charged it all to the taxpayer.

Far below, the late-summer brown of the vast prairie lands gave way to the deep green of the Midwest, and so many cut-up tracts of farmland that he could scarcely believe it. In the West you had ranches, big ranches, spreads that sometimes ran for a hundred miles of bone-dry land. But he'd never been to the East Coast, never wanted to go, either. All he'd ever heard about were crowds and lousy weather, scorching hot, humid summers and icy winters when the sun rarely shone.

Case stepped off the plane at the small Norfolk airport. Within minutes his khaki shirt was soaked, and the thought of food made him queasy. And then, when he'd finally gotten a rental car and a map—along with impossible directions—the traffic was horrendous, mostly military, and he got stuck in a twenty-mile-long pileup. Good God, he thought, and people bitched about Highway 82 into Aspen!

It got better when he turned off the interstate onto a country road that led him into Elizabeth City, a small old Southern port that really was quite beautiful, despite the late-day heat. Trouble was, Elizabeth City was in the wrong direction from the Outer Banks. He'd missed a turn.

It got later. The sun behind him now was slipping, filtering through the enormous trees, casting the fields and small towns in the most incredible golden light, a misty light that Case could have sworn actually smelled old. He drove through the South and thought about that and took in the sights despite the nagging worry at the back of his mind. Beth had been here many times, probably knew the history—what Civil War battle was fought where, and all that. Amazing. She'd been so many places, seen so much and yet . . . He still couldn't believe he'd been her first, her first in that way. He still couldn't fathom the pain she'd held so deep inside all those years, the denial. Unstable. His gut crawled.

The land finally opened up, the odor of sea and brackish water coming in the open window and there was a sign now: Nag's Head, 15 miles. But where was Ocean Sands? Case had seen the ocean. The Pacific, anyway. But this sea was different, he thought as he crossed a long bridge to a stretch of land that was for the most part a mile wide and eighty miles long. This body of water was calmer and bluer, and the smell of the sea was heavy.

He stopped at a gas station and asked directions. He could barely understand a word, so thick was the attendant's accent. But pointing worked. It looked like a left up there, another left, a few miles and a right.

"You wouldn't know the Connelly house?" Case asked, mopping the sweat from his neck.

"Jaysus," the young man said. "Everybody knows dem folks. They's got that big wooden house up dere on that san' dune. C'aint mizz it. It's painted all a gray callah."

"A big gray house?" Case asked.

"Dat's what I said, mister, sheet."

"Ah, thanks," Case said and took off, the air conditioner blasting him in the face now. *Hold on, Beth,* he thought, *Jesus, just hold on.* He was an ass, all right, an uptight, moralistic ass who'd blown the best thing to come down the pike in a long, long time. She was going to hate him, too, really hate him because she'd never believe he'd come for any reason other than his damn job. "Swell," he mumbled. "Sheet."

* * *

Matt greeted Melinda Feinstein at the door to the Aspen house. Immediately he took in her frown and the white-knuckled grip with which she held her briefcase.

"Well, come in, come in," he said, standing aside. "Didn't expect you till tomorrow."

"Thank you," she said stiffly, sweeping past him. "Is there someplace we can talk, Matt? In private," she said pointedly.

"Ah, sure, my office. I'll just get us a drink and we can..."

"No drinks, please," and she cast about for the direction of his office.

"Okay," Matt said when he was seated behind his desk, "let's hear it."

"In a nutshell," she said coldly, "you lied to me. The whole family, it seems, lied to me. Jesus Christ, Matt, I'm Terry's lawyer!"

"Lied?" Matt put on his best, most innocent face, but Melinda only scowled at him.

"Yes, lied," she said. "I spoke to Cynthia on the phone yesterday, and she happened to mention your stepdaughter, Beth, and told me she was concerned about her testimony."

"Oh, Melinda," Matt began, his voice soothing.

"Let me finish. I had to ask Cynthia just what we were talking about, and it seems that last New Year's—that's almost eight months ago—Beth sat at the dinner table in this very house and told the entire family that she'd witnessed Terry carrying, *carrying* Heather Kelly's body down the hall! How could you—how in hell could you keep this from me?"

"Take it easy," Matt said, smiling, unruffled, "it's no big deal."

"Are you crazy? My God, Matt, I should have been told this immediately. Do you realize the implications?"

"Melinda, Melinda," he said gently, "you don't understand our family. We're loyal. I can understand why this might seem as if we were keeping things to ourselves, but that's the way we—"

"Things?" she scoffed. "Just last week Terry and I sat in my office and discussed Beth living with the sheriff, and Terry didn't say a damn thing about this! You call that no big deal? My God," she breathed.

Matt waved his beefy hand in the air. "Look," he said, "Beth isn't seeing that asshole anymore. In fact, she's disappeared."

Melinda's head snapped up. "You mean...you mean, she's not going to show up at the trial?"

"I don't know. She's kind of off-the-wall sometimes. Got a mind of her own—but not about family," he added quickly. "Never that. She's a Connelly."

"God," Melinda said, "I do need a drink. If she does show up, my God, the district attorney might get wind of this and . . . Christ, if he grills her . . ."

"Just object," Matt said, still unconcerned. "Nothing's going to happen."

"You're very sure of that, aren't you?" she said coolly. "But you never know, Matt. If I've learned one thing in a courtroom, I've learned that you can't ever predict what's going to happen."

"Hey," Matt said, rising, coming around the desk and laying his big hand on her smooth knee, "you worry too much."

"You're paying me to worry."

He headed to the door and turned the lock slowly, the feel of her satiny skin a phantom touch on his hand.

"You know," he said, reaching for his belt buckle, "the girl, that Kelly girl, was probably half passed out and Terry was only helping her. Shit, Beth was probably drunk as hell herself that night. Taking medication, too. You can handle this even if it does come up, which it won't," he said, his voice hoarse now, his breath coming quicker. "This trial will make your career, babe. Just stick with old Matt here, it's in the bag."

She twisted her head and looked at him, her eyes lowering to his open fly. "My God," she whispered, "you better be right."

"Trust me," Matt said.

Beth stood in her wet bikini on the darkening beach and heard a faint noise that didn't quite fit in with the cries of the gulls or the hollow rumble of the ocean. She turned her head and listened, and when she saw him she froze.

She watched with a wild pulse as he came down the beach steps and strode across the sand toward her, then finally stopped. The light was pink-tinted, just on the verge of dying, and it bronzed his blond hair and tanned skin. Beth wanted to flee just as much as she wanted to run to him.

But she stood there. For a time so did he, and it was as if all the air had been sucked from her lungs as she stared at him, wanting him, hating him, loving him so much it was agony.

It was Case who finally moved, step by slow step until he stood before her. She opened her mouth to say something but no words came. And it was Case who finally reached out, tucking a salt-stiff strand of hair behind her ear. Without a word passing between them, his head bowed and she tilted her chin and they kissed with a gentle uncertainty.

Later they lay together entwined in the damp, mussed sheets of the bed. Outside, the light finally died, and the fog curled in off the ocean and lay in wet patches against the dunes. Moisture clung to every available surface of the house, the deck chairs, the screens. Even the wood paneling was tacky in the sultriness of the summer night.

But Beth and Case no longer took notice. They clung to each other, mouths searching, tasting, nibbling. First had been the awful questions, the trying to understand and sort things out. Now was the passion that burned and cleansed, cutting away the superficialities and the pain. Now was only togetherness, a joining of their bodies, their souls.

Afterward Case still held her tightly, breathing hard, sprawled over her.

"Am I too heavy?" he finally asked.

"No," she whispered.

"You're sweating," he said, nuzzling her neck, licking the salty wetness.

"You, too."

Outside the open windows the sea hissed and rumbled, soothing, as Beth ran a hand down Case's back, fully sated. She slid her fingers over the warm wetness, down to where his back hollowed, where there was a sprinkling of fine hair and the swell of his buttocks. "You came after me," she said.

"I promised Tripp Maddock." He raised himself on his elbows above her. "This is official business, lady."

She smiled in the darkness. "Of course, you couldn't lie and tell me it was because you . . . wanted me."

"I could have, but it'd be a hell of a basis for a relationship."

"A relationship, is that what we have?"

"Uh-huh."

"A serious relationship?"

"Yeah, I think so. What about you?"

She was silent for a minute. "It's the only good relationship I've ever had in my life."

"Well then . . ."

"Your kids," she said. "You have to think of them."

He bent his head and brushed her lips with his. "That's one big reason I'm here. They love you. They need you."

She mulled that over. "There are other problems, Case, and you know it."

"Yeah, I know it." He rolled off her and propped his head on a hand. "The damn trial."

"Yes, the trial."

"Now look, Beth, I've never said one word to you about Terry or the trial or your testimony, not a word, except to take your initial statement in an official capacity."

"That's true."

"And I won't start now, but you do have to come back to Aspen to testify."

"I was going to go back," she said.

"Good."

"You didn't have to come all the way here to get me."

"I damn well did," he said.

She was quiet for a time, just lying there looking into the inky night, feeling the damp heat of Case's body touching her.

"You know that I saw something," she finally said.

"I don't know a damn thing."

"I'm a lousy liar."

"I haven't heard a thing you've said," Case replied soberly.

"You've heard everything I said from the moment you met me—everything I said and didn't say."

"That has nothing to do with us."

"What if I lied under oath? Would you still want a 'relationship' with me?"

"You're asking a hypothetical question, and I can't answer it."

"Case . . ."

"No, don't. Don't torture yourself. You know what you have to do," he said.

"I don't. I never have. That's the trouble."

"I trust you," he said softly.

"No matter what?"

"Uh-huh."

"Now you've made it worse."

"No," he said, "nothing's changed."

She sat up. "Goddamn you, Case! You think it's so easy! It's easy for you! It's hard for me, real hard."

He put out a hand and laid it on her thigh. "I trust you," he repeated.

She hugged her knees, resting her chin on them, staring into the blackness. "You expect too much."

"Maybe," he said.

"You're hard on the people around you."

"Maybe."

"I'll fail you," she whispered. "Sooner or later, I'll fail you."

"And maybe I'll fail you, too. Hell, I already did."

"Oh, Case . . ."

"I hate this damn climate," he said, wiping his forehead with the corner of the sheet.

"You get used to it." She sighed.

"I don't want to. We're leaving real soon."

"When?" she asked.

"Tomorrow."

She sat there, feeling his hand on her leg, and it was so warm and solid and sure. A small bud of confidence grew in her. "Okay, tomorrow," she said.

"Yeah, we're getting the hell out of here and flying home."

"Home," Beth repeated, savoring the word.

TWENTY-ONE

"The court will come to order this twenty-second day of August in Pitkin County, Colorado, the Honorable Judge Richard Snyder presiding. Opening statements will be heard. Proceed, gentlemen and ladies."

The old Victorian courtroom was full. In the wide corridor outside, a large crowd was held back by a cordon of deputies. Every network was represented, every penny-ante hometown paper and TV station, CNN, the big papers of Los Angeles, New York, Washington, Philadelphia. Outside the building was a mob scene.

The jury was seated; it had taken more than a week for the selection process alone. Neither the defense nor the prosecution was entirely happy, but that was the way it was supposed to work. Cameras would not be allowed in the courtroom, Judge Snyder had ruled, so there were several artists sketching all the players in this drama.

Terence Connelly, with his dark good looks, smiled surreptitiously at the proceedings. The rest of the Connellys were lined up outside the courtroom, serious expressions on all their faces. They would be called as witnesses later in the trail, but for now, they presented a phalanx of formidable strength. Even Edward Crenshaw, Matt's nephew, and his willowy wife, Katherine, were there to display family solidarity. Beth Connelly sat with the family as well, her face pale but composed.

The opening statements were predictable; the press had already explored the possibilities. But the jury became uncomfortable with Melinda Feinstein's cross-examination of Lester Wiggins. The medical examiner was a good witness, straightforward and exuding integrity.

Ms. Feinstein pressed him about the lack of cocaine in Heather's body. "Now, Dr. Wiggins, how do you explain the fact that the lab found no cocaine in Heather Kelly's blood, but found a definite trace on her nose?"

Dr. Wiggins took his time. "Well, I guess there's only one way I can figure it. Someone rubbed cocaine on that girl's nose to make it look like an overdose. But she was already dead and it didn't get into her body."

"That certainly is an interesting hypothesis, Doctor," Ms. Feinstein said, amused. "But I have a better one. The lab made a mistake. Heather Kelly actually *did* have cocaine in her blood. Much simpler, much more plausible. Is that possible, Dr. Wiggins?"

"Well, it rarely happens...."

"But it could have happened, couldn't it?"

"It would be very unlikely. The FBI lab in Denver has an excellent reputation."

Ms. Feinstein skewered him with a glacial look. "Answer the question, Doctor. Yes or no. The lab could have gotten the wrong results on Heather Kelly's blood tests."

Lester Wiggins glared back at her, his bushy brows drawn.

"Answer the question, please," Judge Snyder said.

"Yes," Lester Wiggins muttered.

That evening, sketches of Dr. Wiggins were shown, along with Ms. Feinstein's harsh stare. In general, people were on the doctor's side, because he seemed like a regular guy. Feinstein, by contrast, was definitely one tough cookie.

The next two days dragged by. Evanick, the snowplow driver, testified that he'd witnessed a man walking along the snowpacked drive at the Aspen Health Club, a man wearing a leather aviator jacket similar to the one Terence Connelly owned.

"Objection!" Melinda Feinstein barked. "Your Honor, this man is speculating wildly."

"You'll have your turn to cross-examine him, Ms. Feinstein," the judge said. "Objection overruled."

When she rose to question the snowplow driver, she had a smug expression on her face. "So, Mr. Evanick, you saw this man at—" she checked her papers "—three forty-five in the morning?"

"Yes."

"Describe the weather, please."

"It was snowing."

Melinda Feinstein picked up a bound collection of papers and held it up. "This is your deposition, Mr. Evanick. May I read what you said back in March?"

"Sure, go ahead."

She began reading: "'I couldn't see too well. It was dark and snowing. I'd say he was medium height, dark hair, wearing an aviator jacket.' Those were your own words." She smiled humorlessly. "And you expect the court to believe that you recognized Terence Connelly that night? Really, Mr. Evanick. A man wearing an aviator's jacket, a man you admittedly could barely see because of the weather conditions?"

"I never said I could tell who it was."

"No, but Mr. Maddock wants us to believe that, doesn't he?"

Tripp Maddock shot up, his face tightening. "Objection!"

"Sustained. I'll tolerate no personal remarks in my court, Ms. Feinstein."

"I'm sorry, Your Honor."

But Maddock lost that point. He tried again, but the judge and Ms. Feinstein interrupted so much that finally he had to quit.

The jogger who'd found Heather Kelly's body testified. And even though he'd only made a call to the police, Ms. Feinstein objected three times to his testimony. Maddock didn't get too upset, however, because pretty soon the judge was going to tire of her big-city defense tactics.

Maddock was wrong about that.

The days went on, and more expert witnesses were called. Finally Maddock had about played all his cards.

The employees of the Antler Club were called into the courtroom one by one, and Maddock scored big at last. Several of them testified that Terence Connelly had pursued Heather the night of her death to the point where she'd been getting behind in her work. But then Melinda squelched each of them in turn with a single question: "Hasn't anyone ever been friendly to you while you were working?"

Point made.

All the while, day in and day out, Terence just sat there scratching an occasional note to his lawyer, trying to look interested. One woman in the jury, a pleasant-faced older lady, could not keep her fascinated gaze off Terence. Often he would smile back at her. The *New*

York Times legal expert discussed with his *Washington Post* colleague whether they could ethically make mention of the fact. Over pasta and tenderloin and a bottle of Montrachet '89 in the Hotel Jerome dining room, they decided not to—unless someone else picked up on it first.

Tension ran high in Aspen. Normally packed in August, now it was doubly so. Behemoths of television satellite vans were parked everywhere, blocking the streets for "opinion" pieces.

In front of the courthouse, Main Street was jammed all day long, and people took to driving through side streets to get around. A reporter died of a heart attack while hiking on a popular trail near town. The mention of his death made the back page of the local paper. Only the Connellys were news.

The press was predicting a win for Ms. Feinstein at this point. Maddock had no smoking gun, no eyewitnesses, nothing but a set of circumstances showing that Terence Connelly could have killed the girl. It wasn't enough.

Feinstein called for a mistrial at this point, claiming the whole procedure was a travesty. The D.A. hadn't a shred of evidence. The waste of time and taxpayers' money was disgraceful. An innocent man was being hounded, simply because the inept lawmen of Pitkin County couldn't find out who had killed Heather Kelly.

After careful consideration the judge turned her down. The betting pool at the *Los Angeles Times* had Maddock's chances for a conviction at eighteen to one. Case McCandless overheard two reporters from Denver laughing, one saying, "Talk about reasonable doubt, this whole trial's one big unreasonable doubt."

In the third week of the trial it was finally time for the Connelly clan to testify. Tension reached a fever pitch, and Matt Connelly's jacket was torn by someone in the crowd as he made his way into the courthouse Tuesday morning.

It was oppressively hot in the high-ceilinged old courtroom that day. The tall windows let in too much sunlight, and the room was too full. Even the sheriff had to stand, leaning against a back wall, his arms folded across his chest. Judge Snyder could be seen dabbing his forehead with a handkerchief. Matt Connelly's balding head glistened as he sat in the front row, his face a mask of somber and strict attention. Lee sat next to him, her perfectly manicured hand on his meaty one. There was a two-hour delay when the local fire marshal decided the number of spectators had to be limited. Thirty nonessential onlookers had to be weeded out.

Terence was scheduled to testify last. It had been a tough decision on Feinstein's part, whether or not to let him take the stand. On the one hand it allowed Maddock to grill him about why he'd lied about not being in his bedroom or having sex with Heather. On the other hand, Terry could be a cool customer under fire, and Ms. Feinstein believed the jury needed to hear his explanation from his own lips to create that shadow of a doubt. And if the prosecution was too hard on him, it would create sympathy for Terry, as well.

The first of the Connelly clan to be cross-examined by Maddock after the morning's delay was Buzz Crenshaw. The ex-football player sat in the witness stand with his usual ease and affability, even getting a chuckle from the crowd when he described his inebriated state on the night of December twenty-eighth of the previous year. "Christ," he told the jury, "I couldn't even feel my knees!" Then he turned to the judge. "Ah, sorry, Your Honor."

Cynthia testified, then Lee took the stand, and it started to become painfully obvious that no one in the Connelly house had witnessed or heard a thing after last seeing Terry and Heather in the living room.

"Mrs. Connelly," Tripp Maddock said to Lee, "surely you heard Terence and Heather in the hallway outside your bedroom." He pointed to a map of the house that sat on an easel.

"Objection!" Ms. Feinstein rose to her feet. "Mr. Maddock is badgering the witness. She already testified...."

"Yeah, yeah," the judge said, waving his hand at her, "objection sustained."

Matt took the stand next, and, surprising the whole court, Tripp Maddock was very easy on him, obviously not wanting the public to think he was hounding the eminent senator from New York. The media loved it, and the general consensus was that Maddock had scored big by treating Matt Connelly with the utmost respect.

The *Miami Sun*'s headline read: Aspen Witch Hunt Ends. They sold an all-time record number of papers that morning.

The next afternoon Beth Connelly was called to testify. She rose from a seat just behind Matt and made her way up the aisle, a slight figure in a well-cut black linen suit and pale pink blouse. Her voice trembled for a moment as she began the oath, then strengthened. She took her seat, her gaze straight ahead, answering Feinstein in monosyllables. Tripp Maddock rose, very slowly, very deliberately, and approached the witness, pushing aside his suit coat to hook his thumbs in his suspenders.

"Miss Connelly, please tell the court your relationship to Terence Connelly."

In a clear voice, she replied, "He's my stepbrother."

"He is not related to you by blood, then."

"No, my mother married his father when I was eleven."

"Did you and Terry get along, Miss Connelly?"

"Objection. Irrelevant," Ms. Feinstein said.

"I ask the court's indulgence. This line of questioning is pertinent and necessary," Maddock said.

"Sustained," Judge Snyder said. "Get on with it, please, Mr. Maddock."

"On the night of December twenty-eighth of last year, Miss Connelly, describe to us where you were."

"I went to the Antler Club to meet the family for a drink," she said.

"And about what time did you arrive at the club?"

"Around eleven, I guess."

"And where were you prior to that time?"

Feinstein again objected. "This line of questioning is irrelevant, Your Honor." But the judge allowed it.

"Now," Maddock said to Beth Connelly, "you got to the club around eleven. And before that . . . ?"

"I had a date."

"I see." Maddock sat on the edge of his table, folded his arms and settled into his role. "Had you been drinking on this date, Miss Connelly?"

"I was only drinking soda then."

"At a restaurant?"

She hesitated briefly. "No. I was at my friend's place."

"And your friend is . . . ?"

"Your Honor," Melinda Feinstein said, rising, "I really must object. This whole line of questioning is—"

"I quite agree," the judge said, and he pinned Maddock with a glare. "Get on with it, Mr. Maddock," he said. "The leaves are going to turn before we're through at this rate." The room thrummed with laughter.

"Okay," Maddock said to Beth, "you'd had soda. Then you weren't inebriated when you arrived at the Antler Club?"

"Not at all."

"Tired then? It was getting late."

"Maybe a little."

"Would you say you were alert?"

"Yes, sure."

"I see." He pivoted and scanned his notes for a moment, then looked back at Beth. "Okay. Would you tell the court please at what point you first noticed your stepbrother and Miss Kelly engaged in a conversation."

"Objection," Feinstein said. "It hasn't yet been established that Miss Connelly even knew who Miss Kelly was or that . . ."

"Quite true," Maddock conceded graciously. "Let's go back then, Miss Connelly, and find out when and if you first became aware of Terence and Heather Kelly forming an association. Did you notice them at all?"

"Yes, I did," Beth said.

"And where were they? At your table, the bar?"

"The bar."

"I see. And this was at what time?"

"Oh, maybe a half hour or so after I'd arrived."

"And you'd had one, two drinks?"

"One," she said. "It might have been two."

"Um. And were you still sober? Alert?"

"Yes," Beth said, and she shifted in the hard seat, uncrossing her trim legs, recrossing them. It was clear to the entire courtroom that it was going to be a very long afternoon. For the next two hours Maddock took Beth Connelly through every last detail of the night: the time, the place, her level of intoxication. Artists sketched, a juror yawned, the courtroom was very hot. It was the same old stuff, nothing new, another Connelly who hadn't seen or heard anything out of the ordinary.

"So," Maddock was saying, "you arrived at the Preserve house and everyone sat around having a nightcap?"

"Most did, yes."

"And then Terence and Miss Kelly arrived..."

"Yes, I told you that."

"Yes, you did. So let's talk about when everyone retired. Who was the first to go to bed after Terence and Miss Kelly arrived?"

"I don't really recall."

"Then who was the last?"

"Matt. That is, Senator Connelly. We both went downstairs at about the same time."

"I see. And would you say you were still alert?"

"Alert? No."

"Drunk?"

"I was very tired. Not reeling, just tired."

"I see. So you were still aware of events."

"Yes."

"That was approximately one a.m.?"

Beth shrugged. "Approximately."

"And Terry and Heather were in the living room."

"Yes."

"Was that the last time you saw Heather Kelly, Miss Connelly?"

Beth hesitated only briefly, but it was enough to make even the most seasoned reporters look up.

"Miss Connelly?"

"Yes, I . . ." Beth cleared her throat.

"May I remind you that you are under oath here, Miss Connelly," Maddock said in a gentle voice.

"I am aware of that," Beth said.

"Answer the question, Miss Connelly," Judge Snyder said, and a hush fell in the courtroom. No one rose to go to the bathroom, no one whispered. Artists' pencils paused in midstroke.

"Miss Connelly?" Maddock repeated, and Beth looked down at her hands for a long moment, then raised her head and slowly found Terry's eyes. The room seemed to drain of air.

"Was that the last time you saw . . ."

"No," Beth said.

"That was *not* the last time you saw Heather Kelly?"

"No, it was not."

"Objection!" Ms. Feinstein said, leaping to her feet.

"Overruled. Continue, Miss Connelly."

"I . . . uh . . . saw her later." Beth swallowed. "I woke up later and opened my bedroom door. Terry was in the hall . . . He was . . ."

When she was done, the court was in an uproar. Banging his gavel, the judge called a recess for the rest of the day. Beth was led out by a deputy, past the crowd of newspeople rabid for an interview. Cameras rolled as the slight, dark-haired girl was half supported, half dragged through a corridor cleared by deputies, out of the courtroom and down the stairs. She halted for a moment when she came face-to-face with Senator Connelly and his weeping wife, then straightened her shoulders in a brave, touching gesture that made her an instant heroine to millions of TV viewers, and went on.

The cameras followed her as she was rushed to an official car, where the sheriff of Pitkin County held the door open for her, helped her in with a touch and a reassuring nod, closed the door and sprinted around to the driver's seat and sped away.

Autumn colors painted Aspen's landscape early that year, and the mornings were crisp. The woman shivered and hugged her robe closer to her body. She wrapped both her hands around the steaming mug of coffee as she read the front page of the local paper. The headline was Matt Connelly To Be Returned To Senate. The article began:

> Senator Matt Connelly, father of convicted murderer Terence Connelly, is expected to be reelected by a landslide. The senator and his lovely wife, Lee, visit Terence in his maximum-security prison cell in Canyon City, where he is serving a fifteen-year sentence pending an appeal. Their daughter, Beth, whose testimony convicted Terence, is now living in Aspen, out of the public eye.

The woman put down the paper and looked across the table at the two blond children clamoring for her attention. Beth smiled.

THE CUTTING EDGE
Linda Howard

Brett Rutland was Carter Engineering's top trouble-shooter—the company's obvious choice to solve a case of internal embezzlement. As the firm's accountant, Tessa Conway's position made her his prime suspect.

Brett was a tough man—had to be in his line of work—but not tough enough to resist Tessa. He'd tried to keep his professional and personal lives separate— and hadn't expected to fall in love. Now, on the day that Brett stood to expose the embezzler, that love was about to face the ultimate challenge.

> *"You can't just read one Linda Howard!"*
> Catherine Counter

LED ASTRAY
Sandra Brown

Cage Hendren had chased, and caught, more than his share of women, but he loved only one—the quiet and serious Jenny Fletcher.

A natural born hell-raiser, danger followed him like a shadow. But tragedy struck too close to home when his brother was killed in Central America, leaving behind his broken-hearted fiancée—the one woman Cage had always wanted. He was about to make the biggest play of all—one that could cost him much more than his heart.

> *"One of fiction's brightest stars!"*
> Dallas Morning News

POWER GAMES
Penny Jordan

Self-made millionaire Bram Soames was a powerful, charismatic man racked with guilt over his son's shameful conception. Jay enjoyed the buzz this power gave him over his father and, so far, had manoeuvred to keep any woman from gaining a strong hold on Bram's life. Then the intriguing Taylor Fielding arrived on the scene.

Wary of controlling men, Taylor had carefully created a new life for herself. It was easier—*safer*—to avoid any form of intimacy. But Bram's sexual magnetism and unexpected sensitivity made him dangerously attractive.

She was a woman with no past. A woman Jay would see destroyed—stopping at nothing, not even seduction, to expose her secrets. But more than one life would be in danger if the truth about Taylor were ever made unknown.

"Women everywhere will find pieces of themselves in Jordan's characters."
Publishers Weekly (USA)

MIRA

HOT PROPERTY
Elise Title

Kate Paley plays to win. And she's used her brains, beauty and bravado to become one of Hollywood's heavy hitters. But she's beginning to feel that the price has been too high. She'd sacrificed the love of her life for power. She stood by silently as her best friend's star burned out too soon. When they both return to her life, Kate is faced with her toughest decision—ambition is everything, but is it enough?

"Gripping and dramatic...from the first page to the very last."

Affaire de Coeur (USA)

MIRA

RED
Erica Spindler

Becky Lynn was a nobody. Everybody told her so—the women who snubbed her at Opal's Cut 'n' Curl, the boys who hurt and used her, the family who didn't want her. But Becky Lynn had dreams—and fled to a world where she could make those dreams come true.

Jack Gallagher wanted to be a somebody. He wanted to be bigger than the father who'd denied him, better than the half–brother who'd claimed all their father's love. And he was getting there—fast. As a top fashion photographer, he was hot, he was sexy—and he was damn good.

Now, in a world where beauty and illusion are intertwined, Becky Lynn and Jack command the spotlight. But is the cost of fame too high? Beneath the glittering facade of their world lurk secrets that threaten to destroy all they've fought to achieve.

MIRA

THE TIES THAT BIND
Jayne Ann Krentz

Dark, compelling and mysterious, Garth
Sheridan was no mere boy next door—even
if he did rent the cottage beside Shannon
Raine's. She was intrigued by the hard-
driven executive, but completely
underestimated the sexual power he soon
held over her.

Garth dictated theirs could only ever be a
weekend affair—two days and nights of
sensual enjoyment. He wasn't about to let
Shannon into his other life—a dirty world
of corporate intrigue, secrets and danger.
For Shannon it was all or nothing. Either
break the undeniable bonds between
them…or tear down the barriers
surrounding Garth and discover the truth.

With more than twelve million copies of her
books in print, Jayne Ann Krentz is one of
today's top-selling writers of women's fiction.

MIRA

RAGGED RAINBOWS
Linda Lael Miller

SHAY KENDALL
She had always lived in the shadow of her
movie-star mother, Rosamond Shay. But
now the glamorous star had been forced
into retirement and obscurity, and Shay's
life was spent doing her duty and never
thinking of herself…

MITCH PRESCOTT
He was known as the author of scathing
exposés. A forceful, probing man, Mitch
had expected Rosamond's biography to be
an easy assignment. But he hadn't
anticipated the unsettling presence—or the
unusual pleasure—of Shay Kendall.

*"The most outstanding writer of sensual
romance."*

Romantic Times (USA)

CARDINAL RULES
Barbara Delinsky

RULE 1: NEVER GET INVOLVED
Determined not to repeat the mistakes of her irresponsible parents, Corinne Fremont had never dropped her guard in her professional or personal life. She was all business—all the time.

RULE 2: NEVER RESIST TEMPTATION
Maverick businessman Corey Haraden conducted his love life in much the same way he did business—with flair and enthusiasm. Corinne was not his type, but she intrigued him. That's why he offered her a job she couldn't refuse—just to tempt her.

RULE 3: RULES ARE MEANT TO BE BROKEN

"One of this generation's most gifted writers of contemporary women's fiction"
Romantic Times (USA)